The Wounded Season

MĀNOA 11:2

UNIVERSITY
OF HAWAI'I
PRESS

HONOLULU

The Wounded Season

Frank Stewart
EDITOR
Susie Jie Young Kim
FEATURE EDITOR

Founded in 1988 by Robert Shapard and Frank Stewart.

Mānoa is published twice a year. Subscriptions: U.S.A. and Canada—individuals $22 one year, $40 two years; institutions $28 one year, $50 two years; single copy $15. Other countries—individuals $25 one year, $45 two years; institutions $33 one year, $59 two years; single copy $17. For air mail add $12 per year. Call toll free 1-888-UHPRESS. We accept checks, money orders, VISA, or MasterCard, payable to University of Hawai'i Press, 2840 Kolowalu Street, Honolulu, HI 96822, U.S.A. Claims for issues not received will be honored until 180 days past the date of publication; thereafter, the single-copy rate will be charged.

Manuscripts may be sent to *Mānoa,* English Department, University of Hawai'i, Honolulu, HI 96822. Please include self-addressed, stamped envelope for return of manuscript or for our reply.

www.hawaii.edu/mjournal
www.hawaii.edu/uhpress/journals/manoa/

CONTENTS

Special Focus ✾ **New Writing from Korea**

POETRY

Editor's Note

In late 1998, we watched with mixed emotions the television coverage from Phnom Penh of Khmer Rouge leaders Khieu Samphan and Nuon Chea being greeted with handshakes and smiles by Cambodia's prime minister, Hun Sen. The two elderly revolutionaries arrived in the city by military helicopter following their surrender to the government, officially ending more than thirty years of civil war. If the two looked surprisingly genial and meek for criminals against humanity, it was even more disconcerting to hear them speak. Reporters asked the two whether they felt any remorse for devastating their country and killing more than two million civilians—mostly by execution and starvation in slave-labor camps. "Yes, sorry," Khieu Samphan said as he departed in order to check into a hotel in Phnom Penh. "And we ask our compatriots to forget the past so our nation can concentrate on the future. Let bygones be bygones." Refusing to accept responsibility for the genocide, Nuon Chea added, "Let's consider that an old issue." "Yes," repeated Khieu Samphan, "we must forget the past."

The last two decades have seen the collapse of a number of authoritarian regimes around the world. In the aftermath, citizens of newly democratized countries must often face a test similar to that occurring in Cambodia: how to understand and articulate a national past that may have included various forms of state-sponsored terror and oppression. But a decision to "let bygones be bygones" is particularly difficult when the truth has been suppressed or manipulated for a long period and the "official" versions of people's lives endure unamended. It is natural, of course, to want to forget painful memories, but traumas, as guest editor Susie Jie Young Kim says, "leave a trace: a mnemonic site." Until the truth is told, national and individual traumas persist in the very heart of the present and ineluctably affect future generations.

The fiftieth and twentieth anniversaries of two of the most traumatic events in the recent history of Korea are marked by the publication of *The Wounded Season:* the civil war, which began on June 25, 1950, and resulted in the partitioning of the country into North and South; and the Kwangju Uprising, which began on May 18, 1980, and radicalized a large portion of the population into exposing the ruthlessness and greed of the junta that

Public Hearing in Korea, 1946
Photograph by Horace Bristol
[CORBIS/Horace Bristol]

had come to power the year before. The world knows the military history of the Korean War, but the conflict's impact on the psyches of individuals, families, and communities is fundamental to another set of stories altogether—another history that endures in the memories of people who lived through the conflict. Even more dramatic is the case of the Kwangju Uprising, the truth about which was kept from the Korean people for over a decade by the men responsible for its bloody course. The uprising began in the capital city of South Chŏlla Province the day after General Chun Doo Hwan imposed martial law on the nation, arrested opposition leaders, and banned all political activities. The citizens of Kwangju held anti-government demonstrations that raged for ten days, until Chun sent soldiers, paratroopers, tanks, and helicopter gunships into the city. Officials claimed that 200 civilians died, but local people have always insisted the number is closer to 2,000.

The Korean stories collected in *The Wounded Season* exemplify the way fiction writers are able to give a voice to those who have been silenced or censored. Writers can articulate "counter-memories," as Kim calls them in her overview essay, and in doing so their works make indelible those truths that authoritarian regimes attempt to erase. Powerfully told stories enable people to resolve the painful contradictions that result from suppressed memories, and by telling the truth, they create a way for healing to begin.

Written by some of that country's most accomplished authors, the Korean stories in *The Wounded Season* depict people whose lives are grievously altered by events and then further harmed by inauthentic but officially accepted versions of what has happened to them. The characters include a doctor who may have committed a murder during the Korean War; an unemployed writer who is caught in Kwangju's social and economic turmoil but who learns how to open "up your stomach to look inside without killing yourself . . . to survive"; a professor and his rebellious daughter who are emotionally separated in the same way that their country has been ideologically divided; and a group of friends who must face their betrayal of one of their own after the Kwangju Uprising. In varying and complex ways, each story explores how honor is intertwined with truth and how truth finally emerges from the individual memories of ordinary people.

Also in this volume is "Kyŏngbok Palace: History, Controversy, Geomancy," an essay by Min Soo Kang that describes the recent controversy over whether to demolish the Korean National Museum Building—a structure erected by the Japanese as the headquarters of their colonial occupation government. Kang recounts the labyrinthine and bizarre story of the Japanese attempt to control not only the Korean people, but also the *ki* (life force) of the nation through geomancy and magic.

Ultimately, however, the black magic fails—just as attempts to control or erase individual and national memory must fail. And so it is that these forceful stories and essays from Korea are finally about hope rather than despair.

Hope links our Korea feature with several other works in *The Wounded Season,* including a portion of Dante's *Purgatorio* newly translated by W. S. Merwin. In this centermost canticle of the *Divina Commedia,* the dark aspects of Hell are left behind for a region of flowers, tenderness, and art. In place of despair there is consolation, brought about by the presence of the abundant life that garlands the earth. Shadows are replaced by starry dawn and an end to the wounds caused by hatred and deceit.

A longtime resident of Hawai'i, W. S. Merwin is as well known for his translations from European and Asian languages as he is for his own celebrated books of poetry. In *The Wounded Season,* he joins other distinguished translators in commenting, in concise essays, on the art of translating poetry from Asian languages. For this two-part symposium—the second part to appear in our summer 2000 volume—we invited translators of Japanese, Chinese, Korean, Sanskrit, Vietnamese, and Cambodian to respond to a provocative essay by Tony Barnstone, "The Poem behind the Poem." Some of the responses are accounts of the difficulties of rendering Asian writing into English; others comment on the unexpected places the process has taken the translator—geographically, culturally, and personally. Some comment on the preparation needed to enter the mind of a poem in order to translate it, while others explore the nature of poetry itself.

Among the other works in *The Wounded Season* are superb stories by Vietnamese writer Ly Lan and Uruguayan author Mario Benedetti. In Ly Lan's story, a woman comes to terms with her ghost in a country overrun with ghosts, and defines the Viet Nam War in the most human of terms: as "women's sorrow, misfortune, helplessness . . . absorbed directly into my bloodstream when I was in my mother's womb." In Benedetti's startling allegory, an artist has a crisis involving form and essence—a "lacunae" that transforms him until he is all style and no substance. Americans Robin Hemley and Maria M. Hummel are each represented by an essay. Hemley's "Roy Underwater" is a haunting memoir about a man whose peculiar subconscious wears away each connection to reality until he is so alienated from family and life that he can no longer exist. And in Hummel's "Dr. Nice Day," an American reflects on the chain of events that lead to several deaths in a Thai village and to her acceptance of her role in that tragedy.

The poetry in *The Wounded Season* includes moving work by Ricardo Pau-Llosa and Mộng-Lan. Writing in the aftermath of a visit to a painter's studio, Pau-Llosa contrasts the sensitive impressions created by a work of art with images of the city he is returning to and ponders "how no light can make us see/beauty in the distances." Mộng-Lan, appearing in *Mānoa* for the first time, evokes the transient beauty in ordinary objects and moments.

The art in this volume includes photographs taken in Korea in the 1940s by Horace Bristol. At one time part of a circle that included Edward Weston, Ansel Adams, Imogen Cunningham, and Dorothea Lange, Bristol helped to create a photographic style that combined journalism and art. During World War II he worked under the direction of Edward Steichen in chronicling the war for the Department of the Navy. Over a four-week period, Bristol traveled around Korea documenting what he later described as that country's "honeymoon with liberation": a time shortly after Korea's emancipation from Japanese rule and before the beginning of the brutal civil war. When his photographs seem idyllic, they are all the more moving in light of what we know was in store for the Korean people in the latter half of the century. The other artist in *The Wounded Season* is Hawai'i photographer Paul Kodama, whose images in this volume were taken in Italy and capture the dark and tender tone we find in Dante's *Purgatorio*. The cover images of Korea are by another Hawai'i photographer, Tom Haar.

Finally, we'd like to thank the following people for their help in assembling this volume: Yi Ch'ŏngjun for his assistance in the translation of his stories; Bruce Fulton for his invaluable advice on rendering Korean words into English; Daniel Cole, of the Center for Chinese Studies at the University of Hawai'i, for help with Chinese typography; Ngo Thanh Nhan for his knowledge of Vietnamese; and Jenny Foster for her assistance during the production phase.

L Y L A N

The Ghost

"I tell you this, but don't be frightened. You are haunted by a ghost."

Miss Linh bites her lip as if she wants to take back her words. She waits for my reaction, but I'm not frightened. A ghost is the spirit of a dead person. A dead person can't rob me, murder me, or slander or imprison me. So why should I be frightened?

"I tell you this not because I have any desire for profit, but to warn you. This is a debt from a previous life. You must drive it away."

I laugh. Among the six billion people who live on this planet, this ghost has chosen me. How can I have the heart to drive it away?

But my mother is worried. "You look pale," she says. "Your soul and body seem not together. You seem lost, even when you are with others."

To cure me, my mother takes me to the pagoda. We bring flowers and fruits with us. When we arrive, I prostrate myself before the Buddha, then join the others sitting cross-legged and listening to the sutras.

"*Antapha baphathuat datapha datmatapha batarami . . .*"

My mother requests that I repeat the words. "These True Words purify the three karmas," she tells me. I repeat them. Pagodas on mountains are lofty places, and sutras in Sanskrit are sacred, so it doesn't matter if, when I read them, I don't understand their meaning. Anyway, the sutras are not for me; they are for the ghost.

"*Batarami maphadata mahadatapapha . . .*"

Listening to the sutras, the ghost may be purified and freed from suffering. Or it may leave me, deciding to lead a peaceful existence at the pagoda instead. After finishing the sutras, I walk in the garden. At noon I have lunch, then chant more sutras into the evening. The plan is for me to stay a few days. The pagoda is a beautiful place. In the evening, from the back of the garden, I watch the sun set deep red in the west, then the skyline gradually turn a dark purple.

But on the second day of my stay at the pagoda, my younger brother arrives and angrily drags me home. He shouts at me, "If you fast and pray like an ascetic, you will surely see your grave!" His recommended treatment is rest and invigoration. Meat, fish, chicken, duck, milk, eggs, cream . . . and a can of beer each day—this is the regimen he suggests for good health. The next day he returns from work, announcing, "My office is having a weekend in Vung Tau. Come there with me; we'll go swimming and sunbathing, eat fresh seafood. I bet you'll feel better."

My mother is busy getting ready for the trip, but on Thursday the war in the Gulf breaks out. Friday evening, the entire family sits in front of the TV set.

"E-game," my youngest sister cries. My mother ignores her and complains of how the prices going up make her dizzy. "Those well-fed people know little about war yet. Let them learn!" my elder brother interjects. My father corrects him, saying, "Nobody really knows. You and I have the experience of surviving the war, but only the dead know what war really means." My younger brother announces, "I have a bet with the chief of my office that Iraq can't last more than a week."

He brought home a case of beer from his office yesterday. When the U.S. issued its ultimatum, people in his office wagered whether Uncle Sam would fight—he fought and my brother won the bet. My brother now drinks beer and smiles at President Bush on TV.

I go to bed early so I will be able to get up to take the bus that departs for Vung Tau at dawn.

At Vung Tau the sea is oily; it foams as if boiling. I want to stretch out on the sand, but the beach is dirty. My younger brother rents a cot and umbrella for me. He dives into the surf with his girlfriend; later we will have drinks with his colleagues at a restaurant. The chief of his office sits beside me and offers me cashews and a Coke. I felt sick on the bus and still have a bitter taste in my mouth; I eat a cashew without tasting it. But the Coke makes me belch, and I feel a bit better. My younger brother's girlfriend calls me to go swimming with her. "I can't swim," I call back. "Come on, come play in the waves just for fun," she teases me.

"Thanks, but I'm too lazy," I tell her.

"Lazy?" The girl laughs and smiles. I smile too.

My plan is to walk along the beach to the other side of the mountain and rest there. But the chief of my brother's office comes back to sit beside me; this time he offers me crab and other seafood delicacies. I thank him and eat my crab with great attentiveness to avoid responding to this flatterer whose breath reeks of beer.

"Chief, may I have a cigarette?"

I look up at the speaker. It is a beggar with one leg and a stick who has been working the beach. I look right back down to the sand. The chief is annoyed.

"No," the chief tells him.

"Then, chief, let me have five hundred *dong* to buy a cigarette."

"What?" The chief grows angry at what he perceives to be the beggar's gall.

"Chief, five hundred *dong* is just the cost of one cigarette. Have pity on unlucky me."

"Miss . . ." The beggar turns to me.

I reach into my bag for money, but the chief stops me. He takes a pack of cigarettes out of his pocket and gives one to the man. I'm determined to look straight into the beggar's eyes this time.

"You are . . . ?" I ask him.

"Hoang," he answers. "And you are . . . ?"

"Forty," the chief answers, cutting me off before I can respond. The beggar's face is rough and without shame; his look is savage and cruel. "No problem," he snaps back. I look down at the sand again.

"Please go away," the chief says.

The beggar moves a short distance on his one leg and stick, then stops and looks back at me. The chief thinks to tease me. "Acquaintance?" he asks.

I wonder if knowing a beggar devalues my personality, but I feel no need to satisfy the chief's curiosity. I shrug my shoulders; the chief turns and suddenly grabs the hand of a boy selling nuts. He stretches the boy's fingers out in his hand, and a pair of sunglasses falls out. "I pick it up for you," the boy tells him. The chief tells me to take care of my things as beggars and pickpockets are everywhere.

"Thanks. No serious losses yet," I tell him.

The chief stands up and tells me to go on ahead to the restaurant.

My younger brother is already there sitting at a table. His face is fairly red. The men around the table are in the midst of a noisy debate. "Who bets on Iraq?" "Will Israel play the game?" "Modern war is resolved in three days." "No, I bet this war lasts at least one hundred days."

Are they war analysts, strategists, gamblers, or drunkards? I tell them I'm sorry, but I have plans to visit the neighboring pagodas. They try to call me back, but my younger brother shouts, "Let her be with her ghost!"

Who is my ghost? I have tried to recall all the people I've known over the years in order to guess who might have died and turned into a ghost to haunt me. I have many old acquaintances whom I haven't heard from in decades. Classmates at high school, old neighbors . . . countless men and women I once knew but have long since forgotten. Is the beggar named Hoang among my acquaintances? I can't say for sure. Is the ghost a lost soul following me by chance, or is it the soul of one who loved me but was forgotten? Am I so indifferent?

I stare at the empty space before me, begging, "Ghost, who are you? Speak, please . . ." I hear my own voice speaking. I realize that I'm acting crazy and try to recover my composure.

The stairs up the mountain to the pagoda are steep. I climb fifty steps without stopping, nearly breathless. In the mountain there are caves where monks retreat and hide from the world so they may purify their hearts by seeking truth or the soul's salvation. I know of one of these caves because my mother took me there once, a long time ago, to collect the remains of my grandfather for cremation. Rats may well have been the only things living at my grandfather's side during his last minutes in this world. We found his bones, fresh and clean, scattered in the cave.

"Please come into the pagoda, miss." The voice startles me. The woman seems to have walked right out from the cliff face; her face wears a smile of complete peace and contentment. Is she—was she—my acquaintance? Her look is very friendly. "Come. Today the pagoda makes offerings of rice gruel for all souls," she says.

I prostrate myself and make my offering to the Buddha. There are small dishes of sticky rice on the ground in the front and all along the sides of the pagoda. The woman puts small bowls of gruel next to the dishes of rice: these are for the lonely souls and wandering spirits. I grab her elbow.

"I'm really sorry, but who are you?" I ask.

"I was at the Mercy Orphanage."

"What's your name?"

"Hoa An."

Now I remember. My mother used to give alms to the pagoda and take me there to pray for my father at the battlefront. I was a little girl then, well dressed, holding two big bags of old clothes and toys and standing in front of a dozen children my age. The children stood at the end of the room, leaning against the wall, and stared at the visitors. My mother pushed me forward. "Go and play with your friends." I took some steps forward and gave a bag to a small girl. Her hand had just touched it when her face changed color and horror filled her eyes. She threw the bag down, dragged me to a table in the corner, and pushed me underneath. The sound of an airplane grew near and then died away. The adults pulled us out from under the table and explained that the child was afraid of planes. She had been the only survivor of a bombardment during a mopping-up operation, and a soldier had picked her up out of a heap of corpses. She was named after the abandoned village, Hoa An.

"Why are you here?" I ask.

"It doesn't matter where I am," she says, and smiles. In her coarse clothes and with her hair twisted into a bun, she looks like any other peasant woman.

"How have you been?" I ask.

"I've been doing chores for this pagoda and growing manioc up on the mountain," she replies. After twenty years of swimming in the ocean of misery, she still remembers me. But I didn't recognize her. I am bad. I don't even recognize the ghost who haunts me. I spend the day with Hoa An, harvesting manioc on the mountain till evening. There are no visitors: the pagoda is not marked on tourist maps. When darkness comes, we hear the rhythmic sound of the bells and the wooden fish clanging as if to emphasize the quiet.

We are having dinner in the back room when I suddenly hear my name being called noisily from outside the pagoda. It is my younger brother and his companions. I say good-bye to Hoa An in haste so that the pagoda's peace will not be broken. Outside, my brother grunts at me and says, "You really are haunted."

It is dark as we climb down the mountain, and the way is difficult. My younger brother has a flashlight; I follow the round light as it falls on grass and bushes. Strong winds blow, and I shudder. The boys begin telling ghost stories, joking and laughing on the way down the mountain. The evening is cool. They say there are many ghosts in our country. After decades of war, who could count all the bodies killed in action or in accidents? Dying innocent, the thousands of young soldiers who didn't marry, who never loved, who never kissed a woman became ghosts with no great desire to go to Heaven. Still wanting a life in this world, they haunted young girls or unmarried women alone in bed. The chief raises his fist. "I will settle the matter with *that* ghost."

When we return to our hotel, another group of my younger brother's friends is gathering in the reception room. The words burst onto the screen: WAR IN THE GULF. The chief rushes in. "Have the Americans landed?" he asks. He bet that the U.S. troops would land today. My younger brother's girlfriend smiles at me and says, "Come here. See who will pay the bill tonight." "Thanks, but I'm tired," I tell her.

It is my younger brother who escorts me to my room. He has been drinking a lot, but he's not completely drunk. He tries to comfort me. "Don't be frightened, Sister. Your brother is here. Have a bath and go to bed. Pay no attention to what those guys said. Don't answer the door, except if you hear my voice."

Homesick and lonely, I take my bath, crawl into bed. Last night the whole family sat in front of the TV set. It was the first time in years we'd all talked about one topic. Though he had been a soldier, my father never spoke to us about war. He had fought in battles for at least twenty years. But he was a defeated soldier. When the war ended, he went to a reeducation camp for six years. During those hard times, my elder brother joined the Young Pioneers because his law school had been dissolved. Later, he fought in Cambodia. He returned on one foot, with eighteen scars on his body and lots of medals and citations. Perhaps it was thanks to those citations and medals that he got to go to the university. Four months later, my father also came back home.

All three men in my house drink. My father drinks with old friends. My elder brother drinks with young comrades. My younger brother drinks with his office chief and colleagues. All those years and they had never talked about the war. If war just means fighting, then I know nothing about it, even though I was born and grew up during the war. But if war means women's sorrow, misfortune, helplessness . . . these things were absorbed directly into my bloodstream when I was in my mother's womb.

I hear a knock, then another.

Someone is at the door, which is locked. I remain in bed.

"Open the door!" a voice yells. "I came to kill the ghost."

I place a pillow over my head. My younger brother's voice calls from outside. "Open the door, Sister. Your brother is here." I open the door, and the smell of beer rushes into the room.

My younger brother staggers to the bed and throws himself on it. He slurs his words, dragging his tongue. "No worry. I'm here."

Then enters the chief. He is holding a long gun and stands in the middle of the room, shouting, "Ghost, face the wall!"

The hotel manager enters, trying to stop the chief from shooting the gun.

"Don't joke, chief," I say.

"I'm not joking! I said I would settle the matter with that ghost. I'll kill him."

"But he *was* killed—he is already dead."

"Let him die again. Stand aside, get out of my way."

I step back to the window that opens onto the garden.

Laughing, my younger brother crawls on the bed. "No worry, Sister. It's a toy gun." He repeats the words reassuringly. "A toy gun . . ."

The chief raises the gun, aims, and shoots. "*Bang!*"

My heart is broken. I fall. The men all laugh, and then in a moment they're gone. The door is closed. The leaves are still falling in the garden.

Translation by the author with Kevin Bowen

ROBIN HEMLEY

Roy Underwater

Every family has its casualties, and Roy was ours. My mother's first cousin, the son of my great-aunt Sam, he was both legend and shameful secret at once. His glorious moment and his defeat happened at precisely the same instant: during the Japanese attack on Pearl Harbor. For years I had the story wrong, and told people that Roy was one of seven survivors of the *Arizona.* Actually, I don't know how many people survived the *Arizona.* In my mind, that famous image of the ship blowing up as the bomb went down its smokestack must have melded with the story of Roy. Roy served in the army, not the navy, so he must have been on land, not on the *Arizona.* But another detail of the story, this one not invented by me, had Roy swimming in the fiery waters of Pearl Harbor for three hours.

This was his calling card: Roy, Survivor of Pearl Harbor. I'm not trying to make light of that because his is not a funny story, but it was a fact on a flashcard, an object lesson, something to be memorized whenever I saw him, which was not frequently because he lived in Connecticut with his family. My family was always moving around the Midwest, and we only came together in the summers, at my grandmother's beach house in Long Beach, Long Island. *He swam around Pearl Harbor for three hours! He had to swim underwater.* Never mind that the attack lasted twenty minutes. Roy swam and swam. I envisioned him almost fishlike, diving deeper as dead men bobbed and sank around him. When he emerged, he was changed forever, of course, but not like America: cleansed by its blood sacrifice, reenergized, mighty in its resolve. Oh, he had resolve, I suppose, eager as anyone to win the war, to lick the Japs, but he spent the next year in a mental hospital in Denver, recovering from wounds as deep as the *Arizona,* a ship named after that parched desert state and lying like a contradiction at the bottom of Pearl Harbor, still trying to float, still manned, sending up coded oil slicks to the surface. From the hospital, he sent photos of himself pre-Pearl: pearly youth, his face so open and beautiful, so confident and naive. This was the face he sent to friends and relatives: Roy in pith helmet, arms crossed, not in defense, but in youthful invincibility. I love this Roy, this one I never knew, because, of course, I see myself—all of us, in fact—in him. Such a hopeful gesture; how was it received by my family? I think most likely with a shake of the head. *Poor Roy! Three hours underwater.*

Faintly, he has written of victory on my photo of him: WE'LL BEAT THEM YET!

We did, of course, but not with Roy's help. He was done for, marked by those three hours, those twenty minutes, that stay in the hospital. But outwardly, he hadn't changed much. My mother, whose war job was to teach photography to the Army Air Corps in Denver, visited him in the hospital there and remembers him as sweet and funny. When he returned home, his father was willing to do anything for him. Roy enrolled in the Academy of Dramatic Art. He built toy furniture. He took up photography, which he loved. My mother says he was too scatterbrained to be involved in anything for very long. His father, my great-uncle Rob, was wealthy, made leather desk sets. Roy lived off his father. He saw himself as an entertainer, always smiling. He stayed for a time with my great-grandmother in her large house in Brooklyn, but one day, he burned the bed in his room and narrowly avoided setting the whole house on fire.

He married Muriel, sister to Riva, my mother's best friend. They had met at my mother's twenty-first birthday party, a surprise party arranged by my uncle Alan. My mother hates surprises. Alan invited everyone, she says, friends and enemies alike. She introduced Roy to Muriel at that party, and later they became engaged. She remembers Muriel coming to her house the day before Pearl, before *that* surprise, and then reading the headlines the next day.

On the way back from Rockaway Playland, a Long Island amusement park, Roy tells us the story of the Viper. I'm sitting in the very back of his station wagon with his daughter Lucy, whom I have a crush on and whom I know, I can just tell, has a crush on me. Lucy is my age, and my age is always between ten and twelve. Always. I believe that no matter how old we get, we fix on a certain age, and stay that age until we die. Some people are nine, some twenty-five. I'm between ten and twelve, and Roy, I bet, was always twenty, the age he was in his pre-Pearl photo.

Lucy and I smile at each other and laugh at nothing. Her younger sister, Rachel, sits quietly in the backseat with the youngest child, Martin, who seems like an evil kid, constantly trying to inflict harm on one of his sisters or even me, though I'm a semistranger, hardly fair game by the unwritten Geneva Convention of sibling warfare. He tried to trip me as I hurried to take a seat on the roller coaster at Rockaway Playland, and he ripped off the ball from the paddle ball I won at one of the carnival booths. Roy's second wife, Fran, sits with Roy in the front seat, silent as always. She's known in my family as stern, even harsh, and the only other fact I know about her is that she's a nurse. No bit of information is given innocently: of course she's a nurse; she has to be, to rescue poor Roy the fish from his underwater habitat. According to my family, she's a contradiction, too: nurse shark. Whatever doesn't kill you makes you stronger.

"The phone rang and the woman picked it up," says Roy.

"'Hello? Who is it?'

"'It's the Viper, and I'm three blocks away.' The line goes dead and the woman thinks, Must be a wrong number."

Lucy touches my hand, and I grasp hers.

"The phone rings again, and she answers. 'It's the Viper, and I'm two blocks away.'"

"Daddy, this is scary," says Rachel.

"Shut up," says Martin.

"Don't tell your sister to shut up," says his mother.

"Yeah, shut up yourself," says Lucy.

"Don't tell me to shut up," says Martin, turning around and slapping Lucy, whose hand is in mine. She lets go and starts slapping him.

"Shut up, all of you," says Fran.

"The phone rings again," Roy says. "She doesn't pick it up at first, but it keeps ringing. She could unplug it, but she's scared, so finally she grabs it and yells, 'Who are you?!'

"There's silence on the other end and then a strange voice answers, 'I am the Viper, and I am only one block away.'"

We're all silent now—none of us need to be chided.

"The phone rings again. She pauses over the receiver, then grabs it before it can ring again. She holds it to her chest, but even so, she can hear his muffled voice: 'I am the Viper, and I am at your door.'"

"How does he carry his phone?" I ask, though this isn't exactly what I mean to say.

"He's a ghost, stupid," Martin answers definitively. "He can do what he wants."

"The woman runs to her bedroom," Roy says, "and the phone rings again. She picks it up.

"'It's the Viper,' the man says in an evil singsong, 'and I'm inside your house.' No sooner does she put the phone down than it rings again. 'It's the Viper, and I'm coming up the stairs.' She yanks the phone out of the wall and locks the door and—"

"Daddy," says Rachel, but Roy is engrossed. He's looking at the road, then turns around briefly. His eyes are big. The Viper's in there. I can see it. I take Lucy's hand again.

"She jumps into bed and pulls the covers over her head. She hears the monster outside her bedroom door. *'I'm the Viper,'* he bellows, *'and I'm standing outside your door!'* The doorknob jiggles and she can hear the lock being picked. 'It's the Viper,' he says, 'and I'm in your bedroom.' She pulls the covers tighter around her. She hears the monster bending closer. 'It's the Viper,' he says softly, 'and I'm standing over your bed.' She feels the covers being pulled away and though she wants to keep her eyes closed, she can't. She opens them and she sees . . . she sees . . . an old man standing there with a toolbox. 'I am the Viper,' he announces, 'and I've come to vipe your vindows, lady.'"

All I can say is that I was relieved, tremendously. Anticlimax is what I longed for in that station wagon. Who wants real tragedy, real horror? Maybe on TV or the movie screen or the terrifying rides at Rockaway Playland, but at my frozen age of eleven, I wanted it to be joke, even a dumb one. It's about the only joke from childhood I remember, and I'm terrible at remembering jokes. But I told this one for years, though never as well as Roy did.

Roy is watchful of his daughters. He constantly seems to suspect them of something, or else he's protecting them from something: themselves? their mother? me? the Viper? He wants everyone together, always.

"Here," Lucy says, and she takes one of my hands. With her other, she touches the back of my head and bends towards me. We're out back, behind my grandmother's house, sitting on a stoop in a little alcove, by a dilapidated red toolshed a little bigger than a phone booth. Cats love to lie on the roof of the shed, and my grandmother shoos them off, yelling from the porch or the window of her kitchen. Cats love my grandmother's yard in proportion to her hatred for them: the more she shoos them, the more they frequent her garden.

Lucy presses her lips against mine. Mine are dry and hers are moist, but then mine are moist, too. Of course, I've seen people kiss before, but I haven't been sure until now what it does, what the effect is. Now I know. It makes me aware. I know the placement of things. Mrs. Hoy's house is ten feet away. There's an alley between her house and my grandmother's, and across from the stoop on which we're kissing are other houses, a fence, garbage cans. It's August, and on my grandmother's porch you can almost always feel the breeze from the ocean, a block and a long beach away; but here, I can't feel a breeze, though somehow it's cool on the stoop. We're sitting in the shadows, and my cousin is kissing me, though I don't know where to put my other hand. It's in my lap.

"Lucy!" Roy calls from inside, but not too far away.

"Uh-oh," she says, pulling back, but not too alarmed, smiling. She stands up, looks down at me, and says, "I'll go inside the house first. Then you come inside, but wait a minute. Pretend nothing's happened."

"OK," I say, my voice cracking.

"I'll come to your room tonight."

Pretend nothing's happened? She'll come to my room tonight? What does this mean? I sit there and watch a tabby rolling on its back on the toolshed roof, swatting at something invisible.

Later, we're playing on the patio, the four of us. We're marching around, the army of the flowerbeds—first quiet Rachel, then me, then Martin. We're all in swimsuits—regulation wear for this army. Lucy holds a garden hose and tries to tag us with its concentrated spray. She's chasing Rachel, who shrieks and runs out of range. Martin picks up the tabby that I saw before and throws it on my back. With claws out, the cat shears my skin as it slides down, its claws trying to gain purchase on my wet skin.

That night, I'm lying in bed, the wounds I made such a fuss over no longer hurting. The door opens, and I see a figure standing there. She moves to my bed. I remember her standing over my bed. A minute later, an hour, a second, there's Roy, and he's calling her. He doesn't seem angry, but he wants her out of the room. She tells him she was confused, didn't realize where she was.

Lucy writes to me next year. She tells me of her life in New Jersey. She says she ran away, but now she's back. She says her mom and dad are divorcing. She says she remembers how nice I am. I remember how nice she was—I remember that kiss, and that moment she stood over my bed.

I don't reply, though I want to, and think maybe I'll call. Yes, I'll find out her number. And call. "This is the Viper and I'm in Indiana."

But I don't.

I see Roy once more, in New York, at the apartment of his mother, then in her nineties. Half of the time, I'm dazed. I don't remember who all my relatives are or where they live. I'm too far away in the Midwest, and I've lived away too long from my many and various relatives. Sometimes I can't even keep my grandmother's sisters and brothers—the eight or nine of them—straight in my head. Why am I at Aunt Sam's apartment? My brother Nathan and I were in the city, and he suggested the visit. We show up, unannounced, and have our audience with her. She's sitting in a chair, feeble, and we're talking, about to leave, because there's not much to say between our years, when a man shows up. I don't recognize him, and he doesn't seem to recognize me, though he knows Nathan. They shake hands, and then he sits there beside Aunt Sam, his hands clasped, arms resting on his legs, head bent—distracted, it seems.

"Who was that?" I ask Nathan after we leave.

"Roy, of course," he says. "Sam's son."

"Roy?"

"You know, he was at Pearl Harbor," Nathan tells me.

"Underwater," I say.

"What?" he says, looking at me strangely as we leave Aunt Sam's building and head up the street.

"He was underwater."

Nathan laughs and says, "What are you talking about, 'underwater'?"

I see Roy leaping off the *Arizona* into a ring of fire. He leaps off the sinking bridge and dives under the fire. He holds his breath until his lungs feel like they'll burst, and then he emerges again, takes another breath, and dives. The attack is over, but he doesn't know. Ships are still burning and sinking. He hears sirens, sees dead men floating. How is he to know the attack is over? And when he finally dares to come ashore, he meets my father, who's recovering the bodies washing in. Another thing I imagined. My father was shipped to Pearl Harbor the day the atomic bomb was dropped on Hiroshima, but, confused, I thought he had gone there the day Pearl was attacked and had spent the next month retrieving bodies. I'm sure someone did, but not my father. Still, I imagined them meeting, my father helping Roy into a waiting jeep, and Roy, unhinged, blabbering, "I've come to vipe your vindows."

Even when Roy died a couple of years after I saw him in New York, I didn't know the truth. I still imagined him a survivor of the *Arizona.* I had recently read of another survivor who died, and whose last request was to join his shipmates in their grave. His request was honored, and he was lowered into the sunken hull. Maybe they'd do this for Roy, too.

I don't know what became of Lucy, the cousin who gave me my first kiss, or of Martin, who threw a cat on my back. But quiet Rachel went insane—quietly or loudly I don't know—and was committed. And Roy, for whatever misguided reason, took her out of the hospital, claiming that he could take care of her. What happened next is whispered in my family. No one talks openly of it. One night, she went into his room. I imagine her standing there over Roy, underwater in his dreams. I imagine her underwater, too, because that's where motives lie. I'll never know why she did that because there are certain things we can't ask our families. I can't ask Roy's sister because she doesn't want to remember, and I can't ask my mother because she doesn't know: all I can do is put together these images of people standing over beds—the anticlimax after anticipation.

But somehow I feel cheated, not relieved. Even with the Viper, I wanted to know why he kept calling, why it was so crucial for him to announce his every step. I want to know why Lucy was standing over my bed. *Pretend nothing's happened. Live underwater.* And I want to know why he swam, this man on land, why he jumped into the fiery waters of Pearl Harbor and then dove. Why he told jokes, why he was cheery, and why his younger daughter went to his room that night and stabbed him in the heart with a fishing knife.

I'm tempted to go back through my story, to lie, to combine the two sisters, or to leave the younger one, the mad one, out altogether. She's a cipher, quiet and bleak in the backseat on the way home from Rockaway Playland. You hardly hear a peep from her, except "Daddy, this is scary" as he tells his corny Viper story.

We know there's a kiss of death, but is there a kiss of madness, too? I'd like to say it was she who gave me my first kiss, but it was the older one, Lucy, who did—on the back stoop, hidden from view by my grandmother's falling-down toolshed, beside a dark alley with garbage cans and stray cats, and the faintest hint of an ocean breeze.

GEORGE KALAMARAS

1956

I crave the red moon burning above the bath water
and the tiny boat with plastic sails.
Mother is trying to forget Father's poker
hand and swabs behind my left ear, searching
for the even light of Sunday, for four
forkfuls of pot roast and maybe a massage. Outside
in the gangway, someone is talking in Greek,
ti kaneis, kala, and the sound of a widow's black
shawl crawls across shoulders like a cut
of cold coal over the cat's hump. Father is betting
on a brand new '56 Buick, on straighter teeth,
a larger flat, maybe air conditioning
and one day even college for the boys. I blow
the boat, and it travels all the way to Tanganyika
and Nyasaland. I open the book and touch the red
giraffe and say *pony* and *doggie.* I already want diamonds
and gold, mouthing *Ma-ma, Ma-ma,* and crave the pearl
of Mother's lovely *ooh*s and *ah*s
when I speak. I'm a good boy
lathered in Ivory soap, and I'm there to have my palm-
sized puppy chest rubbed. I want to grow up
and sail back to Greece, but beyond it. Beyond the hurt
in Mother's hair falling red behind her like sad goldfish
fins burning from fluorescent lights
above the bowl. The widow is leaving
Chicago, she swears, and might move south to Homewood
or Flossmore, though all I can hear is a bus grinding
at 64th and Hermitage, smell its exhaust, and a lilac voice
like Mother's down below and Athenian vowels drawn out
as elongated bees in sun and the cat's
claws scraping the fire escape and the sad humming
when Mother scrubs and what a good boy I am

and how I love Mama and will never grow up
to play poker. Father is somewhere with Louie
Khristophoulos and Pete Kappas and Uncle Gus
again, and a few blondes from Halsted.
They are young and curvey. They love Elvis and dancing and
laughs. They will settle for some Greeks from the south
side. Father is sipping *ouzo,* biting his best
Bogie into a Lucky, planning to buy Mother
a new stove and maybe a tight red dress and real silk
stockings with a black line up her thigh. He can't believe
it all ends with six days of 7 to 7
driving truck for his wife's father
at Merchant's Towel Service. He's suddenly 24
and wants to fuck somebody for once
who doesn't have two kids
and require a massage and slow talk and want pot roast
on Sundays. He's looking for the Jack of Diamonds
to make it right. He draws a long, even drag,
and the pressure nearly fills him.
Smoke crowds out over green felt in dusty Aegean clouds.
He's tapping the deck and tapping his smoke,
and the sunset moon at his fingers
is so close it almost burns.

CHOI IN HOON

The End of the State Highway

The afternoon August sun sizzles on the railroad tracks. Open terrain. The rails come from far off and move away into the distance.

The state highway runs alongside the railroad tracks. The highway is faultlessly paved. The asphalt surface, lustrous and oil-rich, is wide and smooth, more imposing than the railroad tracks. For its entire length, the highway also runs alongside a U.S. Army base.

Empty of trains, the railroad tracks burn brightly in the sun. At this hour there is not much traffic on the road either.

From the far end of the road a vehicle appears. The vehicle gradually comes closer, as if it were sliding over the road's smooth surface. It is a civilian bus. Not many people are on it, probably because this is an off-peak time and a weekday. There are six passengers. A man of about fifty is wearing a dull, yellowish shirt with no tie; his bluish, old-fashioned, double-breasted coat is placed over the armrest. He looks like the kind of man who deals in black-market goods around U.S. Army bases. Two men from the countryside are wearing identical white ramie overcoats and faded felt hats. Both have their bus tickets stuck in the bands of their hats. And there are two others from the countryside: young men with mussed-up hair, summer shirts. In the seat at the back of the bus, a pale young man stares out the window at the railroad tracks. Resting on his knees is the kind of tote bag college students often use.

The bus arrives at a checkpoint. An MP takes a quick look inside, and then a civilian police officer steps onto the bus. He examines the ID card of the man with the double-breasted suit.

"Employment?"

"I'm in sales."

"What do you sell?"

"Oh, just trinkets."

The police officer passes right by the two passengers wearing the ramie overcoats. He extends his hand towards the two young men sitting together.

"Are you returning from your physical exams?" he asks as he looks at the travel papers they hand him.

"Yes," they reply sullenly. They seem confident about their ID cards—surer about who they are than the others.

He comes to the young man sitting in the seat furthest back. He looks at his ID card.

"Student?"

"Yes, no . . ." His face turns red. "I was a student when the card was issued to me."

"And now?"

"I'm a teacher."

"For what purpose are you traveling?"

"I'm on my way to my new position."

"Some proof . . . ?"

The young man takes some papers out of his bag and shows them to the policeman.

"An elementary-school teacher?"

"Yes," he answers, a touch of anger in his voice.

The police officer gets off the bus and waves it on. The bus driver waves back cordially and restarts the bus. The young teacher stares out again at the railroad tracks. The empty tracks, burning in the sun, silently follow alongside the road.

At the entry to a bridge, the bus meets a U.S. Army transport convoy coming from the opposite direction. The wave of a hand from the jeep at the front of the convoy directs the bus to move to the shoulder. On this road, one makes way when the lord of the manor passes by in procession. The bus driver, grumbling, pulls the bus to the side of the road and stops. The trucks go by one after another. On the side of each is a wooden placard that in red letters reads DANGER EXPLOSIVES and has a carefully drawn skull and crossbones. Two well-groomed soldiers are riding in the front seat of each shiny, carefully maintained truck. Some men wear caps instead of helmets. There are colored soldiers among them. One looks towards the bus and makes an empty gesture with his clenched fist. Then he grins, flashing his white teeth. The young men coming back from their physical exam duck their heads and laugh.

All of the trucks have their yellow headlights on. One after the other, the vehicles pass by, each with an identical canvas covering, with the identical DANGER EXPLOSIVES sign, with identical yellow headlights, going at identical speed, carrying identical soldiers. The convoy seems to have no end. Vehicles continuously pour out over a distant railroad crossing at the base of a hill. Packed bumper to bumper, they form a line all the way to the bridge. The advance of so many identical vehicles creates the illusion that the procession is going around in an endless circle, the same trucks passing by again and again. It seems as if it will never end. In no time at all, traffic has piled up behind the bus as it continues to stand aside for the long procession. The vehicles behind the bus are of all shapes and sizes: civilian vehicles, military vehicles, large trucks, jeeps, three-quarter-ton trucks, and so on. But the expressions on the faces are all the same: the drivers fret and suppress their anger, waiting for the procession to end.

The final vehicle in the convoy passes by. The bus begins to move again. The teacher again turns his eyes in the direction of the railroad tracks. Burning in the scorching sun, they are still empty.

The bus lumbers for a while down the broad, level road. Then all at once the passengers press forward, craning their necks and staring out the front windows. A procession of loud colors, a resplendent chorus of wailing, is slowly making its way down the middle of the road. Just as for the truck convoy, the bus pulls to the shoulder of the road. All of the passengers crowd to one side of the bus and watch, leaning out of the windows.

It is an old-fashioned funeral procession: a forest of silk banners, mourners dressed in white, their hair loosened. Contrary to custom, however, all of the mourners are women. And none of the women, including the pallbearers, is from the countryside.

The driver watches but without interest, cupping his chin in his hand, elbow resting on the steering wheel, one foot propped on the handrail next to his seat.

"It's a funeral for a Westerner's girl. The mourners are from the bar girls' association," explains the driver flatly, as if to say it isn't anything unusual, of special interest.

The passengers nod their heads. Each banner has a different message on it, such as GOOD-BYE, SISTER or SUSAN, HOW CAN YOU GO ALONE, LEAVING ME?

As the procession wriggles along, moving at a snail's pace, the lament of "To the Other World" is followed by the chant of the chorus: "*Uuh eeh uuh eeh.*" The coffin, which was moving forward, begins to waver, drawing back and writhing. It looks like it will never get anywhere.

The vehicles stacked behind each other at both ends of the procession have turned into spectators. The funeral procession hesitates—almost as if caught up in its own chatter—in the gap between the two lines of vehicles facing each other. It appears the procession will soon turn left, off the state highway and onto a side road. Meanwhile, all the vehicles must wait. The funeral procession wavers forwards and backwards, staggering to the left and right, taking one step forward only to take two steps back. All in all, the procession is more like a band of traveling performers putting on a show in the middle of the street than a line of mourners with a destination in mind. The sunlit sky is a deep blue, and the indigo silk banners flash, tottering and then rising erect. The procession, paying no attention to the spectators, seems bent on taking as much time as it wants. It doesn't appear to have made much progress. There is not the slightest murmur of a breeze. The air is hot. Finally, the procession creeps by. A wailing woman slaps the rump of the bus as she passes. The bus winces and begins to move again. After a while, the elementary-school teacher turns and looks behind. The funeral procession is crossing the intersection where the railroad tracks meet the side road. A sudden dip in the side road causes the procession to disappear. After that, the empty railroad tracks burn brightly in the sun.

A little further on, the bus reaches a small village: Texas Village, a jumble of structures on both sides of the state highway. The stores are packed together, eaves touching. They have signs in English: ARIZONA SHOP, LILY SISTERS' STORE, HONEY CATS, PINK HEART. They are makeshift, hole-in-the-wall stores with canvas roofs; the merchandise inside, however, has an oily luster and looks sumptuous and brassy to the eyes of anyone who has been staring at the empty railroad tracks and the state highway tediously cutting through the rice and vegetable fields. In one of the stores, a young woman holds a black soldier around the waist and strikes him in the back with her fist. The soldier takes the blows, covering his head with his hands. Like the other stores, this one caters to U.S. soldiers. Small houses, also makeshift, are clustered together along an alley behind the stores. The town is so small that the bus can pass through it quickly. But the bus stops to pick up four passengers.

The inside of the bus perks up. One of the new passengers is a woman; from her pink blouse and pink shoes one can tell at a glance that she lives in this town. She carries a suitcase that looks foreign-made. The other new passengers are three drunken young men wearing military fatigues. Their hair is long, falling to the bottom of their ears, and is slicked back with grease.

"Pretty cute face, huh? When did you get here?" one of them asks the woman in the pink blouse.

It is true. She has attractive features. Her silver earrings shake, but she says nothing.

"Gee, she must have a wooden stake in her ears. Are you deaf?"

"If it's a stake, she's got it driven in somewhere else," another one chimes in. The other passengers chuckle weakly. The driver winces. The woman turns and stares fiercely at the young men. The young teacher, sitting on the same side of the bus as they are, feels as if her gaze is fixed on him. He turns his head away even though he is the only one who isn't laughing.

"Huh? You're checking us out? You've got eyes for losers like us too?"

The woman jerks her head back around and stares straight ahead.

"Hey, quit messing around. You ***."

The passengers again chuckle weakly. The teacher's face turns red and he looks like he is about to get up and say something, but he sinks back down in his seat. He thinks that her profile is beautiful as she looks out the window, her face averted. And he thinks that the shape of her lips is pretty. The young men continue to taunt her with lewd comments. The man with the double-breasted coat guffaws each time. The men in the white ramie overcoats grin to themselves. The young men returning from their physical exam giggle. The teacher, turning purple red, steals a glance at the woman each time the men taunt her. The woman keeps her face averted and doesn't look in his direction, so the teacher has no way of letting her know that he is not among those laughing. Tediously, the bus continues to grind along the road, and the vulgarity of the drunken men knows no end. It is quiet for a while, and then one of them starts up again. And again, the passengers chuckle weakly.

The woman snaps to her feet. "Let me off!"

The driver turns around. "But we're in the middle of nowhere . . . ," he responds slowly, facing forward again.

"I don't care. Let me off!"

With the engine revving, the driver puckers his lips and pulls over. "All right then."

The woman picks up her bag and starts towards the door.

"Huh? Getting off?"

"Going to sell your *** in the street?"

"I'll be right there. Wash your *** and wait."

The drunken men keep up their lewd taunting to the end. The woman, feigning that she doesn't hear, descends the steps. She pauses on the last step and turns around sharply. Her voice rings out.

"Sons of bitches—dogs! All of you!" she cries, barely able to leap off the bus as it starts to pull away.

Loaded with dogs, the bus hesitates for a moment as if confused, then picks up speed. Driven by a dog, filled with dogs—some of the dogs with their paws up on the windows and barking—the bus barrels down the state highway like a dog that's been kicked in the balls. It disappears into the distance.

On the deserted state highway, only the woman remains, looking like a small, pink doll. She stares vacantly in the direction of the disappeared bus. After a while, she turns in the direction from which she'd come. The state highway and the burning railroad tracks—two endless lines that converge in the distance and then continue on. At the intersection, a massive replica of a Salem cigarette box towers over the landscape, large as a building. Out of the top of the green box, sitting somewhat askew on tall supports, a third of a cigarette the size of a chimney sticks out, aimed at the sky like a gun barrel. She gazes vacantly at that white gun barrel in the distance. Several trucks pass by carrying U.S. soldiers, laughing and joking, but another bus does not come. She does not look anxious. Immersed in her own thoughts, she continues to gaze at the massive Salem box. She stands there, in the scorching sun, for about half an hour. Finally she picks up her suitcase and starts to walk in the direction she just came from—towards Salem. She walks for some time with tired steps, head down and wrapped in thought. As she steps into the shadow cast over the road by the Salem box, she hears the engine of a vehicle coming up behind her. She turns and looks. A bus. She puts her trunk down in the shade. The bus stops in front of her. She picks up the suitcase and gets on the bus. The door closes and the bus starts to move again. It disappears, melting into the oily luster of the road, burning in the sun.

Two endless lines, the lustrous road and the burning railroad tracks alone mark the plain: each a wordless traveler making its way silently into the distance. The massive green Salem watches them go farther and farther away.

On the city's outskirts, at a crossing where the state highway and the railroad tracks meet, a young boy is waiting . . . in the lengthening shadows of the August evening . . . waiting since the time the sun stood high in the sky at midday . . . waiting in the shade of a metal sign—VITA M—twice as big as his house. Many buses have passed by. The person he is waiting for has not come.

The state highway gradually darkens, and the railroad, like the young boy's final hope, shines a dull golden color in the setting sun. The sound of an engine coming down the road . . . the young boy steps forward. Soon a bus with its headlights on appears on the other side of the crossing. It drives across the rails. And passes by. The young boy squats again. The railroad tracks do not shine anymore.

A train comes roaring up the tracks. The young boy stands, then backs up a little. The engine passes by in a meaningless fury, and the passenger cars follow. Crosses have been drawn on the sides of the cars. The faces of long-nosed Yankee men and long-nosed Yankee women dressed in white appear through the brightly lit windows. A woman wearing a white hat presses her face against the window and stares outside at the darkness, at the young boy. After the passenger cars, flatbeds pass by. Stretched out on the flatbeds are giant artillery pieces. Weighed down by their heavy gun barrels, they look exhausted, like wounded soldiers. Tanks with no treads—crouched like mountaintops and looking bigger than the young boy's house—pass by. Crumpled GMCs, their wheels missing and front ends smashed, go by. They are all wordless, injured, exhausted travelers. It is an endlessly long train. The young boy becomes afraid: if this train blocks the way forever, the bus won't be able to come over the crossing. Even now the bus carrying the person he is waiting for must be waiting on the other side. The young boy squats, making up his mind to wait for it all to go by, no matter how long it takes. He has persevered for a long, long time. All of the travelers on the train finally go by. The young boy springs to his feet and looks across. It's not there—the road is not there. The railroad tracks are not there.

The railroad tracks and the road have disappeared into the night.

The darkness clouding into the young boy's pupils and his heart sinking into that darkness are all that remain. Why doesn't Older Sister come?

Translation by Theodore Hughes

ROBERT HILL LONG

Two Poems

ROOF, TREES, RAINS, CLOUDS

The rains sealing Sarah in Oregon winter sleep
bring down needles of fir, oak leaves steeping
their tannins in the roof's wide pool. No light
sleeper, she sinks where breath is lightless deeps:
her brain a turquoise anemone, opening only
at her mouth to suck in dreaming's placental
atmospheres. When she moved in her mother,
her roof was skin, the blood-salted pool of love's
afterlife. Before us, what was she? It's like
thinking of stars in bed when rain offers the roof
continual denial that night is anything more
than cloud cover. Say one body was a bay,
the other a star falling in. Say each breaks
the other open, and their pieces of broken shine

rejoin as a shoal of fish, near the shore. There,
lovers walk the edge until they know what coupling
is for. Stars school in black water, in love's
astronomy. In love's evolving, rain focuses
into the eyes of one miracle fish, which searched
through our pooled life, and one morning came,
spit ocean out of its lungs and cried its first
human cry: awake in our world an hour,
drinking the milk of forgetting. And in sleep,
where she was engendered, Sarah returns
to her rainy beginnings: under our flat roof,
under firs and oaks where winter rains pull down
fragrant needles and leaves, making a shallow
inland cover for this daughter of salt and star water.

AND THE WATER DRANK ME

The pure pleasure of girls slicing into water,
lifted up by it, to climb out streaming
and slice in again. Eight-year-old girls, white
as white peach flesh, gold as pear flesh,
in one-piece sunflower wrappings, in millefiori
on night-blue backgrounds. Black hair,
gold hair between their shoulder blades,
and the golds and the blacks streaming
clear from their water-combed ends, clear
as the streams off the girls' limbs. To be
embodied and colored so like fruit and yet
plunge through this substance that shines
brighter than any blade. So cleanly they cut
into it, this beckoning, yielding thing
that solves the question of iron. This most
patient thing, nothing as thoughtlessly clear
in meditative action, nothing on earth
more capacious. The fruit of them going
into it, pure pleasure now and pleasure again,
their fruit grows and is not eaten in a day,
but is bathed in the thing it cuts through,
is nourished by what will drink it at last.
Between these neutral infinities, the girls go
as shrieks, as exultings. They laugh and call
and lengthen underwater, they are magnified
and faceted, they disappear, rise and shed
this streaming skin of preservation
and dissolution. They dry hair and shoulder blades
on the grass, dry their bands of flowers
planted in night blue, night black. For an hour
they impose on themselves their best pantomime
of the poise death takes in the old books—
stretched out, still, eyes closed, the peace
of blades, of cut pears, drying in the grass.

MIN SOO KANG

Kyŏngbok Palace: History, Controversy, Geomancy

We live amidst so many rumors. The stratum of rumor is thick and heavy. We call this history and we call it culture.

It is a sad thing to live one's life as if listening to a rumor. When we are no longer satisfied with rumors and seek the place of occurrence, that is when we meet destiny.

Choi In Hoon, *Kwangjang*

Introduction

What follows is partly history, partly rumor, and partly confession.

I will trace the history of Kyŏngbok Palace in Seoul, the royal residence of fifteen monarchs of Korea's Chosŏn dynasty, from its original construction in the late fourteenth century through the destructions and reconstructions it underwent in the following five centuries. My narrative will serve as historical background to the great controversy that lasted from 1993 to 1995 over the question of demolishing the National Museum Building, and will reveal not only a secret history of the palace—one steeped in ancient, mystical beliefs—but also the problematic attitude that modern Koreans have toward their past.

Although I have been trained as an academic historian, this essay is not a work of academic history in the strict sense. I have neither burdened it with a massive list of references and notes to support my findings and interpretations, nor taken on the objective voice of the historian as recording angel. I have set out instead to describe my own sense of wonder, and to explain why I distrust that feeling.

What follows is partly history, partly rumor, and partly confession, but every history is partly rumor and partly confession; every rumor is partly history and partly confession; and every confession is partly history and partly rumor. And I believe that when history, rumor, and confession intermingle, the past reveals itself in its most human form.

What follows is also a dream, or perhaps the recurring nightmare of someone trying to come to terms with a traumatic event. And it is a haunting as well, for what is history but the irrepressible visitations of ghosts

Portrait of an Elderly Man Wearing a Horsehair Hat, Korea, 1946
Photograph by Horace Bristol

seeking to return to life—not as human beings, but as something much more enduring . . .

The Palace of Fifteen Kings

Kyŏngbok Palace lies at the northern edge of Seoul's midtown area, which is surrounded by a series of hills. Although the easiest way to reach the palace is by taking either the third (orange) subway line, which stops right below the palace grounds, or the glistening new fifth (purple) line to Kwanghwa Gate Station, I suggest starting on T'aep'yŏng Road near City Hall and walking northward up the street, in order to get the full effect of the view. As you approach the lofty statue of Admiral Yi Sunshin in the middle of the street, which widens out to become the perennially packed sixteen-lane Sejong Road, you will face the green peaks of Pugak Mountain. Below the mountain is the southern gate of Kwanghwa (Luminous Achievement), a solid structure of white stone topped by an elaborately decorated double-tiered roof. Walk past the statue with the Sejong Cultural Center on your left and the American Embassy complex on your right, and you have to cross the street through an underground walkway to reach the southern wall of the building. You can enter the outer grounds through Kwanghwa Gate—which I recommend to fully appreciate the intricate and colorful designs of the roof—but you will then find your view of the rest of the palace blocked by the high scaffolding that hides the work still being done to remove the remains of the recently demolished National Museum Building. You must walk down the east side of the outer grounds to reach the official entrance, where you can purchase a ticket to be admitted into the central section of the palace.

Most of the tourists will be gathered around the two largest buildings: Kŭnjŏngjŏn (Diligent Rule), an imposing wooden structure that was set upon a vast base of stone and that served as the throne room and the audience hall where the kings conducted their public business; and Kyŏnghoeru (Auspicious Meeting), a grand two-story pavilion on a wide, square pond where royal banquets were held. You have to find your way through a complex network of low roofed walls to reach other places of interest, including Sajŏngjŏn (Thoughtful Rule), the king's private working quarters, which contains a famous mural of a pair of four-toed dragons; Ch'ŏnch'ujŏn (Thousand Autumns), the hall of court scholars where the Korean writing system was invented under the guidance of King Sejong the Great (r. 1418–1450); Hyangwŏnjŏn (Fragrant Distance), a dainty structure on a tiny island; and an obscure corner on the north side of the grounds that marks, with a lone stone tablet, the place where Queen Min, the powerful wife of the penultimate monarch, Kojong (r. 1864–1907), was murdered by Japanese assassins in 1895.

If you go to the palace expecting to see a series of sprawling, multistoried mansions and lofty fortifications in the European manner, you will be surprised. With the exception of the audience hall and the main pavilion, all the buildings are rather small and squat and are separated from each other by interconnected walls that give you the sense of being in a maze. Starting in 1963, most of the dozen or so structures that can be visited today were rebuilt, while the vast majority of the original buildings were either torn down by the Japanese during the colonial era (1910–1945) or destroyed by bombs during the Korean War (1950–1953).

In imagining the grandiosity of the palace in its heyday, you have to keep the horizontal plane rather than the vertical in mind. Rulers of nations made up of flat plains tended to build high edifices that could be seen for miles. But in a mountainous country like Korea, where flat land is precious, the most conspicuous way of exhibiting power was to occupy a great tract of open space and turn it into a place of secrets. The palace contained some 330 buildings, which stood on over 410,000 square meters of land, and was a true labyrinth of dizzying complexity: one through which hundreds of slaves, servants, courtesans, entertainers, soldiers, eunuchs, scholars, generals, ministers, and royalty scurried in service or in pursuit of power.

The Palace in Korean History, 1392–1963

In 1392, General Yi Sŏnggye completed his coup d'état of the Koryŏ Kingdom by ascending the throne as the first king (r. 1392–1398) of the Chosŏn dynasty (1392–1910). The new monarch ruled from the old capital of Songdo—today's Kaesŏng in North Korea—for two years, consolidating his power and negotiating with the Ming Empire of China for recognition of his rule's legitimacy. However, he soon became weary of living amidst the hostile noble families loyal to the previous dynasty. It was also rumored that he became haunted by the ghost of the founder of the Koryŏ dynasty, Wang Kŏn (r. 918–943), after Wang Kŏn's descendants, the royal family of the fallen kingdom, were massacred in a series of bloody purges. The king, therefore, resolved to move the capital to a new city and sent out numerous agents to look for a suitable place. Among the royal emissaries was the Buddhist priest Muhak (a quintessential Zen name meaning "no knowledge"), who was knowledgeable in the art of *p'ungsu chiri* (literally, "the science of wind, water, and land" and the equivalent of the Chinese *feng shui,* which is usually translated as "geomancy"). As Muhak was a confidant of the king, his advice to halt the construction of a city at Shindoan, below Gaeryung Mountain, was heeded, and a site above the Han River called Hanyang (today's Seoul, the capital of the Republic of Korea) was chosen instead. The new site was protected by a series of hills with a single passageway to the northeast. After further study of the area, a location below Pugak Mountain, situated in the northwestern corner, was determined to be the best place to build the new royal palace.

Construction of the palace began in the tenth lunar month of 1394 and was completed in a little under a year. The building was named Kyŏngbok

(Great Fortune) by Chŏng Tojŏn (1337–1398), the king's chief advisor and Confucian ideologue. The name of the palace is composed of the last two characters of a line in the ancient Chinese *Book of Songs:*

> Since you are already drunk on liquor and sated by virtue, your ten thousand years as a superior man will be blessed by a great fortune.

The palace served as the royal residence and the center of the kingdom's administration throughout the reigns of the first thirteen kings of the Chosŏn dynasty. In 1592, the twenty-fourth year of the reign of King Sŏnjo, the Japanese launched a major invasion of the Korean peninsula. As the flimsy defense of the ill-prepared Chosŏn army collapsed before the onslaught of two hundred thousand invaders, the royal court fled Hanyang, which fell a mere twenty days after the Japanese landed at the southern port city of Pusan. The palace was set on fire and burned completely to the ground.

What many tourist brochures and history textbooks will neglect to tell you is that the terrible destruction was not the work of the Japanese. After the court evacuated the city—jeered at and pelted with stones by common people who were disgusted by their nobles' cowardice and incompetence—the palace slaves sought to free themselves by setting fire to the building containing the records of their servitude. The flames spread to the other buildings and eventually reduced the entire palace to ashes; slaves who remained on the grounds looted the palace before the arrival of the Japanese. Although the city was recaptured in a few months by the Ming army, the palace was left in ruins for the next 273 years, and the royal residence was moved to the more modest Ch'angdŏk Palace.

After the brilliant rule of the last two great kings of the dynasty, Yŏngjo (r. 1724–1776) and his grandson Chŏngjo (r. 1776–1800), the kingdom rapidly declined. The subsequent monarchs, who were easily manipulated boy-kings, were mere puppets in the political struggle between the Kim clan of Andong and the Cho clan of P'ungyang. In 1864, twelve-year-old Prince Myŏngbok (King Kojong) assumed the throne. When his father was appointed regent and given the title of Taewŏngun ("Prince of the Great House"), the former drunkard and fool surprised everyone by proving to be a decisive and fearful despot.

The Taewŏngun ruled the country as an absolute dictator for the next nine years, getting rid of anyone who stood in his way. He put a lid on the factional feuds in the court, then slammed the door on all foreigners except the Ching Chinese, ordering the military in coastal cities to fire their cannons at all foreign ships. In 1866, an American merchant vessel by the name of *General Sherman* was sunk on the Taedong River. In the same year, the suppression of Catholicism was ordered, resulting in the slaughter of nine French missionaries and some eight thousand converts. The

French sent seven warships to Ganghwa Island in response, but were driven away by a fierce counterattack. It was at this time that the country came to be known as the Hermit Kingdom.

To wrest power from the nobility and increase the prestige of the royal family, the Taewŏngun then embarked on his most ambitious and foolhardy project: the complete reconstruction of Kyŏngbok Palace. Work began in the fourth lunar month of 1865 and took over four years to complete, employing some 36,000 workers. Against the opposition of nearly everyone in the court, he created a special tax and extorted "voluntary offerings" from the rich to pay the colossal bills. Although the palace was restored in a magnificent fashion and the court returned to it in the eleventh lunar month of 1869, the project nearly bankrupted the kingdom and caused much resentment against the regent. When the king came of age in 1871, the Taewŏngun's daughter-in-law, Queen Min, moved against her unpopular father-in-law and engineered his fall from power two years later.

While King Kojong, at the behest of his wife, ended the Taewŏngun's isolationist policy and opened up the nation to the rest of the world, events had occurred in East Asia that would prevent the kingdom from remaining independent. In 1894, Chinese and Japanese armies marched into Korea under the pretext of helping to put down the Tonghak Rebellion. When the Japanese proved victorious in the Sino-Japanese War of 1894 to 1895, Queen Min tried to counter their dominant presence by making overtures to the Russians. However, in 1895 the Japanese ambassador Miura Goro brought in assassins who slipped into the palace at dawn on October 8, dragged the queen and her ladies-in-waiting to a secluded spot in the northern part of the grounds, and slashed open the queen's chest with their swords before burning her body and those of her attendants. The Japanese army subsequently occupied the palace and ousted all anti-Japanese ministers. King Kojong, fearing for his life and that of his son, fled the palace with the crown prince on February 11 of the following year and took up residence in the Russian consulate. The unfortunate king chose to live in Tŏksu Palace when he left the consulate in 1897, and no reigning monarch set foot in Kyŏngbok Palace again.

Despite desperate attempts by King Kojong to maintain Korea's independence—including sending a secret envoy to the International Peace Convention held in the Hague in 1907—he was forced to sign a protectorate treaty with the Japanese and to abdicate in favor of his retarded son (Sunjong, r. 1907–1910). In 1910, Korea officially became a colony of the Japanese Empire.

In the first years of the colonial era, all but ten or so buildings of the palace were torn down, the entire southern wall was destroyed, and Kwanghwa Gate was moved—stone by stone—to the eastern wall. In 1912, a German architect by the name of Georg de Lalande, who was residing in Tokyo, was hired to design the Japanese Government-General Building in Korea. The construction of the massive, five-story, neo-Renaissance-style granite structure began in June 1916 and was completed in October 1926. The complex was erected on the front part of the grounds, completely eclipsing what remained of the palace.

The Japanese left the country in 1945, after their defeat in World War II, and the Republic of Korea was inaugurated three years later. While there was some discussion of tearing down the former Government-General Building—President Rhee Syngman himself favored the idea—the cost of demolishing the structure was too extravagant for the impoverished nation. Instead it was used as the Government Building of the Korean republic until 1983, when it was converted into the National Museum. Reconstruction and renovation of Kyŏngbok Palace began in 1963, when Kwanghwa Gate was moved back to its original place.

The Controversy, 1993–1995

I first became interested in the history of Kyŏngbok Palace because of the discussions in the Korean media from 1993 to 1995 over the question of demolishing the National Museum Building, which used to be the Government Building, which used to be the Government-General Building of the Japanese Empire. In August 1993, President Kim Young Sam announced that the building, as a legacy of the colonial era, would be destroyed in 1995—the fiftieth anniversary of Korea's liberation from the Japanese and the six-hundredth anniversary of the completion of the original palace. Although the proposal was met with wide approval by the public, it immediately set off a bitter two-year controversy over the fate of the building.

The pro-demolitionists argued that, as Korea now possessed the tenth-largest economy in the world, as well as a truly democratic political system that had brought to power the first civilian president in decades, it was high time the country got rid of what they viewed as a remnant from the time of subjugation. The building that had been erected in front of the palace of the old kings to symbolize Japanese imperial dominance should be destroyed, they argued, in order to demonstrate Korea's transcendence of the great trials of the past and its achievement of freedom and prosperity.

The preservationists, however, thought that it was the height of jingoistic stupidity and a gross waste of taxpayers' money to destroy a perfectly good building that also served as a fine museum. They pointed out that the estimated cost would be 4.8 billion *wŏn* (around $6 million at the time) for the demolition work alone, plus some 23.7 billion *wŏn* (a little under $30 million) for the construction of a building to house the museum artifacts. In addition, it would require 178.9 billion *wŏn* (over $210 million) to clean up and renovate Kyŏngbok Palace. A proposal to move the building block by block to a different location was rejected outright when the estimated cost turned out to be astronomical. The preservationists questioned what practical purpose destroying the building served. They asked, Isn't it time the nation moved on from its obsession with the humiliation of half a century ago? If the building is destroyed, Japan remains the same, but Korea will have squandered over 200 billion *wŏn* and ended up with one less place to put the national treasures. To them, it was a matter of reason versus national hysteria.

Historians were also bitterly divided over the issue. The pro-demolitionists among them pointed out that the Japanese were still unwilling to face up to the crimes they had committed during the imperial era. This was exemplified by their refusal to make a proper apology and award reparations to the surviving Korean women who were forced into sexual slavery (the so-called comfort women) during World War II; the success of Japanese books detailing how ungrateful Koreans are for all the wonderful things that were done for them as a Japanese colony; the movement by right-wing groups to claim Tok Island; and the continued use of outdated history textbooks that contain glaring inaccuracies about both early and modern Korea. We need to make a strong statement of outrage, they argued, by destroying that most prominent remainder of Japanese presence on the peninsula and invite foreign journalists to witness the event so that we can express our discontent with Japan's attitude toward the past.

In contrast, preservationist historians pointed out that, while the building was constructed by the Japanese, it also played an important part in the history of the Korean republic, having served as the center of government for most of the nation's history. During a lively television debate on the issue, one historian brought in an enlargement of the famous 1948 photograph of President Rhee Syngman taking the oath of office in front of the building, before a great crowd of people and below the national flag. The building is an integral part of our own history now, the historian said, and to destroy it is to destroy a part of our own heritage. Another historian said that Koreans ought to preserve the building precisely because it is an odious reminder of the colonial era: not only will its presence keep us from forgetting what was done to us, he said; it will also provide a lesson in what can happen if we become weak enough to lose our independence again. He went on to say that you do not tear down the Pyramids because slave labor was used to build them; nor do you destroy Auschwitz because terrible things happened there. What these monuments teach us is far too important, he asserted.

Following the discussions closely, I found most interesting—and, at the same time, puzzling—the frequent mention of certain ideas from *p'ungsu chiri* (geomancy). As I knew virtually nothing about the ancient art, I was completely bewildered by the great passion with which some of the participants in the debates discussed the National Museum Building and Kyŏngbok Palace in geomantic terms. What also struck me was the fact that their mystical ideas were taken seriously by the media and so could not be easily dismissed as the strange ramblings of a few eccentrics. I knew that geomancy was no mere superstition for many Koreans. For example, it is still common practice to hire a geomancer to look over the land one is thinking of purchasing or building on. An MIT-educated engineer once told me that his first semiconductor business had failed because the factory was built in a geomantically unsound place; and I recently found out that my late grandfather—a devout, lifelong Christian and professor of geography—had consulted a geomancer when looking for a suitable grave site for himself and his wife.

In considering the various debates on the controversy, I had no problem understanding the argument of national pride, the argument of practical economics, the argument of historical outrage, and the argument of historical preservation. But it was difficult for me, as a Western-educated person, to take the geomancy argument seriously. My skepticism was reinforced by recent reports in the media of "geomantic crimes" and "geomantic frauds." People had secretly buried the bodies of their parents on so-called propitious land that belonged to someone else, hoping to bring great fortune to their descendants. Some geomancers had received bribes from real-estate agents to declare certain lands fortuitous in order to increase their value. Other geomancers had declared the grave site of the parents of President Park Chung Hee to be fortuitous because the family had produced a ruler of the nation; but when Park was assassinated in 1979, the land was declared to be unlucky. The same thing happened with the grave sites of the parents of Presidents Chun Doo Hwan and Roh Tae Woo: they were declared to be propitious when the leaders rose to power, but found to be unlucky when the men went to jail in 1996 for corruption. And I understand that the grave site of the parents of the current president, Kim Dae Jung, is supposed to be lucky now and is visited by a steady stream of tourists.

I felt that I needed to learn more about *p'ungsu chiri,* superstition or not, in order to comprehend the passions involved. What I found was not only a complex system of thought with a rich and fascinating tradition, but also a secret history of the places at the heart of the controversy.

The Secret History of Geomancy

Modern Western physiology basically regards the human body as a machine consisting of discrete parts, each with a specific function in maintaining the life of the organism. When a person falls ill, the question is asked, Which part has broken down or is not working properly? Once the source of the malfunction is identified, it is isolated and repaired so that the part may once again perform its role in the mechanical system.

Traditional East Asian medicine, on the other hand, sees the body as a vessel through which *ki* (vital energy) flows, animating the corporeal mass. The *ki* travels through points of vital concentration, called *hyŏl,* which are distributed all over the body. At each of these points, the energy accumulates so that its speed, temperature, and quantity can be regulated. Within this system of medicine, an illness is defined as an imbalance or disharmony in the flow of *ki* that is caused by a leakage, blockage, or weakening along its path and that may have an internal or external cause. Acupuncture manipulates these *hyŏl* points in order to correct the flow or to reroute it to places where it is needed the most. Since *ki* paths are all interconnected, a doctor may treat, say, stomach pain by putting needles in such disparate places as the shoulder, tips of the fingers, and back of the neck in order to restore harmony. Of course, it would be of no use for me to insist at this point that this actually works—especially for chronic pain and psychosomatic disorders that Western medicine can do little about—since few in the West are convinced until they try it. But the effectiveness of such treatment does not necessarily prove the general physiological ideas of East Asian medicine, just as the efficacy of Western science does not validate its world view.

The ancient Chinese art of *feng shui* is based on exactly the same model, but applied to the natural environment. *Ki* flows through the living organism of the earth by means of wind, water, and mountain ranges. When it flows in a harmonious and regular manner, the weather is mild and good for farming, the water and air are clear, and all creatures thrive. When it is blocked or dissipated by an alteration in the landscape—for example, a structure erected in the wrong place—the weather turns nasty, disasters like floods and earthquakes occur periodically, and diseases wreak havoc among the inhabitants. A geomancer is both a doctor of the environment, diagnosing the nature of natural calamities and finding the remedies, and an assessor who determines the geomantic health and value of the land.

One of the most important concepts in geomancy is *myŏngdang* (literally, "a radiant place"). The ultimate philosopher's stone of geomancers, *myŏngdang* is the ideal place to live, establish a settlement, or bury one's parents. The method of identifying such a site is extremely complex; basically, a *myŏngdang* is the geomantic equivalent of a *hyŏl:* a place where a strong flow of *ki* accumulates and is warmed and cooled at the same time because of an optimal conjunction of geographical features. Such a place usually has a circular mountain range, which brings in the *ki,* and is bordered by a river that cools the vital energy down before sending it on.

When you examine the illustrations of the different *myŏngdang* in geomantic treatises, you notice that the concept makes perfect geographical sense as well. A settlement built in such a location would not only be protected by the mountains, but would also be right next to a water source. Even though it expresses itself in the terminology of magic, geomancy is one of the most ancient forms of a comprehensive science of urban and environmental planning. And in a small, mountainous nation like Korea, where there is limited space in which to build settlements, it was an essential art.

The more utilitarian aspects of geomancy, however, went into decline in both Chosŏn dynasty Korea and Ming dynasty China. A minor aspect of the art—the concept of generating good fortune by burying one's parents at a *myŏngdang*—eventually emerged as geomancy's main tenet. Hired mainly to look for such a place, most geomancers became agents of the rich and the powerful—a practice that continues to the present. In the early nineteenth century, the great populist poet Kim Sakkat (1807–1863), in one of his many poems satirizing the greed of the wealthy and the incompetence of scholars, condemned the geomancers as well:

> All geomancers are frauds.
> Tongues wagging, busily pointing North and South.
> If there really is a radiant place in those mountains,
> Why did you not bury your own father there?

Feng shui comes largely out of Daoist thought: elements of it can be found in the sayings of the first masters Lao Tzu (circa sixth century B.C.) and Chuang Tzu (circa third century B.C.). It was introduced into Korea during the era of the Unified Shilla Kingdom (A.D. 669–935), with the first great master of the art, the Buddhist priest Tosŏn, emerging in the ninth century. By the time the Koryŏ dynasty was founded in 918, geomancy was regarded as a legitimate scholarly subject and was taught at major learning institutions. Although it never became a core subject of civil-service examinations, the more ambitious practitioners of the art could take the government's so-called miscellaneous examination. This allowed them to enter the ranks of technical scholars, with the hope of one day becoming the court geomancer, who was consulted on matters concerning building and settlement sites, as well as the all-important site for a royal grave.

The strangest episode in Korean history involving geomancy occurred in the early twelfth century, during the reign of the Koryŏ monarch Injong (r. 1122–1146). The kingdom was in crisis at the time: a major rebellion had just been suppressed, the royal palace at Songdo had been completely destroyed by fire during the conflict, and the Jurchen Chin state of Northern China had begun exerting military pressure on the peninsula. Two of the king's high ministers, Paek Suhan and Chŏng Chisang, and a Buddhist priest by the name of Myoch'ŏng, who was reputed to be a powerful geomancer, urged the king to move the capital to their native city of Sukyung (today's Pyongyang, the capital of North Korea). The men argued that the misfortunes of the kingdom were due to the weakening of *ki* in Songdo. Myoch'ŏng went so far as to claim that the Sukyung site he had in mind for the new royal residence was such a potent *myŏngdang* that moving the court there would not only cause all the problems of the kingdom to go away, but also prompt the Chin Empire to surrender of its own accord and make Injong the master of thirty-six nations. The king consented, and a new palace was built in Sukyung by 1129. But even as the king and his court prepared to make the journey from Songdo, the entire country was shaken by a series of terrible natural disasters. When an enormous lightning bolt struck just outside the newly built residence, it was universally regarded as a bad omen and the move was canceled. Although most historians interpret the episode as an attempt by the Sukyung men to use geomancy to increase the prestige of their hometown—and thus their own status—that does not wholly explain what occurred next. Apparently believing every word of his outlandish claims about the power of the place, in 1135 Myoch'ŏng raised a ragtag band of armed men and occupied the city, declaring himself king. He strutted around for a few weeks, claiming to be a ruler destined to conquer the world, and bullied the local people until they got fed up with him and arrested him and his band. The men were subsequently executed for treason.

Farcical events of this nature were not the only effect of geomantic ideas on the nation's history. If you go up to the observation tower on Nam Mountain and look down on the central part of the great chaotic sprawl that is today's Seoul, you will see that the place is a textbook case of a *myŏngdang:* a network of hills surrounds it to the north, and the Han River borders it to the south. To understand this configuration, we must return to 1394, when the first king of the Chosŏn dynasty chose the site for his new capital and the royal residence.

The tract of land below Pugak Mountain was chosen for the palace because court geomancers determined that it was a *hyŏl* upon which an enormous amount of *ki* poured down like a great waterfall from the heights. The geomancers believed that the energy would accumulate at the palace before spreading out across the land, like the benevolent rule of the king. They also found the place to be propitious since the mountain was in the shape of *tae* (the Chinese character for "great"). It was essential, however, to keep the area in front of the palace clear in order to facilitate the flow of *ki.*

The Japanese tried to destroy Korea during the colonial era in many ways: the policy of slow eradication of the Korean language and culture, the destruction of important cultural artifacts and the rewriting of history, the outright massacres, the killing of people in concentration camps through starvation and forced labor, the medical experiments on live subjects, the forced prostitution of nearly 200,000 women. But the most bizarre was through the use of geomancy.

For decades after liberation in 1945, there were stories that the Japanese had brought their own geomancers to Korea to determine where all the major *hyŏl* were. The colonial authorities had then ordered enormous iron spikes to be driven through those points in order to cut off the flow of *ki,* thus destroying all the *myŏngdang* in the land and sapping the life from the nation—much like putting acupuncture needles at the wrong points in the body. The idea was so fantastic that the only people who took these stories seriously were aging geomancers who had lived during the colonial era and who claimed to have gone to the sites and seen the spikes still buried in the ground. I myself thought these were ludicrous anti-Japanese rumors.

In the spring of 1995, all of Korea watched television open-mouthed as investigative reporters followed the old geomancers to some of these locations and, with the help of heavy machinery, began pulling out one iron spike after another, some of them clearly marked with Japanese characters. The geomancers claimed that throughout the years they had removed approximately one hundred and fifty spikes on their own initiative—out of some thousand they thought buried throughout the country. A subsequent government investigation, however, managed to locate and remove only twenty more.

Then it was asserted that the Government-General Building in front of Kyŏngbok Palace was the greatest *ki*-destroyer of them all because it had an enormous iron dome, which supposedly blocked the energy flowing down from Pugak Mountain. Those who argued for the demolition of the building also pointed out the following. The building, when seen from above, looked like the Chinese character for "day": *nip* in Japanese. Down the street was the rather oddly shaped City Hall, also built by the Japanese: seen from above, it looked like the character for "basis": *pon* in Japanese. By combining the character formed by Pugak Mountain with these, you got the three characters for "Great Nippon" (Japan)—smack in the heart of Seoul! In addition, geomancers claimed that two other major buildings erected by the Japanese—the Seoul Railway Station and the zoo and botanical garden at Ch'anggyŏng Palace—were also placed to disrupt the flow of *ki* through the city.

I believe it was the discovery of these iron spikes that finally allowed the pro-demolitionists to win. During the National Liberation Day celebrations at the palace on August 15, 1995, the iron dome was torn off the former Government-General Building amidst thunderous applause. On November 13 of the next year, at five o'clock in the afternoon, dynamite was set off at its granite base, and the entire structure collapsed in a cloud of gray dust. A few weeks later, after most of the debris was removed, a construction crew working in the basement discovered more spikes buried in the ground.

There were some nine thousand of them.

The Dragon in the Pond

For some blessed countries, history is something that happened long ago and far away. For others, the present is full of the past, sometimes as a great burden that prevents forward movement, and other times as a great storm that sweeps everything up and takes it to some unknown place in the future. A historian living in a fortunate country may complain of the public's lack of interest in the past, but it should be realized that the people to whom history matters the most are those of troubled lands, where the tempest of events is still raging. The passion that is aroused in discussions of the past by Bosnians, Palestinians, or Northern Irelanders cannot be matched in similar discussions by Canadians or Swedes. That is why I find the Korean obsession with history both fascinating and sad.

I am not a historian of Korea. Although I am Korean and know the culture and the language, I lived there for only five years, as a child, returning in 1995, after an absence of eighteen years, to perform my compulsory military duty. Although it would be an exaggeration to call myself an outsider in Korea, I cannot help feeling slightly removed. Even as I travel about in Seoul, conversing with people, acting in the proper manner, following the correct rituals of everyday life, I cannot help feeling like an actor playing a part. I remember as an undergraduate reading Dostoyevsky's *The Possessed* and wincing at Shatov's passionate words:

> Rest assured that those who cease to understand the people of their own country and lose contact with them also lose the faith of their forefathers and become godless or indifferent. Yes, yes, it always proves true; that's why you and the lot of us today are either despicable atheists or indifferent, vicious human muck.

For nearly two decades I grew away from my native land, educating myself in Western history, philosophy, and literature, learning to have greater command of the English language, developing close relationships with Americans, and attending graduate school to become a historian of modern Europe—until I was forced to return and enlist in the South Korean army, the toughest institution I have ever been a part of. I was turned into a soldier and sent to a hellhole near the Demilitarized Zone because I owed it to my country to defend it against communism—six years after the fall of the Berlin Wall and the dissolution of the Soviet Union and the Warsaw Pact. Kim Il Sung, the founder and longtime dictator of North Korea, had died suddenly the year before, and the military situation involving both nations was still tense. The economy of the North was deteriorating quickly, and some speculated that North Korea would invade the South before it got worse. In 1996, when a malfunctioning North Korean submarine was discovered off South Korea's east coast and its crew found dead, the South Korean army went on full alert. While reconnaissance units based in Kangwŏn Province searched for the six infiltrators who had been aboard the submarine, the company I was stationed with went on standby and had to wait in battle-ready condition. Our platoon commander even told us to write a letter to our parents because troop movements on the North Korean side suggested that we might be at war in a few days. I saw some of the toughest men in the platoon break down and weep at the announcement; others lost control of their bladders. That was the first time I experienced what it was like to be a participant in history rather than a scholar. And as I had tasted enough of the trauma, I resolved to avoid the experience for the rest of my life.

A few months after I was promoted to corporal and sent home on leave, I watched the destruction of the National Museum Building on television. As I had closely followed the debates during the controversy, I had strong but ambivalent feelings about the dramatic conclusion. It was only after I was discharged from the army in the summer of 1997 that I considered writing about the event. Trouble then with my visa status prevented my returning to the United States, so I had little choice but to spend more time in Korea. In order to familiarize myself with the history of my native country, I visited Kyŏngbok Palace several times, talked with professors and graduate students at Seoul National University, and spent many hours at the National Library delving into ancient texts.

After I finished my research and wrote up a preliminary draft of this essay, I returned to the palace and walked around the grounds for a whole afternoon before returning home and reading over my work. There were many aspects of this early version that dissatisfied me, but the most glaring fault seemed to be its tone. While I presented every interesting discovery I had made during my research, and every fascinating fact I had unearthed, I marveled at the strangeness and incomprehensibility of it all, as if I were an old archaeologist in a pith helmet walking through an Egyptian maze and exclaiming "ooh!" and "aah!" at every turn. When I returned to my country and reimmersed myself in its culture, what struck me most was the constant presence of seemingly contradictory elements.

If you walk around the teeming streets of Seoul, you will find that it looks, sounds, and smells like a modern metropolis, but that you don't have to delve too deeply to find a second city: one built on a firm belief in the efficacy of geomancy, shamanist rituals, and ancestor worship; a belief in the existence of ghosts, demons, and natural deities; and a faith in history as the manifestation of the Heavenly Mandate. The role of geomancy in Korean history, its persistence in contemporary Korea, and the debate surrounding the demolition of the National Museum Building are instances of contradictions inherent in the modern Korean condition. In the last few months of finishing this essay, however, as I found myself going deeper into the cultural matrix, I came to question whether my descriptions were the proper way to represent Korea's history. It even occurred to me that, as I was writing this for an English-language audience, I might have been "orientalizing" it for the benefit of Western readers.

When the twentieth century began, Korea was still a feudal country ruled by royalty and a small landowning elite. Starting in 1910, the nation was exploited for thirty-five years by a hostile power bent on eradicating Korean identity. When this imperial ruler left, two other imperial powers divided Korea, a country that had been a single nation since A.D. 985. A terrible war then followed, in which, with the help of foreign armies and equipment, we slaughtered each other for three years, razing virtually the entire country in the process. Since then—after nearly forty years of absolutist rule by military dictators—one-half of the country has developed a vibrant capitalist economy and a fully democratic political system; the other half has remained one of the most repressive and xenophobic nations in the world. Despite the current economic downturn, the Republic of

Korea is still a leading exporter of manufactured goods, and its living standards are on the same level as those of advanced developing nations. In the North, masses of people are dying of starvation even as that Stalinist state, one of the last in the world, continues to spend half of its meager budget on the military.

Given South Korea's historical legacy and the daily possibility of being swept into yet another terrible disaster, the elements in Korea's culture that I've described are not incongruous at all but necessary: the results of living in two worlds at the same time while trying to avoid being driven mad by history. In holding on to traditional ideas and mystical beliefs that may seem out of place today, Korea is trying to deal with all that happened to it in this century and to heal the wounds inflicted by modernity. In the face of the irresistible necromancy of history, which does not recognize human time, the victims of the past must use their oldest talismans to ward off the present's darkest magic.

In the last months of 1997, as I was beginning to ponder the history of Kyŏngbok Palace, the Republic of Korea went into major economic crisis: the value of the stock market and the currency plummeted. Conditions continued to deteriorate such that in 1998 the country found itself in the humiliating position of having to go to the International Monetary Fund (IMF) for immediate loans. Meanwhile, major companies and small businesses alike began to go bankrupt and unemployment reached a record high. Despite the obvious fact that the crisis was brought on mainly through overexpansion by the larger corporations and the financing of ill-advised loans by government-owned banks with unsound policies, the media abounded with all kinds of conspiracy theories: they claimed that a nefarious few in the shadows—usually foreigners—had engineered the crisis in order to cripple the nation. Last time I was at the vast Kyobo Bookstore, just down the street from Kyŏngbok Palace, I counted no less than twelve books advancing such ideas.

There was also a newspaper item connecting the economic crisis with a dragon sculpture that was found at the palace. On November 14, 1997, it was announced that while workers were cleaning the pond around Kyŏnghoeru Pavilion, they found in the water a magnificent copper dragon, 146.5 cm in length and 66.5 kg in weight. A remarkably well-preserved creature, it had an extended tongue, a protruding mustache, and a cheerful expression. After an investigation by historians, the creature was declared to be one of two dragons that had been placed in the pond during the Taewŏngun's reconstruction of the palace—probably in 1867. In March of that year, a major fire on the construction site had destroyed many of the wooden structures being put up—a disaster that set back the date of completion by almost a year and caused greater hardship for the people. In East Asian mythology, dragons have power over the watery element, so the pieces were put in the pond as part of a shamanist ritual to ward off more fires.

When it was announced that the dragon would be removed and displayed in a museum, more than a few shamans and soothsayers claimed that taking it from the pond would bring misfortune to the nation. It was shortly after this that the economic crisis began in earnest, and all the mystics screamed "I told you so!" in the media. On February 25, 1998, when the loan negotiations with the IMF were about to begin, an elaborate ceremony was held at the Kyŏnghoeru Pavilion, during which an exact replica of the dragon was placed in the pond by four men dressed in the traditional garb of palace servants. The IMF subsequently agreed to make the loans under conditions favorable to South Korea, and the currency, which had fallen in value from around 800 *wŏn* to the U.S. dollar to over 2,000 in less than three months, steadied at around 1,300.

Before I began writing this latest version of my essay, I paid one more visit to Kyŏngbok Palace. I went there not only to see the palace but also to appreciate the view now that the National Museum Building was gone. It was probably the first time I had visited a place to witness the absence of something. As I stood where Sejong Road begins and gazed at the panorama—the shimmering green heights of Pugak Mountain spread out like a great umbrella above the stolid Kwanghwa Gate—I had to admit that the effect was magnificent.

I believe that acupuncture works, but I don't know if *ki* and *hyŏl* exist. I believe that geomancy was an attempt by ancient East Asians to develop a science of urban and environmental planning, but I don't know if there is such a thing as geomantic *ki* or a *myŏngdang.* I do not believe in fate or prophecy, but it frightens me that the famous old shaman one of my aunts dragged me to told me I was destined by the stars to live in many nations, spend my life writing and teaching, and experience an unexpected setback of three years while I was in my late twenties. She then informed me that the achievement of great success at a young age would mean little to me because the loss of my beloved at the same time would cause me to forswear love and dedicate myself to art for the rest of my life.

I believe that the Korean obsession with history is the product of a sense of victimization created by the calamities of the modern period. I believe that Japan should face up to its actions during the imperial era and make a sincere apology and award reparations to the surviving comfort women. I am the furthest thing from a nationalist, and I believe that all things historical—good and bad—ought to be preserved; but as I stood before that grand view with all its supposed *ki* flowing down to me, I could well understand the point of demolishing the National Museum Building.

Perhaps I also live in two worlds at the same time, to prevent myself from being driven mad by history.

MỘNG-LAN

Three Poems

FOOTSTEPS

the ocean air I smell
a condition attached
to everything
a tongue in every mouth
from the sea
I learn to be still

footsteps
the second hand tocking
a door slams urgent fingers
will the steps come to my door?
inside the walls hands

night burns in the sky
stars like footprints
darkness amber-eaten waves
the shore is a tongue eating itself

a bowl of rice
left by my door
the sea in the salt

A TRACTOR

squats   waiting for its season
the steel hand
hungering the night
music of crickets' whiskers resound
within the wheat-walking fields
hours of black rain
descend like cut hair   the gnawing crevices   moss & mucus
come alive
awaken the clay

THE TASTE

of a sonata   adrift
your blanket   the moon   the sun
through the trees like specks of pepper
night wobbles like a drunkard
at the dialectal borders
something is happening in the world   explosions
firecrackers in the night sky
like the coral's patient act
you untangle yourself from the net
of a dream
love was something you invented
drawing your shadows on the rock

SUSIE JIE YOUNG KIM

Remembering Trauma: History and Counter-Memories in Korean Fiction

History continues because we live. Kong Sŏnok, "Parched Season"

The five stories included in *The Wounded Season,* a feature on counter-memories of historical trauma found in Korean fiction, span a wide period: the Korean War (Yi Ch'ŏngjun's "The Wounded" and "An Assailant's Face"); the war's aftermath (Choi In Hoon's "The End of the State Highway"); and the Kwangju Uprising of 1980 (Kong Sŏnok's "Parched Season" and Im Cheol Woo's "Spring Day"). These stories are not just about past events and past traumas, however; they are also about how traumatic experiences endure and how their memories transcend individual and collective attempts to neatly separate past, present, and future. Over time, these personal memories and the stories they generate become part of history, proving that history indeed continues because we live.

A trauma is a physical or emotional wound that causes stress and shock. Traumas do not occur only to individuals but also to whole communities and entire nations. Whether occurring to an individual or a nation, a trauma usually leaves a trace: a mnemonic site. The Korean stories included in *The Wounded Season* are notable for their attention to this powerful kind of remembering and will force Korean readers to reflect on their own relationship with the various traumas by compelling them to remember the events as well. With the passage of time, a gap widens between those who directly experienced these traumas and those who did not, but younger generations often acquire war memories through the many personal stories that their parents and grandparents pass down to them. Telling and listening to such stories are ways of managing collective traumas: no matter how painful they may be, survivor narratives are retold so that the horrors of a particular trauma will not have been experienced in vain. In many survivor narratives about war, for example, the trauma is seen as the driving force behind individuals' desires to survive and rebuild their lives after the war. In this way, literature and storytelling become powerful tools, generating a history often at odds with the official, authorized one.

In "The Wounded" (1996), by Yi Ch'ŏngjun, the narrator's brother has been a soldier in the Korean War. The source of his trauma, however, is not so much his involvement in the war as a specific experience, which has been haunting him for decades: "Concealed somewhere deep inside the sound of that shot was a vivid memory that had remained with me, despite the numerous gunshots heard during the war." It is due to this memory that the man, who becomes a surgeon after the war, has been "A man who seemed to have no doubts about his present life nor any memories of his past" and has concentrated on the present, taking care of his patients "diligently at all hours." The trauma has forced him to live outside of time, unable to either confront the past directly or derive any substantive pleasure from the present. He is able to live without being overwhelmed by the trauma only because of his work.

However, we soon find that deep beneath the surgeon's calm exterior, the tremendous pain of the trauma remains undiminished by the passage of time. The memory of this experience lies dormant until a seemingly unrelated event causes it to surface: the death of a young girl on his operating table. The unexpected happens in an otherwise routine operation, and when the surgeon blames himself, painful memories begin to inundate his mind. His desire to control this flood of unbearable memories is manifested in his writing a novel: writing seems to be not only a way to contain the memories—by revisiting and confronting the trauma—but also a way of healing himself and changing the course of events. His attempt at first proves futile because the memories cannot be rendered directly; moreover, he becomes so immersed in writing and remembering that he is alienated further from the present. Near the end, while the narrator undergoes transformation from a spectator to a participant of sorts, the brother with reservation reaches his own transformation. This manifests itself in his realization that writing about his trauma cannot change what happened in the past, but only help reconcile him to it.

In Choi In Hoon's "The End of the State Highway" (1966), the trauma of the Korean War—known in Korea as *yugyo* (literally, "June 25")—continues in the war's aftermath. Everything about the landscape in this story, written more than a decade after the cease-fire, is slightly askew or distorted. Even a traditional funeral procession is somehow unseemly: "none of the women, including the pallbearers, is from the countryside"; they are *yangsaeksi,* whose bodies are designated for use by American soldiers. "The End of the State Highway" contains other figures who have been transformed by American military presence in Korea, such as "the kind of man who deals in black-market goods in the areas around U.S. Army bases." For these people, the American military serves as their main referent: their identities are defined almost solely through their interaction with the soldiers. In fact, within this disordered landscape—where Salem cigarette billboards dot the skyline and there is a makeshift "Texas Village," which is comprised of Arizona Shop, Lily Sisters' Store, Honey Cats, and Pink Heart—the ones who seem to be "surer" about their identities are two young men returning from their physical examinations for military duty. Just as telling, citizens must pull to the side of the state highway to let U.S. military convoys pass: "On this road, one makes way when the lord of the manor passes by in procession." The Korean countryside is defiled by monstrous American trucks and weapons of destruction, but it is also tainted by the gaze of the other:

> The faces of long-nosed Yankee men and long-nosed Yankee women dressed in white appear through the brightly lit windows [of the train]. A woman wearing a white hat presses her face against the window and stares outside at the darkness, at the young boy. After the passenger cars, flatbeds pass by. Stretched out on the flatbeds are giant artillery pieces. Weighed down by their heavy gun barrels, they look exhausted, like wounded soldiers. Tanks with no treads—crouched like mountaintops and looking bigger than the young boy's house—pass by. Crumpled GMCs, their wheels missing and front ends smashed, go by. They are all wordless, injured, exhausted travelers. It is an endlessly long train. The young boy becomes afraid.

Trauma and the memories and counter-histories it generates are manifested in an altogether different form in Im Cheol Woo's "Spring Day." Through the framework of a survivor's narrative, this story concerns a more recent national trauma: the Kwangju Uprising in 1980, when the military opened fire on civilians during a peaceful demonstration against martial law. The story portrays the ongoing effects of this trauma on a group of college friends. Sangju, a character who only appears in the narrator's recollections and conversations, is haunted by the ghost of Myŏngbu, a friend who died during the massacre:

> Certainly Myŏngbu's death was a pit he had fallen into and could not escape. . . . Myŏngbu remained an open wound for me as well. I felt as if a large wooden stake had been driven into my chest, creating an injury that continued to fester. But with the passage of time, each one of us had to pull that stake out and go on living as before. When we looked at the wound from time to time, the pain was renewed, but the wound was covered by a scar. We had no idea that for Sangju the wound had never closed, and his memory was like the blade of a knife frantically cutting his heart and soul into pieces.

The guilt Sangju feels at having betrayed a friend crying out for help is symbolic of the survivor's guilt that most Koreans experienced after the

Kwangju Uprising. This story asks difficult questions: How do you move on? How do you keep on living after something like Kwangju? For the narrator, the conflict resides between the two extremes of returning to an ordinary existence and being unable to break out of the cycle of remembering and reliving the trauma:

> It was true: everyone else was carrying on, looking as peaceful as before. New lane dividers had been painted on the asphalt, and pedestrians with absent-minded expressions filled the streets again. Shops attracted customers, old men laid down *yut* boards in the park, and young idlers who had nothing to do roamed the streets, loudly chewing gum. And thick grass had grown over Myŏngbu's grave, which we had recently visited. Yes, everyone was getting along as before. They had erased their memories, large and small, or had nursed them and patched them up and just gone on living.

In order to survive trauma, the story seems to say, one must somehow understand that its effects are not fleeting, but lasting, and that the only way to cope with this dilemma is to "live with those somber memories constantly shadowing our daily lives." The narrator explains:

> a great many things had taken from us the closeness we had felt in the past and changed it into raw emotion. . . . All those things we faced in everyday life now possessed different meanings, smells, textures, hues, and sounds—suddenly calling forth a host of dark and frightening memories from the other side of oblivion.

Yi Ch'ŏngjun's "An Assailant's Face" addresses the reality of living in a divided nation and what this signifies for everyday life in South Korea. On one level, the forced and artificial division of the country makes victims out of all Koreans: "That war didn't take the spirits of only the dead." On another level, this story reveals, Koreans "are all victims of contradictory situations," but the boundaries between victim and assailant can sometimes be blurred and difficult to locate.

Kong Sŏnok's "Parched Season" depicts the lives of marginalized figures who are survivors of the Kwangju Uprising. All the principal characters—an unemployed divorcée with two children, a bar owner whose daughters have different fathers, a mute teenager, a handicapped woman, a disabled man with no lower body, and a former teacher who is now a wandering poet—are peripheral figures of society who have been ensnared by the "specter" of history. However, as the divorcée tells the bar owner, "History continues because we live. We mustn't die. Nothing can be done through death, and nothing can be connected through it." It is a community of such survivors and their stories that will perpetuate a history in which the marginalized are not forgotten.

In the name of progress or some other abstraction, narratives comprising "official history" often promote forgetting rather than authentic remembering. So motivated, official narratives regularly neglect and negate the complexities and multiplicities of the traumas that shape history. The five Korean stories presented in *The Wounded Season* illustrate some of the problematic effects of that erasure and forgetting and attest to the importance of personal remembering and storytelling. They help render a history shaped from and true to the lives of individuals—a history that is therefore alive.

Merchant Sitting in Store Window, Korea, 1946
Photograph by Horace Bristol
[CORBIS/Horace Bristol]

IM CHEOL WOO

Spring Day

Did he really go to Sangju's house at dawn that final day in May? Is it true, as Sangju says, that he just lay there with the bedcovers over his head, even though he knew it was Myŏngbu pounding frantically on his front gate?

Leaning against a gingko tree by the road, I went over that question again and again. I had asked myself the same question before and always arrived at the same conclusion: it was unthinkable. Nevertheless, I kept searching for an answer. As I gazed now at the waves of traffic flowing in and out of the square, that vision of Myŏngbu at Sangju's gate kept coming back to me, troubling me deeply.

The vision begins with Myŏngbu staggering through the fading, indigo darkness. His outline is unclear, his feet are moving frantically, anxiously, and he's gasping for breath. Daybreak's layers of murky darkness surround his body, making it seem as if he's struggling to swim up through the waters of an immense ocean. *Tu-tu-tu-tu-tu . . .* From somewhere I can hear the ominous, metallic rattle of automatic weapons being fired and gradually coming closer—a noise like rocks being churned on a beach, or like waves crashing against the shore. With his back pressed against the alley wall and desperate to evade his pursuers, Myŏngbu edges toward Sangju's house. Before long, he reaches Sangju's front gate, quickly looks around, and in a muted voice calls out: *Sangju . . . Sangju . . . it's me, I'm here. Open up . . . Sang-juuuu.* But there's no reply from inside. *Tu-tu-tu-tu-tu.* The sound of the shots comes closer and closer and Myŏngbu calls Sangju's name more urgently, shaking the front door, but there's still no answer from inside. *It's me . . . I'm here . . . Please, open the door . . . before it's too late.* Myŏngbu desperately shakes the door again. *Tu-tu-tu-tu-tu.* The sound comes closer, and in front of the door that never opens, Myŏngbu collapses to his knees. *Sangju. Help me, please. Before it's too late . . . please . . .* Suddenly, he hears the pounding of heavy boots advancing in a flurry. Myŏngbu shrinks with fright and rises from the ground. He tries to escape, stumbling toward the alley. Soon after, Myŏngbu disappears into the indigo shadows, and from the direction he runs comes the chaotic sound of rifle shots, wild with rage.

I shook the frightening vision out of my head. Surely not . . . no. That just couldn't be. That vision might have merely come from Sangju's own delusions. I shook my head again. But why would Sangju concoct such a wild story, and then start believing it himself? I had no answer. And Sangju's diary, which I held in my hand, did not have the answers either. Though, of course, there's no reason he would have explained everything in notes to himself—it's not as if he had planned from the start to hallucinate . . .

I received a similar assessment of things from Sanghŭi when I met her at a café last night. I had called her the day before to tell her that I was going to visit Sangju in the hospital, and she had told me she had something to give me. She brought along Sangju's diary, which he'd kept until his most recent hospitalization.

"Brother always seemed to think he was being chased by someone. I didn't know why until a few days ago, when I began to guess . . ."

"Are you saying Sangju became paranoid because of Myŏngbu's death?" I asked.

"I'm not sure . . . Anyway, you'll understand after you read this."

"I've glanced at it before. I was wondering if you could answer something else for me?" I hesitated for a moment, as Sanghŭi stared at me intently. "Sangju seems to believe Myŏngbu came to him at daybreak on that final day, when he was being chased, and he was killed on his way back because no one had opened the door for him."

There was no response.

"Don't take this the wrong way!" I said. "I'm only asking because of what your brother wrote."

A shadow suddenly spread across Sanghŭi's forehead, leaving her in an instant and settling over me with a chill. Anticipating her reaction, I continued to try to justify my questions.

"This is all really hard, I know, but what if parts of Sangju's story are true?" I asked, feeling agitated, as if a centipede were crawling around inside my chest.

"No, no. That's only a story Brother made up," Sanghŭi said. "I was home at dawn that day too. Except for Brother, the whole family was in the main bedroom with the bedcovers over our heads, trembling with fear. We were all jittery and on edge, and we would have heard the slightest sound. But we didn't hear anything, *really.* Besides, Brother's room is off by itself, way in the back of the house. So any noise from the front door would have been audible in the main bedroom first. If Myŏngbu had really come to our door, how could we have not known it? Really. It's nothing more than a wild story resulting from Brother's delusions of persecution."

Sanghŭi made all sorts of denials. But what weighed upon my heart was the dark shadow that continued to linger on her face while she adamantly shook her head. Like her, I wanted the story to be nothing but Sangju's wild imagination. Nonetheless, I couldn't get over the few doubts I still had. For example, Sangju's diary recorded the events too vividly and intensely for me to conclude that everything was simply the product of a sick, delusional young man. But what if it were true? Did that mean Myŏngbu's death near Sangju's house—of all places—wasn't merely a coincidence after all? All sorts of doubts wove together inside my head like a tangled web. My head felt ready to burst. I leaned against the gingko tree and closed my eyes for a moment.

When I opened my eyes again, I could see a cylindrical water fountain in the center of the square. The fountain guarded the heart of the square, and from it five paved streets spread out like the tentacles of an octopus sprawled in death. Large and small cars swarmed like flies up and down those tentacles. The province's administrative building, which was now painted white, stood on the opposite side of the square, beyond the old tree that had grown up in front of it. And far off, the blue ridge of the mountain stared down at the city in silence, as always. The fountain had been turned off long ago. Despite the advent of spring, it lay abandoned and ugly, its bare aluminum pipes exposed, having endured the cold of an especially harsh winter.

Sunlight surged into the square, illuminating every corner. The whole world shimmered mysteriously, as if brought to life by the power of the sun's rays. The May sun shone down brightly on the flat pavement and on rooftops of buildings, on windows of cars hurriedly rounding the square, and on light-green leaves newly sprouted at the tips of the gingko trees by the road. The golden rays collided and glittered like fish scales as they beamed down from the sky. I was blinded. For an instant, I stood there feeling dizzy. The expressionless, ghostlike faces of people on buses passed by every few moments, while the pedestrians trudged slowly on, their gait as fatigued and downtrodden as always. As I stood on the corner, dazzled by the May sun, the world felt unreal, as if I were dreaming. Was it because the shimmering objects in the sun-drenched square suddenly seemed so unfamiliar and raw?

Just then, three men from a maintenance crew appeared, hauling a water tank on a cart, and headed toward the flowerbed by the fountain. Each of them grabbed a hose and began watering the area. Whenever the water streamed over the grass and the pansies, the droplets reflected the sun, sparkling like tiny fireworks, and then disappeared. Gazing at them, I felt as if their sparkling beams were like the blue flowers of fire and heat at the tips of acetylene torches, and their sharp points pierced my vision.

Ha ha ha ha . . . Sangju was laughing strangely. *Father, I betrayed you. Even before the cock crowed thrice, I plugged up my ears, closed my eyes, covered my mouth, and denied you. As my unclean body lay cowering beneath my covers, Abel's sinless flesh was being stripped from his back in front of my house. Ha ha ha ha . . .* Sangju held a piece of broken glass in his hand. He brought the sharp edge to his bare chest, then slowly drew a red line across his skin. *As Abel poured incense oil on my head, he left behind a curse. See for yourself. The curse is now engraved in this mark; in the memory of the front door that I locked with my own two hands.* Sangju drew a second line on his chest. *Bless that solid crossbar that was lowered to lock out a friend.* He drew a third line on his thigh. *For our betrayal, which drenched the streets in blood that daybreak.* He drew a fourth line on his forearm. Sangju's gleaming eyes and large, swollen face came rushing toward me. *Ha ha.* A faint smile spread on his twisted lips, an ominous smile that seemed to fill with delight.

I shuddered suddenly, and tried hard to shake off the horrifying image: Sangju naked and alone, slicing at his skin in the dreary back room of a prayer retreat deep in the woods, where sunlight could not reach. This image merged with the violent descriptions in Sangju's diary and made me dizzy.

> *You are after me. You've attached yourself to my back like a shadow and whisper constantly, anytime and everywhere. Even when I'm walking through crowded streets or climbing up and down the footbridge, when I'm reading or sitting down to eat, when I'm alone in a room, or in a café filled with smoke, you are always next to me. In a crowded bus, in a restaurant, on a bench, I always hear your cold, conniving voice. I cannot escape. Will I ever escape you shadowing me? Chills run up and down my spine whenever I discover you mingling with people and laughing freely among them and then find you sitting so naturally in front of me or next to me, sneering and laughing. Please go away. I'm begging you. Just leave, just let me go. Whenever I look behind me, you disappear, and when I face forward, I hear the sound of your breathing like a curse. You hide in my ear and whisper endlessly . . .* Raise your head and answer this, you survivors who remain intact. Where is your brother Abel? Under which mound of dirt did you bury him alive before returning alone? *Why are you asking me that? Am I his keeper? Do I bear all of the blame?* How could you . . . how could you have let this happen? *I don't know. I don't know anything about it.* See for yourself. The blood of the one you abandoned is crying out to me from the dark ground. Your own two hands spilled his pure blood on the earth, and the earth opened its mouth and swallowed his blood. Remember this. You are cursed from this day forth. You will be forever banished from the ground that you stained with your sinful hands. You will not be forgiven, no matter how much you beat your chest or repent and wail with your hair let down. It is too late. Everything is done . . .

I stared at the clock tower on the other side of the square. I wondered how much time had passed since I had arrived. The clock was broken. Dead time hung from the tips of its unmoving hands. When I looked at my watch, it was a little after one, but neither Pyŏnggi nor Sunim had shown up yet. We had decided to meet where we could see the fountain. The first one to arrive was Pyŏnggi.

"Sorry. It wasn't easy getting a cab, being Saturday and all," he said.

He wore a proper suit, and his necktie was tied tightly around his neck. He had started working at a bank four months ago. "Is it true? That Sangju's been hospitalized again?" Pyŏnggi asked. He pulled out a cigarette.

I nodded.

"Wasn't he recuperating at a prayer retreat somewhere in the woods since his last hospitalization?"

"They thought he was better, but two months ago he was transferred from the retreat back to the hospital. It sounds pretty serious this time."

"What do you mean?" Pyŏnggi turned away and stared at the traffic.

"Apparently, he hurt himself. He cut himself all over his body with a piece of glass."

"What?" Pyŏnggi was taken aback. A few buses roared by, and their pungent clouds of exhaust made my eyes sting.

"That fool. It's been two years already! Other people are moving on with their lives as if nothing happened. Why the hell is he the only one still acting like that?" Pyŏnggi let out a deep sigh. For a while we stood there in silence, staring at the fountain in the middle of the square.

It was true: everyone else was carrying on, looking as peaceful as before. New lane dividers had been painted on the asphalt, and pedestrians with absentminded expressions filled the streets again. Shops attracted customers, old men laid down *yut* boards in the park, and young idlers who had nothing to do roamed the streets, loudly chewing gum. And thick grass had grown over Myŏngbu's grave, which we had recently visited. Yes, everyone was getting along as before. They had erased their memories, large and small, or had nursed them and patched them up and just gone on living. But why hadn't Sangju been able to emerge from that nightmare? I could almost picture him locked up in a room, his haggard face smiling contentedly at me through his barred windows—though I had never visited a mental hospital before, I assumed that there would be bars on the windows.

A taxi skidded to a halt in front of us. It was Sunim. She smiled at us as she got out of the cab. I realized the three of us hadn't been together since graduation three months ago.

"You really do look like a teacher. Very respectable," I said. She was wearing a dark-purple dress.

"Oh no, do I really look that way?" Sunim laughed, showing her straight teeth. She had always hung out with us, though she was four years younger. When we had returned to school after getting out of the army, Sunim had thrust her friendship upon us without reservation and we had naturally accepted her. But before we knew it, the five of us had been reduced to three. One was lying in the Mangwŏl cemetery with dirt piled over his head, and another was shut up in a mental hospital.

Now we were on our way to visit Sangju. We walked to the nearest bus stop and waited. The bus going to Namp'yŏng, the city outskirts where the hospital was located, came every thirty minutes. For a while, we were laughing and exchanging funny anecdotes as if we were out on a picnic. By talking about our new jobs, to which none of us had yet become accustomed, or by inquiring about mutual friends, we were able to forget about the depressing purpose of our trip. Buses were infrequent, though, and as we waited, our good feelings soon dissolved into the somber mood of before.

"Wait. How can we go visit Sangju emptyhanded?" Sunim abruptly left our side and went into a flower shop. A bitter smile came over me as I watched Sunim through the shop window. A bouquet of flowers for a patient behind barred windows? I handed Pyŏnggi the notebook that I had been holding.

"Why do you have this?" Pyŏnggi seemed surprised.

"Sangju's sister gave it to me yesterday so I could take it to the hospital. I guess the doctor said he wanted to see it."

Pyŏnggi nodded without saying anything.

Why don't you give it to him yourself? I recalled asking her. I remembered the strange shadow on her face when I questioned her. Did she have a terrible secret she could not reveal?

I don't ever want to go back there . . . Brother doesn't want that, you see. He doesn't want to see any family at all. Especially when mother goes . . . I'd rather not talk about it. I really don't understand how it came to this. In an instant, tears had welled up in her eyes.

"I really don't want to see this," Pyŏnggi said as I held out the notebook to him. "He may be a friend and all, but I don't like prying into someone's personal things."

Pyŏnggi's face reflected his discomfort as he awkwardly took the notebook and examined the cover. Though I wanted to ask whether the notebook was just about Sangju, and whether the story it contained was Sangju's alone, I bit my lip. At that very moment, an air-raid siren began wailing loud enough to split my eardrums.

Uuaaaaannnnggg . . .

Stunned, Pyŏnggi and I stared at each other as the waves of sound contracted and reverberated in the square. The roar poured down from the rooftop of a building across from the administrative building. Turning toward it, we saw the large speaker installed on the building's rooftop and then the yellow flag that fluttered out of the window below it.

"Geez, for a second there . . . !" Pyŏnggi shouted above the noise. "But of course, today is civil-defense-training day!"

"Damn, just our luck to be out on the streets like this!"

Pyŏnggi and I smiled awkwardly at each other, embarrassed at having panicked, if only for a few seconds. In that instant, we had both feared death and destruction and had experienced the terrible foreboding such fear brings. Before we had known it, the peace and safety to which we had become accustomed had been transformed into things totally unfamiliar to us. When we realized that this was only a practice air raid, we were relieved. For a while, the streets were in a state of confusion, as if the orderly movement of cogwheels had suddenly come to a full stop. We heard the sounds of whistles blowing here and there, and people scurried for cover and drivers looked for a place to park. Pyŏnggi and I walked the short distance to the flower shop to look for Sunim.

I stood inside the shop entrance and gazed at the street through the window. A voice blared from the radio sitting on the shop counter: "Our country is now under simulated air attack by enemy planes. Everyone quickly take cover." We could hear the same message being broadcast from the speaker outside.

In an instant, the street and buildings looked like empty ruins. All traces of the people who had been bustling about only seconds before had vanished, and all the traffic had stopped. In the square, where the sun poured down in all of its splendor, there wasn't a living thing in sight. I gazed at the fountain, which stood in the center of the square like a giant coiled serpent lifting its head; then at the rectangular building across the street, the large speaker protruding from the rooftop, and at the indigo ridge of the mountain in the distance. I despaired at the scene: it seemed to say the entire city lay dead. Silently standing beside Sunim, who was holding flowers, Pyŏnggi and I felt like visitors who had come to mourn the city's death.

The shop was filled with the perfume of brilliantly colored flowers. Tulips, chrysanthemums, roses, carnations, freesias, gladiolas, daffodils, marigolds, baby's breath . . . The beauty and scent of the blooming flowers, so unmindful of the season, suddenly made me think of the Summer Festival's Eve of two years ago.

That night, Sangju and I had sat on the grass of the west hill, which overlooked the school's playing field. The darkness of the evening sky slowly descended upon the mountain in the distance, and dusk crept across the campus. On the field, a fireworks display was going off as part of the festival's celebrations. Rumor had it that the organizers had received generous support that year and thus were able to put together an extravagant program. *Pow! Pow!* Accompanied by loud explosions, vibrant colors burst dizzily above us in the inky night sky, and the silhouettes of students danced around the bonfire. It seemed as if nothing had changed. As in all the previous years, people came to the festival without knowing why it was held, fireworks dissipated in the night sky above the campus like fragile flowers, and the luminous incandescence that shot up from the ground filled the sky with fine particles, as if from an atomic explosion. The particles fell gently to the earth, the dust covering the heads of all the sallow-faced students, who in this fallout would age before their time.

"If the senseless deaths of many are nothing but a necessary condition of confirming the existence of good and evil in this world, then why does God exist?" Sangju had been staring blankly at the field below, his arms wrapped around his knees.

I laughed at such a ridiculous question. "A true Jesus freak wouldn't ask such a thing."

"I'm not talking idly. Although our belief has been that God's covenant with us meant that he would punish evil and protect the righteous, throughout human history hasn't it actually been the opposite of that? Hasn't all that just been an illusion that we ourselves created? In fact, evil has always existed in life, slapping its full belly and impudently laughing in our faces. Goodness and justice have existed for us in name only. God has always deceived us, giving us a gospel of lies and saying that life can't be any other way. In reality, evil triumphs over good, and the weak and righteous are trampled by the greedy and powerful."

"That's an extremely pessimistic view."

"That may be . . . but can you keep on dreaming like before? Even now?"

Sangju repeated the question. I pulled a piece of grass from the ground and chewed on it. *Pow! Pow!* Cylindrical flower patterns exploded and slowly flickered on the ink-black canvas of the sky. I knew Sangju was agonizing over Myŏngbu's death again.

"I was always lashing out at him. In the end, I said nothing can be accomplished through intense hatred and anger because they only lead to the destruction of love, and that leaves only devastation . . . But he would scoff at me, saying that what I called love was merely an abstract concept, nothing but vain words. But . . ."

This had been an ongoing debate between them.

"But?" I stared at Sangju. The profile of his haggard face emerged faintly in the darkness. Each time the fireworks exploded, he absentmindedly turned his gaze toward the sky.

"But . . . I think maybe Myŏngbu was right after all. They're not such different things. Hate . . . could turn into love. I didn't know that. When I think about it, how many times have lofty words such as *truth* and *justice* rolled off my tongue. Now he's dead and I'm alive . . . and it's too late. It's far too late."

Sangju dropped his head onto his knees. His body was curled in a spiral, like a snail's. I suddenly became afraid because I sensed that those dark and painful memories, which I had so desperately tried to bury, were about to push open the lid and jump out. And on the other side of those memories stood Myŏngbu, like a departed spirit. I sprang to my feet and shouted at Sangju like a professional therapist talking to a patient.

"Stop saying such tiresome and ludicrous things! Some things need to be forgotten. In the end, forgetting is the only remedy we have for things we can do nothing about. Yes, Myŏngbu is dead! But the people who survived can still do a lot of good things! Living is not at all dishonorable or shameful like you say. It is a blessing, isn't it?"

Fireworks exploded again. We could hear cheers coming from the direction of the field, and the bonfire surged into a huge ball, as if someone had poured gasoline on it. More students began to dance around the fire. All this was in celebration of a deep slumber from which we hoped never to wake.

A few months after the festival, we heard the news of Sangju's first hospitalization. We thought that it was probably just a minor breakdown. Sure enough, we soon heard that he had been released. The following spring, when we began our final year of college, we thought we'd see him on campus. But even before the spring semester had begun, Sangju had taken a leave from school. When we saw him just after he came out of the hospital, he hadn't seemed particularly changed. He had always been a person of very few words and had always preferred to sit by himself, so we concluded that his sickness had been due in part to his peculiar personality.

We thought he was probably resting at home, and when we heard a rumor that he was recuperating at a retreat deep in the Mudangsan Mountains, he gradually faded from our minds. We were also busy with the demanding and cumbersome process of graduating. In the end, his photo was left out of the yearbook and we each found jobs and went our separate ways. By chance I had heard a few days ago the sad news about his second hospitalization. Apparently, his condition had unexpectedly taken a turn for the worse, which was why the three of us had planned to visit him.

> *Remember this. You will have a mute son. As retribution for Abel's blood, which stains your two hands as a sign of your betrayal, I will cut off your son's tongue. And I will make you remember your sin whenever you see the severed stump inside your son's mouth. Whenever you stare into the face of your son, who will beat his chest with his bare fist and stare at you in silence as if his angry eyes are about to explode—as if his heart is about to explode because he is unable to speak his true thoughts—you will recognize the mark of your terrible betrayal. At the end of a ten-year drought, during which even rocks will crumble into white dust, I will gladly bestow on you the joy of harvesting an empty field, and you will gather the bountiful harvest of your sin as you look into your son's silent eyes, as if you were staring into a basket filled with empty heads of grain. And the seeds of retribution that you scattered will take root and bear thousands and tens of thousands of fruits of misery, and these will flourish inside your chest . . . In remembrance of your brother Abel, who ran through the streets at daybreak crying out for help; in remembrance of his wailing as he collapsed in front of your gate when it did not open; in remembrance of you and of your neighbors, who lay beneath the covers with their gate locked denying his screams, I will make your child mute . . . Then I will show you how to teach your child to speak. You will realize that language is not only spoken with the tongue, but conveyed with the hands*

and the feet and gestures involving the entire body. I will make you learn the sign language of the mute . . .

Sangju probably wrote the diary while at the retreat. There wasn't much in it—just a lot of entries with some of the dates missing. He used to write poetry in his spare time, so there were short phrases that looked like they were meant to remain as fragments, along with many crude and frightening scribbles. As I read them over, I realized how insensitive we had been to his anguish, and I berated myself. It seemed as if he was constantly being chased by something. It could have been the spirit of Myŏngbu, or his guilt over Myŏngbu's death. Certainly Myŏngbu's death was a pit he had fallen into and could not escape from. I couldn't accept right away what was happening to Sangju. I was shocked by how strong a hold the memory of Myŏngbu's death had on him. Meanwhile, what happened to Myŏngbu remained an open wound for me as well. I felt as if a large wooden stake had been driven into my chest, creating an injury that continued to fester. But with the passage of time, each one of us had to pull that stake out and go on living as before. When we looked at the wound from time to time, the pain was renewed, but the wound was covered by a scar. We had no idea that for Sangju the wound had never closed, and his memory was like the blade of a knife frantically cutting his heart and soul into pieces.

The three of us heard whistles blowing. A young man wearing a yellow armband and carrying a bullhorn rushed past the front of the flower shop. "The focus of the training exercises today will be drills to prepare for chemical-warfare attack, forest fires, and hotel fires," the man announced.

Pyŏnggi was in the midst of reading Sangju's diary. The sunlight shone through the shop window, creating tiny spots on the pages. "There's a forest fire in progress. Military and civilians need to cooperate in order to stop the fire from spreading as a result of the strong winds—" Over the dull whir of helicopter blades, we could hear the man broadcasting the training-drill scenarios. Sunim held a bouquet of yellow and white chrysanthemums in which a few red roses were mixed. What was she thinking? Somehow her face seemed to have hardened. Meanwhile, at a textile factory somewhere, two thousand employees were quickly taking cover in air-raid shelters after an imaginary attack by enemy planes, and at a high school, students carried out detoxification drills in response to imaginary chemical weapons being dropped on their grounds.

"Due to an invasion by enemy planes, part of the factory was destroyed, leaving seven dead and twenty-five injured, but owing to quick and orderly action, the recovery efforts—" The young man's smooth voice made the imaginary scenarios bloom in the flower shop. It felt as if each empty word was transformed into hundreds and thousands of insects that whirled dizzily inside the flower-scented shop, buzzing and flapping their wings and attaching themselves to the dirty windows. The young man's words were constructing an entirely imaginary situation, a reality made vivid and authentic to us, trapped in the flower shop. It was a linguistic transformation not unlike a miracle. At that moment, we were nothing more than fictional characters surrounded by imaginary words, existing in a fictional space and time. *Remember this, Cain. You will have a mute son. I will personally cut off your son's tongue. Remember this. Remember this.* I suddenly heard Sangju's hoarse voice, as if he were cursing from some lonely road. His gloomy, hollow voice rang out over the sunlit pavement. Next to me, Pyŏnggi sighed as he flipped through the notebook.

> *I see you in the mirror. What perfect revenge. Every morning when I get up to wash the dirt of the night's sleep from my face, you are already sitting in the mirror waiting for me. All right. I won't run anymore. It's been an exhausting fight. I won't run anymore. I'm tired. I'm tired and I just want to lie down . . . I knew the moment you put that mark on the middle of my chest that I would not be able to rest. You took sleep away from me. Because of you, I lost the peace of daybreak, repose of night, and even the comfort of praying. Each night, you hold up bloodstained clothes and sit by my head, waking me with your whispering.* You cannot sleep. You won't be able to enjoy even a moment's restful sleep. I will tightly bind the muscles of your eyes so they will never remember the peace of darkness. Until each of the blood vessels knotted in your eyeballs bursts and dissolves and tears flow down your cheeks and turn into blood—for all of eternity I will not let you close your eyes and rest. *People said that you were dead. People said it as they burned incense, poured wine, and placed flowers in front of your grave. They said the bones of the deceased rot and dissolve into a fistful of dirt where someday a seed of grass will come fluttering and take root. And that root will grow more roots, and those will spread, creating strong, thick grass that covers the field, the hillside, and all the earth. I alone scoffed at them as they wailed. You were not really dead. How could someone say that the rotted corpse with two cartfuls of dirt covering its chest was the whole you? Or the body was the whole you? Or the dirt-stained bones and the foul, decomposed flesh and organs where rusted fragments of metal were trapped? How can a person's life end with the death of his physical self? After I buried your body, you came back from the dead and walked into my memory. And you will live in me until the day I die. Truly, it is a perfect curse. I knew that I would never be able to escape your grasp or be free of the shackles on my legs. Each night you bang on my bedroom door and beg me to open it, saying:* "Where were you? When I called out your name that dawn, where were you . . ."

That was the end of the diary. The entry date was about three months ago, which I guessed was just before Sangju's second hospitalization. By that time, his nerves had weakened and he couldn't control his senses. Sanghŭi had told me what Sangju's condition was like at that time.

"At night, he would lock the door to his room and not let anyone in. He said that someone would always come to his door and call for him. Sometimes he would scream and shout and cry in the middle of the night. In the end, he sat in his room for three days without eating or drinking. Then the incident happened."

Sangju had attempted to escape from the retreat. They didn't think he'd try to leave because he had locked himself in his room and wouldn't move. The guards discovered him running down the hill with a shovel that had been left in the backyard of the retreat. They managed to grab him on the highway at the bottom of the hill and then took away the shovel and told him to go back up to the retreat. Sangju had insisted that he had to go somewhere right away.

"Do you know what Brother said to them? He said that he had to dig up the grave."

"The grave?"

"Yes. Myŏngbu's grave. He said he could never believe Myŏngbu was dead until he saw it with his own eyes."

No. He's not dead. There's no way. He's alive. How can he be dead when he's chasing after me like this and making my life miserable? Let me go. Please. I have to dig up his grave and see his body. The vivid image of Sangju holding a shovel in his hand and screaming appeared before my eyes.

"That night Brother broke the mirror hanging in his room with his fist, then did that frightful thing. When they battered down his door and went in, well . . . Brother was a bloody mess, and he was laughing." At that point, tears welled up in Sanghŭi's eyes and she hung her head.

Uuaaaaannnnggg . . .

The sirens went off again. The yellow flag hanging from the window beneath the loudspeaker had been replaced with a green one. We walked out of the flower shop and onto the street. The cogwheels began to turn again. The people of this city, who had suffered through and survived an imaginary attack, clamored noisily back into reality with the same tired faces. The street, which only a moment earlier had been a desolate ruin, came back to life and was filled with all sorts of sounds and movements. It was the amazing resurrection of the city. Just then, the bus we had been waiting for came staggering toward us from the distance.

When the bus reached Namp'yŏng, it was just past two. We got off at the administrative office of the township. When we asked a passerby for directions to the hospital, he told us it was a twenty-minute walk.

Reaching a fork in the road that split in three directions, we saw a sign that read HOSPITAL. We walked along the main road of the village, dotted with small stores and bicycle-repair shops. The houses soon became infrequent, and before long we saw only fields. On either side of the road, lush greenery filled the vast fields. Whenever a gentle breeze blew over the ears of the barley, verdant waves surged in the field's furrows, making them look like bronze armor. From time to time, frogs would stop singing and leap into the water-filled rice paddies, and wild flowers like Chinese milk vetches and wild violets bloomed in clumps on the banks. We were intoxicated by the dazzling life spread before our eyes, and each of us inhaled deeply. The wind carried the warmth of the sun, the scent of fresh grass, and the aroma of damp earth.

Children coming home from school in twos and threes took turns running ahead of one another as they passed by us. They were holding handfuls of wild flowers whose names they didn't know and were bursting with pure laughter. Several boys walked past us blowing reeds of barley. Seeing this, Sunim ran over to the grass by the road and picked a barley stalk. She broke off the end and held it to her mouth, then inflated her cheeks and blew into it, making a peculiar sound. *Ppeee.* We all laughed.

"It's already May!" Pyŏnggi shouted, letting out a deep breath.

"You're right . . . it's already May," Sunim repeated slowly, as if she hadn't known it. I glanced around at the surroundings for confirmation. It really was May again. The season when the whole world is filled with the joyful force of new life. But for us, that beautiful May day had lost its meaning—or perhaps I should say it had been taken from us. In fact, a great many things had taken from us the closeness we had felt in the past and changed it into raw emotion. The random stains on the asphalt, the smoke rising meaninglessly from smokestacks, the tractors on construction sites, the helicopters, the noise from loudspeakers, the heavy, dizzying weight of trucks moving along the street, the sharp edges of things and their sense of danger, brick fragments and blind alleys, war movies, handbills plastered on walls . . . All those things we faced in everyday life now possessed different meanings, smells, textures, hues, and sounds—suddenly calling forth a host of dark and frightening memories from the other side of oblivion. Before we had known it, we had become diseased. And perhaps there was no other way for us but to live with those somber memories constantly shadowing our daily lives.

We came to a stream and crossed over it on a small concrete bridge. Perhaps because of the drought, the water was shallow. The pebbles in the ripples seemed translucent. The stream curved around the field and flowed into the lower part of Tŭdŭl River. In the distance, slender poplar trees stood in tall rows along the stream. I saw two strangers sitting on the sandy bank near the bridge, looking slightly confused. I figured they had mistaken us for people they knew and walked out of their field to greet us, but at the last minute failed to recognize us. Pyŏnggi, who had been walking ahead, slowed down and began walking beside me. He handed me the diary he'd been holding, then abruptly spoke.

"Sangju was weak. How should I say it: instead of taking action, he halted two steps shy to watch life unfold in the distance. Dealing with the pain by himself, he started doubting everything, and that made him hesitate. Even when he was fighting the enemy, he had already prepared himself to forgive his adversaries. That's why he couldn't really confront anything and do battle."

Pyŏnggi's voice trailed off. The wind blew, and green waves surged in the barley field. For a while, there was only the sound of our footsteps.

"I wonder if the problem didn't lie there. He probably kept waiting for the moment when either the pure hatred or the pure love that he talked about would appear to him. I don't know. Perhaps if such a moment had come, Sangju would have been the most decisive one of us all . . . But in the end, the moments never came. It was just a fantasy created with abstract ideas. It's as if he tried to walk toward the horizon, his eyes gazing into the distance, but tripped over a pebble and fell. It's ironic, isn't it, that he couldn't forgive himself for tripping like that?" Pyŏnggi looked at me for agreement, but I couldn't think of anything to say. I couldn't muster such assurance, but I had to acknowledge that what he said was partly right. I imagined Sangju's haggard face, which had made us jokingly call him "the romantic poet." All at once, his gloomy eyes flickering behind his thick glasses rested heavily upon my heart.

Before we knew it, we could see our destination: a white, rectangular, five-story building standing against the side of a hill. As we entered the main gate, the window of the guard's office opened and the brusque voice of a man stopped us.

"May I help you?" He turned down the volume of his radio and looked us over. Pyŏnggi said we were there to visit someone.

"An employee, or . . ."

"No, a patient."

"If you go through the door over there, you'll see the reception desk on the left. Ask there." The guard yawned as he pointed. Obviously, he didn't want to be bothered. We heard the radio volume being turned up again as we followed a gravel-covered path cutting through the garden and entered the building.

Perhaps because it was Saturday, there were very few people around. It occurred to me then that this place had to be different from a medical hospital, which was the way I had imagined it: nurses in uniform or patients in wheelchairs. We peered into an empty window that had INFORMATION OFFICE above it and stood around for a few moments, until a young woman wearing glasses appeared.

"Which room and which patient are you here to visit?" she asked as she sat down behind the desk and opened the heavy ledger book. I gave her the room number as Sanghŭi had instructed and told her Sangju's name.

"Oh. That patient's visits have been restricted."

"What do you mean? Why?"

"He's been kept in isolation since yesterday morning. His condition suddenly got worse. The doctor left instructions that he not be allowed to meet with anyone, so I can't really do anything. Please come again another time."

"Where's the doctor?"

"He left quite a while ago. It's Saturday," the woman replied. From her officious tone, we could tell that she wanted us to leave. For a moment, we stared at one another in despair. We asked her about Sangju's condition, but she answered curtly that she did not know and even if she did, it was against policy to tell us. Nothing could be done. We stood around the window not knowing quite what to do. I thrust Sangju's notebook toward her.

"What is this?"

"It belongs to the patient in room 58. His doctor had said he wanted to look at it for reference," I explained. Emphasizing her indifference, the woman carelessly pushed it aside on the desk. Feeling a great rage brewing in my chest because of her indifference, I turned and walked out.

The trip back was truly depressing. None of us said anything, keeping our mouths tightly shut as if we had made a pact to be silent. Sunim walked with her eyes cast down, carrying the now useless bouquet, and Pyŏnggi exhaled his cigarette smoke over and over as if he were sighing. I couldn't stop glancing behind me. The many windows of the white hospital building seemed to be shooting daggers at us, as though they were the eyes of wild animals. *Where is your brother? Where is Abel? Under which mound of dirt did you bury him alive so that you could return by yourself?* Someone kept shouting at me from behind. That wounded voice cried like a wild animal—the voice of yet another Abel being abandoned.

We reached the bridge. From there the hospital was hidden by the hill. Beneath the bridge, several children had gathered and were splashing around in the stream. Their bags and shoes lay on the sandy bank, and they were in the midst of pulling something out of the waist-high water. We stopped walking. Countless glittering objects floated on the surface of the water. They were dead fish. The kids were laughing as they scooped up the fish, each barely the length of a person's thumb.

"Some adults are using chemicals upstream. They're catching a whole bunch of eels this big!" the kids shouted to us when they saw us standing on the bridge. We could see two men in their undergarments wading upstream. They were the men we had passed on the way to the hospital. We leaned against the railing and stared down at the shadows cast on the water beneath the bridge. The blue sky was reflected in the water, its image dotted with pebbles in the stream. We could see its blue behind the image of our faces, and on top of our reflected faces were the dead fish, their white bellies turned upward, floating downstream.

"When . . . when do you think he can return to his old self?" Pyŏnggi's face in the water spoke.

"Who?"

"Sangju."

I was busy watching a carp, still wriggling with life, as it floated away on the current. For a while, the silence had opened a gap between us.

"You know what, though? There's still something I don't get. Did

Myŏngbu really go to his house before he was killed that dawn . . ." Pyŏnggi's eyes were fixed on the water as he spoke.

"Maybe—maybe. That may be what happened," Sunim blurted.

"What do you mean?" Pyŏnggi and I stared at Sunim's face. Then Sunim said something even more startling, all the while keeping her gaze fixed on the water beneath the bridge.

"Sangju's mother told me once that on that final day, the family clearly heard someone banging frantically on the front gate. But they didn't open it because they were scared. Of course, Sangju couldn't hear since his room was in back . . . After daybreak they went out and looked, but by then no one was in the alley. I suppose there's no way of knowing whether or not that person was really Myŏngbu, but—"

"N-n-no way . . ." Pyŏnggi suddenly moaned. I thought I could hear the sharp sound of metal pounding somewhere in the distance. I saw Sanghŭi shaking her head vehemently when I talked to her at the café: *No. We really couldn't hear anything.* The strange, dark shadow on her forehead had not gone away.

Suddenly, I was overcome with dizziness. A gentle breeze blew from the other side of the field, heavy with the lush smell of grass and damp soil.

Sunim leaned against the railing with her head lowered and started to cry. Something struck the water below. The bouquet had fallen from where she had clutched it to her chest. Flower petals scattered among the dead fish and sank like tiny, colorful birds. Sunim's drooping shoulders trembled. No one wanted to be the first to speak. We stood there on the bridge a long time, staring at the flowers as they floated away into the distance and became a blur.

Translation by Susie Jie Young Kim

RICARDO PAU-LLOSA

Delft/Miami

After seeing a photograph by Chris del Risco during a visit to his studio

Dust gathers into fates, chalks
and grays in a ladder of light
the window and its burlap rag allow
to fall by rungs of density
into the room. Limelit, the pewter
bracelet—a dark halo with curls
that deflect its cheapness—lies
on the wooden shelf beneath the sill.
A curl of thread from the curtain,
made tungsten by the afternoon's
roulette of light, cracks
the sky of the room without thunder.
All about, the myriad filigrees
of particles in their melodious hovering.
To the bracelet's left a crumpled sheet,
animal in pose and outline,
gleams like a clean moon
with even its crevices blanched,
for that is what the light proclaims
and the artist has chosen to see.

Later, going west on the Causeway
from the Beach into Miami,
against the grain of sunset,
I drive the summer mad
in my air-conditioned shell.
I ponder the obese cruise ship
heading east in the channel out to sea,
and I think the obvious things
to get them on their way—the miracle

of buoyancy, or rather its boring numerics,
and the cost of babbling leisure,
and this hideous piling of decks
on the ever smaller base of ship.
And how no light can make us see
beauty in the distances. Miami readies
its tinseled self for the coming night.
I plunge ever faster into its gape
while the city is still gray against the sun,
leaden in sleep and cannot pay me back
in dream for how I see it.

The Poem behind the Poem: Literary Translation As American Poetry

John Balaban, Sam Hamill, Susie Jie Young Kim, W. S. Merwin, Hiroaki Sato, Andrew Schelling, and Arthur Sze respond to Tony Barnstone

■ **Tony Barnstone**

I came to Chinese poetry originally as an American poet learning how to make the image. Like many other American poets, I was led to China by my interest in Ezra Pound, William Carlos Williams, and other modernist poets who developed and modified their craft in conversation with the Chinese tradition. I came to China, in other words, to learn how to write poetry in English. This is also how I came to translation: as a way of extending the possibilities of poetry written in English. In fact, I would argue that historically the Chinese poem in English has allowed the American poetic innovator to invent a Chinese tradition filtered through the medium of translation in order to find new ways of writing American poems. A translation, after all, is the child of parent authors from different cultures, and however assiduously the translator attempts to remove his or her name from the family tree, the genetic traces will be found in the offspring. What the translator brings to the equation can never be reduced to zero. Translators bring their linguistic patterns, cultural predispositions, and aesthetic biases to the creative act, not merely holding up a mirror to something old, but giving the original text new life in a strange environment. Even a perfectly translated poem—one in which every word magically is turned into its doppelgänger and in which form, sound, and rhetoric are retained—is still a product of misprision, and the translator does not so much create a text in the new language *equal* to the old one as a text that strives to be *equivalent* to selected aspects of the original.

This is particularly true of translators of Chinese poetry. From a set of monosyllabic, largely pictographic characters calligraphed on a Chinese painting, fan, or scroll, the poem proceeds through a hall of mirrors, reappearing on the other side of time, culture, and speech as a few bytes of memory laser-etched on a white page in the polysyllabic, phonetic language of the American translator. The effect is that of moving from the iconic, graphics-based Macintosh operating system to the text-based DOS system. It's very difficult to make the systems compatible because the conceptual paradigms that underlie them are so radically different. We can create a neutral language that will transfer information between the two systems, but small things will have changed: the formatting will have gone awry, certain special characters will disappear if their correspondents are not found, and attached files—such as graphics and footnotes, which modify our sense of the text—may become separated or lost. Raw information will be preserved, but the aesthetic unity, the gestalt of the poem, will be lost in the translation. Literary translation is more than anything else an attempt to translate that gestalt, which a machine isn't sensitive enough to detect, much less reconstruct.

Those who discount the creative element in translation believe that translations should consist of word-for-word cribs in which syntax, grammar, and form are all maintained, and in which the translator is merely a facilitator who allows the original poem to speak for itself in a new language. Poetry, however, can't be made to sing through a mathematics that doesn't factor in the creativity of the translator. The literary translator is like the musician who catalyzes the otherwise inert score that embodies Mozart's genius. In that act, musician and composer become a creative team. However, just because the musician can keep time and scratch out the correct notes in the correct order, it won't necessarily be good music. Musical skill inevitably enters into the equation. *Fidelity*, true fidelity, comes from a musician's deeper understanding of the music. As John Frederick Nims says, "The worst infidelity is to pass off a bad poem in one language as a good poem in another."

From the early metrical and end-rhymed translations of Herbert Giles to the so-called free-verse translations of Ezra Pound, Arthur Waley, and Kenneth Rexroth, Chinese poems have been reinvented as American poems. The Chinese poem in English is like a stolen car sent to a "chop shop" to be stripped, disassembled, fitted with other parts, and presented to the consumer public with a new coat of paint. But despite its glossy American exterior, it's a Chinese engine that makes this vehicle run, and fragments of the poem's old identity can be glimpsed in its lines, the purr of its engine, the serial number, which we may still be able to read. The burden of my essay will be to discuss ways I've found of negotiating between Chinese and American poetic paradigms, and to engage in a limited discussion of what American parts have proved compatible with this Chinese vehicle, which has been a part of Western poetic traffic since the early years of modernism.

Daoist philosopher Zhuangzi says, "The fish trap exists because of the fish; once you've gotten the fish you can forget the trap. . . . Words exist because of meaning; once you've gotten the meaning, you can forget the words. Where can I find a man who has forgotten words so I can have a word with him?" Words are the net we cast upon the waters in search of knowledge, meaning, enlightenment. Ultimately, though, the fish has to come to us of its own volition (Native American hunters believe that when the hunter is in harmony with nature, the animal comes to him and sacrifices itself). So Sikong Tu, a famous ninth-century poet whose *24 Styles of Poetry* is a Daoist treatise on how to write poems, speaks of the need to find poetic inspiration through *lack of effort* in his poem "The Placid Style": "You meet this style by not trying deeply;/it thins to nothing if you approach." There is always something ephemeral about the knowledge behind a poem, about the inspiration that creates it—or creates a translation. To find a poem in translation we need to discover what I call "the poem behind the poem." Sometimes we can't find this metapoem by looking; we also have to see. Sometimes we can't find it by trying; it comes to us while we're doing something else.

Before we discuss the next poem, "River Snow" by Liu Zongyuan—translated by Chou Ping and me—let's take a moment to read it out loud, slowly. Empty our minds. Visualize each word.

> A thousand mountains. Flying birds vanish.
> Ten thousand paths. Human traces erased.
> One boat, bamboo hat, bark cape—an old man.
> Alone with his hook. Cold river. Snow.

"River Snow" is considered a prime example of minimum words/maximum message and has been the subject of numerous landscape paintings. It is terrifically imagistic: the twenty Chinese characters of the poem create a whole landscape, sketch an intimate scene, and suggest a chill, ineffable solitude. To get this poem across in translation, I strove to reproduce the linear way the characters unfold in the reader's mind. The syntax is particularly important because it is perfectly constructed. We walk into this poem as if walking into a building, and the spaces that open up around us and the forms that revise themselves at each step unfold according to the architect's master plan.

The first two lines create a fine parallelism: birds passing through the sky leave no trace, just as human traces are effaced in the mountain paths. It makes me think of the Old English kenning for the sea: *whale path.* Here the sky is *bird path.* In the second line, it's clear that the snow is the active agent in erasing humanity from the natural scene, yet snow is never mentioned. After the last trace of humanity disappears with the word "erased," a human presence is rebuilt in this landscape, character by character, trace by trace: "One boat, bamboo hat, bark cape" and—the sum of these clues —"an old man." These first two lines sketch a painterly scene: the vast emptiness of the sky above and the snowy solitude of the landscape below hit the reader like a glance at a Chinese landscape painting. And then the tiny strokes that create a man in the third line direct our imagination deeper into the poem, as if we had discovered a tiny fisherman's figure on the scroll. The next line tells us what the old man is doing. He is "Alone with his hook." Silence. We take in the "Cold river." The last character sums up the entire poem: "Snow."

Snow is the white page on which the old man is marked, through which an ink river flows. Snow is the mind of the reader, on which these pristine signs are registered, only to be covered with more snow and erased. The old man fishing is the reader meditating on this quiet scene like a saint searching himself for some sign of a soul. The birds that are absent, the human world that is erased suggest the incredible solitude of a meditating mind, and the clean, cold, quiet landscape in which the man plies his hook is a mindscape as well. Thus, there is a Buddhist aspect to the poem, and Liu Zongyuan's old man is like Wallace Stevens's "Snow Man," whose mind of winter is washed clean by the snowy expanse. He is

> . . . the listener, who listens in the snow,
> And, nothing himself, beholds
> Nothing that is not there and the nothing that is.

"River Snow" is a perfectly balanced poem, a tour de force that quietly, cleanly, easily creates its complexly simple scene. To merely paraphrase it in translation is to ignore the poem behind the poem. The translator must discover the poem visually, conceptually, culturally, and emotionally, and create a poem in English with the same mood, simplicity, silence, and depth. Each word must be necessary, essential. Each line should drop into a meditative silence, should be a new line of vision, a new revelation. The poem must be empty, pure perception; the words of the poem should be like flowers, one by one opening, then silently falling. As William Carlos Williams was fond of stating, a poem is made up of words and the spaces between words.

A problem with this technique occurs if the translator takes it to extremes and makes a poem that sounds too choppy. Consider Yip Wailim's translation of "River Snow":

> A thousand mountains—no bird's flight.
> A million paths—no man's trace.
> Single boat. Bamboo-leaved cape. An old man
> Fishing by himself: ice-river. Snow.

Yip is among the best-known contemporary Taiwanese poets, a well-respected translator and translation theorist. His translation is very, very close to mine, and I appreciate what he is trying to do, but I feel that all those dashes and that colon ultimately make the poem seem choppy. Still, the third and fourth lines are almost there.

For the sake of comparison with the translations by Yip and myself, take a look at this quite good but somewhat wordy translation from *Indiana Companion to Classical Chinese Literature:*

> Over a thousand mountains, birds have ceased to fly,
> On ten thousand paths man's tracks have been wiped out.
> In a lone boat, in grass cape and hat, an old man
> Fishes alone the cold river snow.

The translation is fine but, to my taste, prolix: filled with prepositions and articles that make the lines fluid, but dilute them in the process. This prosey version lacks the magical economy of "River Snow."

All three of these translations are very close to the original, and all attempt to reproduce the unfolding of visual clues. My point here is that the addition of a few parts of speech or an unfortunate choice of punctuation can pollute an otherwise excellent and accurate translation and weaken the poem's ability to catalyze a powerful reading experience.

The poetry of Wang Wei—the poet I've translated most extensively from Chinese—is often perfectly clean, like "River Snow." Each character resonates in emptiness like the brief bird calls he records in one of his poems. The inventor of the monochrome technique, Wang Wei was the most famous painter of his day. In his work, both painting and poetry were combined through the art of calligraphy—poems written on paintings. As Su Dongpo said of him, "His pictures are poems and his poems pictures"; and as Francois Cheng has pointed out, painting and calligraphy are both arts of the *stroke,* and both are created with the same brush. I like to imagine each character in "River Snow" sketched on the page: a brushstroke against the emptiness of a Chinese painting—like the figure of the old man himself surrounded by all that snow.

The most famous piece by Zen-influenced composer John Cage was titled "4' 32"." The audience came in and sat down, and for 4 minutes and 32 seconds nothing happened. The audience was the music. Their rustlings, coughs, chatter, the creaking of seats, perhaps the rain on the roof of the auditorium—all this was the music. In classical Chinese painting the white space defines what forms emerge, and in Buddhism emptiness is wholeness. The perfect man's mind, according to Zhuangzi, is empty as a mirror, and according to the Daoist aesthetics of Chinese painting, each stroke of the brush is *yin* (blackness, woman) upon *yang* (light, whiteness, man). All the empty space reacts to one brushstroke upon the page. Each additional stroke makes the space adjust itself into a new composition, in much the way each great poem makes all of literary history readjust itself, as T. S. Eliot said. To make a Chinese poem in English we must allow silence to seep in around the edges, to define the words the way the sky's negative space in a painting defines the mountains.

As I stated earlier, I think the poem in translation must carry on a conversation with other poems in order to discover itself. For me, "River Snow" resonates with Japanese Zen poems and poems of the English Romantics, and it is this conversation that allows me to hear its silence. Consider these lines from a *haiku* by Japanese poet-painter Buson, translated by Robert Hass:

> Calligraphy of geese
> against the sky—
> the moon seals it.

Here's the first clue: the birds are imagined as brushstrokes. Thus the empty sky is like a blank page. Consider now these lines from a poem by Japanese Zen poet Musō Soseki (1275–1351) translated by W. S. Merwin and Sōiku Shigematsu:

> Don't look back
> to this world
> your old hold in the cellar
> From the beginning
> the flying birds have left
> no footprints on the blue sky.

From Buson's image we come to Soseki's image of the flying birds passing through the sky without leaving a trace, as in "River Snow"; and as in "River Snow," there is a contrast of the human world with the natural. Here, the birds' trackless flight through the sky is a symbol of the enlightened mind's passage through the world without grasping or holding or desiring. Compare "On Nondependence of the Mind," a poem by Dōgen (1200–1253)—founder of the Sōtō school of Japanese Zen Buddhism—translated by Brian Unger and Kazuaki Tanahashi:

> Water birds
> going and coming
> their traces disappear
> but they never
> forget their path.

The mind that doesn't depend on the world leaves no traces, just as the "water birds" don't forget their path—a path we can understand as a mystical Way. In these lines from Wordsworth's *Prelude,* he describes his hike through the Alps:

> Like a breeze
> Or sunbeam over your domain I passed
> In motion without pause; but ye have left
> Your beauty with me

Because he is in tune with the natural setting, Wordsworth's meditative mind passes through nature without leaving tracks. The inverse parallelism he sets up (of his trackless passage through nature's landscape versus nature's beautiful inscription in his mindscape) is implicit in "River Snow" as well. "River Snow" is also a poem in which the mind is washed clean, like the sky empty of birds, the paths empty of humanity. Zhuangzi asks, "Where can I find a man who has forgotten words so I can have a word with him?" The fisherman in "River Snow" is that man.

Although I felt it necessary in "River Snow" to make an absolutely literal, word-for-word translation to get at the heart of the poem, in other cases I've translated lines in unusual ways to get at the poem behind the poem: the urgent image, the quiet mood, the sound that I felt resided in the Chinese poem and needed emphasis to be felt in English. Sometimes I've deviated slightly from a literal translation in order to get an effect that I believe is truer to the poet's vision. There are no fast rules; the translator has to feel it. I want to close with a discussion of a translated line that is much more problematic than the ones above.

First, though, I need to discuss what—somewhat idiosyncratically perhaps—I call deep-image lines in Chinese poetry. There are times when Chinese poets create a nature imagery that is almost surreal, incredibly evocative and strange. In order to learn how to recreate these lines in English, I think it's good to look at the school of deep-image poets in America. Most famous among them are Robert Bly and James Wright, though I would classify contemporary Native American poet Linda Hogan as deep image as well (in her practice, as opposed to her literary history). Bly and Wright were deeply influenced by the combination of personal and impersonal perspectives and tones in Chinese and by Chinese rhetorical parallelism, clarity of image, and focus on implication. They blended these characteristics with a late strain of surrealism derived from Trakl, Vallejo, Lorca, and Neruda. It is precisely this mélange of influences on Bly and Wright that opens up a space in American poetry for a blend of the Chinese tradition and the surreal—and that provides a model for translators.

Here are two examples of deep-image lines, the first from Linda Hogan:

> Crickets are pulsing in the wrist of night.

and the second from James Wright:

A butterfly lights on the branch
Of your green voice.

How do these lines work? They invert your expectation, blending the human and the natural or engaging in synaesthesia (as in Su Dongpo's great line "With cold sound, half a moon falls from the painted eaves"). Similarly, in Wang Wei's poems "In the Mountains" and "Sketching Things," nature does strange things; the world is so lush that its green color becomes a liquid that wets his clothes:

No rain on the mountain path
yet greenness drips on my clothes.

and

I sit looking at moss so green
my clothes are soaked with color.

The strange beauty of James Wright's image taps into a profound psychological mystery and opens up a space in the imagination that Wang Wei's lines also reach. Wright makes it possible for us to *see* Wang Wei's synaesthesia, and to *see how* to translate him into English.

As with the Wang Wei lines above, the human and the natural are intertwined in Linda Hogan's line. It works because it imagines the world as a body through which the blood pulses, an intermittent action that is also a sound, the *ba-dump* of the heartbeat. The cricket sound is similarly an intermittent, two-beat sound, and it brings the night into our bedrooms, making it as intimate as our bodies—a small, internal event, like a pulse.

Of course I was thinking of Linda Hogan when translating one of my favorite lines of Wang Wei in which he sets himself the task of getting at the action-pulse of the cricket's song. Wang Wei's line comes from "Written on a Rainy Autumn Night After Pei Di's Visit": "The urgent whir of crickets quickens." I like the sound qualities here, the onomatopoeia, the internal off-rhymes, and the sense that the line is just beyond comprehension, yet intuitively right. However, this line as I translated it—in collaboration with Willis Barnstone and Xu Haixin—is extremely problematic: an example of the product of translation as reinvention. Literally, the line reads:

\ —	/	\	/
ts'u - chih	*ming*	*ji*	*chi*
urge + spin/weave (=cricket)	to sound/the sound of a bird or animal	intense	anxious/urgent/hurried

The urgent whir of crickets quickens.

The first two characters refer to the house cricket and mean "to urge into spinning" or "to urge into weaving"—an idiom derived from the similarity of a cricket's intermittent, two-beat chirp, produced by rubbing its wings together, to the *shhk-shhhk* of a shuttle on a hand loom, or the whir and whirl of a spinning wheel. In other words, the Chinese idiom for cricket has an onomatopoetic element. This element is also present in the English word "cricket," which derives from the insect's characteristic sound, *cricket, cricket.* Of course, we forget that unless the word is heard freshly: the off-rhyme "crickets quickens" is therefore meant to focus our attention on the forgotten music of the word—to make us actively *hear* "cricket," perhaps for the first time.

Now what about "the urgent whir"? Isn't it mistranslating to add this image, using something that is simply an idiom? No, I don't think so. Idioms such as this add an idiosyncratic beauty to language, like the pillow talk of Japanese poetics or the kennings of Old English. A translation that rendered Beowulf's "whale path" as "the sea" would be a very dull translation indeed. The Chinese idiom suggests an image that is inherent in the language, much as "foot of the mountain" bears a comparison, long forgotten, of the mountain to a human body.

This idiom allowed me entry to the poem behind the poem, to a sound that was also an action. I wanted to bring alive the complex image of the cricket wings shuttling like a cranky loom or lost in a whirring blur like a spinning wheel, so I had to analyze the phrase for what activated that metaphor: intermittency, quick action, noise. I imagined the blur of cricket wings rubbing themselves into song, and I imagined that song as both continuous and intermittent, both an act and a sound. The word "whir" suggested both the action of spinning—the insect's blur of wings—and the sound of that action: *whir.* I wanted a line that was musical throughout, wanted the reader to hear the crickets' stuttering dactylic rhythm when he or she hears the line's rhyming, emphatic beat: "The **ur**gent **whir** of **cri**ckets **qui**ckens." This goes beyond the question of whether to be true to the letter or the sense; it's a question of being true to the spirit of the line, which is both image and song. In this interpretive translation, I can't say that I truly got this line of Wang Wei's into English, but I do believe that I brought an analogous English poem to life—one closer to Wang Wei's imagination and to the imagination inherent in the Chinese language than one merely translated as "the cricket's loud sounds speed up."

I have argued elsewhere that Chinese poetry in English has deviated deeply from the form, aesthetics, and concerns of the Chinese originals and that this is the result of willful mistranslation by modernist and postmodern poet-translators. In the first decades of this century, Chinese poetry was a powerful weapon in the battle against Victorian form, and thus it was brought over into English in forms resembling the free verse that it helped to invent. Rhyme and accentual meter were quietly dropped from the equation because—unlike Chinese use of parallelism, caesura, minimalism, implication, and clarity of image—they weren't useful in the battle for new poetic form. However, we are now in a different place in the century and need no longer be constrained by past literary conflicts. While the elimination of rhyme and meter from translations of Chinese poetry has created a distinguished English-language tradition of "Chinese" free verse—one that has influenced successive generations of American poets—it has also denied the poem its right to sing. I don't recommend a return to the practice of translating Chinese poems into rhyming iambics (generally, this overwhelms the Chinese poem with our pastoral tradition). But I do think that as much attention should be given to the way the Chinese poem triggers sound as to how it triggers sight, and that translators should use the whole poetic arsenal—syllabics, sprung rhythm, off-rhyme, half-rhyme, internal rhyme, assonance, consonance, and so forth—to try to give the English version of the poem a deeply resonant life. Too often translators have given Chinese poets the resolution powers of an electron microscope, but have cut off their ears. By being cognizant of the poem's song, we are less likely to be deaf to the poem behind the poem, and less likely to be satisfied with clumsy rhythms and a lack of aural pleasure.

If my examples are notable less for their similarity than for the apparent divergence of the translation principles by which they were created, this is the essence of my argument. There are many roads to China. So that the original's voice and silence can be heard, the poem behind the poem may require word-by-word fidelity—that is, for translators to restrain their inventiveness. Or the poem may require a radical departure from convention to arrive where it began. In either case, the translator must keep faith with the deeper need that poetry fulfills in our lives. Like a cricket's song, a poem is an arrangement of sound and image that is also an action affecting the reader. If we are very quiet, can we feel its tiny pulse fluttering in our wrists? If we listen like Stevens's snow man, if we become nothing long enough, we may discover not what the poem *says* but what it *does.* A poem is a machine made out of words, as William Carlos Williams once wrote, and like a wheelbarrow or a can opener or a telephone, it is a machine reduced to an economic efficiency of parts and designed for a specific function. It doesn't matter whether we take the original poem apart with an Allen wrench or a Phillips screwdriver, or whether we build the translation out of wood or plastic or burnished copper. What matters is that the gears engage and the wheels turn and that the poem's *work* is done in the translation as well. All translation is mistranslation, but a translator's work and joy are to rig something out of the materials at hand that opens cans, or carries hay, or sends voices through the lines. We will never create a truly Chinese poem in English, but in this way we can extend the possibilities of the translation, which may in turn reveal to the imaginations of American poets unforeseen continents.

■ **John Balaban**

Translating Vietnamese Poetry

Tony Barnstone's phrase "the poem behind the poem" offers a useful way of looking at translation. In the translation of a poem—as opposed, say, to a technical document—we are always looking for more than mere denotative equivalencies. We want to feel how the poem felt in its original. We want to inhabit the condition of its first reader or listener. Traveling in English, we seek to cross cultural borders and encounter the poem on native ground. To do this, we must hear "the poem behind the poem."

What lies behind, or even prior, to the poem depends on several things at once. First is the poem's historical tradition, including that tradition's habits of prosody, its abiding themes, its range of language, and its notion of what a poem is (and is not). Second, to hear "the poem behind the poem," we must consider the poet's unique operations within his or her poetic tradition. We must be able to feel the dialectical commerce, as it were, between the poem and the tradition it plays against. And finally, for the above to be working in a translation—for our incognito travel to take place—the translator must possess true talent in English poetry so that all prosodic possibilities seem alive and attendant. As Stanley Kunitz writes in the introduction to his and Max Hayward's beautiful translations of Anna Akhmatova:

> The poet as translator lives with a paradox. His work must not read like a translation; conversely, it is not an exercise of the free imagination. One voice enjoins him: "Respect the text!" The other simultaneously pleads with him: "Make it new!" He resembles the citizen in Kafka's aphorism who is fettered to two chains, one attached to earth, the other to heaven. If he heads for earth, his heavenly chain throttles him; if he heads for heaven, his earthly chain pulls him back. And yet, as Kafka says, "all the possibilities are his, and he feels it; more, he actually refuses to account for the deadlock by an error in the original fettering."

The discovery of "the poem behind the poem" for a translator of Vietnamese is a long prospect. The literary poetry of Việt Nam began in the first century C.E. with poetry written in Chinese. From the tenth century and into the early twentieth, Vietnamese poets wrote in *nôm,* a calligraphic script devised by the literati for Vietnamese phonetics. This *nôm* literary tradition, with its characteristic forms, subjects, and allusions, was heavily influenced by the poetry of China (particularly the T'ang)—even more than the literary models of classical Greece and Rome influenced English poetry.

These literary poetries are only part of the Vietnamese landscape. Alongside and beneath the *nôm* and Chinese poetries, an even older poetry known as *ca dao* runs like a vast river or aquifer. This oral poetry, still sung in the countryside, originated perhaps thousands of years ago in the prayers and songs of the Mon-Khmer wet-rice cultures to which the Vietnamese are tied. The word-stock of *ca dao* is native, bearing few loan words from Chinese. It is a lyric poetry—not narrative—and its power lies in its allusive imagery and brief music. Its references are to nature, not to books; to delta fish and fowl, to creatures of the field and forest, to wind and moon, to village life. It belongs to the farmers of Việt Nam, which is to say that it belongs to most Vietnamese because eighty percent live, as ever, in the countryside.

This repository of images, melodic patterns, aspirations, and beliefs is the cultural center of all Vietnamese poetry. Even literary poets—whether they are working in *lü-shih* regulated verse (*thơ đường luật* in Vietnamese), modern free verse, or the metrics of the oral tradition, like the great classical poet Nguyễn Du—seem always to be working in some relation to *ca dao. Ca dao* is the fixed foot of the literary culture's compass. Representing a folk culture resistant throughout the millennia to Chinese acculturation, it is an important aspect of "the poem behind the poem" in Vietnamese.

Vietnamese is a tonal language, which is to say that every syllable has a linguistic pitch that creates the semantic meaning. *Là,* with a falling tone, is the verb "to be." *Lá,* with a high, rising tone, means "leaf." *Lạ,* with a low, constricted tone, means "strange." There are six tones in the language, indicated in writing by diacritical marks. In prose, these tones fall at random. In poetry, these tones fall at certain places in the metrical line. In *ca dao,* as in the example below, the various arrangements of linguistic pitches give rise to patterns that easily become *musical* pitch patterns, that is, melodies or, more correctly, what the musicologist Trần Văn Khê calls "singing without song" or cantillation. It is just this singing that is *ca dao*'s chief delight to the Vietnamese listener.

How on earth does the translator convey this? One can approximate the rhyme scheme (*dạ/mạ, hàng/ngang/đàng* in the rove rhyme of the *lục-bát* couplet) with "heart/dart," "streaks/leaving/creek," but "the poem behind the poem" is essentially lost. To paraphrase the late critic Nguyễn Khắc Viện, this kind of translating "is like drawing a bucket from a moonlit well at night and losing the silvery shine of its light." For it is the lone voice of the singer that makes one sad for the woman left behind in the field.

Bước xuống ruộng sâu man sầu tấc dạ
Tay ôm bó mạ nước mắt hai hàng
Ai làm lỡ chuyến đò ngang?
Cho sông cạn nước đôi đàng biệt ly?

Stepping into the field, sadness fills my deep heart.
Bundling rice sheaves, tears dart in two streaks.
Who made me the ferry's leaving?
Who made this shallow creek that parts both sides?

In the poetry of Hồ Xuân Hương, who wrote around 1800, near the end of the high tradition of *nôm,* we find poems behind poems behind poems. Almost all of her *lü-shih* or *chüeh-chu* poems, while apparently about natural landscapes or everyday activities, have hidden within them a complete, parallel second poem: a double entendre whose topic is sex. Sometimes, as in the poem below, the translator can succeed by finding words that are both true to the physical landscape she describes and suggestive of other things to the English ear: for example, "cleft," "bearded," "plunges," and "mount." Here, the translator's task is to also set up a double meaning with a single set of images.

ĐÈO BA DỘI

Một đèo, một đèo, lại một đèo.
Khen ai khéo tạc cảnh cheo leo.
Cửa son đỏ loét tùm hum nóc,
Hòn đá xanh rì lún phún rêu.
Lắt lẻo cành thông cơn gió thốc
Đầm đìa lá liễu giọt sương gieo.
Hiền nhân, quân tử ai mà chẳng . . .
Mỏi gối, chồn chân vẫn muốn trèo.

THREE MOUNTAIN PASS

A cliff face. Another. And still a third.
Who was so skilled to carve this craggy scene

The cavern's red door, the ridge's narrow cleft,
The black knoll bearded with little mosses?

A twisting pine bough plunges in the wind,
Showering a willow's leaves with glistening drops.

Gentlemen, lords, who could refuse, though weary
And shaky in his knees, to mount once more?

As scholars have noted, the title "*Đèo Ba Dội*" (Three Mountain Pass) would probably suggest to a Vietnamese reader the range in central North Việt Nam called Đèo Tam-Điệp. But the poem's peculiar grotto would invite suspicion, and of course a literate Vietnamese reader would recognize immediately the pine and willow as male and female symbols, respectively. "Gentlemen" and "lords" *("Hiền nhân, quân tử")* are traditional terms for the elite, mandarin class. Yet Hồ Xuân Hương is anything but traditional. A woman writing in a male, Confucian tradition at the end of the decadent Lê dynasty, she only makes honorific references to men when she is being derisive.

The main aspect of the poem behind the poem (behind the poem) for Hồ Xuân Hương is that she is almost always working against tradition.

Behind her traditional landscapes lies sexual dalliance. Behind her pagoda walls, irreverent fools. In the widow's funeral lament, she hears infidelity. Yet all her poetic subversions are launched in exquisitely made, regulated *lü-shih* and *chüeh-chu:* verse with traditional requirements for line length, rhyme and tone placement, and syntactic parallelism. But here too she is unique and surprising, often using the word-stock of *ca dao* and the aphorisms of the common people where her male contemporaries are content with flowery rhetoric and stock ideas.

In "Three Mountain Pass," the double meaning is conveyed through the imagery; that is, the poetic manipulation of the landscape suggests the second meaning. For the translator—as Ezra Pound learned from his efforts with Chinese—this visual, or phanopoetic, aspect of poetry is a challenge, but an answerable challenge. More difficult to render are Hồ Xuân Hương's poems in which the second meaning is suggested through verbal puns, tonal echoes, and contemporary cultural detail. In the poem below, she makes allusions to the decadent state of the Amida Buddhist clergy.

VỊNH SƯ HOÀNH DÂM

Cái kiếp tu hành nặng đá đeo
Chỉ vì một chút tẻo tèo teo
Thuyền từ cũng muốn về Tây-trúc
Trái gió cho nên phải lộn lèo.

THE LUSTFUL MONK

A life in religion weighs heavier than stone.
Everything can rest on just one little thing.
My boat of compassion would have sailed to Paradise
If only bad winds hadn't turned me around.

The "little thing" that weighs down the monk and keeps him from entering the paradise of the Amitabha Buddha seems to be his penchant for sex. This is not said explicitly but rather with puns, some of them tonal: by changing the pitch of the words she's chosen, you get ones with obscene meanings. For example, in the last line of the original, *lộn* means "to confuse," "to turn about." *Lộn lèo,* then, means something like "to turn over" or "to capsize." But *lồn* with a falling tone means "vagina." *Lẹo* with a low, constricted tone means "to copulate." *Đeo* in the first line means "to bear" or "to carry." With a high, rising tone, it also means "to copulate," as does *trái* ("ill winds") if the pitch is shifted to the monotone, as in *trai gái.* It's not so much that this poem has a clear second line of argument or double entendre as that obscenities unexpectedly seem to be trying to invade the poem, as if it expresses the tormented mind of the monk himself. Finally, balanced against this set of suggestions is the Buddhist notion of perfecting oneself, which is centered around the "perfection"—*paramita* in Sanskrit

—of compassion. With the Buddhist symbol of the journeying boat of the spiritual self, we have a doctrinal echo from the very etymology of *paramita:* "to get to the other side," to the opposite shore.

This Vietnamese delight in covert verbal play reached its apogee in palindromes in *nôm,* with *lü-shih* that could be read forwards *and* backwards to yield a second poem with a different meaning. There is a poem in *nôm* that, read in reverse, becomes a poem *in Chinese* about the same landscape, but of course with a different point of view. Then there is the fabulous cyclical palindrome composed by Emperor Thiệu-Trị in 1848 and set in jade inlay in the imperial city of Huế. In this one sun-shaped *lü-shih,* there are concealed twelve perfectly metrical *lü-shih.* Each can be found by starting at any one of the calligraphic rays and going clockwise or counterclockwise, from the inside out, or the outside in.

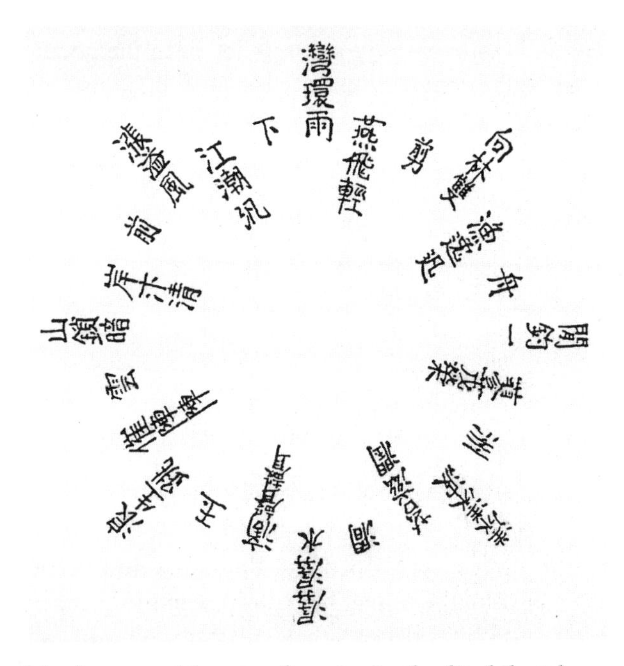

One of the last practitioners of poetry in the *lü-shih* style was Tản-Đà, the poet and patriot who ran a newspaper during French colonial rule in the 1930s. When informed that a more enlightened colonial administration had lifted censorship, Tản-Đà lamented that a direct telling of the news would be too easy.

Two great traditions lie behind any Vietnamese poem: the oral folk poetry of the common people; and the *nôm* poetry of the literary elite. These two great and ancient streams of poetic tradition feed nearly every literary endeavor in Việt Nam, even today, and even in prose. Any effective translator of Vietnamese would have to have traveled some in these two realms of beauty and belief.

Đi ra một ngày, về một sàng khôn. "Go out one day," the proverb says, "and come back with a basket full of knowledge."

■ **Sam Hamill**

Sustenance: A Life in Translation

I was introduced to classical Chinese poetry by Kenneth Rexroth and the Beat poets in the late 1950s, especially by Rexroth's immensely popular *One Hundred Poems from the Chinese,* which included thirty-odd poems translated from Tu Fu, whom Rexroth called "the greatest non-epic, non-dramatic poet in history." I drew inspiration from what I learned of Han Shan in Jack Kerouac's *The Dharma Bums* and Gary Snyder's translations, and from the poets in Robert Payne's *The White Pony,* Witter Bynner's translations, and of course those of Arthur Waley.

Later, after four years in the U.S. Marine Corps, two of which were spent in Japan, where I began Zen practice and learned some rudimentary Japanese, I came to Ezra Pound's adaptations of the notebooks of Ernest Fenollosa, published as *Cathay* in 1915. In an essay in the second edition of *A Poet's Work,* "On the Making of Ezra Pound's *Cathay,*" I discuss the origins and development of this little volume of only fourteen poems, claiming it to be the single-most influential volume of poetry in this century. Here, I'd like to elucidate a few of this book's problems because they present some of the dangers of translating without knowledge of the original.

Fenollosa knew little Japanese and almost no Chinese. His informants were two Japanese professors, Mori and Ariga, neither of whom was fluent in classical Chinese, and thus Li Po became known in the West by his Japanese name, Rihaku. This trilingual effort sometimes produced strange results, as in the poem "Separation on the River Kiang." Pound retains Fenellosa's Japanese pronunciation, *ko-jin,* which means simply "person," mistakenly treating it as a personal name rather than recognizing the two Chinese characters *ku jen.* The *kiang* in the title means "river." So Pound's title becomes "Separation on the River River" rather than "Separation on the Yangtze River." Nevertheless, *Cathay* opened the doors to American modernism. More than any other volume, it is responsible for the personal tone of much of this century's shorter lyrical, imagistic verse.

When I began translating Tu Fu in the mid-1970s, I looked up each character and annotated each poem before attempting my own draft and then turned to translations by Florence Ayscough, William Hung, Rexroth, and others for comparative readings. What I found was often surprising.

Here is my translation of Tu Fu's "New Year's Eve at the Home of Tu Wei":

> Seeing the year end at a brother's home,
> We sing and toast with pepper wine.
> The stable is noisy with visitors' horses.
> Crows abandon trees lit by torches.
> Tomorrow morning I turn forty-one.

The slanting sunset shadows lengthen.
Why should one exercise self-restraint?
I may as well stay drunk all the days of my life.

Rexroth, who is very good at locating the personal voice and situation of Tu Fu in his translations, makes no effort at recapturing the formal end-stopped couplets of the original even though the couplet is the fundamental unit of classical Chinese poetry and Tu Fu its greatest master. Choosing in its stead a typically loose line that may be a run-on, Rexroth's version ends:

In the winter dawn I will face
My fortieth year. Borne headlong
Towards the long shadows of sunset
By the headstrong, stubborn moments,
Life whirls past like drunken wildfire.

Sometimes relying too heavily on Ayscough or the French translations of Hervey de Saint-Denys or Georges Margoulies, Rexroth is clearly led astray by the former in this instance. Ayscough's translation reads:

At bright dawn my years will bridge four tens;
I fly, I gallop towards the slanting shadows of sunset.
Who can alter this, who can bridle, who restrain the moments?
Fiery intoxication is a life's career.

While Rexroth's version makes a fine poem in English, Ayscough's version carries considerable Victorian baggage. Neither poem, I believe, captures the spirit of Tu Fu very successfully. Tu Fu's poem is not about "fiery intoxication." It is not about life whirling past or about the pathetic fallacy "drunken wildfire." Hung's version:

To see the year depart at a brotherly home,
To participate in the songs and toasts with the pepper-wine,
I can hear from the stable the noisy horses of the guests,
I can see the crows leaving the trees because of the torches.
By tomorrow, I shall no longer be forty;
The evening of life will be fast coming upon me.
Of what use is it to be cautious and to exercise restraint?
Let me forget it all by being utterly drunk.

Even if Hung is wordy, he is closest to the original. However, if his penultimate line is far too prosy, the ultimate line is far too generalized. He also inserts an intrusive "I can hear" and "I can see" where none exist in the original; sometimes a first- or second-person pronoun needs to be added in translation, but one should do so only when essential. Elsewhere, Hung also contributes to general misunderstanding, as when he translates this line in what is probably Tu Fu's last suite of poems: "Such is indeed the shining grace of God." Tu Fu had no concept of a monotheistic god. The principal religions of China in the eighth century were Taoism and Buddhism, neither of which accommodates any notion of a monolithic god. Master Tu was a good Confucian in many respects, but not a deeply religious man. Rather he demonstrated a decidedly existential turn of mind. Hung allowed Western civilization to intrude upon Eastern art in a notably ugly translation.

Tu Fu's joy in joining his brother is shaded by deep resignation as the poet considers the conditions of his life. What is implied in the original, and what should appear in English, is the notion that somehow, being Tu Fu, he will *not* waste away sitting before the wine jug. The great poet-out-of-office, unsung in his own time, asks the question every poet asks under such circumstances: Why do we do it? Why not give up and submit to despondency or the numbing effects of wine? The Chinese poet is not embarrassed by direct expression of this conflict.

Another way translators sometimes go wrong is by investing too much in the pictographic elements of characters. Although an excellent essay, the Pound-Fenellosa "Chinese Written Character as a Medium for Poetry" leads many a Westerner to forget that Chinese is a spoken language and that its poetry, like our own and others', aspires to the conditions of music. One of the things immediately lost in translation is the play of pictographic elements, but if we remember that Chinese poetry was chanted, then we can remember how important is the ear in poetry.

There is not much we can do in English with a basically monosyllabic, rhymed five- or seven-character line. Attempts to translate classical Chinese into rhymed metrical structures in English have largely resulted in academic doggerel. In translating Tu Fu, I sought formality enough to represent the couplet-by-couplet construction of the original, including the syntactical parallelism where possible, and also sought to interpret or interpolate within the poem only where I deemed it essential. Chinese has an almost infinitely larger capacity for rhyming than does English. I therefore sought to pay particular attention to assonance and consonance, and to slant and implied rhymes, while struggling to be true to what I perceived the poet said and to the spirit in which his poem was given—meaning the general tone and stance.

I learned early to rely on scholars whose knowledge of classical Chinese was far greater than mine. After nearly ten years of studying Tu Fu, I completed a first-draft manuscript of about one hundred of his poems. A university-press editor asked Irving Yucheng Lo to evaluate my work. Professor Lo was kind enough to comment on each poem, noting exactly where I had misread a Chinese character or misinterpreted a line. His generous offering of time and scholarship was encouragement enough for me to revise the manuscript.

Here is one of Tu Fu's last poems, "Heading South":

南 征

春岸桃花水，chūn àn táo huā shuǐ
雲帆楓樹林。yún fān fēng shù lín
偷生長避地，tōu shēng cháng bì dì
適遠更沾襟。shì yuǎn gèng zhān jīn
老病南征日，lǎo bìng nán zhēng rì
君恩北望心。jūn ēn běi wàng xīn
百年歌自苦，bǎi nián gē zì kǔ
未見有知音。wèi jiàn yǒu zhī yīn

Spring returns to Peach Blossom River
and my sail is a cloud through maple forests.

Exiled, I lived for years in secret, moving on
farther from home with tear-stains on my sleeves.

Now old and sick, at last I'm headed south.
Remembering old friends, I look back north a final time.

A hundred years I sang my bitter song,
but not a soul remembers those old rhymes.

I am perhaps guilty of stating too much by adding "living in secret" where the original suggests simply "refugee." In addition to wanting to do more than just call up the image of the refugee, I needed to fill out the line musically, so I interpolated here. I think "Heading South" is an important poem and have been surprised that David Hinton and other recent translators of Tu Fu have ignored it. After years in exile, the old poet thinks he is about to return home, though still virtually unpublished and unknown but to a few poet-friends. The resignation and frustration articulated in the poem have been given a deeply ironic turn by the judgment of history. Tu Fu died shortly thereafter, never dreaming that he might one day be declared the greatest poet in the history of Chinese.

While completing work on Tu Fu's *Facing the Snow,* I translated a small selection of the Tzu Yeh songs and poems by Li Ch'ing-chao, *The Lotus Lovers;* about fifty poems by Li Po, *Banished Immortal;* and Lu Chi's *Wen Fu.* I found *Wen Fu* to be particularly helpful, not only as a translator's handbook but also as a writer's: "When studying the work of the masters," Lu Chi says, "watch the working of their minds." Among the first poets to discuss poetic form and content, Lu Chi lays out an elegant tradition, a good deal of which may be applied directly to our practice two centuries and another language later. In each instance, my translations were corrected, improved, and clarified by being passed under the eyes of such knowledgeable scholar-translators as J. P. Seaton, with whom I recently translated *The Essential Chuang Tzu.*

I was fortunate to receive a Japan-U.S. Fellowship in 1988 and spent much of that year following Bashō's famous route through Japan's northern interior as I began to translate his *Oku no hosomichi* (Narrow road to the interior), now included in the much more comprehensive *The Essential Bashō.* When I began studying Bashō, I had thought *haiku* was something I would study for perhaps a year. Ten years later, when I finally saw my book in print, I realized that I would continue to be Bashō's student for the rest of my life. The work is never finished. Every translation is a provisional conclusion.

While I knew that my studies in Chinese would be helpful in translating Bashō, just how helpful became clear almost immediately. Bashō's poems and prose are loaded with paraphrases and quotations and echoes of Chuang Tzu, Tu Fu, and Po Chu-i. All during his twenties and thirties, Bashō studied Tu Fu. He claimed to have carried a copy of the *Chuang Tzu* with him wherever he went. To know the working of his mind, it is helpful to read what he read, to understand as much as possible about his Zen practice and the social conditions and traditions within which he came to flower.

Japanese poetry flows from two forms: the *chōka* (longer poem) and *waka* (shorter poem). Over a century of aesthetic discussion and development, the *waka* evolved into *tanka,* both written in syllabic lines of 5-7-5-7-7. Unlike Chinese, Japanese is polysyllabic, and its sounds are much closer to those of Western languages. The Japanese language combines *kanji,* Chinese written characters, with a phonetic syllabary, *kana,* of forty-odd characters. Translated literally, *tanka* and *haiku* usually come out a few syllables shorter in English than in Japanese. Consequently, most Western translators have simply ignored the Japanese syllabic structure, thereby sacrificing the musicality that may be achieved by adhering to form.

Another, and to my mind much more egregious, mistake on the part of many translators is to rearrange the order of perceptions in a poem, often with the intent of creating a kind of formal closure. From R. H. Blyth's renowned scholarship of the thirties to that of recent times, one sees this unfortunately common practice. *Haiku* often opens at the end, rather than closes, as in Bashō's most famous poem:

Furuike ya
kawazu tobikomu
mizu no oto

At the ancient pond
a frog plunges into
the sound of water

How this poem has suffered in English! I can't remember whose version it was, nor can I locate it now, but years ago I read one that went:

An old pond.
A frog leaps in.
Kerplop!

The "translator" wanted a punch line at the end. If we may assume that he knew what the original actually said, perhaps this final line is a poor attempt to achieve onomatopoeia. The result may be economical, but completely misses the whole point Bashō is making. While the translation remains true to the order of perceptions, it ruins the poem by creating artificial closure. *Mizu* is water, *no* is postpositional, and *oto* is sound: "The sound of water." Every translator who has put this frog *(kawazu)* into water has missed the poetry. The frog *plunges*—a word I chose because of its onomatopoetic quality in the context of leaping into water—into pure sound. I wanted to stay close to the original form and remain true to Bashō's final line, which, I propose, is followed by a fourth, unwritten line of silence. The poem opens at the end, leaving the reader-listener listening.

Some say that *haiku* is indebted to the four-line Chinese *chüeh-chu* and that, by leaving out the third line, an imaginative leap is made. I doubt the accuracy of such a theory, but there are some structural similarities. Bashō, like his Chinese predecessors, often sets a scene in the first line; however, he uses the Japanese "cutting word" *ya* to create a kind of emphasis: "At the ancient pond, yes, /a frog." The *chüeh-chu* also makes use of an imaginative leap, usually between the third and fourth lines. But there, similarities end. The Chinese poet has no cutting word.

Another example:

Fuyuniwa ya
tsuki mo ito naru
mushi no gin

A winter garden—
the moon also a thread,
like the insect's song

What does that *mo* ("also") in the second line refer to? If the moon *(tsuki)* is "also a thread," what is the first thread? The insect's song *(mushi no gin)?* Chuang Tzu often speaks of "running out the string of our days." Perhaps Bashō means here the thread of his own life. The ambiguity is in the original, and to fail to represent that complexity is to fail in the service of poetry. One implication might be that the moon is the thread stitching the winter garden to the insect's song. Where there is a deliberate use of ambiguity in the original, I try to create a parallel in the translation.

Sometimes the translator must make shifts, as in this poem:

Uki fushi ya
take no ko to naru
hito no hate

which literally means:

A sad confluence—
young bamboo shoots
 [literally, *take no ko,* "children of bamboo"]
to become
everyone in the end

A revised version reads:

A sad confluence—
everyone in the end becomes
young bamboo shoots

In the end, what is any poem in translation except another blade of grass in the field—not a conclusion but a provisional entryway into the vast ecology of the poem within its greater tradition? It is best to have two or three translations of any classic text: one a strictly scholarly, literal treatment, and one a more imaginative, more interpretive translation, preferably by a sympathetic and knowledgeable poet.

But of course there can be no such thing as a literal translation since even individual nouns and verbs often have no exact equivalents in other languages. Even when they do have acceptable equivalents, we still find problems of translation. When the Chinese or Japanese poet writes of "clouds and rain," he or she may mean only clouds and rain or may mean sexual congress since "clouds and rain" has been a fixed epithet or *makura kotoba* (pillow words) for two millennia or more. In the hands of a good poet, the weather and the personal experience become interlocking parts of a compound metaphor. Since we don't have equivalents in English, we must learn to read the translation as well.

Horace was among the first to warn against *verbo verbum* translation.

Octavio Paz notes, "Every poem is a translation." With roots in Greek, Latin, and German and with an admixture of foreign terms that have become Americanized through common usage, the English language itself is a translation.

My practice as a poet and a translator is really one work evolving as much from my Zen practice as by any wish to "make" a poem. Translation has been for me a simultaneous learning and making. There are few stupidities I have not committed. But since I am an *unsui,* a perpetual beginner in the temple of poetry and along the dharma path, I understand that there is no perfect prescription and that we are all students together. In the company of Chuang Tzu, Tu Fu, Bashō, and Issa, my practice is refined, but perfection remains an elusive ideal rather than an attainable reality, and translation a provisional conclusion.

When Bashō advises his students, "Don't merely follow in the footsteps of the masters, but seek what they sought," I number myself among his students. I feel a solidarity with Tu Fu in his exile despite the fact that we are no longer living in a time of war and I have been fortunate enough to have published more than thirty books while he died an obscure poet. I translate because I want to be in the company of these poets—to comprehend their art, to learn what they learned, and to be shaped by their learning—and because I want to make them available to others.

When an otherwise notable translator like Stephen Mitchell muddies the waters with something as irresponsible as his wild interpretation of Lao Tzu, passing it off as translation, it is like a computer virus that begins to invade other programs. Mitchell writes that he felt no compunction to study the original Chinese because he got the transmission directly from his Zen master and thus felt free to interpret Lao Tzu's *Tao Te Ching* as he wished. In at least a couple of chapters, there is not as much as a single word from the original. The problem here is that the naive reader might assume that the English bears some resemblance to the original, which all too often simply isn't so. Or as Chuang Tzu would say, "Not quite *there* yet, eh?"

To truly understand Lao Tzu, Chuang Tzu, or most classical Chinese poets, we would need a large scholarly apparatus to clarify the allusions and explain the characters and explicate the cultural-philosophical contexts and linguistic differences. Bill Porter's recent translation of *Tao Te Ching* is brilliant—in part because it is accurate and in part because he includes insightful commentaries unknown to previous translators.

Chuang Tzu to Tu Fu, Lu Chi to Bashō, the Taoist and Zen literary masters are the very foundation of my practice as both poet and Zen Buddhist. When I say I "practice" the arts of poetry or translation, I mean as a doctor or lawyer "practices" his or her profession. Poetry in America is not a profession, but an avocation. Nevertheless, one is a *practicing* poet, a *practicing* Buddhist or Christian or Jew—or, in my case, Buddhist atheist. (Buddhism is generally nontheistic.) I've always been moved by Gary Snyder's remark

"As a poet, I hold the most archaic values on earth." What Tu Fu valued, I value; what Bashō sought, I seek. The human condition remains relatively unchanged over a millennium. And I agree with Stanley Kunitz that poetry "has its source deep under the layers of a life, in the primordial self."

We are fortunate to live during the greatest time for poetry since the T'ang dynasty. While academicians bemoan the decline of "the canon," the canon is expanding exponentially. One can't really begin to understand the East Asian canon without knowing Confucius, *The Lotus Sutra* (the foundation of Buddhism), Chuang Tzu, T'ao Ch'ien, and the T'ang poets. Anyone who believes for a minute that Confucius is not as important as Plato is suffering from tunnel vision. To understand something about Tu Fu and Bashō is to establish kinship with a great and powerful tradition.

American poetry has flowered precisely because we have brought these and many other masters into English. When I survey the great literary influences on the poetry of the last fifty years, I must include beside the many East Asians such poets as Rilke, Akhmatova, Rumi, Trakl, Odysseus Elytis, George Seferis, Yannis Ritsos, Valéry, Neruda, García Lorca, Cavafy, Sappho, and Paz. Their influences have provided sustenance, inspiration, and models for hundreds of our poets. There are more terrific poets writing in America today than have lived here in the past two hundred years, and much of what they create—from surrealist to language poetry, sonnets to "organic verse"—is a direct or indirect result of translation.

Kunitz writes in his *Passing Through:* "Through the years I have found this gift of poetry to be life-sustaining, life-enhancing, and absolutely unpredictable. Does one live, therefore, for the sake of poetry? No, the reverse is true: poetry is for the sake of the life." I sit at the feet of the great old masters of my tradition not only to be in a position to pass on their many wonderful gifts, but to pay homage while nourishing, sustaining, and enhancing my own life.

■ **Susie Jie Young Kim**

Entering the Pale of Literary Translation

Translation is a literary practice that has been abused and mistreated in many ways. Literary translations have often been viewed as subordinate and inferior forms that straddle the line separating what is "literature" from what is not. They have often been kept out of standard literary histories because the translator didn't have the appropriate birthplace, and because translations have been plagued by a discourse of equivalence, which assumes that for any given word, there exists an exact equivalent in another language. For translation to operate in this artificial way, one would have to assume that language lacks any adaptability and flexibility and is therefore impervious to the influences of its cultural context; that the meanings of literary texts are fixed and therefore there is only one possible interpretation of every story, novel, play, or poem; and that a translator is able to suppress all the experiences she would normally bring to a text so as to be a sterile medium through which this mechanical process can take place. Literary translation is, of course, a bit more than a mechanical, formulaic, or clinical process in which one text is seamlessly transformed into its equivalent in another language.

In my own academic work, I have encountered translation in one of its most creative forms. In turn-of-the-century Korea, translators were translating just about everything into Korean. Their creations transcended strict notions of "translation": some would technically be considered "adaptations," that is, liberal transformations in which only a skeleton of the "original" text remained. Translators wrestled with a multitude of foreign languages, and some did not even know which language the text that they were translating had originally been written in. Some translators based their work on previous translations done in Japanese, Chinese, English, and even Esperanto. These early translators understood the process as one of literary creation and went about their work with the freedom usually associated with more conventional literature. Rather than gain their rightful place in literary history, however, their role has been simplified to that of helping to introduce Western literature to Korea and thereby make Korean literature more "modern."

Besides the two languages and cultural traditions involved in the translation process itself, there are external factors that affect literary translations. The historical relationship of the two literary traditions also influences the translator's approach to or attitude toward the process. As a translator of Korean poetry and fiction into English, I am very aware of the uneven power relationship between Korean literature and its European and American counterparts that resulted from the cultural imperialism accompanying territorial colonialism in early twentieth-century Korea. And of course, the translator's own position comes into play. Unlike some adherents of more standard notions of translation, I am very aware of the fact that my various identities as a Korean, a scholar of Korean literature, and a woman all leave their respective traces on my translations.

To restate, the act of translation is not merely a process of copying contingent on the linguistic principle of equivalence. The text is filtered and contaminated through the translator and thereby transformed, most obviously in its physical appearance and more subtly in its content. Literary translation, which for practical purposes is an arrested moment of such fluidity, also maintains a fluidity of its own. It is this aspect of the translation process that I aim to achieve in my own work.

What often occurs when I ask people to read drafts of my translations is that they assume the attitudes discussed above. The most frequent comment I get is some version of "We don't say that in English," "We don't have that expression in English," or "This doesn't sound right." Such comments are often justified. I have misread the original text, become myopic—as one inevitably does when spending too much time concentrating on a translation—or, more simply, mistyped. My reader then does her job as a reader: to point out a sentence or phrase that is incorrect. However, it is also often the case that the wording of a phrase or sentence is deliberate on my part, as when I purposefully retain the tensions arising from the translation process. Interestingly enough, I have found that I am given more freedom in this respect when I am translating poetry. This is partially aided by people's assumptions about poetry: poetry is *supposed* to be cryptic; it's *supposed* to make little sense.

In order to illustrate the thinking that underlies my own translation process, I offer my drafts of a poem by Yi Sŏng-bok. Yi Sŏng-bok's "1959" represents the political embodied in the lyrical. The sense of futility, mental paralysis, and despair aptly represents the poem's historical context: a turbulent era in Korean history when the Korean War was still vividly etched in people's minds, the cease-fire having taken effect only a few years earlier. Within the temporal context of the poem, it has been fourteen years or so since the nation regained its independence from the Japanese, but the people are feeling the strain of being trapped under yet another type of authoritarian rule. A year later, in spring of 1960, the social unrest would explode into nationwide protests encompassing people from all levels of society.

1959

Winter passed that year and summer arrived
But spring never came. Peach trees
Bore tiny fruit before efflorescing
And barren apricot trees withered away.
Pus oozed out of boys' genitals without reason
And doctors emigrated as far as Africa.
Friends going abroad for school bought us a round,
And we unexpectedly received a letter from an uncle
Who had been shipped off to the South Seas during World War II
But no surprise could lift us from the lethargy, our frigid state
 of being
We merely embellished our dismal routines more lavishly than the
 year before
Nothing created memories.
Though Mother was alive and my sister vigorous,
Their happiness would be quietly thrashed by these feet
Or crushed beneath a fly swatter.
Each time I saw a painting of spring it looked desolate
That year, winter passed and summer came
We did not fight with spring but morals and phony principles
Spring was not to come
So we voluntarily entered an imaginary prison

The translation above is a version I attempted several years ago. Being something of a perfectionist (like many translators, I suspect), I never question whether or not a translation is "complete." Rather, translation for me is an ongoing process. A hiatus usually appears in the form of an editor's nonnegotiable deadline; it also may come in the form of reaching a creative impasse. In whatever form the break manifests itself, it too is part of the translation process. Although such a break is not an unequivocal cure for such creative woes and frustrations, it is only through time spent away from the translation that one can approach it again with fresh eyes. Revisiting the above version of "1959" after having laid it aside for about four years has given me a fresh outlook on the original poem, as well as on my translation. The hiatus has allowed me to develop alternative readings of the poem that were unavailable to me at the time of my translation.

At times the process of translation involves imaginative negotiations. In general, the negotiations and compromises I was having to make with this version of "1959" had to do with questions of form versus content. Most of the liberties I eventually took were contingent on concerns of not adding too much information for the sake of comprehensibility. Related to this, I also recall, I spent a great deal of time struggling over the rhythm in English. The rhythm in this version is not too bad, partly because I attempted to make it smoother by inserting my own punctuation. With the exception of one comma in the middle of the line that is in the middle of the poem, Yi Sŏng-bok's original contains no punctuation. Also, because Korean does not use case to distinguish between words, Yi Sŏng-bok's poem flows in the natural rhythms of Korean without the pauses and stops created by case changes. In this more recent version, I experimented with the translation by leaving out the punctuation and rendering all the words in lowercase.

1959

winter passed that year and summer arrived
but spring never came peach trees
bore tiny fruit before efflorescing
and barren apricot trees withered away
pus oozed out of boys' genitals without reason
and doctors emigrated as far as africa
friends going abroad for school bought us a round
and we unexpectedly received a letter from an uncle
who had been shipped off to the south seas during world war ii
but no surprise could lift us from the lethargy our frigid state of being
we merely embellished our dismal routines more lavishly than the
year before
nothing created memories
though mother was alive and my sister vigorous

> their happiness would be quietly thrashed by these feet
> or crushed beneath a fly swatter
> each time i saw a painting of spring it looked desolate
> that year winter passed and summer came
> we did not fight with spring but morals and phony principles
> spring was not to come
> so we voluntarily entered an imaginary prison

I have not decided whether or not this works well in English, but one thing that I can say is that I like the fact that the poem is not as cluttered as before. Somehow, leaving out punctuation helps this version to remain much quieter than my initial one did.

Another challenge of this poem lies in Yi Sŏng-bok's line breaks. Korean grammar is such that, more often than not, an English translation must invert the order of a Korean sentence. Thus, the lines "and we unexpectedly received a letter from an uncle/who had been shipped off to the South Seas during World War II" reads in the original more like "during World War II to the South Seas [who was] shipped off the uncle/unexpectedly a letter received." Translating becomes tricky when determining the line break in English, as emphasis will be placed on different things depending on where I decide to make the break.

Rereading my initial translation of the poem, I feel the need to attempt a few modifications. I ponder the word choice in line three: "bore tiny fruit before efflorescing." I like the economy of "efflorescing" because the word conveys the idea that peach trees were producing premature fruit even before they had flowered. A more literal rendition of Yi Sŏng-bok's lines reads something like the following:

> spring did not come peach trees
> before their flowers had bloomed bore very small fruit

To translate this line as "before the flowers had bloomed they bore tiny fruit" seems incorrect because the translation is a bit too drawn out, interrupting the rhythm more than is necessary. However, "efflorescing" perhaps connotes a bit more than I would like it to here. It would sound better to say "flowering" rather than "efflorescing."

In line ten, "but no surprise could lift us from the lethargy our frigid state of being," I made the opposite gesture: toward expansion rather than compression. Yi Sŏng-bok's lines read:

> from an uncle who was drafted to the South Seas during World War II
> we received a letter unexpectedly but no
> surprise could from the lethargy and frigidity
> lure us, it was just that compared to the previous year

In my translation, I opted to elaborate upon "frigidity" and render it as "our frigid state of being" for the purposes of maintaining consistent rhythm in that part of the poem. I made a similar gesture in the final line of the poem, but for different reasons. Here is how Yi Sŏng-bok's lines read:

> we were with moral principles and pseudo doctrines not with spring
> fighting since it had to be that spring didn't come
> we voluntarily went into a prison that could not be seen

"Moral principles" is interchangeable with "morals" in Korean, so I chose to be more economical in this case. With "pseudo doctrines," I wanted to convey the speaker's distrustful tone. "Pseudo doctrines" does not quite encapsulate the cynicism, so I chose "phony principles."

For "a prison that could not be seen" or "a prison that we could not see," I elected for a more liberal rendering. At the time I was working on this version, I was drawn to the notion of an "imaginary" or "imagined" prison: a prison constructed out of that period's oppressive social and political context. The sense of hopelessness and dejection is effectively captured in Yi Sŏng-bok's image of people blindly walking into such a prison. Pondering it now, however, I hesitate. The translation would perhaps work better if the image evoked in this line was emphasized in a more direct manner.

The following is my latest version of "1959":

1959

winter passed that year and summer arrived
but spring never came peach trees
bore tiny fruit before flowering
and barren apricot trees withered away
pus oozed out of boys' genitals without reason
and doctors emigrated as far as Africa for us
friends going abroad for school bought us a round
from an uncle who had been shipped off to the South Seas during
    World War II
we even received a letter unexpectedly but no
surprise could lift us from our lethargy or frigidity
we embellished our dismal routines more lavishly than the year
    before, that was all
nothing created memories
though Mother was alive and my sister full of life
their happiness would be quietly crushed by these feet
if not already smashed beneath a fly swatter
each time I saw a painting of spring it looked dilapidated
that year though winter passed and summer began
we were fighting with morals and phony principles not with spring
since spring was not to come
we voluntarily entered an invisible prison

■ **W. S. Merwin**

Preface to East Window: The Asian Translations

These poems, taken from *Selected Translations 1948–1968, Asian Figures, Selected Translations 1968–1978,* and *Sun at Midnight,* represent my attempts to make poetry in English out of poems originally written in Asian languages, over a period of more than three decades. I cannot remember when I first encountered Asian poetry, but it was in translation, of course, because I know no Asian languages. When I was still a child, I found, in the Harvard Classics, Edward FitzGerald's version of the *Rubáiyát of Omar Khayyám*—the original language not, according to some definitions, strictly Asian, and the rendering, I am told, a distant approximation, but I have remained fond of it ever since, as a great piece of Victorian poetry. By the time I was sixteen or so I had found Arthur Waley's Chinese translations, and then Pound, and was captivated by them both. Their relations to the forms and the life of the originals I will never be able to assess. But from the originals, by means and with aspirations that were, in certain respects, quite new, they made something new in English and they revealed a whole new range of possibility for poetry in English. Poetry in our language has never been the same since, and all of us are indebted to Waley and Pound whether we recognize and acknowledge it or not. Their work suggested, among other things, that the relation between translation and the original was more complicated and less definite than had often been assumed. But in fact the notion of what translation really was or could be had been undergoing change all through the nineteenth century, partly as a result of efforts to bring over into English a growing range and variety of originals. The assumptions inherent in the word "translation" had shifted radically since the early eighteenth century.

When Pope set out to translate Homer, almost everything (as it appears to us) was known beforehand. He knew who most of his immediate readers would be: they had subscribed for the translations. They, in turn, knew—or thought they knew—who Homer was, and they knew the text, in the original. Both the subscribers and the translator took it for granted that the proper form for heroic verse, in English, must be the heroic couplet. Pope's work was expected to display the wit, elegance, and brilliance with which he could render a generally accepted notion of the Homeric poems in a familiar English verse form.

Since the eighteenth century, and especially since the beginning of modernism, more and more translations have been undertaken with the clear purpose of introducing readers (most of them, of course, unknown to the translators) to works they could not read in the original, by authors they might very well never have heard of, from cultures, traditions, and forms with which they had no acquaintance. The contrast with Pope's situation is completed by the phenomenon, which has appeared with growing frequency in the past half century, of poet-translators who do not, themselves, know the language from which they are making their versions and who must rely, for their grasp of the originals, on the knowledge and work of others.

New—or different—assumptions mean different risks. New assumptions about the meaning of the word "translation," whether or not they are defined, imply different aspects of the basic risk of all translation, however that is conceived. Which is no risk at all, in terms of the most common cliché on the subject: that all translation is impossible. We seem to need it, just the same, insofar as we need literature at all. In our time, an individual or social literary culture without it is unthinkable. What is it that we think we need? We begin with the idea that it is the original—which means our (as scholars, potential translators, or readers) relative conception of the original. At the outset, the notion is probably not consciously involved with any thought of the available means of translation. The "original" may even figure as something that might exist in more forms than one, just as it can be understood by more than one reader. But if we take a single word of any language and try to find an exact equivalent in another, even if the second language is closely akin to the first, we have to admit that it cannot be done. A single primary denotation may be shared, but the constellation of secondary meanings, the moving rings of associations, the etymological echoes, the sound and its own levels of association, do not have an equivalent because they cannot. If we put two words together and repeat the attempt, the failure is obvious. Yet if we continue, we reach a point where some sequence of the first language conveys a dynamic unit, a rudiment of form. Some energy of the first language begins to be manifest, not only in single words but in the charge of their relationship. The surprising thing is that at this point the hope of translation does not fade altogether, but begins to emerge. Not that these rudiments of form in the original language can be matched—any more than individual words could be—with exact equivalents in another. But the imaginative force that they embody, and that single words embody in context, may suggest convocations of words in another language that will have a comparable thrust and sense.

By "rudiments of form" I mean recognizable elements of verbal order, not verse forms. I began translating with what I suppose was, and perhaps still is, an unusual preconception about the latter: the fidelity in translating a poem should include an ambition to reproduce the original verse form. Besides, I started translating partly as a discipline, hoping that the process might help me to learn to write. Pound was one of the first to recommend the practice to me. I went to visit him at St. Elizabeths in the forties, when I was a student. He urged me to "get as close to the original as possible" and also to keep the rhyme scheme of the poem I was translating, if I could, for the exercise as much as anything else. He was generous. And eloquent about what the practice could teach about the possibilities of English. He recommended that I should look, just then, at the Spanish *romancero,* and I did; but it was almost fifteen years before I actually made versions of many of the *romances*—and without the original rhyme schemes. I kept to his advice, at the time. When I did come, gradually, to abandon more and more often the verse forms of the poems that I was translating, I did not try to formulate a precise principle for doing so. Translation is a fairly empirical practice, usually, and the "reasons" for making particular choices, however well grounded in scholarship, are seldom wholly explicable. I would have recognized, probably quite early, a simple reluctance to sacrifice imagined felicities of the potential English version, to keep a verse pattern that was, in a sense, abstract. The preference seems to me practical, at least. I think I began to consider the subject more systematically when I was trying to decide on the best form for a translation of the *Chanson de Roland.* I had before me versions in blank verse both regular and more or less free, and one that contrived to keep not only the metrical structure of the Old French but the rhyme scheme: verse paragraphs known as *laisses,* sometimes many lines in length, each line ending with the same assonance. The result, in English, struck me as nothing more than an intellectual curiosity; unreadable. The word order of the lifeless English was contorted, line by line, to get those sounds to come out right. As for the virtues of the original that had moved hearers for centuries and contributed to the poem's survival over a thousand years, there was scarcely an indication of what they might have been. It's easy to multiply examples of this kind of translation. And yet it must be true that in translating—as in writing—formal verse, exigencies of the form itself occasionally contribute to the tension and resonance of the language. But I realized at some point that I had come to consider the verse conventions of original poems as part of the original language, in which they had a history of associations like that of individual words—something impossible to suggest in English simply by repeating the forms. Verse conventions are to a large degree matters of effects, which depend on a familiarity that cannot, of course, be translated at all. The effects of the convention in the new language can never be those the convention produces in the former one. This is true even with forms that have already been adopted. There would be certain obvious advantages in retaining the sonnet form in English, if translating a sonnet from Italian, but however successful the result, the sonnet form in English does not have the same associations it has in Italian; its effect is not the same; it does not mean the same thing. And sometimes an apparent similarity of form can be utterly misleading. The *Chanson de Roland,* again, for example. The original is in a ten-syllable line, and an English-speaking translator would naturally think, at first, of iambic pentameter. But if the poem is translated into any sort of blank verse in English (leaving aside the question of the relative vitality and brightness of that form in our age), the result is bound to evoke reverberations of the pentameter line in English from Marlowe through Tennyson—echoes that drown the real effect and value of the Old French verse.

The whole practice is based on paradox: wanting the original leads us to wanting a translation. And the very notion of making or using a translation implies that it will not and cannot be the original. It must be something else. The original assumes the status of an impossible ideal, and our actual demands must concern themselves with the differences from it, with the manner of standing instead of it. When I tried to formulate practically what I wanted of a translation, whether by someone else or by me, it was something like this: without deliberately altering the overt meaning of the original poem, I wanted the translation to represent, with as much life as possible, some aspect, some quality of the poem that made the translator think it was worth translating in the first place. I know I arrived at this apparently simple criterion by a process of elimination, remembering all the translations—whatever their other virtues—that I had read, or read at, and sat down, thinking, "If the original is really *like* that, what could have been the point of translating it?"

The quality that is conveyed to represent the original is bound to differ with different translators, which is both a hazard and an opportunity. In the ideal sense in which one wants only the original, one wants the translator not to exist at all. In the practical sense in which the demand takes into account the nature of translation, the gifts—such as they are—of the translator are inescapably important. A poet-translator cannot write with any authority using someone else's way of hearing.

I have not set out to make translations that distorted the meaning of the originals on pretext of preserving some other overriding originality. For several years I tried to maintain illogical barriers between what I translated and "my own" writing, and I think the insistence on the distinction was better than indulging in a view of everything being the (presumably inspired) same. But no single thing that anyone does is wholly separate from any other; and impulses, hopes, predilections toward writings as yet unconceived certainly must have manifested themselves in the choices of poems from other languages that I preferred to read and wanted to translate, and in the ways that I went about both. And whatever is done, translation included, obviously has some effect on what is written afterward. Except in a very few cases, it would be hard for me to trace in subsequent writings of my own the influence of particular translations that I have made, but I know that the influences were and are there. The work of translation did teach, in the sense of forming, and making available, ways of hearing.

In the translations in *Asian Figures,* I let the sequence of the ideograms (which in most cases I had in front of me, with their transliterations) suggest the English word order, where that could be done without destroying the sense. The series of translations from Ghalib—made from literal versions, scholarly material, and direct guidance supplied by Aijaz Ahmad—were part of the same impulse. My first drafts remained close to the original *ghazal* form, and both Aijaz and I thought them papery. As he planned to include in the eventual publication the original texts, literal versions, and his own notes on vocabulary, the whole point of the enterprise was to produce something else from the material: poems in English, if possible. The rule was that they were not to conflict with Ghalib's meaning, phrase by phrase, but that they need not render everything, either. Translation was viewed as fragmentary in any case; one could choose the fragments, to some degree. Considering the inadequacy of any approach to translation, I had been thinking of Cézanne's painting the Montagne Sainte Victoire over and over, each painting new, each one another mountain, each one different from the one he had started to paint. I imagined that in translating a poem something might be gained by making a series of versions bringing out different possibilities. I still think so, though I realize that versions, however many, from a single poet-translator are likely to sound like variants of each other, and echo the translator's ear at least as clearly as they do the original.

The Ghalib translations are among those made without any firsthand knowledge of the original language, as I have explained. I don't know that such a procedure can be either justified or condemned altogether, any more than translation as a whole can be. Auden, for one, thought it the best possible way of going about it. I suspect it depends on the circumstances: who is doing the work, and the collaborators' relation to each other and to the poetry they are translating. I have had my doubts about working this way, and have resolved several times not to do any more translation of this kind (as I have resolved not to translate anymore at all), but I have succumbed repeatedly to particular material.

I should make it clear that the only languages from which I can translate directly are Romance languages, and that I am less familiar with Italian and Portuguese than with French and Spanish. All the translations in this collection were based on someone else's knowledge. I continue to go about this in different ways, certain that no one translation will be absolute, for the obvious reason that it cannot be the original, and the original, as long as anyone is interested in it, will be heard in ways that gradually come to differ more and more among readers who use the second language in changing ways.

After 1978, my principal attempt at translation from an Asian language was the collaboration with Sōiku Shigematsu on the poems of Musō. I met Shigematsu-sensei in 1976, and we began talking about Musō, as I remember, almost at once. For years I had been interested in what I had read of Japanese poetry from the earliest period through Bashō and his disciples, and in the relation between much of the poetry and Buddhist insight.

Shigematsu-sensei is a Rinzai priest and a professor of American literature (particularly the Transcendentalists) in Japan, who had been working on literal versions of Musō's poems for years and was looking for a poet with whom he could collaborate in English. We worked together on Musō's poems, mostly by correspondence, for over a decade.

When I look back at the various attempts to make in English something whose life seemed to me to suggest what was alive in the original, I am not sure that "translation" is the right word for some of the ways of trying to do that, but no other term seems adequate either, and the restless search for one becomes part of the practice of translation—an enterprise that is plainly impossible and nevertheless indispensable. The fond hope that has led me is fed by the same spring, I think, that sustains poetry and language itself.

■ **Hiroaki Sato**

Forms Transformed: Japanese Verse in English Translation

In translating poetry, no one is *wrong,* except when the literal deciphering is. I remember, for example, a translator working on some poems of Hagiwara Sakutarō (1886–1942) and misreading the Chinese character (*kanji,* in Japanese) for *sara* ("plate" or "dish") as the one for *chi* ("blood"). This was years ago, and I no longer remember the lines, as translated by him, that contained the misreading, although, checking my own translation, I see it must have occurred in places such as "I would like to steal and eat that love-plate of skylarks, which gleams in the sky," "I ate too much of the plate of *cabbage* this morning," and "I looked through the whitened plate." Sakutarō's imagery in these descriptions may be odd enough for this particular misreading not to matter much—at least to the reader ignorant of the original; still, it is an error.

But Hagiwara Sakutarō is mainly known for his *jiyū-shi* ("free verse"), which does not employ any discernible syllabic patterns. My focus in this essay is on two traditional forms: the 5-7-5-7-7-syllable *tanka* and, Japanese verse forms having developed genealogically, its grandchild, the 5-7-5-syllable *haiku.* Most translators routinely render these in five and three *lines,* obviously because the two forms consist of five and three syllabic units. The question is: does the 5- or 7-syllable unit constitute a "line"? Also, in view of the recent emergence in the United States of translators who employ the same syllabic count in their translations of classical Japanese verse, you might ask what happens when they do so.

The first thing you find when you step out of the realm of traditional forms, where inherited notions may hold sway, is that, yes, the 5- and 7-syllable units can each be a "line." Miki Rofū (1889–1964), for example, wrote *"Furusato no"*—a poem that became famous because it was set to music—in lines that alternate 5 and 7 syllables:

Furusato no
ono no kodachi ni
fue no ne no
urumu tsukiyo ya.

In her village
in a stand of trees by a field
a flute's sound
blurs in the moonlit night.

For that matter, the rendition by Ueda Bin (1874–1916) of Paul Verlaine's *"Chanson d'automne,"* likely the most memorized French poem in Japanese translation, is done in a series of 5-syllable lines.

Yet, at the end of a prolonged period of verse experimentation—from the latter half of the Meiji Era (1868–1912) and well into the Taishō Era (1912–1926), when Western notions of poetry and poetics swamped the land in one wave after another—Hinatsu Kōnosuke (1890–1970), a scholar of English literature and a poet, concluded that neither the 5- nor the 7-syllable unit had "a general suitability in engendering poetic effect in Japanese." Indeed, among non-*tanka* and non-*haiku* poets, the usual practice was to compose poems with lines variously combining the two classical syllabic units. For example, the lines in the poem *"Isago wa yakenu"* (The sand is burnt), by Kambara Ariake (1876–1952), employed 7-5-7, 7-5-5, 5-5-7, or 5-7-5 syllables. In another famous translation of his, Ueda Bin gave 7-5-7-5, or a total of twenty-four, syllables to each line of Baudelaire's sonnet *"L'albatros."* Also, before free verse originating in France reached Japan and prevailed, poets worked out new syllabic patterns, such as 6, 8, and 9, and combinations thereof.

So, first, it may legitimately be asked: if the 5- and 7-syllable units in *tanka* and *haiku* are to be automatically regarded as "lines" because each forms a pattern, what to do with those "lines" Ariake composed? What to do with newly created syllabic patterns?

Second, free verse also affected the realms of *tanka* and *haiku,* prompting a substantial number of poets to stop using syllabic units and counts. I'll give one example from each genre.

Toki Aika (1885–1980)—who critically influenced the famous *tanka* trilineator Ishikawa Takuboku (1885–1912) and continued to experiment with *tanka* throughout his long life—has left some impressions of New York, which he visited in 1927. Here's one of them:

Sotto yorisotte waki no shita ni mugon no pisutoru o sashimukesō
na otoko no aida o tōru

I pass between men who have the air of quietly sidling up to you
and turning silent pistols up against your armpits

The original, written as one line, consists of forty-one syllables—ten more than the standard form—and cannot really be scanned.

As an example of the *haiku* genre, I cite Ozaki Hōsai (1885–1926):

Taikū no mashita bōshi kaburazu

Right under the big sky, I don't wear a hat

Also written as one line, the original consists of fifteen syllables, or two less than the standard seventeen, and, again, it is tough to scan, though the second half does form a 7-syllable unit. (I used this *haiku* as the title of a collection of my translations of Hōsai's work; as a reviewer noted, it is a rare book that has a complete poem for its title.)

Third, most *tanka* and *haiku* poets, along with their commentators, regard the *tanka* and *haiku* as one-line forms. But, as you may discern from my use of the word "most," there are lineators in both genres. This fact has enabled the erudite popular writer Inoue Hisashi—not a poet as far as I know—to comment on Takuboku in this fashion:

> Had Takuboku followed the approach that no one had doubted till then and written tanka in one vertical line, or in two lines at most [the latter for reasons of space], he might have been able to make something like
>
> *Kishikishi to samusa ni fumeba ita kishimu kaeri rōka*
> *no fui no kuchizuke* [31 syllables]
>
> Creakingly stepping in the cold the boards creak as I go
> back in the hall a sudden kiss
>
> but he would not have been able to make
>
> *Aru hi, futo, yamai o wasure,* [12 syllables]
> *ushi no naku mane o shiteminu—* [12 syllables]
> *tsumako no rusu ni.* [7 syllables]
>
> One day, suddenly, I forgot my disease,
> and mimicked a cow mooing just to see—
> in wife and child's absence.

Inoue's point is that a deliberate use of space, here manifested as lineation, makes a big difference. Put another way: when poets string words together without spacing, they are aiming to create a certain effect—shall we call it agglutinative?—which they evidently feel they lose when they break the poem up into lines. And this is the sentiment of the majority. (As

I show in my new introduction to the revised and expanded *Howling at the Moon* [Green Integer, forthcoming], Hagiwara Sakutarō, who took the *tanka* form very seriously, also tried to break up the 31-syllable form into lines, but in the end decided that doing so was unnatural.) Something similar can be said about the *haiku* form.

Fourth, a few centuries back, a group of poets led by Kagami Shikō (1665–1731) tried to create a new poetic genre called *kana-shi.* The general idea was that the units of 10 (5+5) and 14 (7+7) syllables would each form a "line," with the former corresponding to a 5-character line and the latter to a 7-character line in *kanshi* (verse composed in classical Chinese). This is significant because *kana-shi* rhymed in the manner of *kanshi* and, therefore, the concept of "line" was stronger.

Finally, to state the obvious, syllabic value differs from language to language. Japanese is a polysyllabic, vowel-laden tongue; English isn't. English can express, on average, twenty to twenty-five percent more than Japanese can with the same number of syllables. You can guess what happens when the 5- and 7-syllable formations are applied in translating traditional *tanka* and *haiku:* the result usually says more than the original does.

Well, does all this matter? After all, Japanese and English are so different. Because the languages are different, shouldn't the assumption be that forms can't be transferred? Japanese poets may regard *tanka* and *haiku* as one-line poems, but it's highly doubtful that they have any notion of the "line" in the Western sense and, anyhow, one-line poems are non-poems in English—even though, yes, come to think of it, there's something called the monostich in the English poetic tradition. But of the monostich, the *New Princeton Encyclopedia of Poetry and Poetics* says, "It is an interesting question whether a one-line poem is possible," doesn't it?

So are Japanese views and practices, linguistic realities and such, of any import?

Not really. In large measure, the answer depends on what you are after. Some American poets have found my one-line approach intriguing because they'd never thought that the *tanka* and *haiku* are conceived as one-line poems, but these writers are a minority. In this, as in many other things, American views and practices are the mirror images of Japanese.

As I said at the outset, in poetry translation no one is *wrong*—or *right,* I would add here. To show this, and to conclude, here are some translations of one poem from *tanka* and *haiku* each.

Murasaki Shikibu, author of *The Tale of Genji,* is represented in the canonical *Hyakunin isshu* (One hundred poems by one hundred poets) by the following *tanka:*

> *Meguriaite mishi ya sore tomo wakanu ma ni kumo gakurenishi*
> *yowa no tsuki kana*

The poem comes with a headnote: "Someone who was my childhood friend very early—I came across her years later, briefly, around the tenth of Seventh Month, but because she hurried away as if racing with the moon [I made the following poem]." (The original doesn't specify the gender of the friend.) In my translation the *tanka* reads:

> We met again but before I could tell I saw you, you hid in the
> clouds, midnight moon!

Steven D. Carter—who explains that in his translations he exploits such "natural resources" of English as "punctuation, capitalization, spacing, and a 'jogging' of lines"—has rendered the tanka this way:

> Quite by chance we met,
> and then before I was sure
> who it really was,
> the moonlight had disappeared,
> hidden behind midnight clouds.

You will see that Carter has allocated exactly 5-7-5-7-7 syllables, although, as far as syllabic fidelity goes, he for some reason has ignored the fact that the opening phrase of the original is hypersyllabic, consisting of 6, rather than 5, syllables.

In contrast, consider this translation by F. V. Dickins:

> I ventured forth one moonlight night,
> And then saw someone hastening past,
> Ere I could tell who 'twas aright,
> With dark clouds was the moon o'ercast,
> Whose pallid ray
> O'er th' middle night held tranquil sway.

Dickins, a physician attached to the Royal Navy, did, as far as I know, the first complete translation of an anthology of Japanese verse—the *Hyakunin isshu.* He worked on the translation in the 1860s, and it shows every sign of someone groping to find meaning in the opaque and obscure original, as he honestly admitted. Also to his credit, in his preface he didn't say the *tanka* was a 5-line verse form, though that's probably because his Japanese informants didn't.

One hundred sixteen years later, another Englishman, Richard Bowring, gave this poem a try. With the headnote, his translation reads:

> I met someone I had known long ago as a child, but the moment was brief and I hardly recognized them. It was the tenth of the tenth month. They left hurriedly as if racing the moon.

Brief encounter:
Did we meet or did it hide
Behind the clouds
Before I recognized
The face of the midnight moon?

In the headnote, Bowring, perhaps in an attempt to avoid gender identification, uses "them" when its antecedent is "someone"; the same attempt is discernible in the poem as well. This may be a reflection of the time: by the mid-1970s, the use of "he" when the sex wasn't known or didn't matter was fast becoming a no-no.

What about translations of the other genre, the *haiku?*

In 1689, Matsuo Bashō carried out his famed journey to the interior of Japan and, in his celebrated account of it, included about fifty *hokku (haiku)*. One of them, along with its preceding prose passage, may be translated:

> The glory of the three generations lasted only as long as a single nap. The place where the main gate stood was one *li* this side. Hidehira's site had turned into paddies, with only Kinkeizan retaining its shape. First, we went up to the Takadachi and saw the Kitagami was a large river flowing from Nambu. The Koromo River flows around Izumi Castle and below the Takadachi pours into the large river. The old site for Yasuhira and others was on the other side of Koromo Barrier, with the Nambu side fortified for defense, it seemed, against the Ezo. The most loyal among his loyal vassals were selected and put up in this castle, but their fame lasted only for a moment and turned into clumps of grass. "The country destroyed, the mountains and rivers remain. In the castle it is now spring and the grass has turned green." Sitting on our hats laid on the ground, we shed tears for a while:
>
> *Natsukusa ya tsuwamono-domo ga yume no ato*
>
> Summer grass: where the warriors used to dream

Here, I will cite only translations by those who prepared the complete translation of Bashō's account, *Oku no hosomichi:*

The summer grasses:
The high bravery of men-at-arms,
The vestiges of dream.

—*Earl Miner, 1969*

A mound of summer grass:
  Are warriors' heroic deeds
    Only dreams that pass?

—Dorothy Britton, 1974

        A dream of warriors,
and after dreaming is done,
        the summer grasses.

—Helen Craig McCullough, 1990

Summer grasses:
all that remains of great soldiers'
imperial dreams

—Sam Hamill, 1991

Of these four translators, Britton and McCullough use 5-7-5 syllables; Miner and Hamill don't, though Miner goes beyond the allotted seventeen syllables and Hamill arrives at exactly seventeen—accidentally perhaps. The effect of an inevitable amplification, which was only vaguely discernible in Carter's translation of Lady Murasaki's *tanka,* is here loud and clear: the padding creates fancy results, such as "high bravery" (Miner), "heroic deeds" (Britton), "dream . . . dreaming" (McCullough), and "great . . . imperial" (Hamill).

But are they wrong? I don't think so.

▪ Andrew Schelling

Manuscript Fragments and Eco-Guardians: Translating Sanskrit Poetry

Nature Literacy

A quality I find more and more compelling in Sanskrit poetry and its related vernaculars is the deep, ancient regard shown for the natural world. There is in our current historic period an intense debate over the status of wilderness regions and nonhuman species. It's put poets on the alert for insights into nature or wilderness that distant artistic traditions might offer, and the best Sanskrit poems seem to hold something instructive. Rooted in Paleolithic habits, they balance a fine-tuned eco-literacy with a cosmopolitan delight in language, social patterns, and erotics. Studied with a close, unsentimental eye, wild creatures were daily familiars to the classical Sanskrit poets, not far removed from the human realm, as in this poem by Apanagara:

Stag and doe
hard short lives
ranging the forest for
water and grass
they don't
betray each other they're
loyal
till death

For American poets working to become nature-literate on home territory, it is profoundly interesting to see the ease with which figures of the natural world can become citizens of standing in a poem. The Sanskrit vocabulary for flowers and trees is particularly abundant and botanically accurate. Happening on this tradition at the remove of a thousand years, you might slip past it, but the nonhuman elements of the landscape were carefully regulated inside the Sanskrit lyric. Poets worked specific flowers or blooming trees, particular birds, animals, or phases of weather into compressed cultural ciphers. The mere hint of fragrance off a nearby forested hill told not only in what calendrical moment of what season the poem was located, but also evoked a constellation of human relationships, a precise mood, and vivid moments echoed in other poems.

There's good evidence this use of landscapes came into classical Sanskrit from the somewhat earlier Tamil tradition of the south. Classical Tamil poets (circa 100 B.C.E.–250 C.E.), writing in a Dravidian tongue, devised for their intricately erotic short poems an alphabet of natural elements, which they calibrated to distinct landscapes—what we now call bioregions. By invoking the name of a plant or animal native to a certain habitat, they would summon an image at once natural, cultural, and resonant with a particular emotion. The Tamil poets identified five wilderness regions, which we would call montane, riparian meadow, forest, littoral shoreline, and arid desert. Each landscape set the scene for a particular erotic mood. Plant companions are so abundantly featured in Tamil poetry that A. K. Ramanujan's good book of translations, *Poems of Love and War,* includes a botanical index. It reads like Thoreau's "List of Plants" at the end of *The Maine Woods.*

In a looser vein, the Sanskrit poets, from the founding of the Gupta Empire in 320 C.E., used this type of alphabet for their own lyrics, introducing the kind of attention to seasonal changes in various bioregions that has been the stuff of natural history, and superimposing on the natural orders a sophisticated psychology of human life. Regional plants, weather patterns, bird migration or animal habits, and seasonal cycles were all used emblematically—yet the poems lend sound testimony to Ezra Pound's counsel that "the natural object is always the adequate symbol."

Aside from a hundred rather fierce lyrics by Bhartrihari (circa seventh century)—who was very likely both an accomplished linguist and a bark-clad yogin at different times in his life—little Sanskrit poetry was written by hermits. The poets formed a professional guild—some doing double-time as philosophers or scholars—and rarely chose to live outside human settlements or to develop yogic powers among the wild, nonhuman orders. The fact that poems minutely familiar with nature were not written by recluses gives Sanskrit short poems a different flavor from the Chinese: the settings or landscapes seem closer to home; there are few brooding mountain escarpments, few unvisited gorges along thundering rivers.

In Sanskrit lyric, the human and nonhuman orders seem linked in unsensational daily intimacy. Local villages with birds in flowering trees. The whiff of odors from a nearby forest grove. Farmland crops or native grasses in fertile alluvial soil. Sweet-smelling blossoms along a village path. To put it another way: what flowering creeper shares the details of your life because you walk past it every day to fetch water? What pliant reed did you collect one spring night to weave a mat for your lover?

Transcendentalist Tracks

The tricky, many-forked paths a poet takes into other centuries and other literatures are hard to trace. Sanskrit poetry—indeed, the thorny old language itself—seems a curious place to end up, and it's hard to be sure how I got there. There's a good poem by Dharmakirti—it has a postmodern flavor—that might serve as an entry point. Dharmakirti was a Buddhist scholar from South India who, late in the seventh century, wrote seven razor-witted treatises on Buddhist logic, a number of sutra commentaries, and lyric poems, a handful of which survive. Here is one:

> No one visible up ahead,
> no one approaches
> from behind.
> Not a footprint on the road.
> Am I alone?
> This much is clear—
> the path the ancient
> poets opened
> is choked with brush,
> and I've long since left
> the public thoroughfare.

I grew up in Transcendentalist country: the prerevolutionary townships that spread west of Boston. This meant that as a child I became familiar in a native way with the forests and meadows Henry David Thoreau surveyed. I dodged watchful rangers to swim the ponds he washed in or wrote about, and I lived on close terms with the little holy places of Emerson, Margaret Fuller, and the Alcott girls and their eccentric, philosophic father.

An airy mixture of Asiatic books and thoughtful Romantic philosophies (which read like poetry) hung over the region. Thanks to early curators Ernest Fenollosa and Ananda Coomaraswamy, local museums offered world-class collections of Indian sculpture and Chinese paintings of mist-wrapped landscapes. These exposed viewers to archetypes of consciousness in Indian sandstone and forested crags in Chinese ink that suggested the way one's own mind was fashioned.

Something similar had happened to Thoreau, though in a rougher way. In *Walden* he tells of waking at dawn and walking to the pond's edge to get water. When he gets there, he notices a Hindu arriving the same moment at the Ganges and filling his own little water pot. This leap—what could it mean? That the Bhagavad Gita, the Upanishads, some Buddhist sutras, the Hindu Puranas were, by the middle of last century, cross-fertilizing among New England hemlock, maple, and oak? Perhaps even the geographic error reflected in our use of the word "Indian" for this continent's native peoples expresses some unarticulated karmic link between North American landscapes and South Asian texts? Emerson and old man Alcott thought so.

It was the holy books of Sanskrit that I encountered first. Full of thunder and wind, craggy metaphysics, humorous folklore, tingling insight, they felt like poems. No matter that the available translations were largely in an unlively prose. When I finally settled down to get what I could of Sanskrit into my head, it was because the familiar translations, many from last century, no longer felt close enough. What did those British and German philologists leave out? Looking into their translations, I caught something tawny, a muscular flex just back of the language: like turning your head in the forest—an instant too late to identify the creature that's gone into the trees. At the time, I did not know there was also a classical tradition of poetry—secular, tenderly amorous, refined, instructively nature-literate—lying in wait. As I am an American, this would have been hard for me to know.

There have been few good translations of Sanskrit lyric poetry. Mostly there's been indifference, even contempt, shown towards Sanskrit verse. Because there are no good translations? Or is it the other way around? Introducing his collection of translations, *The Jade Mountain: The 300 Poems of the T'ang Dynasty,* Witter Bynner states, "I doubt I could ever feel any affection for the ornate, entranced poetry of India." This is seventeen years after the first Imagist manifestos: two decades of Pound, H. D., Williams, Marianne Moore, and a handful of other writers working out that lean American hunger for poems shorn of adornment.

The English translations Bynner would have seen by 1929 could only have confirmed his estimate. Most of them are worthless. British and American scholars put Sanskrit poems—surprisingly compressed, fleet-footed, and alert in the original language—into Tennysonian iambics. Furthermore, for complex reasons the translators seemed to require three or four times as many English words as Sanskrit. Given the distance between the two languages—one heavily declined, the other quite analytic—I realize it would be nearly impossible to define what constitutes a "word." But a survey of bilingual books on my shelf suggests that translations of Chinese poetry—because Chinese has no verb tenses or pronouns and not much in the way of prepositions, all of which translators into English supply—often use about one and a half to two English words for each Chinese ideogram.

A longwinded translation of a sprightly poem—Chinese, Indian, or any other—misses the one thing that counts: the poetry. John Dryden said it for all of us: "I cannot, without some indignation, look on an ill copy of an excellent original . . . a good poet is no more like himself in a dull translation, than his carcass would be to a living body." When in my studies I encountered *kavya* (Sanskrit's short lyric poetry), I was unprepared to like it and so was surprised to see how much vigor it had. Only two modern scholars have recognized this vigor, gone to the poetry on its own turf, and done good work: Daniel H. H. Ingalls, who has devoted himself to it and written the best overview of Sanskrit poetry; and Barbara Stoller Miller, who throughout her life produced clean, modern translations based on good scholarship. Without their efforts, the trail might still be lost.

It is instructive to consider the effect China and Japan have had on American poetry. By contrast, India seems nearly invisible. There are two, possibly three Sanskrit words in Pound's *Cantos. The Wasteland* has three, all drawn from a single episode in the Upanishads (Eliot studied Sanskrit as an undergraduate at Harvard). Only with Kenneth Rexroth's post-WWII poetry does Indian mythopoetics enter our tradition in a compelling way.

Few Sanskrit scholars appear to like the poetry. The standard reference books—British scholars compiled them during colonial times—treat it with dismay or a sneer. D. D. Kosambi, a Marxist and coeditor of the important twelfth-century anthology *Subhashita-ratna-kosha,* dismisses it for other reasons. Following Plekhanov's theory of literary production, he is convinced that good poetry can only be written by newly emergent classes that are advancing the means of production. The Sanskrit poets were courtiers or courtesans, scholars or schoolteachers—not revolutionaries. Their poetry, says Kosambi, "necessarily carries with the rank beauty of an orchid the corresponding atmosphere of luxury, parasitism, decay."

If the professionals don't like it, readers will be indifferent. Predictably, the books get harder to find. Only a half-dozen libraries in our country have a workable collection. Where I live, along the front range of Colorado's Rocky Mountains, we're a thousand miles—the width of India—from the nearest Sanskrit collection of note. A few dealers in Calcutta and

Delhi have helped turn up useful books, but many volumes are hopelessly scarce: they went out of print in Bombay or Poona a hundred years ago.

Ragged Manuscripts

Classical Sanskrit poetry was written over the course of about eight hundred years, beginning around 320 C.E. During those centuries, Indian civilization reached its height: the culture was abundant and cosmopolitan, drawing Chinese pilgrims, Arab merchants, and Greek philosophers; and most of India's exquisite sculpture, architecture, and mural painting, the manuals of science, erotics, theater, linguistics, and philosophy were also produced. All these arts came to a violent end during the eleventh and twelfth centuries, when Muslim warriors on horseback rode over the Khyber Pass and down into the Gangetic Plains, taking control of the cities and highways. They drove out the Buddhists, who had compiled good libraries in their *viharas* (universities). Some manuscripts managed to survive in India, hidden away. But the *viharas* were sacked or burned, and the libraries vanished.

Buddhist monks lucky enough to escape fled to Tibet, carrying what manuscripts they could: sutra literature and Buddhist exegeses, but also volumes of secular writing. One of the notable examples is the *Subhashita-ratna-kosha,* compiled between 1100 and 1130 by a likable scholar, Vidyakara, who served as abbot of Jagaddala *vihara* in Bengal. A Buddhist monk with a keen ear for poetry, he saw no contradiction between his religious training and the teeming, playful, erotic poems he collected. His anthology—translated by Daniel Ingalls as *An Anthology of Sanskrit Court Poetry* —is open-minded and tolerant. Its 1,738 poems contain hundreds of erotic epigrams, cameos of tender moments, and portraits of lovers, children, poor people, rich people, animals, and the seasons. There's wit, despair, humor, irony, bitterness, affection; and many of the poems are love poems as good as those written in any language.

Vidyakara's anthology was entirely lost until this century, when two explorers a few years apart happened upon a readable twelfth-century palm-leaf manuscript, probably Vidyakara's personal copy, at the Ngor monastery in Tibet, about a day's journey by foot from Shigatse. In 1934 Rahula Sankrityayana—an Indian *pandit* who was a good scholar and good Sanskritist and was probably up in Tibet as a British spy—found the manuscript in a barn attached to the monastery. Some years later Giuseppe Tucci, an Italian collector and scholar of Buddhism, also came across it. Each managed to produce, under challenging conditions, photographic plates of very poor quality ("execrable," says one account) and to transport them out of Tibet.

Working from these plates, which they compared against photos, manuscript fragments, and newer anthologies housed in libraries in Nepal and India, Kosambi and fellow Indian scholar V. V. Gokhale managed to edit a clean edition for Harvard University Press's Oriental Series. Here, from Kosambi's 1957 introduction to the volume, is a representative estimate of the estate of the old poems:

> A chance still remains of getting better materials from Tibet, including the original manuscript or good new photographs. . . . This was in fact promised me at Peking in 1952 by the authorities of the People's Republic of China. . . . [However,] Tibet being completely autonomous in such purely internal matters, the new evidence will not be forthcoming as long as the manuscripts remain sacred possessions of the monasteries, to be worshipped unread, or sold in fragments for pilgrims to use as charms. There is no doubt that the Tibetans themselves will soon develop a modern scientific attitude towards their priceless treasures, which are India's treasures too. This implies the development of systematic archaeology, which will open up images and stupas in which many manuscripts may have been immured.

Two things about this little account strike me. One, though many went unread, the old Sanskrit manuscripts were considered sacred. That they were regarded as sacred was both why they were preserved and why outsiders rarely got wind of them. The other notable thing is that decades before global tourism entered the Himalayas—trekkers in Gore-Tex, college students with granola bars, high-tech trophy mountaineers, international dealers in cheaply bought antiquities, and all sorts of other travelers willing to trade hard cash for old goods in the little mountain villages—manuscripts were already being broken apart by monks and sold to visitors or, more interestingly, being ritually inserted into religious icons. Might entire pages of high-quality Sanskrit poetry, tied into bricklike amulets, be lying unread inside gilded icons or little prayer boxes? Of course, two years after Professor Kosambi wrote his introduction, Chinese soldiers moved artillery into Lhasa, the Dalai Lama fled, and the People's Army set out on a savage wrecking spree that may not be over yet. Many religious images were destroyed or melted down for bullion; others were hustled away at great personal risk by Tibetans and secured in remote caves.

Lady Shilabhattarika's Poem

Six short poems, distributed through several anthologies, bear the name of Shilabhattarika, who most likely lived in the ninth century. Whatever else she wrote has been lost. Her best-known poem is of a quick, almost unendurable beauty. If one believes Shila to have written it from direct personal experience, she would have lived as a young woman in one of the villages or towns along the Narmada River, on one side of the Vindhya Mountains in West India. Her poem occurs in at least two versions; here is the one from a fourteenth-century anthology, the *Paddhati* of Sharngadhara:

Nights of jasmine and thunder,
torn petals,
wind in the tangled *kadamba* trees—
nothing has changed.
Spring comes again and we've
simply grown older.
In the cane groves of Narmada River
he deflowered my
girlhood before we were
married.
And I grieve for those faraway nights
we played at love
by the water.

According to ancient and modern critics, this version has a flaw. Poetic convention does not permit the *malati,* a jasmine, to bloom in Caitra, the lunar month of March to April, or spring. If Shilabhattarika got the botany wrong, the critics' assertion would be a sound eco-critique of her best poem.

Did Shilabhattarika herself make this mistake? Or could her poem, going into the *Paddhati* five hundred years after she wrote it, have been rewritten by someone unknowledgeable about poetic convention or botanical detail? Shila certainly recalls the *malati* blooming—blooming that season she made love all night on the riverbank as a girl. But having aged, has she confused the season with another? Mislocated the event?

Sanskrit's enormous vocabulary is full of words with complex overtones or several related but distinct meanings woven into each other. Because the meanings are sometimes linked by something as subtle as a fragrance, no word-by-word translation can hope to catch the *rasa,* the mood or flavor, of a good verse. I find several early lexicographers give *malati* the additional meaning of "virgin." The scent of jasmine, the newly opened flower releasing its fragrance. Without denying the botanical fact, the image could stand for the poet herself on those faraway nights of Caitra.

The other version is from Vidyakara's anthology:

The one who deflowered me
is still my lover
the moondrenched nights haven't changed.
Scent from the newly
bloomed *malati*
blows in from the Vindhya hills
and the girl is still me.
But her heart?
It grieves for those nights
we stole off and made love forever
in the riverside cane.

Having gone deep into the jasmine-scented darkness, deep into the dictionary, deep into the poet's rhythm (set in a meter provocatively known as Tiger's Play), both poems grip me. Which would you give up: the moon-drenched nights *(candra-garba-nisha)* or the breeze-torn *kadamba* blossoms *(kadamba-anilah)?* If you could have only one, which would it be: the Vindhya Mountains or the Narmada River?

The Sanskrit short poem is a compressed moment of bedrock human emotion set into an accurately drawn landscape. Shila's temperament and training would have required a strict economy of language to reach that conjunction. Perhaps to write both mountains and river into a single poem was not in the Sanskritic grain. But the wild fragrant nights, wind off the hills, flowering branches, and moonlight; the abandon with which a girl takes her first lover; the bittersweet recollections of a middle-aged woman looking back on it all: it seems hardly extravagant to make two separate poems. What does it matter the critics consider one a bit ragged?

Nature Sentinels

From *Kavikanthabharanam,* a twelfth-century treatise on poetic training by Kshemendra, comes this good counsel:

> With his own
> eyes a poet
> observes the shape of a leaf.
> He knows how to make
> people laugh
> and studies the nature of each living thing.
> The features of ocean and mountain,
> the motion of sun, moon and stars.
> His thoughts turn with the seasons.
> He goes among
> different peoples
> learning their landscapes,
> learning their languages.

There's no explicit scholarship to cite, but it is my belief that the way the Sanskrit poets continually and accurately named their trees, creepers, rivers, mountain ranges, and weather patterns reveals an archaic, magical habit of language. Recurring in endless variants, phrases like "newly opened jasmine," "black clouds mount the horizon," and "wind from the Vindhya Mountains" did not originate as descriptions of nature, but were spells set loose to summon the spirits controlling these events. The poetic handbooks, which were carefully consulted—their exacting rules cover not only grammar and metrics but also natural history—have similar roots in shamanic habit. They keep watch over the local calendar: animal migration and fertility, plant growth, weather cycles, river floodings.

The composers of the Vedic hymns (circa 1700 B.C.E.) had left India with a legacy of ritual verse that summoned the forces of a dramatic wilderness: thunder, wind, boiling clouds, sky-rending bolts of lightning, forest spirits, even frogs. We know those early poet-priests were specialists who compelled local spirits by ritual use of plants, animal products, and fire—maybe even human bones. After a lapse of two thousand years, the poets of classical Sanskrit took up the old energies and redirected them, bringing the poem to focus on human affairs. The archaic grain was not lost; the innovation was simply to lay patterns of human life across the old mythic orders.

From this perspective, most collections of classical Sanskrit poetry are ritual accounts of the Indian year. The short poems come down to us in anthologies ranging from collections of a hundred lyrics to over four thousand. A quick glance shows the anthologists ordered their books by seasonal and diurnal cycles, and patterned both alongside or on top of the rounds of human life: erotic, social, and biological. You can therefore read the anthologies as almanacs. The habits of animals, the tree groves, the seasonally flooding rivers, clouds gathering over the mountains, the fragrant blossoms—as in so much old poetry, these are the good companions, spirit guides on the human journey.

And the task of the poem? One of the oldest. To bring humans into right relation with denizens of the plant, animal, and geological kingdoms. Some of these spirits went into the Sanskrit poem, others into sculpture, architecture, painting, folklore, and the varied range of Hindu and Buddhist texts. A popular term applied to them was *lokapala,* protective figures that guard the eight directions or the neighborhood holy places: a temple door, a clear little runnet dropping out of the forest, a hillside grotto, the meadow at a bend in the river. Local and cosmological, they are "world guardians," sentinels of place.

What the Sanskrit poets accomplished was to secularize these sentinels and then to regard them with the naturalist's careful eye. It gives their writings a precise sense of ecology that seems nearly contemporary. Perhaps Kshemendra, Shilabhattarika, and their comrades—their writings scattered through fragmentary old manuscripts—can offer a few useful models as North Americans develop a poetry both cosmopolitan and minutely adapted to our own terrain. A poetry of romance, stout friendship, the sharp unforgettable image, the easy native wit. But also bristling with residents of our own ecosystems: cacti and piñon trees, granite outcroppings, songbirds, the hardy native flowers of our upland meadows.

Won't the poets of old India clap their hands when they hear of it.

Translating a Poem by Li Shang-yin

The translation of Chinese poems into English has always been a source of inspiration for my own evolution as a poet. In 1971, as a student at the University of California at Berkeley, I majored in poetry. Also studying Chinese language and literature, I became interested in translating the great T'ang dynasty poets—Li Po, Tu Fu, and Wang Wei, among others—because I felt I could learn from them. I felt that by struggling with many of the great poems in the Chinese literary tradition, I could best develop my voice as a poet. Years later, in 1983, after publishing my third book of poetry, *Dazzled,* I translated a new group of Chinese poems, again feeling that it would help me discover greater possibilities for my own writing. I was drawn to the clarity of T'ao Ch'ien's lines, to the subtlety of Ma Chih-yuan's lyrics, and to Wen I-to's sustained, emotional power. In 1996, after completing my book *Archipelago,* I felt the need to translate yet another group of Chinese poems: I was particularly drawn to the Ch'an-influenced poems of Pa-ta Shan-jen and to the extremely condensed and challenging, transformational poems of Li Ho and Li Shang-yin.

I know translation is an "impossible" task, and I have never forgotten the Italian phrase *traduttori/traditori:* "translators/traitors." What translation does not in some way betray its original? In considering the process of my own translations, I am aware of loss and transformation, of destruction and renewal. Since I first started to write poetry, I have only translated poems that have deeply engaged me; and it has sometimes taken me many years to feel ready to work on a particular poem. In many instances, I have lived with a poem in Chinese for a long time before ever sitting down to translate it. I remember that in 1972 I read Li Shang-yin's untitled poems and felt baffled by them; now, more than twenty-five years later, they strike me as veiled, mysterious, and full of longing: some of the great love poems in classical Chinese.

To show how I create a translation in English, I am going to share stages and drafts of a translation from one of Li Shang-yin's untitled poems. I like to begin by writing out the characters of the Chinese poem on paper. I know that my own writing of Chinese characters is awkward and rudimentary, but in writing them out in their particular stroke order, I can begin to sense the inner motion of the poem in a way that I cannot by just reading the characters on the page. Once I've written out the characters, I look up each in Robert H. Mathews's *Chinese-English Dictionary* and write down the sound and tone along with a word, phrase, or cluster of words that help mark its field of energy and meaning. Doing this groundwork, I go through the entire poem. After I have created this initial cluster of words, I go back through the poem and, because a Chinese character can mean so many different things depending on its context, I remove from the list I've made the

鳳	尾	香	羅	薄	幾	重
male phoenix	*tail/s*	*fragrant*	*gauze, thin silk*	*thin, slight*	*how many*	*layers, folds*
feng^4	wei^3	hsiang^1	lo^2	po^2	chi^3	ch'ung^2
碧	文	圓	頂	夜	深	逢
green jade	*elegant, refined*	*round*	*the top*	*night*	*deep*	*meet with*
pi^4	wen^2	yüan^2	ting^3	yeh^4	shen^1	feng^2
扇	裁	月	魄	羞	難	掩
fan	*to cut*	*moon*	*form, shape*	*shame, blush*	*difficult*	*conceal*
shan^4	ts'ai^2	yüeh^4	p'o^4	hsiu^1	nan^2	yen^3
車	走	雷	聲	語	未	通
carriage	*departs*	*thunder*	*sound/s*	*word/s*	*not yet*	*get through*
ch'e^1	tsou^3	lei^2	sheng^1	yü^3	wei^4	t'ung^1
曾	是	寂	寥	金	燼	暗
once, already	*is*	*silent*	*empty*	*gold*	*ashes, embers*	*dark, cloudy*
ts'eng^2	shih^4	chi^4	liao^2	chin^1	chin^4	an^4
斷	無	消	息	石	榴	紅
cut off	*no, without*	*— ebb and flow —*		*liquid measure*	*pomegranate*	*red*
tuan^4	wu^2	hsiao^1	hsi^1	tan^4	liu^2	hung^2
班	騅	只	繫	垂	楊	柳
mottled	*piebald horse*	*only, but*	*tie, bind*	*hang down*	*— willow —*	
pan^1	chui^1	chih^3	hsi^4	ch'ui^2	yang^2	liu^3
何	處	西	南	任	好	風
what, which	*place*	*— southwest —*		*allow, confide in*	*good*	*wind*
ho^2	ch'u^4	hsi^1	nan^2	jen^4	hao^3	feng^1

words or phrases that appear to be inappropriate and keep those that appear to be relevant. In the case of Li Shang-yin's untitled poem, I would then have a draft that looks like the illustration on the previous page.

In looking at this regulated eight-line poem, I know that each of its seven-character lines has two predetermined caesuras, so that the motion in Chinese is 1-2/3-4/5-6-7. I therefore try to catch the tonal flow and sense the silences. I know that the tones from the Mathews's dictionary only give me the barest approximation. T'ang-dynasty poems are most alive when they are chanted. The sounds are very different from the Mandarin dialect that I speak. Yet I can, for instance, guess that the sound of *tuan*^{4}, the first character in line six, is sharp and emphatic. I also feel that characters three and four in line six—*hsiao*^{1} and *hsi*^{2}—have an onomatopoetic quality to suggest ebb and flow. In looking at the visual configuration of the characters, I am again struck by the first character in line six, *tuan*^{4}. Here the character contains the image of scissors cutting silk, and I wonder if this can be extended to develop an insight into the poem—if I can make any use of that possibility in my translation.

I proceed by writing a rough draft in English: trying to write eight lines in English that are equivalent to the eight lines in Chinese. I realize immediately that the translation is too cramped. I look back at the Chinese and decide to use *two* lines in English for each line of Chinese. I also decide that it might be a good idea to emphasize the second caesura of each line in Chinese so that in English there's a line break after the meaning of the fourth character in each line of the Chinese original.

I write out another draft in which sixteen lines in English now stand for the eight lines in Chinese. All of the lines in English are flush left, but the blocklike form does not do justice to the obliquely cutting motion of the poem. To open it up and clarify the architecture, I decide to indent all of the even-numbered lines. I go through another series of drafts, which oftentimes incorporate English words that I've listed on the page with Chinese characters, though I don't feel compelled to use all of them. At this transitional stage, I have something that looks like the version below (without any of the crossed-out or underlined words):

phoenix tails, fragrant silk,
↓ *folds*
how many thin ~~layers~~.

under the ~~elegant~~ green round canopy
opens to ↓
she ~~encounters~~ the deep night.

the fan cuts the moon's shape
↓ *but* ↓ *blush*
~~and~~ can't conceal her ~~shame~~.

a carriage goes, thunder sounds,

↓ *didn't*

the words ~~can't~~ get through.

a while in the desolate quiet

x

gold embers in the dark.

nothing now but ↓ *the ebb and flow of*

↳ ~~cut off, no word, who could~~ be pouring

~~a measure of~~ red pomegranate wine?

a piebald horse is yet tied

↓ *dangling*

to a ~~trailing~~ willow.

↓ *from*

x and where is the place ~~in~~ the southwest

where the fine breeze can blow?

At this point, if there are books of Chinese translations that I think might be helpful to me, I look at them to see if they have any commentaries that are relevant. In *Chinese Poetic Writing,* I find that lines one and two "describe the bed curtain of a bridal chamber," that "to pluck a willow branch" means to visit a courtesan, that red pomegranate wine might be served at a wedding feast and that it connotes explosive desire, and that the southwest breeze alludes to a phrase in a poem by Ts'ao Chih (A.D. 192–232): "I would become that southwest wind/waft all the way to your bosom." I find these comments insightful but do not want to incorporate them overtly into my translation: because Li Shang-yin's great strength is his oblique exactitude, I want my translation to hint at these elements.

I now look at my very rough translation and go back to the original Chinese. My understanding of the poem is that a woman is lamenting the absence of her lover and longs for him even as she worries that he is unfaithful. I go back through my translation, cross out certain phrases, and substitute new phrases wherever they seem better. With the second line, I decide that it is more appropriate to have the silk in folds than in layers. In line three, the phrase "elegant green round canopy" is cumbersome; I decide the word "elegant" is too explicit and should be removed. It's so hard in a contemporary poem to use an adjective like "elegant" and not cause a boomerang effect. I read on and decide that "encounters" is too neutral. To make the longing more overt, I change it to "opens to the deep night." In line six, I change "and" to "but," and substitute "blush" for "shame." I'm happy with this last change: the "blush" will help foreshadow the "red pomegranate wine" and also suggests the red of desire. In line eight, I change "can't" to "didn't," though I'm not sure this is better. In line nine, I mark with an *x* and a double underline the word "desolate." This word is another loaded adjective, but nothing comes to mind as a good replacement, so I mark it with an *x* to tell myself to come back to it. I am totally dissatisfied with line eleven and strike it out. I go back to the page with characters and reincorporate "ebb and flow." With line fourteen, I am uneasy about "trailing" and insert "dangling." Line fifteen strikes me as too wordy, but again nothing comes to mind, so I mark it with an *x* and a double underline.

At this point, I put the translation away for a few weeks. I brood on it and, if some changes come to mind, jot them down on the side. But I usually wait until I feel I can revise with intensity and clarity. When I finally sit down and rework the translation, I decide that "the deep quiet" opens up the emotional space in a way that "the desolate quiet" can't. I decide to foreground the gold embers and make them a more active presence; the verb "scintillate" leaps into my mind. To suggest that red pomegranate wine connotes explosive desire, and to make the configuration of sounds more alive and poetic, I replace the static "a measure of red pomegranate wine" with the active "pulsing red pomegranate wine." I also decide to alter the symmetry of the indented lines by further indenting the very last line; I think this heightens the cutting effect of the ending. You can see these significant changes incorporated into the final version of this untitled poem by Li Shang-yin:

Phoenix tails, fragrant silk,

so many thin folds.

Under the round green canopy,

she opens herself to the night.

A fan cuts the moon's shape

but can't conceal her blush.

The carriage goes, thunder sounds;

the words couldn't get through.

A while in the deep quiet,

gold embers scintillate:

nothing now but the ebb and flow of

pulsing red pomegranate wine.

A piebald horse is yet tied

to a dangling willow.

And where out of the southwest

can the fine breeze blow?

Casting Shadows, Umbria, 1995
Photograph by Paul Kodama

Purgatorio: Canto XXXIII

"Oh God, the heathen have come," the ladies were
singing in alternation, now three now four,
beginning a sweet psalmody, and weeping,

and Beatrice, sighing and pitying,
listened to them, overcome by it so
that Mary at the Cross was scarcely more so.

But after the other virgins gave her
place to speak, she rose onto her feet
and was the color of fire as she answered,

"A little while and you will not see me,"
and again, "my belovéd sisters,
a little while and you will see me."

Then she put all seven in front of her,
and behind her, simply beckoning, she put
me, and the lady, and the sage who remained there.

So she went on, and I do not believe
that she had set a tenth step on the ground
before she struck upon my eyes with her own,

and with a tranquil look, "Come more quickly,"
she said to me, "so that if I speak to you
you will be well placed to listen to me."

Once I was with her, as I was meant to be,
she said to me, "Brother, why do you not
venture to question me, now while you come with me?"

As those who are too reverent, speaking
in the presence of persons greater than they are,
cannot bring the voice to their teeth still living,

so it happened to me, and with only part
of a sound I began, "My lady, you know
what my need is, and what is good for it."

And she said to me, "From here on I would have you
disengage yourself from fear and shame
so that you no longer speak like a man in a dream.

Know that the vessel which the serpent broke
was and is not; but let the one at fault believe
that God's vengeance cannot be frightened off.

Not for all time will the eagle be without
an heir, who left the feathers on the chariot
which became a monster and a prey.

For I see clearly and so tell of it: there are
stars near us already bringing us,
undeterred by obstacle or barrier,

a time when a five hundred, ten, and five
whom God will send, will slaughter the whore
and the giant who offends with her.

And it may be that my somber story,
like Themis and the Sphinx, is harder to
believe because it darkens the mind as they do,

but events, before long, will be the Naiads
that will solve this hard enigma without
flocks or harvests being paid for it.

Take note exactly as my words are said
by me; teach them to those who are living
a life that is a race they are running toward death.

And when you come to write it, bear in mind
not to keep back what you have seen of the tree
and how, twice over here, it has been ruined.

Whoever robs it, or whoever harms it
with an act of blasphemy, offends God
who for his own sole use made it sacred.

For a bite of it, in craving and torment
five thousand years and more the first soul longed
for Him who in Himself punished that taste.

Your intelligence is asleep if it does not
think there is a singular reason for its height
and for its reversal at the top,

and if thoughts turning in your mind had not
been the water of Elsa, and your delight
in them a Pyramus to the mulberry,

from such circumstances alone
the justice of God would have been known
morally, in the forbidding of the tree.

But since I see that your mind has been turned
to stone, and has acquired a stony hue
so that the light of my speech dazzles you

I would have you also carry it away
within you, painted even if not written,
as palm wreathes the pilgrim's staff, and for the same reason."

And I, "As wax under the seal, that does not
alter the figure that is stamped into it,
you are imprinted now upon my brain.

But why is it that, longed for as they are,
your words fly above my sight so far
that the harder it peers the more it loses them?"

"So you may know," she said, "that school which you
have followed, and see whether it can follow
with its doctrines the things that I say,

and may see that your way is as far away
from the divine as the earth is from that
heaven that turns at the greatest height."

Then I answered her, "I do not remember
ever having been estranged from you, nor
is it something I feel the bite of conscience for."

"And if you cannot remember it," she
said, smiling, "bear in mind that this
is the day on which you drank from Lethe.

And if from smoke you can argue a fire,
this forgetfulness proves clearly that your
will was doing wrong when it turned elsewhere.

Truly from now on my words will be
as simple as they will have to be
if they are to be clear to your rude vision."

Now, shining brighter and with slower pace
the sun held to the noon meridian
that moves back and forth depending on the angle of vision.

When, as one who goes ahead, escorting
others, comes to a stop at finding
something strange, or the remains of it,

the seven ladies stopped at the margin
of light shadow such as that which the mountains
cast on cold streams under green leaves and dark boughs.

I saw before them, it seemed to me,
the Euphrates and Tigris rising from
one fountain and, like friends, parting slowly.

"Oh light, oh glory of humankind, what is
this water that from one beginning flows
and takes away, out of itself, itself?"

When I asked her this she said to me, "Inquire
that of Matilda," and that beautiful lady
answered, as someone who wished to be

freed of blame, "I have told him that,
and other things, and I am sure that
the water of Lethe did not hide it from him."

And Beatrice, "It may be that some greater
  concern, which can make one not remember
  sometimes, has darkened the eyes of his mind.

But see Eunoe flowing away there;
  lead him to it and revive, as you are
  used to doing, this weakened power of his."

As a gentle soul, with no excuses,
  making of another's will her own
  once an outward sign had made it known,

so when she had laid her hand on me
  the beautiful lady moved on, and gracefully,
  in the way of ladies, said to Statius, "Come with him."

Reader, if I had more space to write
  I would sing something at least about that
  sweet drink that I could have drunk forever,

but since all the pages that were laid upon
  the loom for this second cantica have been
  filled, the curb of art lets me go no farther.

From the most sacred waters I returned
  remade in the way that trees are new,
  made new again, when their leaves are new,

pure and ready to ascend to the stars.

Translation by W. S. Merwin

Stars and Stripes, Pisa, 1996
Photograph by Paul Kodama

YI CH'ŎNGJUN

The Wounded

For several days I hadn't been able to add anything to my new canvas; it overpowered me completely. After the students were gone and the studio grew quiet, I stood back from it and lit a cigarette.

Something peculiar was preoccupying me. My older brother was suddenly writing a novel, and the business seemed to be profoundly connected to an incident that had occurred a month ago, when his scalpel had carved the soul out of a ten-year-old girl. The operation's failure had not been entirely my brother's fault. No one blamed him—neither the girl's family nor I, who had been watching him operate without incident for nearly ten years. For that matter, my brother didn't think he was entirely responsible either. From the beginning, the operation had had less than a fifty-percent chance of success, and the girl would have died for certain without it. Moreover, operations of this sort fail all the time—even in large hospitals. Still, the girl's death was a terrible blow for my brother. After it happened, he began to neglect his work. At first, he would occasionally go downtown and then return home drunk at night. But then he closed the clinic for good. He would shut himself in his room all day long, not allowing even his wife near him. In the evenings, he would go out and then come back so drunk he could hardly catch his breath.

Then I heard that while he was shut up in his room during the day, he supposedly was writing a novel. At first I was not particularly interested in this so-called novel. As literature, the thing would be incomprehensible to me—a mere art student running a studio for a living. I was curious, though, to know why the girl's death had caused him, a doctor, to start writing a novel, of all things. Then one evening, having come across the manuscript in his room, I was startled by what I read: my brother was writing about his experiences as a straggler during the war—which had ended ten years earlier—experiences he had kept to himself for all too long.

My brother always described himself as having led a quiet life during his decade as a surgeon, "cutting open, cutting off, opening up, and sewing together." A man who seemed to have no doubts about his present life nor any memories of his past, my brother never tired of his work, taking care of his patients diligently at all hours. But despite the many patients he treated successfully, giving new life with his skilled hands, he was not satisfied. He desired more and more patients, as if it was his mission to save as many lives as possible. Cautious and precise as a surgeon, he had not had a single mishap until the incident with the girl.

Apart from these facts, I knew little about my brother. But I could perhaps say a few things about my sister-in-law. I am sorry to say this about her, but she is a woman who is talkative and not too bright. Nevertheless, my brother had carried on a long and exhausting rivalry for her with another man. I didn't think my brother would win her, given what I considered his lack of tenacity, but he did. After the marriage, his calmness and her colorlessness meant they had few serious disputes. When minor problems did arise, it was not due to personality differences, but to their lack of children. Childlessness can cause friction in any marriage, however. All in all, I was inclined to think that he was able to get along so well in life because of his positive attitude toward all humanity, though I could not say this with certainty. And that was all I knew about him.

I had always been curious about my brother's being caught behind enemy lines near Kanggye during the Korean War. At the time, a brutal battle was underway near the thirty-eighth parallel. I knew that he killed one of his fellow stragglers—I'm not sure how many there were altogether—and afterward managed to cross nearly four hundred kilometers of enemy-held territory, finally making it back to safety. My brother never talked to me directly and openly about the circumstances under which he had become a straggler, however, or which of his fellow soldiers he killed and how and why he did it; nor did he say how he managed to get away, or what it was like during the escape. In fact, only once, when he had come home dead drunk, did he tell me that he was able to escape and stay alive because he had killed one of his fellow soldiers.

The story was strange. There was a lot I couldn't understand, but afterwards my brother pretended he had never said such a thing at all, and I was in no position to verify if the incident had really happened. Now, in writing the novel, he had begun retelling that very story. Simultaneously, the canvas I was working on had begun to seem immensely imposing to me. My brush trembled in my hand—all because I had secretly started reading my brother's manuscript. The trouble was that he had stopped making any progress at a crucial part of the story, and while he was at a standstill, I couldn't carry on with my own work. Speculating about the story's ending hadn't helped me add a single line to my unfinished canvas, and now it was tormenting me. Until the outcome of the story was revealed, I couldn't do anything.

Night at last flooded in through the window, filling my studio with darkness and leaving only my square canvas white. I finally rose from my chair, and it was then that I noticed Hyein had stepped just inside the door, like a shadow. When I turned the light on, she looked as if she had been standing there for a long time. Her body was motionless, and her shoulders sagged as if from fatigue. The sudden brightness caused her to lower her head a little and turn away.

"Shall we go out?" she asked.

I turned the light off.

Why had she come? Did she still have feelings for me that she hadn't sorted out? When she had stopped coming to my studio, without telling me why, I had had no trouble figuring out how I felt about her.

Hyein, a recent college graduate, was an amateur painter who had started coming to my studio to study art at the urging of my brother's friend. One day, when my other students had left early, Hyein stood alone in front of a plaster bust. I walked over to her and stood close behind her, breathing softly. Suddenly, she turned and kissed me. She later said she'd kissed me because I was an artist. Then one day she told me she would not be coming to the studio anymore and would have nothing more to do with me. She said it was because I was an artist, and then without another word she closed her beautiful, flowerlike lips. I wasn't in a position to demand anything from Hyein. Actually, I was angry at myself because I knew that my feelings for her would pass quickly, and it would be easy to let her go. As she said, I was just a painter.

Now she sat across from me in a teahouse. Taking out a white envelope, she said, "I came to give you my wedding invitation."

I smiled foolishly. I felt nothing as I realized that she had truly left me. Hyein, too, showed no emotion. She was marrying a doctor who owned his own clinic, she said. It had been decided even before she had stopped coming to my studio.

"It's the day after tomorrow. Will you come?" She fumbled with the envelope containing the invitation while I sat staring blankly. Her voice sounded very distant.

That evening, when I told my sister-in-law about Hyein's wedding, she sounded delighted. "Do you want to go, then?"

My sister-in-law is the kind of person who enjoys humiliating actors by applauding when they miss their lines. I was baffled by her tone and felt oddly like an actor being applauded by her. How did I respond? I think I said I would hire someone to attend the wedding and that person would be perfectly fine for conveying my congratulations. It wasn't jealousy. In fact, I wasn't interested in anything about Hyein or the wedding, even as I recalled her days at the studio and thought of her fumbling with the invitation as she talked about the ceremony.

"It's strange that you aren't angry," my sister-in-law said.

I replied with a yawn.

"You know," she said, "you have an awfully dark streak in your personality." My sister-in-law enjoys talking about other people's business, but not necessarily because she cares about what happens to them.

"Before you got married, weren't you afraid you were going to lose out on something? Did my brother have any kind of trick that got you to marry him?" As I spoke, I was actually thinking about Hyein's wedding and my brother's novel.

"There was something persistent about him, so I guess I assumed he was uncomplicated. A complicated man cannot be persistent about one thing, and women hate complications. To put it frankly, I thought I could depend on him completely. Wasn't that a natural way to think? A woman past marrying age doesn't dream extravagant dreams."

My sister-in-law's assessment of my brother was not completely accurate. But I did not want to pass judgment on her thinking or generalize about women's minds.

At the teahouse, suddenly reminded of my brother's novel, I had said to Hyein, "I've got some work to do." I finished my coffee and rose quickly. My large, unfinished canvas flashed painfully before my eyes.

Hyein had risen, too. "You haven't answered me." She stood in the doorway as if determined not to move until she'd gotten a response.

"Forget about that girl," my sister-in-law said. "A woman can be heartless in a situation like that." The concerned look that my sister-in-law gave me wasn't appropriate in Hyein's case: Hyein wasn't playacting, as women apparently like to do.

I glanced around. As expected, my brother had not come home yet. I'll bet he's dead drunk, I thought. As soon as I finished eating, I went to his room and searched his desk drawer. The novel was in the same place as always. My brother did not seem to be hiding it from either his wife or me.

"Suddenly you seem to regard your brother as a great writer," my sister-in-law said from behind me, though she had no real interest. Ignoring her, I opened the manuscript to the last page; the story, however, hadn't progressed. Given the discarded pages in the wastebasket and my sister-in-law's assertion that my brother had been at his desk all day long, it appeared that he at least had been trying very hard to write. Nevertheless, something about the ending of the story or, more precisely, about the killing, was keeping him from finishing. I felt annoyed, as if my brother was purposely teasing me—and after I'd spent the day sitting in front of my suffocatingly large, unfinished canvas.

Putting the manuscript back in his drawer, I returned to my room. I arranged the bedding and lay down earlier than usual, but my eyes were wide open. Sleepless, I was preoccupied with thoughts about how I would end the story.

The novel opened with a vivid image—a memory from my brother's childhood—though of course I could not be entirely certain that the narrator and my brother were identical. The narrator told of following a group of deer hunters. In those days, hunters always came regularly to the narrator's home town during the hunting season. They hunted wild boar in the autumn and deer in the winter and early spring, bringing with them a big aluminum pot in which to cook the game they killed. Particularly in winter, the hunters would hire a few villagers to go along with them as beaters, whose job it was to flush the deer and boar from the mountains by banging on pans. The villagers accepted this work because they didn't have any other employment during the winter; if the hunters failed to show up, the villagers would become anxious.

One winter day, when the snow blanketed the mountains, the young narrator had returned to his home town for a vacation; joining the beaters, he went with the hunting party to the mountains. For most of the day, they saw no game at all. When evening came, the narrator and one of the men sat together on the mountain ridge eating frozen riceballs. Just then a shot echoed from the other side of the valley. My brother had written:

> When I heard the shot, I felt as though the food I had just eaten suddenly lodged in my throat. A chilling sound . . . unquestionably murderous in intent and merciless, it echoed through the snow-covered valley, and I began to regret having followed the hunting party, which I had done only out of curiosity.

However, the shot didn't kill the deer. Spraying blood on the snow, the injured deer ran away. The hunters and beaters pursued the wounded animal, following the red drops. They thought that eventually they would find the fallen deer bleeding to death in the snow. The narrator reluctantly joined them, even though his heart pounded when he saw the bloody trail turning the white snow red. When he had heard the shot, a feeling of regret had arisen from the depths of his chest. He had wanted to flee down the mountain. But he had hesitated, and though his heart was pounding and it was getting late, he found himself unable to leave. The blood trail seemed endless, and finally when night came, he was able to go home. Almost immediately, the young narrator was struck with a high fever and sent to bed. He only heard later through rumors that the hunters had had to trek over three more ridges before they finally found the fallen deer. Just hearing about it was enough to make him shudder violently.

That, roughly, was the opening section. Of course, at first I did not read from the beginning; I started somewhere in the middle. But that made me so tense that I had to go back to the start. Reading this passage, I felt a strange, unsettling parallel between the sound of the gunfire and the spots of blood. Even from the beginning, my brother's novel was saturated with a dark unease and coldbloodedness.

Of course, my interest in my brother's past had a lot to do with why his novel made me nervous; an even greater reason for my interest was that I thought his personal history might somehow be influencing my painting. This was all happening at the same time that Hyein left me and I had a sudden impulse to draw a human face. It's true that I had had such a vague desire for a long time. So I can't say that my desire to draw a face came when Hyein and I broke up. But certainly around that time, the urge intensified.

I hate to talk about my painting. It's unbearably painful. I can't explain even a fraction of what I think about my art nor what I wish to express through brush and paint. I can say, though, that this whole thing with my brother made me think more deeply about the fundamental nature of human beings. I'd been thinking about the garden of Eden, Cain and Abel, and what qualities are inherent in human nature. Like a one-celled animal, each person in Genesis seems to have a different essence. Abel's concept of good, for example, and then Cain's jealousy, which God condemned forever as evil. Perhaps God was alarmed by man's desire to rise above his nature and by the complexity of humans. Anyway, from that time on there's been an infinite mixture of good and evil.

Still, no human face had ever moved me deeply enough to want to paint it—to make my brush tremble with excitement. Perhaps I had been wandering aimlessly in a sea of interesting faces. What was frustrating me now was that I had a strong premonition of a certain face. I hadn't actually met a person with that face, but I sketched an outline, using a firm oval—this was unusual for me—that was full of tension. For several days, I agonized over the outline.

One day, the day before he began writing his novel, my brother showed up in my studio. It was still daytime, but he was already drunk. I was taking care of my students, completely neglecting my own work. My brother stood in front of my canvas and then said to me belligerently, "Hmm! The person Teacher is drawing looks lonely. You didn't give this person any facial features."

He examined the sketch intently, as if it were a finished painting. I stared at him blankly. "I've only just started," I said.

"Well, depending on how you look at it, it could be a finished piece even though the face has no features. It could be God's most faithful son—with no eyes or ears, living by merely following God's will. But once it gets eyes, a mouth, a nose, ears, it'll be different, won't it? By the way, Teacher, which condition do you prefer?"

My brother glanced back and forth between the drawing and me. His eyes were searching for something, though he seemed to know that he wasn't going to find it. I was totally puzzled.

"Well, you're ignoring my questions," he said. "I'm sure an artist like you will agree with a doctor like me that the inside and the outside of a person cannot be explained solely in terms of logic, right? If you agree, what I'm about to say may be at least partially true. What do you think? Should I say it?" My brother often said things I couldn't make heads or tails of. I only knew that right now he was excited and wanted very badly to say something.

"I think a newly created person's eyes and lips should show vengefulness," he said. "What's hopeful about this—of course, this is only my opinion—is that the line is so intense." I found it strange that my brother was commenting on my drawing.

That evening, for the first time in a long while, my brother and I left the studio together to get a drink, at his invitation. It was raining so lightly that it didn't matter if we had no umbrellas. In front of the construction site of J Bank, there was usually a beggar kneeling on the sidewalk: a girl about ten years old who would sit with her head drooping below her shoulders and her arms stretched out, palms open on the ground. There were always a few blackened coins in her hands. As we were passing in front of her, my brother, who was walking several paces ahead of me, absentmindedly stepped on the girl's hands. I was even more shocked than the girl. I guess he didn't feel the soles of his shoes crushing the girl's hands because he never slowed or broke his stride. What was even more bizarre was that the girl, who raised her head in shock, didn't cry out. She just stared at my brother's back as he continued walking. I looked down at her hands. They seemed unhurt, and she merely resumed her pose.

I was angry at my brother but said nothing. I thought that perhaps he was trying to prove something to himself and it was related somehow to what he had been saying in the studio. I guessed that his behavior was a result of the surgical mistake he had made a few days earlier, even though his patient's death hadn't been his fault entirely.

When we reached an intersection, my brother turned around to look at me. A question was in his eyes. They were the eyes of a man who took pride in asking questions that he believed I could never answer.

"You did that on purpose," I said nonchalantly when we sat down in a bar he had taken us to.

"What?" my brother replied, seeming to feign ignorance.

"You stepped on that girl's hands," I said, irritated. For a brief instant he looked perplexed, and then he was upset. "You must be accident-prone, older brother. Your feet must have been out of control, right? The girl didn't look like she was in pain, but then you couldn't have known that because you didn't turn around to look."

The following day my brother started writing his novel, and I was no longer able to work on my painting.

After describing the deer incident, the novel moved to a South Korean army camp before the outbreak of the Korean War. It focused on two men in the camp. One of them was O Kwanmo, a sergeant who always carried a bayonet in his hand. He was short and had pale lips, and when he got angry, his eyes became triangular, like those of a poisonous adder. When a new recruit joined the unit, he would brandish his bayonet under the recruit's nose and with his triangular eyes threaten him into submission by saying, "Any man who slouches in front of me, I'll cut his belly open with one swipe!" Such threats taught the recruits not to let their bellies stick out, but he never actually cut any of them open.

Then one day a new recruit joined Kwanmo's unit. He was the other male character in the story, and was simply called Private Kim. He had a beautiful face, like a girl's, and was a little pudgy. Other than the fact that Private Kim's nose was "stubbornly stuck up," he was so submissive that there was no reason for Kwanmo's eyes to turn triangular. However, for some odd reason, Kwanmo began to beat Private Kim from nearly the first day in camp, acting like an angry snake whose tail had been stepped on. At first, the narrator of the novel suggested humorously that Private Kim's stuck-up nose was costing him dearly, but that kind of lightness was only temporary.

> I was returning from the mountain, carrying poles I had cut for a makeshift stretcher in the medical section. My route took me around the back of the unit, by the outhouse, and that's where I saw Kwanmo holding a broomstick. Private Kim was lying on the ground, and Kwanmo was flogging him in a frenzy, like a man trying to kill a dog. As soon as Kwanmo saw me, he threw the broomstick away and grabbed one of the poles I was carrying. I stood dumbfounded while Kwanmo, breathing heavily, used the pole to strike Private Kim across the buttocks, each blow making a heavy thud that sounded across the valley. But Private Kim submitted to Kwanmo's flogging with a frightful composure. There was a rumor that what irritated Kwanmo was the way Private Kim passively accepted his constant abuse. Indeed, Private Kim was unbelievably calm. Meanwhile, Kwanmo was sweating profusely and making strange cries. It was a dreadful sight. It seemed like Kwanmo was begging Kim to give in. Then something truly odd happened, causing me to intervene in this weird contest between Kwanmo and Private Kim. Kim, whose body had seemed immobile, slowly raised his head and looked up at me. At that moment, the look on his face made my breathing stop.

What the narrator saw was the expression in Kim's eyes. Each time he was flogged below his waist, a "blue flame" would shoot through his eyes.

My brother described that look at considerable length. Even so, he seemed doubtful about whether he'd done it adequately because he left two empty pages before moving on. Perhaps he wanted to change the description of the blue flash to make it more convincing. At any rate, it seemed that my brother, at the moment of the recollection, was enduring an intense experience, as if he were witnessing the blue flash all over again. My brother's literary imagination could not have concocted such a thing.

> Private Kim exposed the ghastly whites of his eyes, twisted his lower body to the side, and groaned, "Ugh! Ugh! Ugh!" On the verge of crying out, Kwanmo jumped on top of Kim's writhing body, jerking his hips to and fro in a frenzy.

After that, the narrator saw the bizarre contest often. Each time that he watched the blue flame flash across Private Kim's eyes, he wanted Kwanmo to flog him even harder. The narrator himself would shudder with excitement and nervousness.

> It was strange. I did not know why I was so nervous and excited; nor did I know whose side I was on. And so without my knowing a single thing about this, and with the strange confrontation between these two men not yet over, the Korean War broke out.

This section of the story ended here. The true focus of the story, however, had not yet been revealed. What I mean is the incident in which my brother became a straggler, killed someone, and then, because of this murder, was able to escape from enemy territory. Starting a new section, my brother concentrated in minute detail on that very incident.

The setting was moved to a cave in a valley somewhere around Kanggye. It was snowing outside, and near the mouth of the cave the narrator was lying on his stomach with his head sticking halfway out, being snowed on. Inside, Kwanmo was sitting in a relatively clean uniform while Private Kim was at the back of the cave, covered by a pile of dead leaves. They were defeated soldiers, and the mood in the cave was tense. Even as the narrator gazed into the valley below, where he could see the deep snows of winter beginning to pile up, his mind was on Kwanmo. The sergeant was chewing on and spitting out dry stems. The corners of his mouth were beginning to foam with thick spittle, and his eyes were fixed on the narrator's back. My brother described this desperate moment by writing simply, "It was because the first snow was falling." Such compressed writing made the narrator seem even more on edge. Private Kim's right arm had been severed—this was explained later in the story, but I thought it best to mention it now—and his eyes looked utterly blank, as if he were not even conscious of the other men.

> We didn't even know where we were, except that it was north of Kanggye. We were told by other troops in the area that we might be able to see the Yalu River in a day or two. At dawn, however, we were unexpectedly attacked by the Chinese Communist forces whose intervention in the war had been only rumored. Until then we had advanced without engaging in any serious battle. Now, for the first time, we spent the entire day pinned down by gunfire and artillery shelling. Both sides held out, not yielding an inch of ground. The following dawn, while I was looking for injured soldiers, I found Private Kim with his right arm severed at the armpit. I carried him to a shelter beside a boulder and began giving him emergency aid to stop the bleeding. Suddenly, the sound of gunfire started moving toward us. Partly because Private Kim hadn't regained consciousness but also because the gunfire was moving to the south so quickly, I wasn't able to do anything but take cover where I was. Soon I could hear the

Chinese troops calling to each other as they passed over the hill. By daybreak of the following day, the main Chinese line had left the valley. Still, for half a day I was unable to leave the protection of the boulder because the last of the Chinese troops continued to filter by. Gradually, the sound of artillery fire disappeared to the south.

That evening, Private Kim became semiconscious. The following day, the sporadic artillery shelling faded completely and there were no longer any traces of Chinese troops. As in all wars, what's left behind after a battle is over either perishes on its own or becomes powerless to participate in the war. Even if the Chinese troops had guessed that there were a few wounded stragglers, they would still have abandoned the battlefield as they did. The valley was now filled with silence and the autumn sun, but I continued to feel uneasy. I scavenged the battleground, finding a bag of hard biscuits and a few cans, and, supporting Kim, I set out to find a safe place to hide. Kim's wound was healing relatively well, but it was impossible to look for the rest of the South Korean forces once the sound of battle had disappeared. Perhaps the noise would return. Until then, we would need a safe place to wait.

Kim and I climbed up the valley and came out through a pine grove into a field that stretched to the top of the mountain. I found a cave and was peeking inside, with Kim leaning against me, when a voice behind me shouted, "Who the hell is peeping into someone else's house without permission?!"

I turned around, startled. From the opposite side of the woods, there was a man aiming a rifle at us, smiling. It was Kwanmo.

"I almost pulled the trigger because I felt like eating some meat," said Kwanmo, putting his rifle back on his shoulder. He ran over to us. "Oh! You look useless," he said, clicking his tongue. Then he tapped my shoulder. "But I ought to be thankful since you guys waited for me. They sent me out to do a reconnaissance, but when things became ugly, everyone ran for his life."

From here, the novel shifted back to a point when it had not yet begun to snow. Sergeant Kwanmo spat out the dry reed he had been chewing and walked out of the cave carrying his carbine. He went out to look around and hunt for signs of other troops. He was shrewd enough to check whether it would be safe to fire a rifle in the valley without it being heard. Just Private Kim and the narrator were in the cave now.

First we gathered food left on the battlefield, having found it mostly in one place, and carried it back to the cave. We made numerous trips down the mountain over a period of several days, and each time carried one or two days' worth of supplies. Kwanmo and I each went down the mountain separately, leaving Private Kim in the cave. But several times Kwanmo seemed to want to be alone with me, out of Kim's hearing. Inside the cave, he always seemed to be hemming and hawing, as if he wanted to tell me something. But when we were alone, he couldn't bring himself to say what was on his mind. Instead, he just beat around the bush.

But on the last day of our forays into the valley for supplies, Kwanmo stopped suddenly and turned around to face me. "The sound of artillery isn't going to start up again, is it?" he asked abruptly.

"We'll have to wait until the winter is over," I replied without thinking, drawing a deep breath. Kwanmo smiled a little.

"How long can we survive on this?" he asked, punching the rice bag on his shoulder. Then his expression changed. "There is no way we'll make it," Kwanmo said, quickly turning around, "except to reduce the number of mouths to feed." He began climbing the mountain again. At first, I didn't understand what he meant. I was walking behind him, pondering his words, when he stopped again and turned around.

"Leave everything to me. A sparrow-heart like you can just watch. A medic isn't fit for this kind of work. By the way, when would be the best time?" He gazed into my face, then spoke curtly to me as if everything had been decided. "I think the first day of snow would be good. If the sound of artillery comes back in the meantime, we can rethink it." Kwanmo stared at the sky as if snow might fall that very day.

That night he approached me again, but I had been appalled by what had happened the previous night and violently drove him away. After I'd fallen asleep, I suddenly opened my eyes, disturbed and uncomfortable. I felt a stubby lump thrusting against my buttocks. Someone was breathing heavily in my ear. Disgusted, I twisted my body, but the bastard locked his arms around my chest.

"Stay still," Kwanmo panted into my ear. I couldn't stand it. The bastard was coiled around me like a snake. With a violent push, I flipped over onto my back and glued myself to the ground. He held his breath for a while, then rolled away, rustling the dead leaves, resigned to leaving me alone. I closed my eyes, remembering what Kwanmo had said that afternoon about finding Kim "useful."

That night might have been the first time that Kim allowed Kwanmo to have him from behind. The next day, Kim's expression had not changed much. Instead, he appeared calm as usual. When I told him about the sound of artillery, and that it might soon return, the life seemed to come back to his eyes.

Kwanmo bothered Kim less after that, and Kim's wound remained stable, though it was serious enough that it could never heal entirely under the care of a mere medic like myself. A few more days went by without change, and then one evening Kwanmo came to me again, breathing heavily. He said that Kim stank. I chased him to the back of the cave. After that, he never got close to Kim again.

It was true that the smell from Kim's wound had become unbearable. I again tried to talk to him about the sound of artillery, but the light was gone from his eyes. He even refused my daily application of disinfectant and no longer got up at all. Three days passed during which he ate nothing, not even the biscuit-crumb soup I made for him. Finally, when our hope of hearing artillery was gone, the first snow fell.

As darkness came, I watched Kwanmo walking up from the valley. He would climb a little, then stop for a while, looking up at the cave. I felt my arms and legs growing numb with dread. I rushed over to Kim and looked into his eyes. His pupils were fixed on the ceiling, and his optic nerves seemed to have stopped functioning. His eyes contained nothing but emptiness. The only sign that he was still alive was an occasional slow blink.

"It's snowing, Kim," I said softly. I looked into his eyes, but there was no response. "Kim, it's snowing," I said a little louder. When his expression still did not change, I quickly unwrapped the bandage, stiff with dried blood, from around his wound. Startled, I heaved a sigh. The flesh around the injury was crumbling like a mud wall. Again I gazed into Kim's eyes. Tears welled up in them. Did he understand what I was saying, I wondered. Or was he listening to the last sounds of his life, letting himself sink into the deepest corner of whatever was left? Then his eyelids stopped moving, and soon his eyes became dry, as if the tears had stopped forever. His gaze remained fixed on the ceiling. And it was then that I thought it would be all right for him to die.

The story stopped here. Although the man my brother said he had killed was apparently Kim, it still was unclear who had actually done it and what role Kwanmo had played in the murder. Anyway, it really didn't matter to me who the killer was as long as my brother had gained the strength to escape. My brother had apparently already committed the murder once, and by retelling the story he was reliving the murder. But he hesitated to act. This reminded me of the hunting story told in the opening section of the novel: the narrator had nervously hesitated, unable to do anything, just as he now hesitated in deciding between Kwanmo and Kim. I still had no idea why my brother wanted to write about the murder and what it had to do with the operation in which the girl died.

Every night I read through the novel, hoping for the story to end. But Kwanmo always lingered down below in the valley, and Kim lay in the cave, awaiting my brother's decision. Most important of all, while my brother hesitated over finishing the novel, I couldn't do any of my own work in the studio.

The following morning my brother didn't show his face until after I'd eaten breakfast and left. I was determined to concentrate on my work and not think about his novel, so I went to the studio early. Even so, I knew that unless I was emotionally ready, I wouldn't be able to get any painting done. I walked to the window and lit a cigarette. The students would be coming to the studio in the afternoon. As always, I sat in front of that large canvas, feeling dizzy and doing nothing except think about my brother's novel. It was as if one of the story's characters was trying to appear on my canvas. Of course, I could infer an ending to the story. After all, my brother had said that he had killed his fellow soldier. But he might have meant that his passive response to Kwanmo's actions had made him complicit in a homicide. If that was the case, my brother was pathetic and I'd loathe him. He was a superb intellectual, but he always hesitated, agonizing over other people's actions, imagining they were his, and never acting on his own. Caught in a paradox, he was trying to prove he had a conscience by tormenting himself over the death of the girl, even though it wasn't entirely his fault. My brother seemed to want to affirm his moral identity in order to find new strength to go on.

Lately, however, my brother was becoming wishy-washy even about things that were all in his mind. Though he pretended to be cruel, he was simply a coward. Perhaps his clever conscience wouldn't allow him to be anything else.

I walked through the studio and looked at my students' canvases over their shoulders, then ended up going home well before dark. My brother, of course, wasn't there. I went to his room to check the manuscript. It was the same as the day before. I put it back in the drawer and left. I took a shower, ate dinner, and exchanged a few jokes with my sister-in-law. All the while, I couldn't help feeling angry. I felt like pouring out all the abuse I could think of. My anger wasn't directed only at him, however; I would curse anyone in order to release the frustration that was building up inside me. When my sister-in-law left the house for some fresh air, I went back to my brother's room. I could wait no longer. I carried his unfinished manuscript and some blank sheets to my own room and began venting my anger on Private Kim. I pounced on him the way a leopard pounces on a rabbit. Of course I didn't know if this had actually been the case, but I concluded the story by having the narrator drag Kim out of the cave and shoot him. As for my brother's escape, that part really didn't matter to me. I fell asleep near dawn, after writing about the thumping of my brother's "sparrowlike heart," which Kwanmo had called "hesitant and scared."

The following day, I worked on my painting a little, though for some time I couldn't shake off a strange feeling of excitement. Perhaps subconsciously I was thinking of Hyein's wedding. In fact, at one point it occurred to me that it would be appropriate for me to attend the ceremony. But I soon forgot about this because at last I was making progress on my canvas. After returning from lunch and while I was waiting for my students, a letter arrived unexpectedly by special delivery from Hyein, who must have been in the wedding hall right at that moment. I tossed the letter in a drawer, thinking that I would open it the next day or else forget about it completely. I was anxious for my students to arrive. I thought it would be better to have them around. Suddenly someone flung open the door and walked in. It was my brother, who looked around with bloodshot eyes. Of course, I hadn't assumed that he would simply ignore what I had done to his manuscript the night before. But because I was at last able to paint, and because I was also distracted by thoughts of Hyein's wedding, his visit came as a surprise.

My brother leaned in the doorway as if he had walked into the wrong place, scanned the room, and then slowly walked toward me.

"Was that girl's name Hyein? Aren't you going to her wedding?" my brother said as he gazed vacantly at my painting. His voice was steady, but his forefinger trembled as it touched the canvas. Since Hyein initially had come to my studio with an introduction from my brother's friend, he no doubt knew about her, her wedding, and even her fiancé.

"I didn't think you were interested in that sort of thing," I replied calmly.

"You are quite levelheaded, except for when you lost her," he said, laughing. He was beginning to make me uneasy.

"I guess you didn't come to thank me," I said to change the subject.

"Of course. However, I didn't want you to misunderstand," he replied, pressing his finger into my canvas until he tore a hole. I stood up. But with one hand he continued to widen the tear, and with the other he motioned me to sit back down.

"I just want an intelligent younger brother, that's all. I hope you don't get mad. I'm in too good of a mood to put up with any angry looks from you. This painting is all wrong, you know. You've definitely misunderstood things, as you'll soon find out. But in any case, I have to go to the wedding; I know the groom. I think I'm already late."

At that, my brother left the studio—swaggering slightly, it seemed to me. I gazed out the door after him. When I turned back to my canvas, I saw that it hung askew, like the sail of a ship that's been caught in a storm. Suddenly remembering, I took Hyein's letter out of the drawer. I considered its thickness for a moment and then opened it.

I'm leaving. Why say this now, you ask? Last night, you didn't even give me the chance to tell you. You would say it's because you hate pretentiousness. Well, I'm not going to ask you to congratulate me. I should've already said my final goodbyes to you, but since I couldn't, I suppose you'll think that I'm once again putting on an act.

You don't need to be alarmed just because this is a letter from a bride-to-be on the eve of her wedding. You never wanted to take any kind of responsibility, and my attempts to pressure you to be responsible never succeeded. I realized finally that there is nothing you can take responsibility for anyway. Perhaps you are under the impression that not taking responsibility is a responsible act in itself. You think that an emotional problem can be solved like a geometric equation, but that merely proves you're incapable of taking responsibility. Your answers always end up going in circles.

What made you that way was perhaps the strange wound you have. The man I'm marrying tomorrow calls your brother a Korean War casualty. At first I didn't know what he meant. But after hearing about the incident in your brother's clinic, his recent novel writing and drinking—yes, you may be surprised, but my fiancé is a friend of your brother's—I can understand to a certain extent. What I don't understand, though, is you. I thought of you when my fiancé told me that your brother's war wound had never healed, that he's still suffering from it. You, on the other hand, have a wound with no origin. I wondered then what kind of casualty you are, suffering from a wound that isn't a wound. Your symptoms are more serious, and your wound is more acute because you have no idea where it's located or what kind of wound it is. I don't know where your brother's strength comes from, but he stood his ground and fought to win the woman he wanted.

I'm not saying this because of a few kisses and caresses. I wanted to help you heal, but I realized it's something only you can make happen. I can only pray that you will.

And now, I want to be happy no matter what. I know I have to forgive myself before I can forgive anyone else. With that faith, I'm going to stop here.

To the lord of the castle with the tightly sealed door,
Hyein

"Has a strange wind blown into this house today?" my sister-in-law asked, smiling, when I returned home, having barely taught my students.

"What strange wind?" I replied, stealing a glance into my brother's room, which was empty, as usual.

"You look different today," she said. Actually, I thought her expression was different, too.

"What happened?"

"Your brother says he's going to start working again—beginning tomorrow," she said, grinning as if she'd been waiting all day to tell someone a secret.

I rushed to my brother's room, opened the drawer, and took out the manuscript. Holding back my emotions as best as I could, I opened the novel to the last section. I rapidly scanned the words, feeling once again as though I was falling into an abyss. My brother had deleted the part of the novel that I had written and in its place had written his own conclusion. I couldn't tell to what extent the events he described were factual. For all I knew, the last part could have been complete fiction. In any case, my brother's version entirely rejected mine.

The narrator kept pacing in and out of the cave until Kwanmo showed up. When the sergeant arrived, his face was shining with sweat in the darkness.

"Are you just going to lie there and stuff your face with the excuse that you've been wounded?!" Kwanmo shouted at Kim. "Today you have to help us get ready for the winter." Kwanmo began dragging Kim to his feet and pushing him out of the cave. The narrator grasped Kwanmo's arm to hold him back, but Kwanmo turned on him with a vicious look. The narrator let go and looked away and said nothing.

"You just watch," said Kwanmo in a low voice. He started down the mountain, pushing Kim in front of him. The narrator thought he heard Kwanmo's voice yelling, "You sparrow-heart!" Kim descended calmly, though once he suddenly turned around to look at the narrator. There seemed to be nothing in those blank eyes. The two men stumbled on, leaving black footsteps in the snow. Until their tracks disappeared into a pine grove, the narrator felt paralyzed, as if his feet had been nailed to the ground. The snow stopped falling. The wind sweeping over the snow rustled through the bushes, making an eerie noise. Through the broken clouds, the stars streamed westward. A little later, a shot from the valley broke the silence. The sound circled the ridges once, then trailed off to the south. The shot caused the narrator to jump, as if he had been startled out of a long sleep.

> Concealed somewhere deep inside the sound of that shot was a vivid memory that had remained with me, despite the numerous gunshots I had heard during the war. It was that same merciless, murderous, cold sound that had echoed in the snow-covered mountain when I went deer hunting as a boy.

The blood traces that had spread across the snow-covered mountain when he was a boy reappeared before the narrator's eyes. Then another shot echoed. The narrator shuddered, picked up his rifle, and went down the mountain, following the tracks of blood still vivid in his memory.

> I'm going to see that deer, the one that has fallen down and is spitting blood. You just wanted me to watch? Is that it? The feast has always been yours.

The narrator kept repeating these words over and over while following the blood tracks vivid in his mind.

> The tracks seemed to continue on and on. I ran. My forehead struck a low branch, and the impact brought me to my senses. I realized that the bloody tracks were the footsteps of Kwanmo and Kim. The aching in my forehead caused me to stop and rest. I spun around and saw a thorn bush the size of a man. It seemed to be holding its stomach and laughing. I found myself in a large pine grove. When I touched my forehead, my hand came away sticky and black. I decided to continue on when a sharp voice startled me: "Where are you going?" I turned quickly. Kwanmo was standing downslope, on the trail where the footsteps had disappeared, aiming his rifle at me. His white teeth shone in the darkness, as though he were smiling. When I stood still, he lowered the rifle and took a step towards me.
>
> "A sparrow-heart like yourself is better off not seeing this. Didn't I tell you to pretend as if nothing's going on?" Kwanmo spoke in a low, caressing voice.
>
> But tonight, I've got to find that deer, the one that has fallen down spitting blood, I thought. I turned around slowly, ignoring Kwanmo's orders.
>
> His voice followed me. "Don't go!" he said, strangely calm. The sound of his carbine loading a shell into its chamber sounded in my brain. My head was aching. I was conscious of a black muzzle pointing at me from behind, like a serpent's eye.
>
> I'm giving him my back again—my back, I thought.
>
> "There is no hope of our artillery units returning. When we run out of food, we have to leave and try to find our lines. I still need you, and you need me just as badly," said Kwanmo. He paused. "Turn around."

Right, I have to turn around. I can't keep my back exposed like this, I thought.

When I turned, Kwanmo looked relieved. He lowered his rifle, which he had been aiming at my back, and started toward me again. He looked as though he were about to put his hand on my shoulder. At that moment, my rifle went off and I threw myself flat on the ground. Kwanmo fell, too, and almost simultaneously more shots rang out, breaking the silence in the valley. It all seemed to happen in a flash.

A heavy silence once again surrounded us. I raised my head and looked at Kwanmo. He was sprawled on the snow, motionless. Moving my body slowly, I determined that in the confusion, Kwanmo's shots had been off target and that I hadn't been hit.

Looking back at Kwanmo, I saw a pool of black liquid spreading over his chest. My gaze fixed on the blood. I slowly stood up and walked toward him, my rifle ready. The blood that flowed out of his chest ran down his neck. The same blood flowed toward my boots. The trees loomed over us, and a strange loneliness seeped into my bones. Suddenly, Kwanmo's body stirred. He moved a little at a time, with the motion of a sand castle crumbling. I began to be afraid. The blood had spread over the snow now and was touching my boots. I watched him fearfully for what seemed like a long time. A salty liquid streamed into my mouth from the cut on my forehead.

Kwanmo stirred more and more. I thought he might sit up at any moment. The salty liquid kept flowing into my mouth. Slowly I raised my rifle and aimed at him.

Bang!

The noise of that shot rebounded across the valley, as if trying to chase away the silence before it vanished over the ridge. A profound longing clutched at my heart, riding on the echo of the shot. Before my eyes, a shadowlike face appeared, as though shimmering on the surface of water. The face seemed to be smiling. I felt that if only the face were to become a little more distinct, I would recognize it. It was a face I'd been yearning for, like a face I had known in my mother's womb, a face I had known forever. If only I could remember. But the face shimmered faintly, like a shadow, and then gradually disappeared. I closed my eyes. And I pulled the trigger again and again. The shots echoed through the valley. The salty liquid kept flowing into my mouth. When my ammunition was gone, the sound of the shots stopped.

I saw a smiling, blood-covered face. It was mine.

Having finished the novel, I remembered the cold food on the table and my sister-in-law, who had been waiting. I took a shower and went to the dinner table but sat without looking at her. My conjecture about my brother had been completely wrong. But that didn't matter. My brother had completed the novel in haste; nevertheless, I could see that the face he had talked about had been firmly and indelibly outlined. That was the reason he had torn up my painting earlier this afternoon. I could also understand his decision to resume working tomorrow. And the mystery behind him successfully making the four-hundred-kilometer escape after killing a fellow soldier—the answer to that was in the novel, too.

After finishing dinner, I went outside to sit and smoke a cigarette.

"He finished the novel, didn't he?" my sister-in-law asked, sitting down next to me.

"Yes. Have you read it?"

"No, I don't think it's that interesting." Women's intuition is uncanny. Like an extremely sensitive insect, they can sense things with their skin. "It's strange. I don't understand your brother."

I knew what she meant. "It's OK not to understand," I said.

"You're unknowable, too—like him."

"There's something you don't understand about me?" I asked.

"You've stopped drinking recently. Are you trying to take revenge on that woman?"

My sister-in-law disliked complicated stories. Whenever the story became difficult to follow, she would always make me backtrack a great deal.

"She got married today."

Shortly after eleven o'clock, the gate opened and I heard my brother coming in. I listened as he staggered up the stairs, apparently dead drunk. Ignoring his wife's questions, he went into his room, huffing and puffing like an angry beast. A little later I heard him come out of his room, vigorously tearing up some papers. I heard him go outside and strike a match. Then it was quiet. He seemed to be humming a song, and then he murmured something to himself. His wife must have been standing next to him, watching. She never helped him when he was drunk—not that my brother expected her to.

A red flame was reflected in the window.

What is he burning? I wondered.

I jumped to my feet and went outside. My sister-in-law looked at me, expressionless. My brother was sitting on the front step, tearing up his manuscript page by page and throwing it into the fire he'd built. After a time, he turned his head and looked at me with a sneer, then went back to burning the manuscript.

"You stupid fool," he muttered. At first I wasn't sure if he was speaking to me. His voice sounded too exhausted to be directed at anyone other than himself. But no doubt it was aimed at me. Then he looked straight into my eyes.

"Did that charming girl really not like you?"

I almost said, "She called you a Korean War casualty." But since I knew there was something more he wanted to say, I merely nodded.

"You idiot," he said, speaking forcefully this time and looking at me as he continued to tear up his manuscript and toss it into the fire. "And you wanted to draw the face of the girl who left you, huh?"

I decided to put up with him a little longer. My sister-in-law glanced back and forth between us.

"Everything is useless . . . a misunderstanding," he muttered. I thought it would be pointless to ask him to explain why he was burning the manuscript. Instead, I turned to go back to my room.

"Stay!" he yelled, starting to get up. "You are pathetic, killing Private Kim. So, you've been reading everything from the beginning? . . . Poor Private Kim . . . It's only natural that she didn't like you."

Though his thoughts were all jumbled up, it was clear to me what he was trying to say. I stared back at him, but then looked down, unable to bear his eyes. He continued to tear up the manuscript and throw the pages into the fire, all the time staring at me.

"You are a stupid fool! Understand?!" he yelled again. Then he nodded a few times, as if affirming that what he had said was exactly right. "By the way," he said, dropping the remainder of the manuscript and grabbing me by the ear. As he pulled me close to him, the smell of alcohol on his breath burned my nose and eyes. He placed his lips close to my ears, whispering so his wife wouldn't hear. "You haven't asked me why I'm burning the novel." His tone was so intense that I tried to look up, but he held on to me. "By the way, since you've read it, you know that man I killed—Kwanmo? Well, I met him tonight." Pausing, he slowly examined my face. His eyes looked as if they were soaked in alcohol, but that wasn't the only reason his mind was far away. In a loud voice that was also a sigh, he said, "So, this turns out to be useless, you idiotic bastard!"

He shoved me away and then picked up what was left of the manuscript.

"But it was strange . . . the bastard couldn't recognize me. And he didn't seem to be pretending either." My brother continued to look into the fire. "Since I had killed him off for good, I was thinking of starting work tomorrow. Then, as I got up from my seat to leave the bar . . . that's right, I only had a few more steps to go . . . someone tapped me on the back and said, 'Hey, you're alive!'"

At times I couldn't tell if my brother was aware of my presence or if he was just mumbling to himself.

"I turned around, startled. Well, it was that bastard—Kwanmo. He said he was sorry . . . backing up, all scared. Maybe over the years he had grown afraid of me. Of course he's afraid of me! In any case, I walked away, and as soon as I got out the door, I ran. What good is *this*"—he threw the rest of the manuscript into the fire and shot a glance at me—"if that bastard is still alive?

"You sparrow-heart, what are you listening to? Get back into your cave!" he screamed so loudly that I fled back to my room.

I felt as if I were being skinned alive. I think it was my brother's pain. He had been living with that pain, enduring it, and he knew where the pain was coming from. That's why he was able to endure it. The pain enabled him to stay alive, caused him to stand his ground. My brother's mind was not shattering into pieces; it had already survived colliding with something heavier and more burdensome.

Even so, my brother will soon start working again, I thought. He had the strength and courage to accept himself honestly. Whether or not Kwanmo's appearance had been a hallucination, my brother at last had the power to destroy the painful castle of abstraction that had sustained him—and that had now collapsed. Above all, he now knew the location of his pain. That knowledge would give him strength to wield his scalpel again. It could also be an incredible source of creativity. But . . .

I tried hard to collect my thoughts as I lay down on my bed. Where did my pain come from? As Hyein had said, my brother was a war casualty, but I had a wound without a source. Where is my wound? Hyein had said that there ought to be no pain where there was no cause for pain. If so, was I just making a fuss over nothing?

My work, my canvas, lay in pieces like a broken mirror. I might have to lose even more before I could start over again. Perhaps I would never be able to find a face. Unlike the one behind my brother's pain, there was no face in mine.

Translation by Jennifer M. Lee

Captive's Gaze, 1996
Photograph by Paul Kodama

MARIA M. HUMMEL

Dr. Nice Day

In real life, we never choose our mothers. My father had at least three: the one who bore him and died after the birth of his youngest brother; his step-mother, my Oma, who sold their furniture for potatoes during the poverty of World War II Germany; and Tante Bella, the aunt who practiced medicine in Alabama. Tante Bella sent him a steamship ticket to come to America when she found out that he, twenty-one and restless, was failing out of Frankfurt University.

My own mother is just as generous and formidable as these women were. After sewing, baking bread, knitting, and even sugaring the neighborhood maple trees for syrup for her four children's pancakes, she has launched a political career in the Vermont legislature. She writes to me in free moments on Statehouse stationery. I also had a mother in Thailand, where I volunteered in my own twenty-first year to teach English at a small college. I loved her as one loves a strict grade-school teacher: first out of obligation, later from memory and with respect. I never would have chosen her. Her name was Dr. Nice Day.

After dinner we would stretch back from the small table, her nieces busily clearing the dishes away, whisking the wood clean with an old rag before they disappeared. She would take her perch on a polished, cushionless teak couch, as hard and comfortless as the floor, where I lounged. It would have been the perfect time to smoke or drink tea, but Thai women don't smoke unless they are prostitutes and she never offered tea. Staring at the green TV set, she might question me about English, or I might ask her about her country, or the nieces might come in shrieking with a baby gecko they'd captured on the garage wall. Flailing in a plastic bag, head too large for its ugly body, it was doomed to be squashed by a brick in the driveway.

It was traditional to kill those particular geckos, called *too-kays* for the two-syllable noise they made at night while claiming their territory. Heavy eyed, blue-green or orange-brown, depending on the color of the wall they climbed, they ate the smaller lizards, left shiny turds everywhere, and were rumored to inflict painful bites. She kept dogs to hunt them. The dogs' names were Good and White, and she treated them with more care than most families did, allowing them to sleep in the garage at night, promising Good every time she got pregnant with another litter that she would spay her.

In return, they loved her, wiggling in timid ecstasy when she returned from the market: two mutts the color of the land bleached from exposure to the sun. At times, I felt like them, unsure of my position, wagging my way in the door night after night. Dr. Saowanee, whose Thai name translates in English as "Dr. Nice Day," had adopted me for the year I lived at Ramphaipanni Teacher's College. She invited me to eat with her family, which included the nieces who stayed with her so they could go to schools better than the ones in their hometowns. O and May were chubby adolescents, O distinctive for her high-pitched and frequent giggle, May for her sullen sighs. Mon, the eldest, was a student in business at Ramphaipanni and showed up every evening at six on her yellow Suzuki Love to pick me up. Climbing on back, I would speed with her up to Dr. Saowanee's house, Mon's shower-damp, long, black hair whipping my face.

The first time we arrived at the house, I noticed the long, thin trees out back: strange, sickly poles dripping fat orange tears. These melancholy trees bore papaya, a sweet, heady fruit I learned to like and, later, to hate. Masked by a guava tree, the front of the house was shabby from withstanding so many rainy seasons. All human residences in Thailand, including my own rust-stained, concrete dormitory, paled in comparison to the bright jungle that encroached on them. It was as if you could build nothing there that would last forever, and if you left, even for a year, all traces of your existence would disappear.

To be a foreigner in Europe is one thing. There's always some nice Scandinavian fluent in six languages who can rescue you from the Parisian vendor who insists it *was* ten dollars for your hot dog. To be a *farang* is another. *Farang* is the Thai word for a white stranger, as well as their word for guava, an ungainly green fruit that tastes like a juiceless apple.

As a tall, blond guava, I was a traffic hazard, causing motorcyclists to crane their necks long after they passed me. *It's like being famous for a year,* another teacher had written in a letter to me. My boyfriend, Tom, and I had chosen rural Thailand because we wanted to live entirely outside our own culture; to complete that immersion, we had even decided to live fifteen miles apart, at separate schools. We paid for this decision by becoming novelties, creatures of pale skin and light hair, who dressed differently, spoke differently, even ate differently, raising our forks instead of our spoons to our mouths.

Although it had been my choice, I hated being on stage constantly. *Farang, farang,* I would hear in the market as I glided through like the ghost I was, buying vegetables and fruit, expensive peanut butter from the grocery store. Once, Tom traced me all over town by asking where the blond *farang* had gone. Everyone knew—noodle-stall owners, postal workers, the bank clerk—pointing thin, dark fingers, *There, there.*

In a country where the language roared and pulsed around me like a river I could not stop—the rising and falling vowels, the paralyzing twists of tongue and breath—actions meant more to me than words. For months, I heard so many things I did not understand, ignored so many menus and signs with their strange curling alphabets, that my senses heightened to who brought me fruit, or gave me a lift on a hot afternoon, or asked if I needed anything from town. Thais are extraordinary hosts: curious about foreigners and generous gift givers.

I was lonely and accepted their hospitality greedily, hating the spider-cracked walls of my dorm room, the hard gym mats that made up my bed. There were many who promised to teach me Thai cooking, to show me around Chantaburi, the town where I lived. But only Dr. Saowanee, who had studied for her doctorate in math for seven years in Los Angeles, understood how long the hours were between teaching and sleep. Hers was one of the few houses I stepped inside the entire year I was there. She was the only one who said, "I want you to be like my family," looking away with her hard, black eyes.

She wasn't pretty and had never married: the only child from her nine-sibling family who finished high school. Isolated by her intelligence and learning, she was rarely visited by these siblings, although she dutifully took in their children. Her wiry black hair and wide nose suggested Cambodian ancestry, thought less attractive by the Thais than the high cheeks and straight hair of their own physiognomy. Her face had set into a seriousness I saw on very few citizens of the country that was known as "The Land of Smiles." After dinner she bossed her nieces around with quick barks, and the few times she was away, they grew giddy with freedom, eating extra dessert, swatting each other as they dried dishes, singing.

"When the cat's away, the mice will play," I said in English. Mon looked up from scrubbing the wok.

"Say again?" she said, soap bubbles climbing up her wrist.

I translated. She interpreted my Thai for O and May, who laughed as if they understood me for the first time.

My students also occasionally invited me to join their sprawling families, taking me with them to Loi Grathong, a November festival in which palm-leaf boats are set, candle-lit, on lakes and rivers for the water gods, who receive everyone's wishes for the coming year. I don't remember what my wishes were, except not to be killed by the wayward fireworks that showered hot sparks over the small lake. Five girls, all in my classes, held my hands as we walked through the maze of crowds, buying roasted coconut rice in hollowed bamboo, grilled corn, and our own set of firecrackers to set off. I remember watching a red-haired *farang* wandering pale and dazed through the throngs. Her face was strained with not seeing all those who stared at her, and I realized it must be a mirror of my own. "Your friend," my student Noi said, and nudged me. But I didn't want to talk to the *farang*, didn't want her to invade my Thailand, and answered in Thai that I wanted to see the *caa-bum* (their word for bumper cars). There must have been some urgency in my voice because Noi led me back into the mass of black-haired, coffee-colored faces, offering me a strip of roasted chicken the way a father pleases and quiets his daughter with a lollipop.

As the cool fall season gave way to the warmer months of winter, the first of March neared, the start of the longest school vacation of the year. I remember complaining to Dr. Saowanee one night about how restless the students were, how unwilling to study. The same ones who took me to Loi Grathong were just as sweet and pleasant, but they refused to answer questions in class, fanning themselves with their damp notebooks and letting their gaze trail out the open, screenless windows. Dr. Saowanee said the weather would get worse and worse until no one would even be able to lift a pen. Our discussion made me dread the upcoming English Camp.

My school had never had this kind of event before (I guess the last volunteer had had the savvy to avoid it), but about a month before the break, Ajaan Nipa, the head of my department, approached me. A sharp-faced woman who loved Robert Frost, she told me about English Camp as if it were an already established fact. It was Thai tradition to require *farang* teachers to plan and execute a two- or three-day event celebrating English. The idea was that no one was to work too hard and everyone was to have fun—except for the *farang* who was in charge of making it all happen. Fine. I knew it was coming. I had thought of the excuses I could make, but I also wanted my chancellor's permission to leave the country during vacation and go trekking in Nepal. Getting his permission in exchange for arranging the camp was a fair trade.

I invited Tom and my friend Lisa, also teaching English in Thailand, and asked their schools to excuse them. I drew up plans for games like scavenger hunts and grammar jeopardy. I planned a day at a national park, where we could play outside in the morning and spend the afternoon hiking to a waterfall. The other *ajaan*s (Thai for "teacher") were in charge of ordering food, arranging transportation, and so forth. My chancellor was reportedly buying his first pair of jeans to wear for the occasion.

I didn't see Dr. Saowanee in those last weeks, feeling irritable at the Thai race in general for burdening me with their expectations of a good time. All the teachers were very excited, the students grumpy because they weren't able to go home as early as they had wanted. The days sped by: the last week of classes, exams written and taken, then English Camp.

Mon was forced to go by Dr. Saowanee, although she was not an English student like the rest. She came, reluctantly, in plaid shirt and jeans—the attire of all the students, who insisted on wearing the grunge fashion of Seattle in their tropical climate. Mon and I had grown to be friends mostly through gesture, although my Thai had limped along well enough to learn that she had no boyfriend and blamed it on the rigid curfews of Dr. Saowanee. It seemed that most weeknights she wanted me there, leading us in aerobics to her one English music tape before her aunt came home. I think she liked me in the intrigued way that White, the friendlier of the two dogs, did: he always sniffed me curiously and bumped my hand as if he thought a *farang* might pet him differently.

On the way back from the national park, Mon rode the bus with me, Lisa, and Tom while most of my English students crammed on cafeteria benches in the back of a huge, green lorry. Those students had guitars with them and sang their way down the mountain, ahead of us. The day had gone well, the mountain air cooling the glare of the approaching season. The students especially liked the game in which one person leads a blindfolded partner to a tree, gives him a moment to study it with his hands, and leads him away again. When the blindfold is removed, the partner must find the tree that his hands know, but his eyes have never seen. I watched as the blindfolded students groped the air clumsily and their partners responded by growing gentler, leading their awkward children through the confusion of roots and fallen leaves.

Later, on the wide, flat rocks of a waterfall, the students' youthful aggression returned. They splashed each other in their sneakers and jeans until the denim slicked against their legs like a shiny second skin. The mossy stones on the river grew dark and slippery, and many students fell, then rose again, unhurt and laughing. Nineteen and twenty, they played like fifteen-year-olds—the girls shy about their bodies, the boys getting drunk from flasks of whiskey they thought I couldn't see.

Because the sky had grown overcast and threatened the afternoon rain that so often came in Chantaburi, I had turned down the students' invitations to join them in the lorry. I watched them call and sway as the truck steered ahead of us down the steep hills. I remember feeling old that day—tired of the games I made them play, of the glistening water of the falls—and wondering how I could amuse them that night. I had planned a dance—and prizes that so far had not been bought. The students were exhausted, I could tell, and would just as soon pack their bags that night so they could leave the next morning. The lorry pulled over to get some gas. Our bus went on. I leaned against Tom and closed my eyes, listening to the patter of rain on the steamed windows, already opaque with our breath.

When we got back, Tom, Lisa, and I took turns showering in the cold water of my dingy, yellow-tiled bathroom. Clean and wearing fresh clothes, we walked out to find Ajaan Nipa to discuss the dance. The courtyard of the girls' dormitory where I lived was crowded with students. The white-flowered bushes by the gate gleamed with new rain while my students leaned against their motorcycles or squatted on their haunches in the pebbled drive.

"Accident!" Noi called out to me.

"What?" I asked, quickening my pace.

"Accident. The big car," another student started and then began lapsing into Thai. I understood the words "students" and "hospital" and remembered the green lorry packed with bodies, the songs streaming behind them into the bus's open windows, and the last time I saw the lorry: pulled over in a gas station.

I understood "rain," and "accident" again, in the chorus of voices trying to explain. I pulled Tom and Lisa along with me to find another English teacher named Dissaya, who could tell us what had happened. Walking up the hill to the school, I looked back once to see the girls still gathered at the edge of the gate, as if they were afraid to cross it. There were so many of them, and yet I could only see the empty spaces between their huddled bodies: the white gravel shone like the skin of all those who were missing.

Later that night, as some students returned from the hospital, staggering on crutches or wearing white bandages that glowed in the dark like strips of the moon, Lek came up to me, limping.

"*Ajaan,* my friend is dead. What do I do?" Lek was a student who could rarely dredge up more than "hello" from her English vocabulary.

"I'm sorry," I said, my own capacity for speech failing. She introduced her parents mechanically. They stood behind her in the shadow of their truck, smiling the tragicomic smile we all have when we are too nervous or sad to control our faces.

"My friend is dead," she repeated, leaning towards me in a half-embrace, then limped away. I already knew which friend—skinny, smart Rojana. There were a few others in my classes: Cheeradet, Songsak, Daeng. The lists had come in at the office while we waited with Dissaya, and I recognized the names I struggled over the first months, those collisions of letters I had to memorize. I also learned how the old lorry had experienced an electrical failure in the heavy rain and spun out, flinging students onto the pavement, crushing some of them as it fell on its side. It took several hours for all of them to be taken thirty miles away to the hospital in town, and many lay in the rain all that time, shivering in their soaked clothes. Those of us who had taken the bus were pronounced lucky; many times that night I was told how lucky I was not to have been on the lorry, as if fate had split us in two that day and some had made the right choice, others the wrong one.

"What do I do?" I wanted to ask back. What was a *farang* to do? I had no car in which to go to the hospital. Disturbed by my open, red-faced grief, the other *ajaan*s suggested I go to bed, that I stay inside. Tom had taken Lisa back to his house; I would join them tomorrow. Tonight I stood in my window, ill at ease with the bright stars, with the sound of cars, parents arriving to take their living children home.

The next morning I woke up sweating after dreaming of a *too-kay.* The entire dream consisted of the gecko staring at me with its huge green eyes, an ugly creature stepping out from the shadows, a permanent outsider. To avoid remembering the depths of its lonely gaze, I rose quickly to dress in the already hot room and walk to school. My face was still puffy. When I reached the main office to hear the report of who had died during the night, a few names had been added to the list. The secretaries were busy writing telegrams to parents, answering the shrill phones. The chancellor was a blur among them, his expression strained.

"Dr. Saowanee is looking for you," Dissaya said when she appeared in the office entrance, closing the blue umbrella she carried daily to shield her skin from the sun. She watched me from behind her large glasses, adding, "Dr. Saowanee was very worried when she heard about the bus, and didn't know if you were on it. She told me she loved you like a daughter."

I nodded, feeling sullen and resistant to this declaration. My real mother would have found me by now. "I'm sure I'll see her," I said. "What are you going to do?"

"I am going to the hospital." She named another *ajaan* as driving. It was clear I was not invited.

I nodded again and walked away from her, into the bright glare of pavement that led to the cafeteria. Halfway up the walk, I ran into Dr. Saowanee. I remember she was wearing a white ruffled blouse because, within a minute of seeing her, I burst into tears and she drew me towards the stiff lace of her collar in an awkward hug.

"It's OK," she said firmly, patting me on the neck. I was half a foot taller than she and so drooped unsteadily against her shoulder. "You come to my house and Mon will make you some lunch."

"But I have to correct my exams," I protested. I was embarrassed by my outburst and afraid her sympathy would prevent me from regaining control of myself. Instead of my ugly tears, I wanted to have *jai yen,* a perpetual calmness prized in Thailand, especially in bad circumstances. *Jai yen* meant "cool heart," but mine was a raw, hot lump in my chest—an erratic pump I could not control.

"Bring the exams with you," she insisted. She marched me to my office to collect them, then drove me to her house, calling a few curt directions out of the window to Mon, who was sitting at a table in the open garage.

Mon nodded and rose, smiling when she saw me.

"I was worried about you," Dr. Saowanee said, staring at her steering wheel. "I thought maybe you were on that truck, but Mon said you were with her on the bus."

I opened the door. "Yes," I said. "I guess I was lucky."

Mon made me squid soup and watched TV while I corrected the exams, some of which belonged to students who had died the day before. I held the papers they had touched just a week earlier, remembering their earnest pens, the blue and black inks marking the white paper like severed bits of veins. On top of the stack lay Cheeradet's, his penmanship fast and awkward. In his final skit for the class, he had posed with friends in a male beauty pageant (narrated rather skimpily in English). In my mind flashed the gangliness of his arms, his shy head turned away from the audience—but then I forced myself to turn numbly to the next paper, setting the dead in their own, silent pile.

When Dr. Saowanee came home, she sat on her hard couch and began counting a wad of cash and making marks on an official-looking sheet of paper. The *ajaan*s were contributing money to give to the parents, she explained, because the school had no insurance to cover the accident. I offered to pitch in. She shook her head.

"It's not your responsibility," she said. "It's not your country."

A few nights later, she took me to a wake for three of the students. On easels their pictures stood in heavy gold frames, garlanded by flowers. Monks in orange robes chanted and shook cymbals. The concrete floor was lined with stiff metal chairs. I understood nothing, taking a seat next to her and trying not to look around.

Ottaporn, Naiyana, Cheeradet, Songsak, Rojana, Daeng. The names of the lost ones rang through my head as a young girl brought everyone a small white string. The other *ajaan*s tied it neatly around their left wrists. My larger hands fumbled and slipped. After a minute, Dr. Saowanee sighed and tied the string for me, pulling gently at the knot so it wouldn't be too tight on my wrist. Even with it secured, I couldn't forget how the string had slid, smooth and resistant, through my fingers, how the series of names still accused me of not keeping the students alive.

No one would blame me for the accident, although I had moved our English Camp to a national park. If I had kept the games confined to our campus, everyone would be alive. But I was bored with Ramphaipanni, and certain the travel time would reduce the number of activities I would have to plan. I eagerly encouraged us to go up those mountain roads, ignoring the fact that it rained every afternoon.

Secretly, I wanted the accident to be the fault of the lorry driver, who had run away after the wreck. People said he would turn up at a temple in a few weeks, asking for sanctuary. Yet no one blamed him either. "Electrical failure," Dr. Saowanee had said, her tongue blurring the *r*s and *l*s, as if this failure was as inevitable as a hurricane or flood. No one talked about seat belts or other safety guards—lessons to be learned from the accident. You can't learn a lesson if you don't think you made a mistake, and no one thought it was a mistake.

"It was their time," Dissaya had said to me simply one afternoon when we ate *moo satay* together. "It was time for some of them—that's what we believe." And when I left Thailand the next October, on my good-bye card, Ajaan Nipa had written, *We know some thing that happen here make you think badly about our country. We ask you to remember the good times, too*—as if hoping to prevent me from carrying my grief out of Thailand.

I touched the knot Dr. Saowanee made for me. The skin of my wrist still glowed where she had held it—the way my scalp would often feel warm for minutes after my mother had finished tugging my hair into a braid before school. I raised my head. The monks were reciting prayers in Sanskrit, and I felt relieved that no one else around me understood the language in this last ritual between life and death. For several minutes, we were united by incomprehension, and waiting. I saw incense rise around the photographs and mask them. Rain came daily now, and I took it for granted that I would arrive home soaked, my skirt clinging to my legs, my umbrella too small to keep the fierce drops from my face.

Soon after I handed in my exams, Tom and I flew to Nepal, spending three weeks trekking in the high, clear air and looking down mountains so sharp and steep that the valleys were clefts of shadow. On the dangerous drive from Katmandu to Pokhara, where we would begin our trek around the Annapurna range, I saw six trucks wrecked in the ravines that washed down from the narrow road. Any one of those accidents could have been my own; any one of the sicknesses I caught in Nepal, including giardiasis, could have meant my death.

When I returned to Chantaburi—my legs muscular and thick from climbing, my lungs accustomed to gulping great breaths of air—I felt clean and strong. Somewhere on the edge of a Nepali village, where the spun prayer wheels whispered softly beneath the wind, I had watched a vulture tear at the bloody carcass of a yak that had fallen out of reach of the village and I realized that death was not an injustice, but an inevitability. When I got back to Ramphaipanni, I calmly accepted the news that all the students had left the hospital but one more had died.

My Thai improved. My classes, bereft of some of their best students, acted like the amputees they were: clumsy at first, then gaining a strength they had never had before. We produced a play together, all in English, and in performing it for the rest of the school, not one of the students forgot his or her lines.

Chantaburi grew used to me, and I realized that those who stared must be strangers themselves. I made a few more friends, and went to Dr.

Saowanee's house less often—once or twice a week instead of four or five times—greeting her like a guilty daughter every time. Part of me needed to be free of her so that I could be free of the person I was before the accident: the overgrown child who wanted to be cared for, who wanted a mother. When I entered the cool depths of her house, I thought she treated me like someone who no longer needed her generosity; or perhaps the novelty of the *farang* had finally worn off. When I came for dinner, I felt I was pressing that same luck that had gotten me to take the bus. I was asking too much.

Still, I remember some dinners when I had made them all laugh as I tried to open a steamed crab or cut an unfamiliar fruit the wrong way. Then she was patient with me, picking up her own blade to pare a clean strip of skin from the orange flesh. "This way," she said gently, and took my hand to show me the steadiness of her own.

"Dr. Saowanee is in the canteen if you want to say good-bye to her," Ajaan Nipa offered as she got in the passenger seat of the van that would take me to Krating, where Tom and I would catch a ride to Bangkok. It was my final day at Ramphaipanni. I was going home—the last of the long, hot days marked off on the calendar. In less than a week, I would see my family, eat Ben & Jerry's ice cream, and go to a movie in my own language. I would walk down the street, and no one would stare at me.

"I said good-bye to her yesterday," I answered, although that wasn't really true. I had gone to see her a few days before, but only Mon was there, in the shabby house, reading. I didn't want to see Dr. Saowanee now because I couldn't bear for her to wave at me casually or, even worse, to cry. "It's OK. We need to hurry," I urged.

Ajaan Nipa nodded and slammed the door, sending a warm wave of air across me in the air-conditioned interior. It smelled sweet, like a ripe papaya ready to fall away from its stem.

One day I may dream myself back there. I will be at dinner again with Dr. Saowanee, eating my way through green curry and roasted chicken, through fried kale and piles of white jasmine rice. The nieces will move gracefully, raising their plump arms to dip into one dish, then another, layering their plates. Mon will say a few words in English, blushing as her tongue stumbles over an *r*. Afterwards, they will clear away the dirty dishes, and Dr. Saowanee and I will sit back, just the two of us, stretching our warm stomachs.

"You are not my mother," I will say sternly, and Dr. Saowanee will laugh. For the first time, she will look at me, and in her eyes I will see all the days I longed to end, all the hours I read novels to escape the heat, while the jungle grew its green tangle around the balcony where I sat, overlooking the wall of the school. I will see the faces of the students I lost, calling to me from the swaying lorry, telling me not to be sorry, even if I must be sad. I will see the white string I could not tie, tumbling from my hands to make the waterfall where we all waded those last hours we had together.

In the dream, she will become a country, ribboned with plantations of durian, darkened with rubber trees dripping their white sap down the scars of their carved trunks. She will become the hot ache of sun on the eyelids in the afternoon, the flashing temper of rain where clouds meet on the foreheads of mountains. She will be high white rapids, and the lowland rivers of slow brown water. She will be waiting for me, always, and I will return to her someday, because I still want to be loved by that place I left so easily, because I want to be remembered as a daughter.

KONG SŎNOK

Parched Season

There is no end to the noise. Though the street behind the apartment building hasn't been properly paved yet, the traffic on it isn't much lighter than on the main road, because it leads directly onto Namhae Highway. In fact, drivers trying to avoid the congestion on the main roads prefer this side street. I wouldn't mind so much if it were only buses, taxis, and cars going by, but the smoke and dust belched out by the dreadful procession of muddy dump trucks, concrete mixers, and oil tankers—all rumbling from I don't know where—are suffocating and the noise is deafening. The noise makes me short of breath and bores into the marrow of my bones with its sharp sensations, and trapped behind a wall of noise, I end up putting my head between my hands and crying.

The children play in the corridors of the apartment building. They use the cold, hard concrete floor as a playground where they jump rope, draw lines with crayons, and play rock-paper-scissors. They yell back and forth as if saying to the din of the traffic, "Let's see who wins—you or us!"

The noise of the cars is loud, so the children's voices grow even louder, and since their voices grow louder, it's inevitable that television volumes also go up. The smaller noises are swallowed up by the din, and all of it makes one huge mass of noise.

On Sundays, when the children don't go to day care, the corridor turns into a crucible of more noise, the children sounding as if they are fighting rather than playing.

That's how the noise is behind and inside the apartment building. Then there's the noise in front.

The apartment complex is made up of five buildings: numbers one, two, and three in the back, and numbers four and five in the front. Each building is fifteen stories high and has twenty apartments per floor—three hundred households per building. Fifteen hundred apartments in all. Because of the number of households, it was only natural that the large square would serve as a common area. But the "square" is actually a parking lot. This is the source of the problem.

Have you ever seen the parking lot of one of these "permanent rental apartment complexes" in the middle of the night? It's a truck stop, a vast garage filled with heavy vehicles.

Once, having seen all the trucks in the parking lot after visiting me, my friend who lives in an apartment complex run by a large corporation could not restrain herself from exclaiming, "This is it—the horror of real life."

There is not one single car in the parking lot—not even a tiny Tico, the so-called people's car. The only small vehicles amid the large cargo trucks are a few motorcycles, bicycles, and carts.

But the truly disturbing part of this happens in the mornings, when the big trucks move. It's frightful.

Each dawn it's as if a huge mountain comes crashing down and the ground splits open. My child cries out, "Mom, I'm shaking, but I'm not moving!"

Not knowing what else to do, I pull my child closer to me. "Just wait a bit. It's not an earthquake."

After the large trucks leave, the kids are awakened a second time by the arrival of the garbage trucks. Since there are so many households, it takes a long time for the trash to be cleared away and the noise to stop.

Each morning begins this way: a symphony of aggressive noises blasting from the back and the front of the building.

Finally I couldn't stand it any longer. Wasn't there some way to stop the racket, at least on one side of the building? If it couldn't be prevented out front, couldn't a soundproofing wall be put up in the back?

Trying to suppress my rage, I called Korea Housing Corporation, the contractor that built the apartment.

When I called the first time, the female employee I talked to said in a polite voice, "I'll submit a request to have someone look into the problem."

When I called the third time, frustrated because nothing had happened, the same employee said, "Why don't you submit a petition?"

Resolving to get a petition started, I went to the head of the neighborhood association to ask her to put the matter of a soundproofing wall on the agenda for the next meeting. She told me to my face that she would do it, but once again nothing happened.

When I respectfully asked the head of the association about my request, she said, "You should just put a lid on those emotions of yours."

But I felt like I couldn't possibly "put a lid on those emotions" once they'd been stirred up, so I made time in my busy schedule to visit the apartments near me.

I knew that there'd be no one home in 302, the apartment right next door to me, because the occupants peddled from a cart during the day. I rang the doorbell of number 303, across the hall.

This was the first time since I'd moved here a month ago that I'd talked to the woman in 303. She was getting ready to go out.

"I live in number 301. Don't you find it a bit noisy here?"

"I don't know."

"But what about all those trucks behind the buildings?!"

"Is there really anything we can do about it? Besides, isn't it good enough that we're able to live in a place like this?"

After that I gave up the idea of a petition. She was right. Wasn't it enough to be living in an apartment such as ours? Wasn't it enough not to have to rent rooms in other people's houses? Was it right to complain about the noise or the surroundings? It's an old saying that if a monk doesn't like living in the temple, he should leave.

There was nothing I could do but suppress my emotions and just get on with my life.

That's how my fate crossed with that of the woman in number 303.

We introduced ourselves.

"I guess introductions are belated. I'm Aram's mom."

"Is that so?" Yujŏng's mom said. She hadn't seen me before because she was so busy trying to eke out a living. She said she was on her way out to take care of urgent business matters, and then she invited me to stop by her bar for a drink sometime.

"Do you take Yujŏng to work with you?"

"Well, there's no one to look after her."

"Why don't you leave her with me so she can play with my children when they return from nursery school?"

The woman thanked me, said how glad she was to have met such a kind neighbor, and left five-year-old Yujŏng with me. I had to watch over Yujŏng until my own children, who were in the all-day class, came home from school. But Yujŏng amused herself by playing with my children's toys and humming sorrowful songs.

Those were stressful days for me: I was racking my brain trying to write a damn novel—something I'd never done before—because I had impulsively promised a publishing company that I would write one. Trying frantically to weave together some ideas, I realized after a while that the rustling sound of toys had stopped and felt there was an absence behind me. I stopped wrestling with the keyboard and the word processor, straightened my back, and turned around.

Yujŏng, with her mournful lyrics and solitary playing, was nowhere to be seen.

I ran out the front door to look for her. The corridor was filled with the ear-splitting din of children playing, but Yujŏng was not there.

"Yujŏng!"

Horrified, I ran down the stairs.

In the open square in front of the apartment complex, the daily "Respect the Elderly" celebration was going on. During the day, the huge, empty parking lot was a perfect place for recreation. Elderly residents of the complex were melancholy and unable to sleep at night if the square went unused. Thus, "parties" for them were arranged daily.

It was the height of spring, and sunlight poured gently onto the asphalt of the square. The senior citizens had put up a marquee, CHŎNNAM UNIVERSITY DEMOCRATIC ASSOCIATION, and were in the middle of playing a game.

Grandmothers were on one side, and grandfathers on the other. Yujŏng was on the side of the grandmothers. The women were tipsy and danced merrily about, and five-year-old Yujŏng was fluttering among them as innocently as a butterfly. When I called out to her, Yujŏng just stared at me blankly, without blinking an eye, and kept fluttering her hands. Then she fluttered toward me, every bit like a butterfly.

It was strange, but when the child's eyes gazed at me so innocently, I got all choked up inside. I held Yujŏng tightly on this spring day as sunlight poured warmly down my back.

My children played with Yujŏng in the noisy corridor of the apartment building. We'd been there for over a year now. When she was at home and not at day care, my older child, who is timid and weak-minded, refused to play anyplace in the corridor where our door was not in plain sight. Yujŏng, who was younger, and my second child had no choice but to play in the corridor with my older one. Even when it got dark, Yujŏng did not go home, but simply slept over. So I unexpectedly became a mother to three children.

It was a summer night, and rain was pouring down. After managing to put the kids to sleep, I went out to the balcony and quietly started to sing old songs. On rainy days I was sometimes comforted by singing songs from my childhood. It was probably only because it was raining, but I was feeling a little lost inside. I don't know if it was resignation or acceptance, but by that time I had almost begun to tolerate the big trucks massed in the apartment square. Without any animosity I stared at them parked in the rain. When I couldn't remember the words to a song, I hummed or made up my own words. As I gazed at the trucks, pushcarts, and covered carts, a feeling akin to sadness came over my heart. It was just then that the phone rang.

"Are the kids asleep?"

It was Hyŏnsun, Yujŏng's mom. We had become close, like sisters.

"Yeah."

"If they're asleep, why don't you come over to the bar."

"Why, are things slow again?"

"Things are slow, it's raining, and my mind's wandering—I don't think I can go home in this state."

I caught a cab outside my apartment building. Rain poured down heavily. On a night like this, even the upbeat hymn playing on the cab's radio made my heart ache.

Shedding our burden through God's grace,
even this world that is full of sorrow
will become like Heaven.
Alleluia.

Operating a business late at night was illegal, so the stairs leading to the underground bar called Sojŏng were dark. As soon as I walked in, the smell of alcohol and humidity swept over me. In the middle of the bar having drinks were two women: Hyŏnsun, the owner, and Miss Cho, an employee.

For someone who worked at a bar, Miss Cho could not drink very much. As soon as I sat down, she stood up.

"I'm going to go now. It doesn't look like there will be any customers anyway."

"That's fine."

Hyŏnsun gave cab fare to Miss Cho, who rose, the long skirt of her dress draping over the bottom half of her body. Because of her dress, I couldn't tell before she began walking that she was handicapped. The rippling folds of her skirt concealed a prosthetic limb. With Hyŏnsun's help, she climbed the stairs.

After seeing Miss Cho off, Hyŏnsun returned, sat down, and began to lament her lot in life. I didn't have a chance to ask about Miss Cho's crippled leg. Hyŏnsun was tormented by the pain of unrequited love, and I had to muster all the comforting words I could think of.

From a small room in the back of the bar Hyŏnsun brought out a drawing of a man. I couldn't tell if it was an accurate portrait or not. With thick curly hair and a high nose, the man in the picture resembled the ideal European—come to think of it, his well-defined ears, eyes, and nose resembled the features of Christ in religious paintings. Hyŏnsun tore up the picture that she had painstakingly drawn of her lover's face and started to cry.

That night, this forty-year-old woman who had twice failed in marriage cried while I, a thirty-three-year-old divorcée, struggled to find words to comfort her.

We left Sojŏng and raced by cab through the rainy streets to a dining place where we could buy *haejangguk,* the soup that soothes hangovers. The covered carts packed together in the rain in Kwangju Park had a strange air about them. Hyŏnsun suggested that we should go to a stand because the covered carts overcharged you, and it was annoying when it came time to pay. The proprietress of the stand was sleeping; she looked like the pig's head that lay on top of the bar counter beside her, its eyes closed. Hyŏnsun was no longer crying bitterly. She no longer talked of the lover who had betrayed her; instead we talked for the rest of the night about the election.

"In any case, Kim Dae Jung should be elected."

"What if he doesn't win?"

"Then we all have no choice but to bite our tongues off and die."

Hyŏnsun's brightly painted red lips moved impatiently as she spoke. It was summer, so it was odd to be talking about the election and politics. Looking back, I realized it had been a strange evening.

Though summer passed and autumn came, Hyŏnsun's business still did not seem to be doing well. When I discovered apartment 303's maintenance bill, which had been left unpaid in the lobby mailbox for three months, I was overcome with sadness. If Hyŏnsun didn't pay her bill, she could be sued under the house's eviction rules and regulations for "being delinquent with several payments for more than three months" or her apartment could be put up for sale.

My writing wasn't going well either. Since I couldn't write and wasn't able to find a job, I was in danger of falling into a similar predicament with my maintenance bill. Amidst these worries, the melancholy season of autumn arrived at the complex.

Oblivious of their mothers' economic woes, the children ran up and down the noisy corridor and played with all their might.

The rental complex was inhabited mostly by senior citizens and single mothers with children. Once a month the staff from each building distributed rice to "protected tenants"—the elderly—in a corner of the building. The old people stood solemnly in line, each person holding a rice sack. This scene reminded me of one of those books of documentary photographs taken during the Korean War, except the senior citizens in our rental complex were healthier and more robust-looking than the emaciated, worry-filled people in those photographs. Nevertheless, for a moment I felt as if I had gone back fifty years, to a time when I hadn't even been born yet. The old people in line survived on relief food—just as old people back then probably had. To the "protected tenants" of the rental complex, the 1990s probably didn't seem that much different from the 1950s. Not being a "protected tenant" myself, I had to make money with my own two hands to buy my daily food. I made up my mind to get a job and was on my way to inquire about a help-wanted ad in the regional newspaper when I brushed past the elderly receiving their rationed rice. Their line had formed where they could catch the warmth of the low autumn sun. I had calculated my household budget's Engel's Coefficient: the light and fuel payments (bills for heating and municipal gas), which were late; the bill for the telephone, which was on the verge of being disconnected; late fines; legal costs if action was taken because I couldn't make the back payments (something rare for the complex); and rent. This was the frightening reality of trying to survive.

When I arrived at the employment agency, the woman glanced at my haggard face and shapeless body and shook her head.

"Lady, you look like you should eat more protein, not just rice."

As I came out of the employment agency, my legs were trembling, perhaps from lack of protein.

That day I walked all over town on my shaking legs. Though I lived in the cheapest housing in all of Korea, not only was I unable to pay the rent, but I had even dared to complain about the noise. It wouldn't have been so bad if my complaints had remained just that, but I had had the audacity to try to gather signatures and make phone calls to people who didn't care. Unable to bear my loneliness and feeling sorry for myself, I walked around aimlessly. Maybe there was some point to this wandering because I ran into the neighborhood poet. When I used to live in a rented room in a neighborhood high up on the hill, the poet had lived next door. He had been a teacher originally but had been laid off during the National Teachers' Union strike and now spent his days writing poems.

The poet walked toward me on the cold, wind-swept road by the Kwangju riverbank, looking very much like a poet because of his melancholy face and the turned-up collar of his raincoat. Was it just because it was autumn?

The poet asked me where I was headed.

"I was trying to get a job, but they said that I can't because I don't have enough fat on my body."

"That's a difficult one. Don't you have to get a job first so you can put some fat on your body?"

"That's what I'm thinking."

"If that's the case, why don't I fatten you up a bit today."

Tired from wandering about on trembling legs, and seeing that it had turned dark without my realizing it, I accepted the poet's offer.

I don't know if the poet did this just to make sure I had enough to eat, but he ordered enough pork for two people and didn't eat any himself; he only sat with me and drank *soju.*

As I chewed, I became worried thinking about my children, who were as protein deficient as their mother. But I couldn't just leave, so I kept on chewing.

The poet spoke.

"You've got two stories published, both in the journal *Ch.*"

My shoulders involuntarily tensed.

"It's time you left Kwangju. The new generation—those in their twenties and thirties—aren't staying. For them, it's 'Still Kwangju? Why Kwangju?'"

The piece of meat I was chewing rolled around in my mouth like a stick of gum that had lost its sweetness.

After leaving the poet, I felt rather lonely. The right thing to do would have been to go home right away to apartment number 301, where my hungry kids were waiting for me. That was a mother's duty. No matter what the reason, to let young children who didn't know how to feed themselves go hungry was a crime.

Nonetheless, my fat restored, I wandered the streets—an immoral mother.

The leaves of the trees lining the street were falling in the cold autumn evening. How were we going to buy food in the coming winter months? Even creatures in the wild, mere animals, were making preparations for winter, but how was I going to buy food and warm clothes for my two children?

I saw a help-wanted notice at a textile factory that was recruiting housewives, but when I went in, the factory was in the middle of a strike, so they told me that they would contact me later. The person at the employment agency had said to come back after I'd fattened up a bit, and since I'd filled myself up with meat, I decided to go back there the next day. If they shook their heads, I'd have to pop open my stomach and show them how full it was. But there was no way to open up my stomach without killing myself. This dilemma was unbearable.

Hey, Hyŏnsun. Perhaps you can answer this. Is there a way to open up one's stomach without killing oneself? Just like the Rabbit standing before the emperor, I had to somehow slit open my stomach, or my children and I would starve. "You really think the Rabbit opened it up? All you need are wits and wisdom to survive."

I went to Hyŏnsun's bar, where she yelled at me, saying that my kids were to be pitied. She pulled my tired body into the back room of the bar.

"What's this for?" I asked, my eyes bulging at the sight of so much food.

"It's my birthday. This is all my daughter's doing."

That was when I found out that Hyŏnsun had a child older than Yujŏng.

"She can't speak or hear, but she's clever with her hands and she's got heart."

Hyŏnsun was starting to cry. Chandi, Hyŏnsun's daughter by her first husband, had come down from Seoul for her mother's birthday. She attended a high school for the disabled, which Hyŏnsun spoke very proudly of.

"What about school?"

"She's taking a few days off because she's not feeling well."

Even though she was suffering from a chronic fever, Chandi had painstakingly prepared her mother's birthday dinner and then had returned to the rental complex.

"Let me tell you what kind of girl Chandi is. I was ashamed of having a child by myself—without a husband—so I had gone into hiding in a village in the middle of nowhere, where the ghosts of the Kwangju Uprising are buried. I gave birth on the floor, but something was wrong: I couldn't stop bleeding. I lay there thinking that I was going to die. Chandi, who was only ten years old, went out in the middle of the night in a heavy rainstorm to a pharmacy ten *li* away. This child who can't speak or hear banged on that pharmacist's door with her feet and hands and managed to get some pain-killers. I took them and became unconscious. When I opened my eyes sometime later, she had her ear on my stomach, as if she was listening for something, checking to see if her mother was dead or alive."

I mumbled something about it being Hyŏnsun who was pitiful. I tried very hard not to cry, but since it's not my nature to hold back, I ended up crying anyway. No matter how tough you are, if you have the slightest bit of human feeling, how can you not cry after hearing such a story?

Hyŏnsun's daughters often move me, though I don't know exactly why: Yujŏng, who dances and flutters about, and Chandi, who is able to lay out a birthday dinner for her mother even though she can't speak or hear. If there's something wrong with one of a person's senses, usually another sense becomes more developed. Just as a blind person's sense of hearing or touch surpasses an average person's, Chandi's sense of taste seemed particularly developed, and she was also very good with her hands. Unable to speak or hear, she cooked and created all sorts of things with those hands.

It didn't seem like there would be many customers that night either. Hyŏnsun said that business was bad not because of her location or because she was inept but—she blurted this out after a few drinks—because the government was taxing people's savings.

"And since they make it illegal to run your business during the hours when customers really start drinking, people in remote places like this are suffering."

Hyŏnsun called out for Miss Cho. I realized then that I had completely forgotten Miss Cho was there. Not only did Miss Cho not drink, but she also didn't speak much. I shouted so that both Hyŏnsun and Miss Cho could hear:

"Hey, madame proprietress, do you really think you can do business with such a quiet waitress?"

Miss Cho slowly emerged from a corner behind drawn curtains. She wore a loose white dress that I had seen her in before. She walked toward me slowly and thrust out a glass. I poured a drink for her. She stared at the glass and then emptied it in one gulp. When she was done, she pushed the glass toward me. I accepted. There was something oddly serene about Miss Cho; her gestures were delicate and quiet.

It was very strange. Were the feelings I sensed in other people only a reflection of my own vulnerable emotions? I stared at the drink Miss Cho had poured for me and then I drank, just as Miss Cho had.

Good-for-nothings celebrating a good-for-nothing's birthday.

Hyŏnsun snapped her fingers and began chanting something that sounded like an old shaman's song. Amid the discordant sounds that she made, Miss Cho's own faint singing could be heard. Hyŏnsun kept pouring drinks for herself and carrying on while Miss Cho continued to sing.

. . . So, what if I got rid of this place and tried one of those singing bars?

What . . . you're saying that I can't have one of those singing whatevers with just a security deposit of one hundred and twelve per month?

It takes wisdom. Opening up your stomach to look inside without killing yourself. The wisdom to survive. Hyŏnsun, who had been talking to herself, abruptly raised her voice and started to sing a marching song.

. . . If those days in May should return, angry blood will pour from our hearts . . . that day in May . . .

The song was so unexpected that it startled Miss Cho and me, but since we knew it, we were obliged to sing along. We even pounded our feet while Hyŏnsun pounded her feet and swung her arms. Afraid that once we got to the end of this rousing song we would all be depressed, we sang with as much energy as possible.

"What's with the old song?"

Preoccupied with our singing, we hadn't noticed that someone had come in. We stopped singing and stared at the man standing in the bar's entrance. Hyŏnsun's eyes shone brightly, like those of a cat who has just spied some food.

"Look at me! I completely forgot about my business. Thanks to my daughter, I was letting off steam." In a split second, Hyŏnsun had put on the welcoming face of a bar proprietress. Slowly, Miss Cho stood up too.

The celebration was over. The only thing left for me to do was go home. Thinking of my poor, starving kids, I got choked up, and as I did, my legs buckled. Forgive me my sins, O God of Drinking. I finished my drink with a contrite heart and stood up.

I raised my hand to take leave of Hyŏnsun, thinking that this was how things always ended up: I was always saying good-bye.

"Hey lady, it's illegal to be operating your business this late at night."

"What do you mean illegal? When did having a birthday party with your sisters become illegal?"

"Hey, you there trying to leave! Come back down."

The man's use of impolite speech annoyed me. I stopped climbing the stairs and turned around.

"It's one o'clock in the morning! If you're going to stay open illegally, at least turn off your sign, put the shutter down, close the curtains, and be quiet about it—who do you think you are?"

The man was not a customer but a policeman out to enforce the curfew, and it looked as if Hyŏnsun, Miss Cho, and I would be hung with the same rope.

There was no way to prove that the bar wasn't operating illegally. I slumped down on the stairs, fearing that now I wouldn't be able to go home to my poor kids at all. The policeman told us to follow him.

"Hey you, you'll have to come along as well."

Though the policeman used polite speech with Hyŏnsun and Miss Cho, he used impolite speech with me, even though I wasn't the one who had been illegally operating her business at night. If I had been, there probably wouldn't have been any customers. While I was annoyed with the policeman for making Hyŏnsun out to be a criminal when she was merely keeping her lights on late at night, I was especially annoyed at the way he was speaking to me. That's why I didn't get up. Hyŏnsun came to my defense.

"She's my sister—she came to wish me a happy birthday."

Because the policeman had used impolite speech with me, Hyŏnsun spoke impolitely to him.

"Is there any proof she's your sister?"

"If I say that she's my sister, she's my sister. And she's a writer at that."

At this, the policeman's brows, which had been furrowed in anger, rose in complete mockery.

"Why don't you name some of the titles of your books?"

I was used to restraining myself when mad—even when I wanted to spit in someone's face—so I quietly stared back into the policeman's mocking face, remaining composed enough even to smile. Hyŏnsun again spoke up for me.

"She's written a respectable novel—a suspense story. It's called *The End of Love,* and it's going to be published soon."

Though Hyŏnsun didn't know what kinds of things I wrote, she knew that I played around with writing—but since she'd never read my work, she had to make things up. The policeman's anger subsided, almost as if Hyŏnsun's explanation had convinced him. It looked like he might be willing to ease up on her. The writer of *The End of Love* rose from the stairs where she'd slumped and left the bar.

As I walked through the door, the bar's neon sign blinked out. The illegal night operation had now truly begun. I checked the cab fare that Hyŏnsun had thrust into my hand, raised my poverty-stricken arm, and waved frantically toward a cab coming my way.

I was thirsty. It was unbearable: the heartburn and thirst came over me all at once. The discomfort became so unbearable that I turned on the light. Tonight, four kids were sleeping at my house: Yujŏng, Chandi, and my two little ones. Their sprawled bodies formed an elaborate diagonal shape, with Chandi as the focal point and the kids spread out around her. This was how kids whose mother led a fast life looked. Nausea, along with heartburn, climbed up my parched throat. After glancing at the sprawling kids, I muttered some profanities and went down the hall, into the kitchen. I tilted the water kettle over a glass, but despite the steep angle, no water came out of it. There was no water in the refrigerator either. There was no tea, so I turned on the cold-water faucet. *Garrgh.* A coughing sound was all that came out of the spout. Were there plumbing repairs going on somewhere? There had been water that morning, but now nothing. I turned on the hot-water faucet, and water gushed out. I had no choice—I drank it. Hot water is still water. It didn't help my thirst, but my heartburn was a bit better.

That's about the time water rationing began, due to the drought. Oddly enough, despite the restrictions, hot water continued to come out of the tap every day.

The sound of flowing water from the apartment below started about the same time. Every other day, when we didn't get cold water, there was no sound. But on the days that cold water flowed out of the faucet, the rushing of a waterfall came from below. Night and day without fail, I could hear the water running in apartment 201.

At first I couldn't stand the sound, but I tried to bear it. Hadn't it been the same with the car noise? When you put up with an annoyance and just get on with your life, it somehow disappears, as though you had become numb to it. I tried to regard the water noise in the same way. The owner must have gone out and forgotten to shut off the faucet on a day when the cold water hadn't been turned off. But the owner would surely return soon. Every day I told myself, "I only have to endure it for a day." Soon, a month had gone by. I had been hearing the waterfall noise every other day for thirty days.

Autumn passed quickly, and winter came. Though the season changed, the water noise didn't. Finally, I called the apartment-building office. In an urgent tone—and biting my lips and regretting that I hadn't reported it sooner—I said, "There's a noise of running water. The noise is one thing, but the water's also being wasted."

I could not get the words "Perhaps there's been some sort of accident there" out of my mouth. There couldn't have been such an accident—surely not.

But the reply from the office was unperturbed.

"There's nothing we can do if the door's locked. When the occupant returns, please give him or her a good scolding."

Wait until the occupant comes home and then "give him or her a good scolding"? I rang the doorbell of 202, the apartment next to 201.

"Do you know where the occupant of 201 went?"

"Come to think of it, I haven't seen her around lately."

"Does she live alone?"

"Yes, she's a 'protected tenant.'"

Hearing the words "protected tenant" from the woman in 202 made my hair stand on end. But I hid my emotions.

Like a detective I asked, "Is there somewhere she could have gone?"

"Well, let's see, she did say that she had a daughter somewhere. Maybe she went there. Why do you ask?"

"You know how they shut off the water every other day? Well, on days the water's turned on, there's a noise like a waterfall in 201 and it doesn't stop."

"Do you live upstairs?"

"Yes."

"Then it's really not your business to be worrying about it. Why don't you report it to the office?"

"All right."

I had no choice but to climb the stairs toward my apartment, my shoulders drooping like those of a begging puppy dog. I called the office again, just as the woman in 202 had told me to, but the reply was the same as before: there's nothing we can do, so let's just wait until the occupant returns and then reprimand him or her. It made me mad, but I said all right and hung up. In effect, they were saying that they didn't care whether or not a person was dead.

An elderly tenant has died at the rental complex. She was discovered a few months after she died by a woman living upstairs who became suspicious of the constant noise of running water coming from her apartment.

The water is loud. And it's being wasted in this drought. These words came to me easily. But for some reason I could not get the really important words—that perhaps someone might be dead—out of my mouth.

While I struggled with the problem of the water noise, Hyŏnsun was sent to jail—and incurred a huge debt at the same time. One day, two pretty young girls had come looking for work at her bar, saying that they had to pay off their ailing father's medical bills and their brother's school expenses. "Is that so? Isn't that admirable?" Hyŏnsun had said. Frankly, she was desperate to attract business, so she advanced them the sizable sum of money that they had asked for and put them to work. But that very day she got caught in a raid. The girls disappeared with the money, and Hyŏnsun was put in handcuffs and charged with employing underaged kids.

I went to visit her. She was wearing a blue prisoner's uniform and rubber shoes, and I complained to her at length about the water noise, even though she was, in her own words, "in debt, out of business, humiliated, and turned into a con because of the crime of not knowing that those girls were damned underaged kids!"

"How's our Miss Cho doing?"

It was then that I realized I hadn't seen Miss Cho even once.

"She's probably doing fine. She can't be worse off than you."

"No, her boyfriend died the other day. She was crying when she came to visit me."

"Of course she'd cry because of her boyfriend. But soon she'll start dating someone new."

"It would be all right if it were as simple as that. But for her, it's not."

"What do you mean?"

"Her boyfriend was in the citizens' army during Kwangju. After he got out of prison, he got sicker and sicker over the next ten years, and then just died, even though he was still young. She lives in apartment 914. Go visit her for me and comfort her."

Because we talked so much about Miss Cho and her dead boyfriend, we ended up not really being able to talk about ourselves.

"So, did Miss Cho hurt her leg that May?"

"No. She said that it happened in an accident. She lost both her parents and one of her legs in a train accident. Before she moved to the apartment, she was living by the railroad tracks. When the security guard at our building introduced us, she didn't seem very lively, but I hired her anyway because it was a pitiful sight to watch her struggling to survive. She then started dating her boyfriend, but he didn't seem very healthy either—physically or mentally. Miss Cho's also responsible for two younger siblings."

I had no choice but to take care of Yujŏng while Hyŏnsun was in jail. According to Hyŏnsun, five-year-old Yujŏng was just big for her age—bigger than my seven-year-old. But her size made people suspicious. When a notice came requiring me to enroll my daughter in school, I told Hyŏnsun about it and she confessed that Yujŏng was actually old enough to start school.

"What should I do?" she asked. "I didn't even put her on the census register."

"Whose last name are you going to use?"

"Her father's last name is Pak, but since there's no way of locating him, there's no choice but to use my name. Hey, that works out perfectly. My Chandi's father's last name is Kim, so her last name is Kim. I'm also a Kim, so Yujŏng is also a Kim."

Hyŏnsun was so pleased with herself that she began to kick up her feet.

Since Yujŏng had been transformed from a Pak into a Kim, Hyŏnsun decided to give her daughter a new first name as well. On the spot she came up with a given name as well as a family name to be put on the school register: Kim Hyanga.

Hyanga. Hyanghang. I left the jail and went into a bar called Hyanghang, whose sign had caught my eye. I couldn't tell whether my stomach was upset or my heart was aching, but in any case I sensed that the burning feeling inside would dissipate only when I had a drink. So I forced myself to drink two bottles of *makkŏli.* In the bar Hyanghang—Hong Kong—I imagined I really was in Hong Kong. I saw Hyanga smiling on a Hong Kong pier.

The next day, I took a letter of attorney in Hyŏnsun's name—which I myself had written up—and went to the town office with the late fee of 50,000 *wŏn* and registered Kim Hyanga for a certificate of residence.

As a result, I forgot all about Miss Cho. I didn't mean to forget about her, but I did. And then I twisted my ankle and had to lay in bed for two days.

How did I sprain my ankle? It had to do with the water noise. It was loud. I clenched my teeth, telling myself I could live with it just as I could live with the noise of cars and trucks. Let's say that the noise was bearable.

But what about the water being wasted, running down the drain in this drought and nothing being done about it? After a while I couldn't stand it. The amount of water being wasted was at least a day's worth of water used by the whole apartment building. I was sure it wasn't less. On days that the water was turned on, it gushed on and on without ceasing.

Was it really the water being wasted that caused me to act? The truth is that I wanted to go in there . . . yes.

The old woman was probably dead—most of her body probably rotted away by now. I wanted to show the Korea Housing Corporation civil servants—are they civil servants or not?—the grisly sight of the old woman's body. *Should a person just wait around for the occupant to return when something like this happens? Don't you people have parents? An old woman is dead, and all you can say is there's nothing we can do except wait?! Just like you people to let a person die!*

Since the front door of the old woman's apartment was locked, I tied a rope to the iron railing of my balcony, thinking that I'd enter through the sliding glass door on the balcony. If the glass door wasn't open, I would break the window. I would go in and then show the old woman's body to the heartless civil servants in the building office. And I'd give *them* a severe reprimand. *Do you people think you can continue to collect maintenance fees for the apartment building when you let things like this happen? What do you mean by charging people security fees when you don't care whether or not someone dies?*

Maybe it was because I'd had a few drinks at Hyanghang: my mind, confused from the alcohol, compelled me to remember my code of ethics. I had no choice but to lower myself on that rope to the floor below. People should not be heartless. We shouldn't have to live in a world so bleak that people don't want to hear about a dying neighbor.

Someone whistled from below.

"Hey you! You a burglar?"

I lost my grip on the rope and fell onto the grass below. That night, even though I wasn't a burglar attempting to rob an empty apartment, I had become a rope thief. Without getting permission from the maintenance office, I had taken the rope from the basement.

The day after I got hurt, I went to register Kim Hyanga for school. The pain was bearable that day, but after that, my ankle began to throb and swell. So I lay in bed for the following two days.

When a person is lying down, sleep comes easily. Foolishly, like a cow, I simply waited for the swelling to go down. I thought that after a nap it would probably be better without my even knowing. Then I opened my eyes. I looked down at my ankle. The swelling remained the same. I started to feel disappointment, but then I noticed that there had been a change of another kind, so I didn't need to feel disappointed after all. The water noise. I looked at the clock. It was one in the afternoon. It was time for the water to be on, but there was no sound. There had been a reason after all for my spraining my ankle. My foot still hurt, but I wanted to go to the balcony to see if the second-floor's sliding door was open. If it was open, then they had probably discovered the old woman's body. I was just about to stand up when the interphone rang.

"Someone just died. Can you please come down and identify the body?"

I forgot all about the pain in my ankle. I rushed down to the second floor and tried to open the door to apartment 201. But it would not open, and there was no one in the second-floor corridor. Instead, people were gathering behind the apartment building. There the wind was gusting, and the snow that had fallen the day before had not yet melted. Shaded by the building, the area was terribly bleak. People stood in the cold.

The body was frozen blue. I saw that the moisture that had collected on its lower half was turning into ice, coating the prosthetic leg.

I was unable to get near the body. The police had come and would not allow anyone to approach it. Miss Cho was turning blue on the cement ground in the cold shade where not a bit of sun shone. People gazed at the body from a distance, as if across the space between death and life. Just as the dead body was freezing, so were the living.

A few days after Miss Cho died, I saw the old woman from 201 purely by chance. As I entered the lobby, she was standing there holding her heavy bags and receiving a severe scolding from a security guard.

"If you're going somewhere, let us know, and if you don't want to inform us, then make sure that things are in order before you go out. The water kept on running so that we had to mobilize a ladder, just like in the civilian-defense drills!"

The old woman kept bowing her head, like someone who had committed a serious crime.

"Let me carry that for you," I said.

The old woman smiled, her lips pursed.

"Did you go somewhere far?"

"My daughter just had a baby. I was with her to help celebrate the baby's first Hundred Days."

The old woman stopped in front of apartment 201. "Thank you," she mumbled meekly with a toothless smile. I turned around without saying a word.

As I turned to go to my apartment, something warm gushed out of my eyes for no reason. Not knowing why the person who had carried her bags was crying all of a sudden, the old woman became flustered, as if she had been the cause of my tears. I climbed the stairs. I passed the third floor where Hyŏnsun's and my apartments were and kept going up. I had made up my mind to finally go up to the ninth floor, where Miss Cho had lived. As always, the stairwell was filled with echoing noises, and just as often everyone endured them. I pushed through the noise and climbed the stairs. My tears dried as I climbed.

The door to 914 was shut tight, so I rang the doorbell of 913. At first I thought that the man who poked his head out of 913 was really short, but that wasn't the case. The lower half of his body had been amputated. He opened the door and with both of his hands pushed the top half of his body outside as if riding a sled.

"Is there anyone next door?"

"The young woman's siblings, but they went out. They'll be back at night."

The man in 913 was holding an iron rod that he seemed to use to open the door since he couldn't reach the doorknob. I felt really bad for ringing the doorbell—I hadn't known who was inside—and fumbled to help him shut the door. As he disappeared inside, the man bowed, and I heard him pushing what was left of his body into a living space of twelve feet square.

I stood in front of the locked door of Miss Cho's apartment, where she no longer lived, then looked at the door of the apartment next to hers, which had to be opened and closed with an iron rod, and then stared at the ground below: the patch of cement that Miss Cho had surely chosen in advance as the place where she would land. I was dizzy. Was it acrophobia? I heard a ringing in my head that was distinct from the traffic noise. Miss Cho's voice. I felt as if her hard plastic leg was nudging me in the back. If there's a crime, it's to still be alive, to have survived. A bitter cold blew against me from behind. I grasped the railing in the corridor so that another wrong wouldn't occur. Just then, the door of 913 suddenly opened, and the cripple was sitting there and glaring at me. No, in his own way he was standing. The blue muscles of his arms, as he pushed himself up from the floor, were shaking.

He glared at me and shouted, "Don't do something stupid! Even I keep on living! Even someone like me is still living!"

I came down from the ninth floor as if I were being chased. The cripple kept on screaming from above, "Go down, keep going down! Go down and live! Do whatever it takes to live! Live even if you have to crawl on the ground!"

I visited Hyŏnsun in jail. She had told me she was hemorrhaging again, so I took some thick sanitary pads to her. I reported the registration of Kim Hyanga and told her about Miss Cho's death. As was her habit when she suffered trauma or felt deep sorrow, she twisted her lips and opened wide her already large eyes.

"It's *—ing,*" she said.

"What?"

"The present progressive form."

"What is?"

"Even if we want to stop talking about it, stop covering it up, stop crying about it, stop it all, we can't. That's how history is. The reform of 1894 doesn't exist on its own, and neither does what happened in 1919. In the same way, the Kwangju Uprising doesn't exist by itself either. Just as the March First Independence Movement of 1919 is connected with the 1992 Independence Movement, the Kwangju Uprising of 1980 begins again as the Kwangju Uprising in 1993. History is a specter. It latches onto the people who are connected to certain events, and it even drags off those who just happen to know those people. When an unconnected person encounters a connected person, she unexpectedly gets eaten up by that voracious specter. There's not one free person in history. That's just how it is."

Hyŏnsun kept on saying, "That's how it is." I was starting to get tired of her saying that, so I shouted at her, "That's not it! Miss Cho died because Kim Dae Jung wasn't elected. Why do you complicate such a simple thing? You've no right to. You're just a corrupt merchant who employed underaged kids."

I ranted and raved senselessly at Hyŏnsun, who sat there in her blue prisoner's uniform. Words jostled against each other in my mouth.

"Don't talk about history when you yourself are just a corrupt merchant who employed underaged kids. You have no right to talk about history. Why do you have to start with death? History continues because we live. We mustn't die. Nothing can be done through death, and nothing can be connected through it."

Hyŏnsun didn't get mad at my senseless shouting. There wasn't time to get mad. Hyŏnsun got mad at not having time to get really mad, and I got mad because I hated myself for getting mad for no reason. Visiting hours were almost over, so Hyŏnsun spoke fast.

"Is Kim Dae Jung her grandfather or something?"

"You said so yourself that if Kim Dae Jung didn't become president, we should all bite our tongues off and die."

"I just meant that we should be *prepared* to die. Why should we kill ourselves—for whose benefit?"

Spring has come again. The noise that seemed to pierce the eardrum and bore into the brain continues as always. Hyŏnsun's sentence was reduced to a fine, but she's still serving time because she has no money to pay it. The drought is still not over.

"Due to the water shortage, we will be increasing the number of 'shut-off days' for water rationing from every other day to three days at a time, so please be advised."

I rush to fill up a basin with water. It is strange. My thirst continues no matter how much water I drink. I dunk my head inside the tub and drink like mad. A warm fluid flowing from my eyes mixes with the cold water. I keep my head submerged to hide this. The kids come home.

"Mom. Don't wash your face in there! We have to drink that water for three days!"

"You're right. Sorry."

I raise my head. I can't have my children drink this water mixed with tears. I discard the half-filled tub to fill it again. But the faucet has already started to cough. The moment I try to refill the tub, the water is shut off. My daughter yells at me.

"Why did you throw the water away? See, now there's no more coming out!"

The child is about to cry. I rush to her to try and calm her down.

The children leave me flustered and run out into the corridor. Before long, I hear them shouting. The sun pours down relentlessly onto the apartment square, where the protected tenants are enjoying themselves again.

It is the height of spring, when everything is resplendent in all of its glory, and just when I am about to go down there—thinking that maybe I too should dance among them and contemplating whether an era of civilian government for a respectable "new Korea" is truly beginning—I see massive container trucks arriving at full speed, forcing the protected tenants who were having a good time to scatter in a flurry.

Translation by Susie Jie Young Kim

Piazza Tipica, Firenze, 1996
Photograph by Paul Kodama

MARIO BENEDETTI

The Expression

Milton Estomba had been a child prodigy. When he was seven years old, he could already play Brahms's Sonata Op. 5, No. 3, and when he was eleven, his concert tour throughout major cities in the U.S. and Europe was accompanied by unanimous public and critical acclaim.

However, when he became twenty years old, one could see that the young pianist had undergone a transformation. He had started to become inordinately preoccupied with pompous gestures, the ostentatious look on his face, his frown, his ecstatic eyes, and other such related effects. He called all of this his "expression."

Little by little, Estomba started specializing in expressions. He had one for playing "Pathetic," one for "Girls in the Garden," and another for "Polonaise." Although he rehearsed in front of the mirror before every concert, the frenetic, addicted public nevertheless regarded his expressions as spontaneous and would welcome them with loud applause, cries of "Bravo!" and feet stomping.

The first disturbing symptom appeared during a Saturday recital. The audience realized something strange was happening, and their applause was eventually infiltrated by an incipient stupor. The truth was that Estomba had played *Submerged Cathedral* with the "expression" for the *Turkish March.*

Six months later, a catastrophe occurred that was diagnosed by doctors as lacunal amnesia. The lacuna in question concerned scores. In the span of twenty-four hours, Milton Estomba forgot, forever, how to play all the nocturnes, preludes, and sonatas that had been notable in his wide repertoire.

What is amazing, really amazing, was that he didn't forget any of the pompous and ostentatious gestures that had accompanied every one of his interpretations. Although he could never give a piano concert again, there was some consolation. To this day, on Saturday nights his most loyal friends still meet at his house to attend silent recitals of his expressions. The unanimous opinion among his friends is that his *capolavoro* is the "Appossionata."

Translated from the Spanish by Harry Morales

YI CH'ŎNGJUN

An Assailant's Face

1

From late June to September 1950, the eighth-grade boy attended K Junior High and lived with his married sister in Hyehwa-dong. On three separate occasions during those months, people came to their house looking for his brother-in-law. Even if his brother-in-law had wanted to escape danger, he couldn't have avoided being captured and dragged away by these people—except for the last visitor, whose purpose and circumstances differed from the others'. For a time, all had been part of P Federation, so they all knew each other's motives and circumstances. The first and second groups came to arrest their former comrade in order to have him serve their factions. Perhaps it was best that the boy's brother-in-law left with the first group, thus speeding up the process that was inevitably headed toward disaster. However, the boy and his sister had no idea that that would be the last time they saw him.

The boy's brother-in-law had graduated from O professional college at the end of the Japanese colonial period and immediately afterwards had taken a teaching position at J Junior High. During that time, his ideological beliefs had inclined toward the left, and after Liberation on August 15, he had become a member of the left-leaning national teachers' organization. There were times when he had been more enthusiastic about political organizing than teaching. But after the formation of the Republic of Korea government in 1948, the political climate was no longer favorable for leftist activities. Furthermore, the brother-in-law's youthful enthusiasm for socialism had cooled. To mark the end of that part of his life, he had publicly signed an oath, pledging that "he repented his past mistakes and would work for the newly established democratic government with all his might." He had done this in a desperate attempt to protect himself, and had joined the right-wing organization called P Federation for the same reason. Afterwards, he had joined a campaign encouraging people with similar pasts to join the P Federation. Then he had returned to his old teaching job. For about two years he kept a low profile, and nothing major happened. Finally, the incident occurred that June.

The boy's brother-in-law was in a state of confusion and could make neither heads nor tails of what was happening around him. The morning of June 26, when the people from P Federation came to the brother-in-law, the boy and his sister thought it was to protect him and help him escape from the predicament he was in. Early that morning, rumors had begun to spread that recent developments at the battlefront were unfavorable for the South Korean government.

"Comrade Kim," the people from P Federation asserted, "how can we just sit here and watch when the country is in danger? We've decided to fight for the government even if it's from behind the front lines. So, let's go to our meeting place now. Don't we all have a history of recanting? You know very well that our recantations are unforgivably treasonous in the eyes of the leftists. If the battle takes a wrong turn, this is the only way to survive. We mustn't miss this opportunity to show our allegiance!"

Their concern seemed genuine, expressed out of loyalty to a comrade, so the brother-in-law had no reason to doubt what they said. That's probably why he readily left with them. When the next group of people from P Federation arrived, intending to cover up their own recantations by accusing the boy's brother-in-law of being a traitor, the boy's sister was glad that her husband had already gone south.

This second group appeared near dusk on June 27, before the North Korean army crossed Miari Pass. They were fundamentally different from the first group. There were still many people in Seoul who had received the federation's protection in return for recanting their leftist positions, even though these pledges were only a formality. However, when the war broke out, people like the ones in this second group resumed their original colors and waited in secret for the North Korean army to march into Seoul. Perhaps this was their way of protecting themselves in the event of a lightning attack by the North that would make them vulnerable to retribution. At the first sound of the North Korean artillery, they frantically began hunting for "traitors" to scapegoat.

It was the night before the South Korean army retreated across the Han River. "This is traitor Kim's house, right?"

As if Seoul already belonged to their side, they did not even bother to hide their motives. From the beginning they were bloodthirsty, as if in search of a criminal. When they found out that their quarry had already fled south, they ground their teeth in spite.

"That bastard didn't recant for his own protection or to go undercover. He recanted ideologically!" exclaimed one.

"That's why he was able to go back to his old teaching job. He's a traitor of the People! But then, how far can he run?" said another.

Without capturing the boy's brother-in-law, they left, and his wife shuddered. She was relieved that her husband had chosen to go with the first group, and the boy, too, felt that that choice was a hundred or even a thousand times better. But it soon became evident that their sense of relief and hope had no foundation.

Eventually, Seoul fell under the enemy's control. There was no other news from the boy's brother-in-law. Since it was impossible to send him a message, the boy and his sister could only pray that he had escaped and gone farther south. That was what they wanted to believe. Then a rumor began to circulate that caused them to despair.

"It's being said that the P Federation people who went south all died before crossing the Han River," the boy's sister reported to him after she had gone out to check the word on the street. She had heard the news from one of the families of a P Federation member in a similar predicament.

"Their coming to our house, you know, was actually the preliminary arrest or something like that. That's why they took your brother-in-law. It's like the losing side setting fire to war supplies or barracks so that nothing will fall into the hands of the enemy—even people . . . They couldn't arrest everyone in such a chaotic situation. But since your brother-in-law had recanted, they thought he was unreliable . . ."

The boy's sister seemed to give up on her husband a few days after she heard this news. Perhaps she was more concerned with the imminent danger of being a family member of a reactionary, and the severe glances that it brought from the red-armband gang.

"I think your brother-in-law may be dead," she told the boy. "I don't trust every word they say, but I think it's true that when the Han River bridge was destroyed, many people like your brother-in-law got hurt. There were dead bodies everywhere around the West Gate—not only in prisons and police stations but in schools and chapels, too."

For a few days she went around the west side of Seoul, looking for traces of her husband, or his corpse. One day, she suddenly said to the boy, "It was your brother-in-law's fate when he followed the first group without really knowing what was going on, right? No matter what, death awaited him. He would've met the same fate even if he had stayed at home . . . So, from now on we have to start thinking about the future and how we're going to get through this crisis."

After that she stopped looking for her husband. The red-armband gang became more active, and with their encouragement she began following the wartime mobilization camp. She endlessly repeated her conviction that her husband's recanting and his joining the federation had been a ploy to save his life or he had been forced against his will to recant. As if she were avenging her husband's sacrifice, she worked at the labor camp enthusiastically, like a heroic warrior for the People. However, the strange story of the boy's brother-in-law did not end there.

After a long July and August had passed, the sound of artillery again started to come from the West Gate. In the early hours of dawn one day, the invaders were preparing to retreat when they were pursued by the

South Korean soldiers who had come to reclaim Seoul. That night, when the boy's sister went to work at the mobilization camp and the boy was left shivering and alone in the house in Hyehwa-dong, someone knocked carefully but impatiently on the window. This was the third time after the war had started that someone from P Federation came to the house. But this person didn't come in search of the boy's brother-in-law. In fact, it was a young man who was in a similar predicament to that of the brother-in-law; and even though he was on the run, he had come to the house to relay a message.

The boy had hastily opened the front gate before he knew who the man was. The young man looked anxious and frightened as he quickly came through the gate. When the man learned that there was no one else in the house, he said to the young boy, "I was with your brother-in-law. I was with him until recently. He is still alive." Then he incoherently told the boy, as if pleading for help, about the predicament that both he and the brother-in-law were in.

"I don't know what's going to happen to your brother-in-law now. I was a captive like him, and that's why I escaped. Your brother-in-law and I were captured by the people from the North. We were compelled to do hard labor around the suburbs of Seoul. But recently the situation changed, so we knew we would be killed on a forced march to the North or be massacred here . . . We couldn't just wait for that to happen."

The essence of the young man's rambling explanation was that the boy's brother-in-law was still alive somewhere in Seoul—a prisoner of the people from the North, but now faced with being either exiled in the North or executed.

"Your brother-in-law and I promised each other that whoever escaped first from the grip of those bastards would relay a message to the other person's family. So, I got the chance to escape first. I risked my life to get away and come here."

After he had said this much, he carefully examined the alley outside the door and looked for traces of others inside the house, as if he didn't believe there was no one else home. Recalling the horrible experience of his escape made him tremble. The boy could guess how dangerous the situation was, but he did not know what he could do for his brother-in-law, and the young man did not spell out the kind of help that he himself needed. Instead, the man simply hesitated, as if he still had something to say to the boy.

"You don't need to know where your brother-in-law is at this moment, and even if you knew, it would be of no use. We never stayed in one place for very long. If they are still on the move, it is good for your brother-in-law," the young man said.

The boy nevertheless felt the need to ask where his brother-in-law was, and this clearly annoyed the young man. The only thing the boy could do was hope for his brother-in-law to escape, and the young man's mission seemed to be to instill this kind of hope in the boy.

Having delivered his message, it was at last time for the man to go. The boy grew impatient, knowing that because he and his sister were considered a reactionary family, their house was under constant surveillance. He had neither the time nor the maturity to fully comprehend the young man's behavior. Outside there were sounds of people being chased. In this situation, it was easy to get hurt or killed. Having a fugitive inside the house was like inviting death. Moreover, it was getting light outside. The young man would have to leave the house soon, before anyone caught sight of him, but he continued to hesitate as if he still had more to say.

"So, that time . . . around late June, I went to P Federation and . . ."

He ignored the boy's nervousness, adding explanations as he continued to glance around the house, uneasy and impatient, as if he were waiting for another person to arrive.

"Soon our retreat to Seoul became impossible, so we moved our camp toward the Map'o area of the Han River. I can't be certain, but I believe the original plan was to evacuate us south of the river. We all believed that. Do you understand what I'm saying? But then, I found out later that the P Federation members we had left behind in the areas of Miari and Tongdaemun had suddenly begun to welcome the North Korean troops marching into Seoul. Without knowing what was going on, we were divided into a small group of five or six people, and as a temporary measure we were then divided into even smaller groups. We were incarcerated in prison cells and in government and public offices; sometimes churches or classrooms . . . You understand? And from then on, we were treated like criminals and kept with prisoners who had been captured before us. I don't know whether this treatment was planned from the beginning or whether it happened because of a misunderstanding. There was a rumor that a very large number of P Federation people were executed at once. Can you understand me?"

As if wanting to impress something into the boy's mind, he kept repeating "Can you understand me?" He also seemed to be trying to delay his departure by including lengthy and elaborate details.

"So, I met your brother-in-law when a larger group was divided and we were put in the same group in a chapel cellar somewhere. And from then on we were together. Two of the federation people in the cellar were taken out, and there was no sign of them afterward. Can you understand me? We were simply waiting our turn to die. Then from somewhere we heard an explosion that shook the earth. We called out, but no one came to get us. We learned later that the Han River bridge had been destroyed and our captors had run away to save their own lives. Can you understand me? But even then we didn't know what had happened . . . Well, even if we had known, there wasn't a place where we could find refuge. We were trembling with fear. It was only with the North Koreans' help, after they entered Seoul, that we were able to see daylight again. Can you understand this? Can you?"

Since the boy kept silent, the young man became even more impatient, fidgeting and repeating "Can you understand?" as if he were pleading for the boy's help. Nonetheless, the boy felt that there was nothing he could do, so nothing registered in his head. The boy became more agitated as time passed, because the man looked as if he had completely forgotten about the imminent danger. His elaborate explanation seemed to have lost its main point, and the boy became annoyed. But he could not stop the man from speaking or ask him to leave the house, or push him out the door. He had to wait for him to finish his story or realize that he was in danger and leave the house of his own accord. The boy fretted in silence. Slowly, the man's voice began to lose vitality, as if he at last sensed the boy's wish.

"Because of what they considered to be our traitorous recantations and our answering of the federation's call for mobilization, we were branded enemies of the People—reactionaries who couldn't easily be forgiven . . . Fortunately we still had some use, so we were sent to a labor camp under the pretext of reeducation training and self-criticism. So, we were able to survive until now. But the wind changed again and we became entangled in another kind of deathtrap . . . Can you understand this?"

The man again repeated "Can you understand?" but this time it wasn't intended to urge the boy to do something. As if he had given up on getting a response from the boy, he averted his eyes. For the last time, he glanced around the house for any trace of another person.

"OK, remember what I said and tell your sister. I trust you, so I'll go now. Bye. Take good care of yourself, understand?"

Unexpectedly, he bade farewell, leaving his last few words to the boy unclear. He rushed out to the street, where dawn was breaking and people were beginning to come and go.

2

The boy grew up and became a professor. He got married around the same time he began teaching. Every time he reminisced with his wife about the hardships he had experienced during the war, he would finish with the story of his brother-in-law.

"So, it was like both sides were chasing after my brother-in-law to kill him. Paradoxically, that helped him stay alive a little longer. The first federation group, in fact, saved him from being killed outright by the second group. Then, when he was trapped by the first group, the second group came and, in a way, rescued him. So, it was like a rabbit being pursued by two eagles: in the midst of their fighting over the rabbit, he was able to survive . . ."

But the professor had long ago given up hoping that his brother-in-law and the young man might still be alive. And it seemed there was nothing more to say about either of them: the young man who had set out on a dangerous and unplanned escape, or his brother-in-law, who had been heading north, towards his own execution.

"I figured out later that the young man had no place to hide in Seoul, so he couldn't have survived the bloodstained path he was on that dawn. My brother-in-law, dragged away and entangled in the chains of death, couldn't have survived either. After that there was no more news from either one of them. That was common at the time. Either my brother-in-law got killed trying to get away, or remained in their clutches and was executed. Even if he was lucky enough to avoid execution and go to the North, the result might have well been the same. He would've died, either from hunger or from the bombing. If he or the other man had survived, don't you think there would've been some trace of them when Seoul was reclaimed, or when the South Korean army marched to the North? But there was no news after that. Later, my sister searched all over the city, hoping to find his body. She was relieved that his corpse didn't turn up, but then she waited endlessly for news of him . . ."

He shuddered at the dreadful memories and seemed to be relieved that he himself had survived the chaos without much suffering.

"People who discuss class consciousness and ideology usually like to talk about that time, drawing a line and saying this side was like this and that side was like that. But there was no such choice for my brother-in-law and for that young man. On either side, death waited for them. Being on one side or the other usually means you have made some kind of choice, but for them there was no choice. To pick up a gun and pledge to die for a certain camp—that's one thing. But for them it was like struggling to get out of a deathtrap that surrounded them on all sides. Someone like myself, who was fortunate enough to survive and probably did not comprehend the full extent of the situation, can only shudder. Despite it all, I'm thankful for my fortune and good luck."

But gradually his feelings of being lucky to have survived that chaotic time without much pain began to change. Even before his newlywed years were over, the professor's friends—who were in their midthirties—started one by one to die. And every time someone died, he would be in distress, grieving and sighing.

"That war didn't take the spirits of only the dead. Although I wasn't very old at the time and was lucky enough to escape danger, I was also severely wounded by the experience. People like me received injuries that cannot be healed easily. I think those who died early were the ones who couldn't endure those invisible wounds. I often feel a kind of abject despair for no reason—like I'm losing my life's energy and spirit."

After the April 19 student revolution, the university students shouted, "Let's go to North Korea and embrace the people there and weep!" For the first time, the professor had the students who visited his home sit down while he stood in the middle of them and expressed his opposition to their ideas.

"You don't know the North's political system and haven't experienced how their ideology works. Their aim is not national harmony or reunification. They're only interested in Bolshevik struggle and reunification by conquest. Didn't the Korean War prove that? If we're going to talk about national harmony and reunification, then those people from the North who started the war should apologize first. Reunification is only possible when they truly want it to happen. Shouting 'National harmony and reunification!' from this side only abets their cunning strategy. It is like inviting another tragedy."

He had chosen his side and was now standing his ground. It had been impossible to do that during a war. By choosing a side now, he was trying to establish a strong position to believe in, one that would enable him to identify himself with the victims of the war—as opposed to the aggressors.

When cases of North Korean spy infiltration began to occur frequently, his view of himself as a victim merged with his staunch opposition to communism to make him increasingly sensitive. His feelings reached their peak after the attempt on President Park Chung Hee's life by Kim Shinjo in January 1968.

"Those belligerents! Of course, their cruel nature hasn't changed. This assassination attempt is a sign that they have recovered materially from the war. From now on, they will continue to infiltrate our country like deadly spirits. It'll be a cause of many headaches for us."

Just as he predicted, that winter there were frequent incursions by armed espionage agents from the North. When infiltrations by guerrillas in the areas of Uljin and Samch'ŏk were reported, he was speechless with anger, and his lips trembled and turned blue.

However, the events that followed did not allow him to enjoy his privileged position as a victim. He had exaggerated his sense of victimhood—perhaps to distract himself from something that was eating him up inside.

As a result of several Red Cross conferences held on the threshold of the 1970s, the July 4 joint declaration was issued by the North and South. It said, "Let's find a way for the people of North and South to communicate." From this time on, the professor's attitude slowly changed. Like most citizens, he expressed indifference about the joint declaration.

"I know that the intention is more than admirable. Sooner or later that kind of effort should be initiated. However, the problem is so deep, it won't be solved by one declaration. It's not a matter of getting all excited and hastily trying to work it out."

After the joint declaration was issued, people from the South and North travelled back and forth for the Red Cross conference and the coordinating committee meetings. One day the professor said something in passing to his wife that was surprising.

"Do you think there is a possibility that my brother-in-law might still be alive in the North? I know it seems impossible, but maybe by chance he got dragged up to the North safely and in one piece."

At the time, it was natural for people to dream or hope that their family members might be in the North. The professor's wife didn't think much of her husband's hope, which he himself regarded as unrealistic. But for some time this dead brother-in-law was being resurrected in his mind.

"You know, recently there have been cases where family members and relatives have come forward, recognizing faces among the North Koreans on TV. I think some people secretly seek news of their family members in the North."

He concluded that the young man who had escaped and come to his house had no possibility of surviving either in the South or North. But he could not ignore the possibility that his brother-in-law might be living in the North. As if he had been entertaining that possibility for a long time, he anxiously asked, "But then, what if he is still alive and secretly sends someone to ask for news of my dead sister?"

Thereafter, whenever people from the North came to the South to attend a conference, he would be glued to the TV, watching anxiously. But his anxiety wasn't caused by the possibility that his brother-in-law might appear or send someone to ask about his sister, who as a result of the trauma of the war died before the age of forty.

One day, the professor confessed his painful thoughts to his wife. As if he was repenting, he expressed them in a tragic and frank tone of voice.

"That young man came to look for a place to hide. I realized this when my sister reproached me severely after she returned home late that day. To be honest, I knew it even before my sister returned. After the young man told me of my brother-in-law's predicament, he didn't want to leave. He continued to implore me by saying, 'Can you understand this? Can you understand?' . . . It was something like the fatal pride of someone being pursued . . . He wanted desperately to ask for something, but he couldn't possibly ask it of a frightened child. His last 'Understand?' was his way of begging for refuge. My brother-in-law and he had exchanged addresses so that they would have a place to hide, where they could seek help. They had prearranged this meeting—I could read that in the way he was trying to delay his departure. I could see it in his face, but because I was so frightened, I completely blocked it out. I knew I had to hide him, but to the end I ignored my inner voice telling me so . . . And I pushed him out into that deadly street that dawn."

In point of fact, the professor was not so much distressed because of his brother-in-law or the premature death of his sister. He was in anguish because of that nameless young man he had cruelly pushed out the door.

Thus, when he confessed to his wife, he willingly exchanged his comfortable position of innocent sufferer for the painful position of guilty participant. Like the criminal who, believing that he has committed the perfect crime, suddenly realizes there is a crucial witness to his actions, he fearfully and remorsefully awaited news of his brother-in-law's reappearance. When the phone rang or when he heard a door being knocked on late at night, he would suddenly start. Without realizing it, he would become pale and tense.

Soon, as he had predicted, the confrontations and tensions between the South and the North intensified. The North Koreans set traps in the South's territorial waters and dug tunnels under the border, and the number of spies dispatched to the South reached unparalleled numbers. The professor tried not to show his feelings, but every time such news was reported, he could not tear himself away from the television set, and his attention would suddenly be concentrated on the alley alongside the house.

After a while, his wife could tell that her husband was waiting for someone, as if he were still the nervous schoolboy. She could read her husband's expressions, and she sensed that nervous schoolboy's restlessness. He might be waiting for his brother-in-law, or for a person who would bring news of him. He might even be waiting for news of the death of the young man who had come to his house. Perhaps rather than hoping to hear such news, he might be praying for just the opposite: that no news would reach him. She noticed his impatient and anxious expressions and wondered, "When did we ever have peace? Why is he becoming like this over some minor incidents in the news?"

The professor had in fact been standing outside the house like that little boy for a long time. Concerned that he had been reduced to trembling and walking back and forth restlessly outside the door, she suggested moving to a different neighborhood.

"I think the value of the real estate in this area went up recently," she told him. "All our neighbors had their houses remodeled a long time ago. Our house is the only one that looks old and shabby. But since we can't afford to remodel the house, why don't we sell this property and move to a bigger place in the suburbs?"

Her husband replied by telling her something she had never heard before.

"Do you think I've stayed here, losing money on this property, because I didn't know about its value? This house . . . I can't sell this house. My sister entrusted it to me before she passed away. She asked me to stay here because there is no other place my brother-in-law could send news of his whereabouts."

In other words, the boy in his mind had been restlessly pacing back and forth long before the joint declaration of North and South Korea—even before his sister had passed away. It had begun when the young man had come to deliver the news of his brother-in-law and then had disappeared onto the dangerous road toward death. Certainly then. It was common for people who had experienced the traumas of war to continue to see themselves as victims, as if they had received physical wounds. Her husband was forever that young boy standing outside. All these years, he had been secretly living with guilt and anxiety. When the joint declaration had been issued, his identity as a victim had begun rapidly crumbling, and now he had finally lost that privileged position.

She could now understand her husband's recent distress. When his friends had begun to die from war trauma, he could not escape the feeling of being different: that he was not a victim like them, but one of the victimizers.

The boy inside her husband could not leave the alley, the old and shabby *hanok*-style house in Hyehwa-dong. Disregarding his wife's pleas and requests, he remained there, paralyzed. Then, in the early 1980s, rounds of negotiations between South Korea and North Korea resulted in several general conferences. He showed no outward changes in emotion when various meetings took place between the leaders or when he followed KBS TV station's heated campaign for the reunion of separated family members. He acted as if it was inevitable that he would soon receive news of his brother-in-law.

"Do you know why someone insignificant like myself is still alive when all my important friends are already dead? I have to live until I hear some news of my brother-in-law. And it looks as if that is not completely impossible at this point."

Despite his repeated assurances, his wife felt that the boy inside her husband wasn't waiting only for his brother-in-law: tortured endlessly, he was also waiting to escape fear and anxiety. He became more and more pale as he struggled to confront his shameful past and to free himself from that painful debt he had incurred and from his guilty conscience. It even occurred to him that he was using his friends' deaths as an excuse to dream of his own death, and this too was a reason for self-reproach. His anxious waiting continued for several more years.

3

In early summer 1987, Sujin, Professor Kim Sail's only child, stayed home to hide. In her first semester, she had plunged into the student movement. Finally, she could not even go to school.

Kim Sail still had not heard any news of his brother-in-law, though his painful waiting continued. Around this time, he began to quarrel with his daughter over her involvement in the student movement. Their friction was a result of their differing opinions regarding the reunification of North and South Korea. Contrary to his daughter's radical view that the reunification should go forward at once, without any preconditions, Kim Sail was of the opinion that reunification should take place gradually. He insisted on a moderate approach, saying that understanding and trust between both the left and right, between the people from South and North Korea, should be established before anything else happened. The disagreement between father and daughter was so severe that they stopped speaking to each other. They lived in the same house but completely ignored each other, like people on separate planets. They did not even want to sit together at the dinner table. The break in their communication and their mutual distrust had become that bad.

Mrs. Kim could not understand their logic, but neither could she watch her husband and daughter be indifferent and hostile to each other. One evening, she called Sujin—who as usual had tried to go up to her room quickly after having eaten a late dinner alone to avoid her father—and sat her down. Meanwhile, the father had finished eating and was sitting in the living room. Mrs. Kim tried to get to the bottom of their conflict by asking Sujin, "What is it? I need to know! It's ridiculous that both of you share the same belief in the need to reunify the two nations, but live with your backs turned to each other because of different opinions on how reunification should come about. Your father believes in the need for reunification, so how is his position different from yours?" At this point, the argument had split into three parts: the father's, the mother's, and the daughter's.

It wasn't easy for Sujin to open up. Her mother's question was unexpected, and on top of that, her father—her rival—was sitting nearby. Professor Kim kept staring into the newspaper as if he hadn't heard a thing. The daughter tried to stand up quickly, indicating with a gesture, "If you want an answer to your question, why don't you ask Father?"

But her mother grabbed her arm, pulled her back forcefully into the chair, and continued to press her for a response. When Sujin could no longer endure her mother's interrogation, she answered reluctantly and curtly, "I believe that, in order to achieve reunification and harmony, both sides have to meet with each other as victims who have suffered unjustly. Father, on the other hand, believes that the two sides have to meet as aggressors who have harmed each other. That's the difference."

"But why is that so important? Why is this distinction so important in achieving national harmony and reunification that father and daughter have to fight over it?" asked Mrs. Kim.

The words "victim" and "aggressor" triggered unsettling images in her mind, but she continued to pressure her daughter in order to get to the heart of the conflict. Her daughter became more heated and outspoken. "I said that we should meet each other as victims because then it would be easier to come together as one people belonging to the same nation. We live in a divided nation as South and North, right and left. That is our historical reality. Because of imperialism and foreign influences, our people and the country as a whole have been divided. Under the dominant capitalist ideology, our people were suppressed and exploited. And our basic human rights were taken away by the authoritarian government . . . Aren't we all victims of these circumstances? So, in order to overcome this situation and heal the national division, we all have to have a common bond—our victimhood. This is absolutely necessary, and the only way. So I don't understand why Father clings to the aggressor's position . . . Who knows? Maybe Father believes the old superficial idea that being an aggressor is the same as being victorious."

Sujin had fought with her father before; nevertheless, Mrs. Kim was surprised by her daughter's ability to put forth an impressive and articulate argument. The mother no longer had to press her daughter to speak.

"So, you think I'm misguided?" asked Professor Kim, unexpectedly jumping into the conversation. "To me, the idea of the aggressor is not superficial." He had been silent, pretending to read the newspaper, and now he spoke as if he could no longer endure his daughter's sarcastic remarks.

"If you really don't understand, I'll explain it to you again clearly . . . As your mother said, you know very well that I, like others, hope for reunification and national harmony. But even if reunification is our nation's most urgent issue, it shouldn't be achieved at the expense of one side injuring the other or demanding a sacrifice."

Unlike in previous arguments, when he would throw down the newspaper and leap to the attack, Professor Kim lowered his voice and spoke calmly, not wanting to act improperly in front of both wife and daughter.

"You are saying that the reunification can be expedited by publicly making us all victims. But even if that were possible, there can't be a victim without an aggressor. Surely an aggressor as a sacrificial scapegoat becomes necessary. For the purpose of harmony and reunification, an aggressor—someone to blame—is needed. But if one side takes this role, it incurs a new debt toward the other, and a vicious cycle develops. You can't possibly argue that this would be a good thing. The reason that I'm cautious about your proposal of making us all victims is that I'm certain it would create this vicious cycle of blame. You're trying to find outside forces to blame and to identify as the aggressor—such as foreign influences and ideology—but confrontations and arguments take place right here among us. Our antagonists are right here. I said this to you before: in a sense, we all are aggressors and victims at the same time. Like you said, we *are* all victims, but maybe you see what I mean by saying it's better if we take the position of aggressors rather than victims."

Professor Kim spoke as if he was trying to appease his daughter, but he also meant to explain himself to his wife. When he finished, he paused for a moment, as if waiting for their reactions. Mrs. Kim, however, could not fully understand what her husband was trying to say. And because a significant part of his thinking was influenced by the fate of his brother-in-law—which he had rarely talked about in front of Sujin—his daughter, too, did not understand it all. His wife knew he had been suffering silently for a long time because of his brother-in-law, and it was only natural that he was sensitive to the reunification issue. She knew it was reasonable that in order for reunification to happen, aggressors and victims needed to be sorted out and identified. But her husband was insisting on their being thought of as aggressors. She wondered whether this wouldn't just encourage more people to identify themselves as victims, thus perpetuating the vicious cycle he talked about. But before she could ask her husband that, he started talking again.

"Speaking from my own experiences, it was difficult during the war to distinguish between victims and victimizers. For a while, both sides were victims and assailants at the same time." He began in simple words to explain further.

"After some time passed, people who had been victims enjoyed the right to an excessive aggressiveness in defending themselves, and gradually, without knowing it, they became the assailants in the conflict. And those people who at first had been the assailants began to present themselves as the new victims, and their voices became louder and louder. The two sides went back and forth—from assailant to victim—in a cycle of revenge and indignation, hostility and suffering, that resulted in endless rounds of more, deadlier aggression and victimization.

"It is ridiculous to assume that the passage of time will change each side's self-image as assailant or victim. Instead, we should all recognize that we have been assailants and try to repay our debts and think about our past mistakes—especially about the one million families separated during the war because of ideology. National harmony and the campaign for reunification are important. The joint declaration between both sides and the students' movement are also important. But for a meeting to take place between individuals, there need to be understanding and harmony. By adopting this attitude that I'm proposing, each side has less potential to continue to injure the other . . . Don't you think so?" Professor Kim finished talking.

Mrs. Kim could understand his feelings. He was talking about his own suffering and his own sense of guilt. Because of his fear and confusion, he had driven away the young man who had come to seek refuge. Now he wanted to repay the debt he owed because of that tragic mistake, and he could only do that by identifying himself as an assailant with a guilty conscience. He had been living with his guilt, anxiously awaiting the reappearance of his brother-in-law or news of him—forever the small boy waiting. Holding on to his guilt was his way of putting his relationship with other people in the right perspective. His strongly held beliefs in the way to achieve reunification were derived from his personal experiences. Understanding this, his wife agreed with him.

However, Sujin was unable to understand her father's position. She had never heard in detail the story of her uncle, a victim of the Korean War whose body had never been found. And since she had never experienced the chaos of war herself, it was only natural that she could not understand her father's profound feelings of responsibility for having harmed someone.

"You're only looking for a pretext to stop reunification because you fear it," Sujin said. "With your method, when do you think reunification would come about? Achieve harmony between people first and then give everybody a guilty conscience—it's only a pretext to postpone reunification, isn't it?"

Sujin's conclusions were spare and simple. Professor Kim began to retreat, as if he no longer had the energy to struggle against his daughter's sarcasm.

"OK, think what you want. A generation that did not wage war on others—there's no point in trying to get them to have a guilty conscience, to feel as if they had done something harmful to someone else. That's the privilege of an inexperienced generation like yours—rightly so—and it's the difference between the younger generation and the older, experienced one."

Sujin could not tolerate her father's backing out of the argument this way.

"Please don't try to simplify the issues by calling us the 'younger generation,' the 'immature generation,' the 'inexperienced generation.' Father, as a member of the 'wiser generation,' what did you see and experience? What did you do that was so terrible, and to whom did you do it, that makes you always talk about being an assailant—as if you were a criminal? I might not understand everything, but it seems to me you safely escaped that chaos. Until now you have lived comfortably, so how can you be an assailant or, for that matter, a victim?"

"Stop it! The question of how one can call himself a victim is something your father could ask you." Mrs. Kim intervened on her husband's behalf when she sensed that he was about to let the conversation drop. Since she was the one who started it, she felt it was up to her to say something in response to her daughter's cruelty.

"Why don't you explain yourself first? How are you suffering? What do you lose by North and South not being reunified? Why do you insist on calling yourself a victim of the division, and being so quick to raise your voice about reunification?"

"I said before that we are victims of a distorted history and of the reality of the unnatural division of our nation. But I didn't mean to say that you hadn't been wounded at all. I think you are much closer to being a victim than being an assailant, as you claim. I was asking you what kind of exertion it requires to create these distortions and contradictions. At the same time, I want to know what kinds of efforts the older generation made to overcome these problems, either as victims or assailants. You torture yourself about being an aggressor and about your unproductive and spiritless past . . . That's why the younger generation is pressing the older generation on the issue of reunification. You want to know how I'm wounded by the situation? The damage from the distortions and contradictions in our country's history hasn't just been suffered by your and Mother's generation—these things have been holding back my generation as well. Reunification is the only way this kind of national suffering can be eliminated so that we can overcome today's antihistorical and antinationalistic forces. But, Mother, you don't understand that. And when you don't understand, you should just keep quiet."

Sujin said this abruptly, as if she wanted to reproach her mother and then ignore her altogether. She then tried to turn to her father, but her mother would not give in.

"OK, it's true that I don't know about this to the extent that you do. As you said, I don't know how serious the contradictions caused by the division are—or the damage. But I can say this with certainty. What you just said about the historical contradictions and suffering experienced by your father and me—it's not that important to us. As your father said, our present livelihood is our reality. And the reunification issue is also part of our reality. But what you said about contradictions and distorted history and their negative effects—I don't know if it's because your words are so eloquent and abstract, but they seem unrelated to what we're really talking about. That your father has been carrying around a guilty conscience is not due to something ideological. He has tried to speak very concretely and directly . . . and I know that he has lived all his life with his mind on practical matters."

"What do you mean," Sujin said, "when you talk about being concrete and practical? And how did that enable Father, or our family, or our nation and society as a whole, to play a creative role in our nation's powerful historical trajectory?"

"I don't know how to answer such a high-sounding moral question. But I do know that your father is unable to leave this house because of your uncle. I don't know whether I'm saying this because I just want to be a common housewife or not. But this house is saturated with nightmares, as you already know. If we had sold this house and moved into a different one, we could've been better off materially and psychologically. But your father has long denied himself that kind of comfort and instead endured difficulties—even now. Inside your father, there is a young boy who couldn't grow up because he has been waiting in fear and anxiety for news of his missing brother-in-law. If you compare this to suffering on a national scale, his is nothing but a small, private story. But speaking on that personal level, I can say that his suffering has almost been unendurable. And about taking on the identity of a victim—what about this deeper, paradoxical victimhood? The kind in which righteousness is not so clearcut. Your father looks to me from time to time like a victim, but only by having an assailant's guilty conscience can he truly become a victim—and even then, perhaps only in the eyes of a future generation."

No doubt because she and her husband shared similar experiences and had sympathy for each other, Mrs. Kim was able to articulate her husband's thoughts, and her response to her daughter grew more passionate. But Professor Kim intervened in his wife's unexpected defense of him, almost as if he resented it.

"I think it's best that we stop here. Let's not exaggerate something . . ."

The argument was coming to an end. He turned to his daughter.

"And as for you, there is no need for you to try to win this argument, because no matter how the argument ends today, you'll eventually emerge the winner. The future lies with your generation, so in that sense, compared to me you were born the winner. And not just on the reunification issue. I'm saying that anyone who comes after us is the winner. And that means you."

Professor Kim was trying to calm his daughter down. He added in a deep, quiet voice, "As your mother said, I guess I'm nothing but a victim like all the others. But if you truly want to be the winner, I think you need to be patient and wait a little longer. Don't ask about the past. Let us forget about the right and wrong of what happened, so that we can come together and work toward reunification. I think that's what you are thinking. Perhaps we live in a world where we are too involved in the past. It seems there are a lot of people repenting for having had that attitude, and it seems to be the fate of our generation that we can so easily discard our past. But our generation is slowly disappearing. I know I'm part of a generation that experienced a lot of things, and our self-consciousness holds us powerfully in its grip. But I'll soon disappear, and I accept that. If reunification happens today, I'll have to step back immediately. So, I think it's best that you wait a little. You can build your victory on my failure, and by acting with deliberateness, you can make your winning more worthwhile."

Sujin did not know how to take his advice; she remained silent, a pained expression on her face. Mrs. Kim was in a deeper abyss. For a long time, her husband had remained in one place; suddenly, the boy inside him had aged without actually growing up. She could not bear to see him like that, so she quickly spoke in his defense.

"You're right. It's easier to win when you prolong the prosecution. We are too wrapped up in our emotions, so let's end it here today. I think it would be ridiculous if we became a divided family as a result of talking about reunification. I'm afraid that our arguing will turn us into one of those separated families." She made this last remark lightly, as if making a joke.

That night the confrontation between Kim Sail and his daughter ended. But that was not the conclusion of the matter—merely a prelude to a more serious event. After a few days of staying in her room, out of sight, Sujin departed without a trace, except for a letter she left for her father.

I'm sorry, Father. I can now understand your and Mother's generation. Perhaps I knew or understood your generation even before I heard what you two had to say . . . But I realize now that even though I understand you, I can't be by your side. In your life, everything has been experienced and completed. That experience belongs only to you and Mother; it can't be my experience or part of my life, don't you agree? Suffering and violence have changed your character, and what you said about failure is not shameful or a retreat—it is something upright and ideal . . . I'm afraid that it is so remote from my own life, however, that I can't bear it. Although you know that your generation must withdraw in order to open a door for mine, you are not about to step back soon, are you? In the end, there is nothing I can do but leave. I still lack so much. Emptiness seems like my lot. So rather than staying with you or Mother, I'd rather be with others who are as empty as I am and slowly fill the space by myself. I believe that rather than wait for my life to be completed in beautiful sadness, I can make my life more worthwhile by searching for and blazing new paths . . .

Please don't wait for me. And forgive me. As you know already, Father, filling the empty space or seeking out a new space is not easy.

After having read Sujin's letter, he showed no sign of surprise or disappointment. He spent the next day in silence, and the following day he began to mumble to himself when he sat down at the dining table, where his daughter was missing.

"Ah . . . at my age, I again have to wait endlessly for another person . . ."

His wife could not think of a reply, but later in the evening, at dinner, she turned to him and spoke carefully. "I know . . . How wretched that she's turned us into people who can do nothing but wait . . . She doesn't realize that her action has made you a most pitiable assailant."

Translation by Jennifer M. Lee

Reviews

■ FICTION

The Descendants of Cain by Hwang Sun-wŏn. Translated by Suh Ji-moon and Julie Pickering. Armonk, NY: M. E. Sharpe, 1997. 180 pages, paper $19.95.

The Rainy Spell and Other Korean Stories. Edited and translated by Suh Ji-moon. Armonk, NY: M. E. Sharpe, 1998. 283 pages, paper $21.95.

Hwang Sun-wŏn is modern Korea's most accomplished writer of short fiction. A good assortment of his stories is available in English translation, but his novels have fared less well. Three have been translated—*Trees on the Cliff, The Moving Castle,* and *Sunlight, Moonlight*—but all the translations were published in Korea, none was marketed overseas, and none is a first-rate translation. *The Descendants of Cain* is the first translation of a Hwang novel to be widely available in the English-speaking world.

The Descendants of Cain is one of the few fictionalized accounts, and certainly the best known in Korea, of one of the more tumultuous events in modern Korean history: the land reform begun in 1946 in the Soviet-occupied northern sector of the peninsula. Hwang and his family were directly affected by the upheaval, fleeing their ancestral home for present-day South Korea. The book's title refers to the blood spilled between Koreans during the land reform and suggests the internecine conflict that would erupt in the civil war of 1950 to 1953.

The Descendants of Cain vividly describes how the land reformers manipulated traditional class divisions in Korean society to mobilize peasants against landowners. Land reform posed hard choices for the landless tenants. Should they remain loyal to landlords who, though sometimes oppressive, offered them lifetime security? Or should they accept land of their own and with it the challenge to survive without the social safety network that a kind landlord could offer? In North Korea in 1946, this collision between self-interest and mutual benefit was a matter of life and death for some peasants. In one ominous scene in Hwang's novel, peasants assembled by the reformers raise glinting sickle and axe blades to signify their agreement to brand various landlords as reactionaries.

The Descendants of Cain is also significant for its portrayal of the two protagonists, Pak Hun and Ojaknyŏ (properly "Ojangnyŏ"—the rendering of Korean names in this translation and *The Rainy Spell and Other Korean Stories* frequently deviates from the standard romanization system). Hun is the scion of a landed family, and Ojaknyŏ is the daughter of the steward of the Pak family's land. Hun is a delicate, indecisive man. Ojaknyŏ, by contrast, has a visceral vitality, but in combination with the modesty and reticence traditionally valued in Korean women. Duality is a strong element in Hwang's worldview, and he does not allow his characters to become stereotyped. Therefore, it does not strain credulity when, at the very end of the novel, Hun, a passive target thus far, burns the deeds to his land and sets out in search of blood. In this and other novels and stories, Hwang creates such pairings as Hun and Ojaknyŏ to implicitly question traditional Korean gender-role expectations and to comment on the weakened state of the fatherland. During Hwang's lifetime, the Korean nation has faced continual challenges to its autonomy: colonization by the Japanese from 1910 (five years before Hwang was born) to 1945, military occupation by the Soviets and the Americans, a brutal civil war, and a succession of political and military strongmen. More recently, the economic restructuring imposed on South Korea by the International Monetary Fund in December 1997 not only shattered the illusion of the country's "economic miracle," but made South Koreans question their nation's autonomy.

Despite these political and gender-role dynamics, Hwang's novel at times reads like a collection of short stories linked by common characters and a common theme. Hwang is a superb storyteller, but some readers may be accustomed to novels with a firmer structure. I would urge such readers to try Hwang's story collections *Shadows of a Sound, The Book of Masks,* and *The Stars and Other Korean Short Stories.* They will find there the preeminent short-story writer of modern Korea.

The Rainy Spell and Other Korean Stories is a new edition of Suh Ji-moon's 1983 collection, which has long been out of print. The original edition contained such major authors as Yi Kwang-su, Ch'ae Man-shik, Hwang Sun-wŏn, Yun Heung-gil, and Pak Wan-sŏ; in this new edition, Suh has added three important contemporary voices: Yi Mun-yŏl, Ch'oe Yun, and Shin Kyŏng-suk. As with the great bulk of modern Korean fiction, there is much to learn about the country from these stories: the impotency of Korean intellectuals during the Japanese occupation (Ch'ae's "My Idiot Uncle"); the bleakness of peasant life (Kang Kyŏng-ae's "The Underground Village"); the tribulations of refugee life during the Korean War (Hwang's "Pierrot"); the family tragedies resulting from the division of the peninsula into North and South Korea (Yun's "The Rainy Spell" and Ch'oe's "His Father's Keeper"); and the cross-cultural abrasions suffered by Korean villagers encountering U.N. forces during the civil war (Pak's "A Pasque-Flower on That Bleak Day"). Collectively, these stories bear witness to the flux of modern Korean history.

The historical range of the selections—1920s to 1990s—is commendable, as is the inclusion of authors represented seldomly, if at all, elsewhere in English: Yu Chin-o, Chŏng Pi-sŏk, and Kang Kyŏng-ae. The anthology also contains a good sampling of women's voices: Kang, Pak, Ch'oe, and Shin. Women in Korea have traditionally been stifled in their attempts to give public expression to their artistic aspirations, and the literary realm is no exception. Although women have been actively involved in modern Korean literature since its beginnings in the late 1910s—writing for publication, working for literary magazines and book publishers, and, in recent years, attaining unprecedented commercial success—their participation in the literary establishment has always been limited because of the great power wielded by Korean scholar-critics, of whom an estimated ninety-five percent are male.

A danger in translating between two cultural traditions as dissimilar as those of Korea and the English-speaking world is that authors and works esteemed highly in Korea do not necessarily translate well into English. In *The Rainy Spell,* Kim Tong-in's "The Seaman's Chant" (part of the literary canon in Korea) and Choi In Hoon's "My Idol's Abode" seem to have miscarried during their passage across the Pacific.

Another potential danger for the anthologist-translator is that the distinct voices of the authors may end up sounding like the single voice of the translator. When a translator specializes in work by one author, it is inevitable, even desirable, that the author and translator merge in a unified voice. In an anthology, though, the overlay of the translator's voice upon the authors' may deprive readers of the opportunity to savor the distinctive voices of the latter. With some of the stories in *The Rainy Spell*—especially the title story and Hwang's "Pierrot"—I feel as if I am reading Suh Ji-moon rather than the author. Suh, a university professor who specializes in Victorian literature, is at her best when she translates refined narrative. Authors such as Yun and Pak, whose language is highly colloquial, or Ch'ae, who is a gifted writer of dialogue, pose challenges to such a translator.

Readers with little exposure to modern Korean fiction will find *The Rainy Spell and Other Korean Stories* a useful introduction. More seasoned readers may wish to continue on to book-length translations of the authors represented here: Ch'ae's *Peace Under Heaven,* the story collections by Hwang cited above, Choi In Hoon's *The Square,* Yun's story collection *The House of Twilight,* Pak's *The Naked Tree,* and Yi Mun-yŏl's *Our Twisted Hero* and *The Poet.*

With *The Descendants of Cain* and *The Rainy Spell and Other Korean Stories,* M. E. Sharpe's East Gate Library of Korean Literature series reaches half a dozen volumes. Two of the books are introductions to premodern literature, two are modern novels, and two are anthologies of contemporary fiction. High on the wish list of Korean-literature specialists is a foundation grant that would enable M. E. Sharpe to publicize and distribute these books more widely and to price them within the means of the university students who constitute much of their readership.

BRUCE FULTON

East Goes West: The Making of an Oriental Yankee by Younghill Kang. New York: Kaya, 1997. 425 pages, paper $16.95.

East Goes West: The Making of an Oriental Yankee is one of the best novels of the immigrant experience to come along in years, despite the fact that it was originally written in 1937. Sixty years later, Younghill Kang's novel of a Korean immigrant's arrival in America and his struggle to find a place in society despite discrimination is as relevant as ever.

More than an immigrant tale, this is one of the rarest of literary species: a novel of ideas. Lyrical and moving, it has as its backbone a subtle social critique, and as its backdrop a marvelous portrait of New York City in the 1920s. Kang's big-hearted hero, Chungpa Han, is a sensitive young classical scholar who lands in America via Japan with four dollars and a suitcase full of Shakespeare. He approaches the New World with bravery, generosity, and a kind of stubborn ambition, yet all the roads he takes lead to marginalization. Like many other immigrants, he works at menial jobs and lives in squalor but continues to try to carve out a place for himself.

> My bread was almost gone. I had known the famines of poor rice years in Korea. Now, in utter solitude with a chilling heart, I feared pavement famine, with plenty all around but in the end not even grass to chew. While in the shadow of New York's skyline, sunny hours were few, evenings seemed to be cold, dreary, long. In my unheated room during the cold hours, I spent some monstrous intervals in studying Shakespeare. But it was hard to concentrate, even in the midst of Hamlet's subtlest soliloquies, I could think of nothing but food. I often passed that charitable soup kitchen, but it, too, wore a closed and alien look and I shrank from passing myself off in there.

After seeing lavish banquets, Han covets the wasted food. The disparity between lack and plenty begins to eat away at his blind faith in the American dream. Han's one hope, aside from literature and the refuge it offers, is a bond forged with other immigrants—Siamese, Italian, Filipino, Chinese, Japanese, and Korean—from whom he seeks guidance in things American. A series of jobs as a waiter, door-to-door encyclopedia salesman, department-store clerk, and lowly assistant to an evangelical minister leads him to construct a persona that is neither Korean nor American. He becomes a kind of chameleon, changing in response to the occasion—the first step in the making of a Yankee:

> Soon I became convinced that everyone in New York felt . . . the need of sustaining a role, a sort of gaminlike sophistication, harder and more polished than a diamond in the more prosperous classes, but equally present in the low, a hard shell over the soul of New World children, essential for the pebbles rattling through subway tunnels and their sun-hid city streets.

Ultimately, the gross excesses of materialism and the lack of opportunity lead to Han's spiritual disenfranchisement. Meanwhile Korea, for all intents and purposes, is no longer the country he remembers. However, Han holds on to the classical traditions of his besieged homeland, just as he tries to understand the modernity of New York City, and though his idealism eventually gives way to realism, he is never bitter:

> We floated insecurely, in the rootless groping fashion of men hung between two worlds. With Korean culture at a dying gasp, being throttled wherever pos-

sible by the Japanese, with conditions at home ever tragic and uncertain, life for us was tied by a slenderer thread to the homeland than for the Chinese. Still it was tied. Koreans thought of themselves as exiles, not as immigrants.

East Goes West charts the "making of an Oriental Yankee" just as it charts his unmaking. It is a journey that ultimately leads to rebirth—or rather, what Han calls the "death of the state of exile"—and an acceptance of belonging everywhere and nowhere.

As Kang's friend and colleague Thomas Wolfe wrote, Kang was "a born writer, everywhere he is free and vigorous; he has an original and poetic mind, and he loves life."

We owe a great debt to Kaya for reissuing this brilliant novel and for its addition of "The Unmaking of an Oriental Yankee," an afterword by Sunyoung Lee. Lee details Kang's failed efforts to obtain citizenship (despite the fact that he married an American), the vicissitudes of his writing life, and the difficulties he faced in publishing his work. Lee also describes Kang's relationship with Maxwell Perkins, his editor at Scribner (the original publisher of *East Goes West* and Kang's first novel, *The Grass Roof*), and offers examples of reviews he received at the time. Sadly, these often focused on Kang's personal life, using his successful enculturation (he attended Harvard, became a university professor, and married an American) as proof of his complete assimilation, and failed to detect the book's underlying social critique. This edition includes all perspectives and also offers a chronology and valuable biographical information.

Every once in a while a book comes along that, even if not destined to be, deserves to be a classic. Younghill Kang's *East Goes West* is such a book.

LEZA LOWITZ

■ POETRY AND POETICS

Sacred Vows by U Sam Oeur. Translated by Ken McCullough and U Sam Oeur. Minneapolis: Coffee House Press, 1998. 226 pages, paper $15.

In words that are both horrifying and startlingly beautiful, the poems in *Sacred Vows* tell the story of a journey that begins in the early stirrings of civil war in Cambodia and continues through the brutal reign of the Khmer Rouge and the regimes that followed. It is a haunting book of loss and longing, speaking to the ability of the human spirit to survive the most unthinkable events with resilience and compassion.

This rare volume—the first collection of modern Cambodian poetry translated into English that I have seen—spans nearly half a century. U Sam Oeur's poems take us from the battlefields of Cambodia to the murder of his newborn twins by the Khmer Rouge to a recent job at a urethane factory in the U.S. And while this book is distinctly Cambodian—steeped in Khmer culture, mythology, and history—it is also universal: it gives voice to the hope and anguish shared by many refugees and exiles.

U Sam Oeur was born the son of a prosperous farmer in Svey Rieng Province in Cambodia in 1936, when the country was still a French protectorate. In 1962, he came to the U.S. to study industrial arts. However, when some of his writings were discovered by the executive director of the Asia Foundation, he was persuaded to enroll in the fine-arts program at the University of Iowa's Writers Workshop. Here he met Ken McCullough, who would later help translate *Sacred Vows.* After finishing his studies in 1968, U returned to Cambodia, where he worked in light industry and was elected to Parliament. He and McCullough continued corresponding until he had to stop because of mail censorship.

When the Khmer Rouge captured Phnom Penh on April 17, 1975, U was among the two million people forced to evacuate the city and work in labor camps in the countryside. The Khmer Rouge executed the educated and the wealthy, former military and government personnel, members of ethnic minorities, and anyone suspected of having ties to the West. U survived by pretending to be illiterate and using the knowledge of farmwork he had gained as a child. During the next four years, approximately two million Cambodians died of execution, starvation, and disease, among them many of U's relatives.

When McCullough learned in 1984 that U was still alive, he resumed their correspondence. He eventually helped U travel to the U.S. to work on *Sacred Vows,* which both of them translated into English.

Sacred Vows is divided into five parts, each of which represents a period in Cambodian history and U Sam Oeur's life. Part one, "Prophecies & Études," describes the beginnings of the conflict in Cambodia and roughly corresponds to the reign of Prince Sihanouk. It opens with a poem about the American war in neighboring Viet Nam: "Thunder in the East makes the sound *traDOK!*/the local elders cross their arms and cry." This section, full of prophecies and metaphorical allusions to the various factions and powers involved in the war—the Republic Army, the Viet Cong, and the Khmer Rouge—is made more haunting by the fact that some of the poems were written long before the Pol Pot regime came to power. For example, the poem "Oath of Allegiance" is dated 1952, the year before Cambodia gained independence from France.

From this early poem also comes the collection's title, which refers to the author's vows to his country and people—a theme that recurs throughout the book. These vows had ramifications for the author: after the 1979 Vietnamese "liberation" of Cambodia, a pro-democracy poem was discovered in U's desk, and he was harassed and forced to resign his position as Assistant Minister of Industry. Even now in the U.S., he continues to receive death threats.

Part two, "The Wilderness of Nightmare," refers to the period April 1970 to 1975: the reign of General Lon Nol and the height of the civil war, in which an estimated one in ten Cambodians died. U was a captain in the Cambodian army; of this time he writes, "The explosions of mines,/the roaring of heavy artillery/from frontier to frontier, shake every/grain of pollen from the champa flowers." The section ends with "Grandpa Suos's Lullaby," dated February 1975, just two months before the Khmer Rouge victory: "Don't cry, grandson./Don't be afraid—the tigers have no claws."

"The Kingdom of Hell," part three, describes life under the Khmer Rouge—the "tigers"—from April 1975 to January 1979. These poems chronicle U's departure from Phnom Penh, the terrors of the concentration camps, the strangling of his newborn twin girls by two Khmer Rouge midwives, and the forced march, led by the Khmer Rouge, to escape the invading Vietnamese. In counterpoint to these horrors are mystical references and the reiteration of U's vows to his country, even as he witnesses Cambodia being ripped apart. The section ends with "The Krasang Tree at Prek Po," which gives us the unforgettable image of a *krasang* tree "withered, its thorns/adorned with the hair of babies, its bark bloodstained." Around it lie the skulls of infants who have been smashed against its barbed trunk by the Khmer Rouge.

"The Wilderness of Trakuon," part four, covers the period from the Vietnamese invasion in January 1979 to the U.N.-brokered peace agreement in 1991. It begins with a haunting poem in which U describes searching for his father's grave: "O grass of thickets, grass/of sticking burrs, where is/the skeleton concealed?/Tell—and I shall ask no more of you." The poems in this section are boldly critical of the Vietnamese occupation, lamenting the attendant corruption, poverty, and violation of human rights and reminding us that the suffering in Cambodia did not end when the Khmer Rouge were driven out.

In September 1992, U came to the U.S. to work on *Sacred Vows.* He brought with him, as McCullough writes in his introduction, "a small suitcase full of tattered reference books and a few scraps of notes—the rest of his work was in his head." Part five, "The Quest for Freedom and Democracy," concerns U's life in the U.S. up to 1998. "Genuine Bliss," for example, describes working overtime in a factory where "Cambodians, Vietnamese, Thais, and Mexicans/work side by side like vegetables stirred in a soup." "Lunar Enchantment" skillfully weaves a description of a night in Iowa City with Cambodian mythology of the moon and the author's longing for peace in his homeland.

Khmer is a vivid, poetic language with rich textures and rhythms that are impossible to capture completely in English, and as I read these poems, I found myself wishing I could hear them recited in Khmer. In his foreword, McCullough describes the "operatic quality" of U's chanting and tells us that "passages which revolve around loss . . . are delivered in a manner comparable to the most emotionally charged aria." Although this quality may be impossible to render in English, McCullough and U's translation does succeed in conveying a sense of the operatic, a depth of passion and grief. And for those readers to whom many of U's references to Cambodian culture, language, and history will be unclear, there is a section of notes at the back of the book. I found these helpful in understanding U's layered poems, but wished they could have been more extensive.

While several moving, well-written Cambodian autobiographies and biographies exist—as well as many books on recent Cambodian history—this is to my knowledge the first volume of contemporary Cambodian poetry that has been translated into English. The reasons for the rarity of such a book are no doubt numerous and complex—rooted in the destruction of Cambodian tradition and culture by the Pol Pot regime, the devastation of decades of war, and the separation of many younger Cambodians raised overseas from their culture. U and McCullough state in the introduction their hope that *Sacred Vows* will help inspire this younger generation to "immerse themselves in their heritage and make those traditions once again vibrant living entities." I can only hope that it will, and that this volume will be the beginning of much more Cambodian literature in English to come.

SHARON MAY BROWN

No Trace of the Gardener: Poems of Yang Mu. Translated by Lawrence R. Smith and Michelle Yeh. New Haven and London: Yale University Press, 1998. 239 pages, cloth $35.

No Trace of the Gardener presents a selection of poems written between 1958 and 1991 by Chinese poet Yang Mu. Born Wang Ching-hsien in Taiwan in 1940, he used a variety of pen names, including Yeh Shan, up until 1972, when he began using Yang Mu.

Growing up in Taiwan, Yang Mu learned Mandarin, Taiwanese, and Japanese. In 1964 he came to the United States, where he attended the University of Iowa and received his master-of-fine-arts degree in 1966. He then went on to study at the University of California–Berkeley and received a doctorate in comparative literature in 1970. He currently teaches at the University of Washington and serves as dean at National Dong Hwa University in Taiwan. Yang Mu's biculturalism is a source of strength in his writing, and he brings the tradition of classical Chinese poetry into modern times.

No Trace of the Gardener presents Yang Mu's work in four sections, arranged chronologically. The early poems have a tender, haunting lyricism. In the opening poem, "The Woman in Black," the presence of the woman is mysterious, yet immediate, and although in the second stanza the speaker says he will wipe off her various influences, one feels he will be unable to do so:

> Drifting here and there between my eyelashes
> standing outside the door, remembering the ocean tides
> the woman in black is a cloud. Before the storm
>
> I wipe the rainy landscape from my window
> wipe the shadow off the *wutong* tree
> wipe you off

The poems in section two reveal a deepening vision and display greater complexity. "Nocturne Number Two: Melting Snow" is in three parts; the third is outstanding in its keen articulation of rhythm and a musical tension that harnesses sound and silence:

> At last it falls like irresistible
> melancholy. Touch it, you wouldn't know
> that it's tears—ripe fruit
> biting wind, autumn of DNA
> Perching crows set the tune. If you don't believe it
> sit down and listen with all your sleep
>
> At first I thought
> the strings broke in protest against war
> in fact it was hunger, three thousand miles of hunger
> flapping wings across a night of mounting tension
> followed by ubiquitous fatigue
> gracing the anticipated harvest: pick a branch or tree at random
> listen well as it moistens and floods
>
> an autumn-water night

In addition to writing in the lyrical, meditative mode, Yang Mu—as was the case with many classical Chinese poets—does not shy away from a social and political critique. However, these political poems are never heavy-handed, and they follow Emily Dickinson's injunction to "Tell all the truth, but tell it slant." In "Kao-hsiung, 1973," when the speaker of the poem witnesses "thirty-five thousand female workers leaving work at the same time," the situation is presented in the form of reportage rather than in the form of social critique. The poem creates a wonderful tension between the factual presentation and the emotional undercurrent that periodically rises to the surface.

From sections three and four, it is clear that Yang Mu has assimilated a variety of influences from the West. There are sonnet sequences, as well as poems that show that Lorca and Coleridge are active forces incorporated into his wider poetic vision. In "Someone Asks Me about Justice and Righteousness," it is moving to see how a simple line can become a refrain that acts as a musical bass line that grounds the wide-ranging meditation of the poem.

In the introduction to *No Trace of the Gardener,* Yang Mu says, "If poetry, or the organic life of culture as a whole, is to be worthy of persistence, we must seek its definition in the process of experimentation and breakthrough." For me, the overall effect of reading through this collection and surveying the evolution of Yang Mu's work is impressive. He has a restless energy and formal command that always make his work engaging.

Lawrence Smith and Michelle Yeh have done a superb job of translating Yang Mu's challenging work into English. The translations are sensuous, vivid, and alive. *No Trace of the Gardener* is essential reading.

ARTHUR SZE

Of Flesh & Spirit by Wang Ping. Minneapolis: Coffee House Press, 1998. 102 pages, paper $12.95.

Of Flesh & Spirit, a collection of new poems by Shanghai-born poet and novelist Wang Ping, is filled with the mutilation of the flesh and spirit of women by husbands, mothers-in-law, language, and ideology. These poems are by turns angry, strident, mournful, and earthy. Wang Ping is a fearless poet, unafraid to give offense and uninterested in creating cool, clean surfaces of language; she prefers questioning, recovering, screaming.

One of the most prominent images in *Of Flesh & Spirit* is that of the bound and mutilated feet of aristocratic Chinese women. For her, bound feet are a metaphor for repressed sexuality. In the title work, a prose poem, she proclaims her ridicule: "For a thousand years, women's bound feet were the most beautiful and erotic objects for Chinese. Tits and asses were nothing compared to a pair of three-inch 'golden lotuses.' They must have been crazy or had problems with their noses. My grandma's feet, wrapped day and night in layers of bandages, smelled like rotten fish."

Remembering what happened to the women in her family is Wang's central theme. In "Female Marriage" she writes, "I think of what happened to my grandmothers, what's happening to my mother and my sister, all those years of not knowing where or who they are. I'm not taking that road. But the only way to help is to think back through my grandmothers and my mother." At the heart of the book is the ten-page poem "What Are You Still Angry About," in which Wang creates a maternal genealogy with verse, prose, and lists. The poem loops back from her mother to her great-great-great-great-grandmother and then forward to herself and her sisters so that "the names of my female ancestors [won't] just vanish like tadpole tails." She describes how her maternal grandmother, Chen Duoni (*duo* means "extra"; *ni,* "girl"), indentured herself as a laborer to a textile factory so that her baby sister wouldn't go the way of the previous five girls: death by drowning in a chamber pot. And she tells us that her great-great-grandmother, Wu Hehua, was sold into marriage at age five and had her bound feet reset by her mother-in-law: each toe was pulled straight, then bent back further towards the arches.

Wang is at her best when her poems approach memoir, when she uses her anger as a tool to recover the missing pieces of her family history. Often, this anger causes her to dwell on the harshness of women's lives. In "Female Marriage," she lists the proverbs and curses that the Chinese have for women—like "cheap stuff" and "losing money commodity"—and tells us that in Chinese the word for woman, *nu,* means "slave." In "Resurrection," she writes to her grandmother's ghost: "Do not wave your bandages at me. My feet have grown as hard as white poplars in our native town. I'll make a pair of wings with them, to carry your soul into spring, into the forest and grass, into a world without memory. Be a bird, a bee, or even a fly. Just to live again, with joy." "In Touch with America" describes her relationship with her mother: "Each day I run to my mailbox to see if my mother has written to me./When a letter arrives, I leave it unopened for weeks on my desk." The women Wang writes about, including herself, are brutalized, so she creates a community of survivors by giving them a voice.

Wang's concern for those without names and voices extends beyond her own family and gender. "Song of Calling Souls," for example, is about a group of Chinese illegal immigrants who died when their ship, *The Golden Venture,* sank off the coast of New Jersey. In the poem, the dead plead to be remembered:

> Please, oh please
> call our names
> Chen Xinhan, Zhen Shimin
> even if you can't say them right
> Lin Guoshi, Chen Daie
> even if you don't know
> our origins or age
> Wang Xin, Huang Changpin

When Wang's attention wanders from her family, her poems tend to become talky and self-conscious, as when she relies on such rhetorical pronouncements as "Language, like woman / Looks best when free, undressed" (from "Syntax"). Nevertheless, her anger at injustice and her willingness to take chances in her poetic forms are admirable. And Wang has no easy answers: as she writes in "These Images," "It is beyond the gods / why we hold on to our sorrows / so long, and so stubborn."

LISA OTTIGER

Hojoki: Visions of a Torn World by Kamo-no Chomei. Translated by Yasuhiko Moriguchi and David Jenkins; illustrated by Michael Hofmann. Berkeley: Stone Bridge Press, 1996. 91 pages, paper $12.

Hojoki: Visions of a Torn World, by Kamo-no Chomei (1155–1216), is both historical testament and poem. As historical testament, it relates much of the sense and feel of late-twelfth-century Kyoto, a city that for all its noted artistic refinement and cultural achievement was frequently subjected to disaster, both manmade and natural. Kamo-no Chomei experienced these disasters firsthand: fires, floods, earthquakes, and famines. This narrative poem recounts those experiences, and struggles to come to terms with what meaning life can have in a world buffeted by change and shaped by events beyond an individual's control.

Kamo-no Chomei became a Buddhist monk at the age of forty-nine and left Kyoto to live in relative seclusion in the nearby mountains. Four years later, he moved deeper into the mountains, built a hut near Hino, and composed *Hojoki;* the title refers to the size of his hut and means "Writings from a Place Ten Feet Square."

A Japanese classic for nearly a thousand years, *Hojoki* has been translated by Yasuhiko Moriguchi and David Jenkins and is now accessible to English-language readers. The poem is narrated by a persona Chomei creates, a character who charms his way into the reader's heart. Perhaps more than anything else, the poem's strength resides in the authority of this speaker. Chomei was there. He suffered. We see what he sees—the streets littered with dead and dying, starved and starving—and find the view compassionate and alive. His voice is angry and joyful by turns.

For all its historical detail, Chomei's world also brings us face-to-face with our own search for understanding, peace, and a spirituality that is grounded in reality. In a thousand years, the human heart has not changed much, and we remain as vulnerable as ever to war and natural disasters. And this is why Chomei's poetry remains new.

Some of the real beauty of *Hojoki* resides in the way it moves through time. Built of many small, songlike stanzas that weave their way through the work, *Hojoki* carries the reader forward and back, through harrowing experiences and lighter moments. The general movement reminds one of a Noh play in which the dancer moves so slowly that the viewer feels physically drawn into the drama by the studied tension that each step creates.

Throughout, Chomei's narrator longs for a quiet heart. His hut brings some measure of peace, but he has chosen to live in exile and poverty. Aware of the flow and flux and constant change of human existence, he aims to liberate himself from the mental disquiet brought about by worldly cares. He wants to live light, to grow with less:

> A house and its master
> are like the dew that gathers
> on the morning-glory.
>
> Which will be the first to pass?

Chomei doesn't have an answer for the suffering he sees in the world, but he does have a way of living with it. He transforms anguish into compassion. Nowhere is this more poignant than in his befriending a ten-year-old boy, which he describes towards the end of the poem:

> We pick buds and shrubs
> and gather bulbs and herbs.
> Or go to the fields
> at the foot of the hill
> and gather fallen ears of rice
> and make different shapes.
>
> When the day is fine
> we climb to the hilltops
> and look at the sky
> above my former home.

Chomei savors life and shares it bounteously. He has time for the child because he knows how the world can be, because he walked streets where starving children clung to the breasts of their dead mothers. The difference in the ages of Chomei and the boy is the difference between innocence and experience: "to understand the world of today hold it up to the world of long ago." Despite all he has experienced, or because of it, he is capable of this love—*Hojoki* is testament.

The conclusion of the poem is in keeping with the work as a whole. Chomei questions his own thinking and attachments, few though they are. Speaking to himself, he asks:

> Has your discerning mind
> just served to drive you mad?
>
> To these questions of mind,
> there is no answer.
>
> So now
> I use my impure tongue
> to offer a few prayers
> to Amida and then
> silence.

Throughout *Hojoki,* Chomei has cautioned against being too dependent on material comforts, and here, at the end of the poem, he realizes that he loves his little hut, the *biwa,* and his books of poetry—and realizes he ought to know better. He imposes silence on himself, and his voice suddenly departs from us, underscoring what he has been saying all along: that our existence on earth is brief.

When Chomei finally stops talking and heads back into the forest of twelfth-century Japan, we want to follow. Left with silence, we feel the ache of loss, but it is an ache we trust will open into a larger, more compassionate world within us.

GREGORY DUNNE

Breeze Through Bamboo: Kanshi of Ema Saikō. Translated by Hiroaki Sato and illustrated by Ema Saikō. New York: Columbia University Press, 1998. 246 pages, paper $15.50.

Breeze Through Bamboo is a book of poems as refreshing as its title suggests. It takes us back to the poetry of Tokugawa Japan, which has its roots in classical Chinese *kanshi.* For women to be included in the rarefied circles of male poets writing in Chinese was unusual during the period—Ema Saikō and her peers Chō Kōran and Hara Saikin were three of the exceptions. To find that Saikō was also free-spirited and independent is even more surprising.

Saikō differs from other women poets in early Japan because she wrote *kanshi.* Hiroaki Sato's introduction to Saikō's work provides a wonderfully detailed discussion of the historical background and technical aspects of *kanshi,* in addition to a fascinating personal account of Saikō's life. Saikō might have found in *kanshi* the freedom to cover a wider range of subject matter than that afforded by *tanka* or *haiku.* Almost portraitlike, Saikō's *kanshi* offer glimpses not of court life or entangled love affairs, but of the poet's physical environment and artistic and spiritual development.

Saikō is a pen name derived from a line by the Chinese poet Tu Fu: "When the wind blows [the bamboo] is delicately fragrant." Sato writes, "Because of this allusion, the name may figuratively refer to a 'breeze soughing through bamboo,' a name her teacher . . . suggested." Having learned to write in Chinese as a child, she also became an excellent artist, often creating ink paintings of bamboo. As a woman who never married or bore children, Saikō devoted herself to her poetry and art. In her work she catalogued the daily rituals marking the passage of time, as well as the disruptions of those rituals, such as earthquakes or floods. The *kanshi* thus collected in *Breeze Through Bamboo* form a kind of daybook, an artist's poetic diary. And because they were written in a "foreign" language, Saikō might have had a certain freedom—the distance to imagine outside of oneself and one's culture.

Saikō paid homage to her literary antecedents in the following poem, which refers to a thirty-volume anthology of verse by over four hundred Chinese women poets:

Reading *Ming-yüan Shih-kuei* under a lamp

The hushed night deepening, I can't take to my pillow:
the lamp stirred, I quietly read the women's words.
Why is it that the talented are so unfortunate?
Most are poems about empty beds, husbands missed.

No such laments exist in Saikō's work. Many of her poems allude to her active literary life—reading, writing, studying, meeting with one of the many poetry groups she belonged to, and visiting Kyoto to see her poetry teacher, Rai San'yō, with whom she is thought to have been romantically involved.

Saikō's poems are sensual and evocative, smelling of jasmine and incense, sounding of rain water and music, tasting of tea and *sake*. Suffused with resignation and wisdom, they possess lightness too. The poet often remarks that she composed a poem "just for fun" or that she "happened to write" a poem. Here is an example of such a work:

Solitary Living in Early Winter

This innermost room, with little to do,
is adequate to commit my plain life to.
Drink a bit, and forget my clothes are thin,
an idea, and I let my brush run aslant.
Wind at the eaves, and the maple sheds its leaves,
on the wet stones chrysanthemums fade.
All day with no guests visiting me,
I've perused books, delighted to learn.

In Saikō's poems, seasons change, blossoms fall, friends and teachers die, the body fails, but art remains as a refuge and an escape. In addition to finding refuge in art, Saikō also performed the duties of an ordinary woman, which included taking care of others.

> Impromptu
>
> Tending someone ill, I haven't gone out for a hundred days.
> The new greens near the eaves have covered up my window.
> So fine, flickering, the evening rain draws me into drowsiness
> as I stand by a screen, dreaming of blossoms falling.

Saikō did not care about publishing her poems while alive. After her death, relatives and friends sifted through over 1,500 poems, chose 350, and assembled them as *Shōmu Ikō* (Manuscript left by Shōmu), published jointly in 1870 by five publishing houses. This work, all but forgotten, has been brought to life again in *Breeze Through Bamboo.* With few writers and scholars these days able to read *kanshi* and *kanbun* in the original, Hiroaki Sato was fortunate to have available the work of scholar Kado Reiko. Sato's finely wrought translations, based on Kado's annotations of *Shōmu Ikō,* are evocative and assured. Copious notes and a detailed scholarly introduction, along with reproductions of some of Saikō's paintings, provide an in-depth picture of the life of this spirited, talented poet—considered by Tu Fu scholar Kurokawa Yōichi to be one of the "three greatest women poets in Japan."

LEZA LOWITZ

At My Ease: Uncollected Poems of the Fifties and Sixties by David Ignatow. Edited by Virginia R. Terris. Rochester, NY: BOA Editions, Ltd., 1998. 136 pages, paper $13.50.

David Ignatow's career presents the reader with a significant test of free-verse practice in twentieth-century poetry. Ignatow goes beyond his masters, Walt Whitman and William Carlos Williams, in constructing verse outside the bounds of traditional meters, nowhere conceding a line to a regular metrical pattern unless it is also the plainest speech. The poems in *At My Ease: Uncollected Poems of the Fifties and Sixties* are typical of Ignatow's mature practice, which eschews regular patterns of rhythm, as well as other repetitions. The lines generally break at grammatical junctures, and the sentences collect into irregular verse paragraphs. Here, in fact, is "prose chopped into lines": the bugbear of critics who would deny the validity or the existence of free verse. Ignatow, then, is a prosodic test case: if one can defend his practice as *poetic,* the various charges of diffuseness and formlessness leveled by conservative prosodists against free verse throughout much of this century can be put to rest.

To read David Perkins's brief account of Ignatow's career in his 1987 *History of Modern Poetry,* one would not get the impression that Ignatow continued to live and write until just this year. The entire entry is in the past tense. And it does seem as if Ignatow's radical simplicity and pessimism have become unfashionable in a period when postmodern irony and bland confessionalism are ascendant. Perhaps necessarily, Ignatow led an almost posthumous existence in the last decade of his life, for his work is incompatible with the comfortable vision of the self ushered in by the right-wing hedonism of the Reagan revolution. Perkins notes Ignatow's "romanticism," remarking that it was derived from Whitman. The real source of Ignatow's romanticism, however, was the very unromantic floor of his father's book bindery, which he found antithetical to his hopes for his poetry, despite the fact that he took over the business as a way to support his family when his father was old. It is his hatred of the factory that blinded Ignatow to the fact that poetry, too, is a form of production, though I'd argue that it is this very blindness that gives such a passionate tone to much of his poetry.

The value of the collection is that, by completing the oeuvre of a poet recently deceased, it invites us to evaluate the writer's accomplishments as both poet and theorist of poetry (for the theory of poetry as an act of perception is never far beneath the surface of Ignatow's poems). In "My Story," he writes,

> I accept the candle handed to me
> out of the dark where I hear
> the thunder of Roman troops.
> The candle is lit, floating down
> from over the heads of the fighters
> against Rome. I place it
> in a candle holder and set the light
> beside my bed. In its ray
> the thunderous troops recede.
> I pick up a history of the Jews
> and read. My story.

The three ten-syllable lines refuse to be exact pentameters, but that very refusal declares the poem's responsibility to be a record of the process of perception rather than an aesthetic object. Also interesting are the four lines containing punctuated caesuras. If Ignatow has no official prosody, he substitutes for it the rhetoric of the sentence. In a poem in which the majority of lines are straightforward clauses, the four medially broken lines set up a rhythm of expectation and perception that controls the poem. The process of perception is meant to be shared; it is a social, even political, act.

Ignatow employs two basic "prosodic" arrangements in these poems. The first consists of the grammatical line and the verse paragraph; the second moves toward the prose paragraph, including end-stops within the structure of the line. It is this second sort of arrangement that in the late seventies would lead Ignatow to the prose paragraph as a poetic form. There are no prose poems in *At My Ease,* but many of the poems seem to yearn for the freedom of the prose sentence.

In certain respects, to be a poet is to be dead to the rest of the world. Ignatow, on the evidence of these poems, is among our most alienated poets, as disconnected from mainstream values as was Edgar Allan Poe. The biographical details revealed in *At My Ease,* and more directly in his *Notebooks,* present an unhappy and conflicted man. Though committed to his marriage and family, he resented them for getting in the way of his writing. He also relates the psychiatric illness of his son, for which he takes responsibility. His treatment of his son seems to reproduce his anguished relationship with his own father; here is a passage from *Notebooks* about his son:

> Of my son I ask forgiveness with the handbag in my grip as I stand waiting for him to come and meet me out of his room and in the hall. Forgive me and grow well. I'll be your father and disappear and be glad for it, leaving you to be yourself. I will disappear from your sight and be lost too, no longer aware of myself as being but only knowing that you are well again, dressing to leave and combing your hair.

Beginning in the seventies, in several interviews Ignatow said openly that his great theme—or the feeling that pervades his poems—is guilt. What is most useful about the poems from the seventies is the way they transform personal guilt and a sense of absolute loss into works of art that are available to readers. Here is "Summary" in its entirety:

> In life we solve no problems,
> just bend them like crowbars.
> A person takes one up
> where we laid it aside
> and advances upon us.

The poems intend to be politically effective, though not didactic. Ignatow's demonstration of the ways in which it is possible to transform personal bitterness into art is one of the chief values of *At My Ease.* What makes the work *poetic* is nothing less than the encounter, through the medium of language, with the disappointments of reality.

With the possible exception of the 1991 *Shadowing the Ground,* Ignatow's poems seldom arrange themselves into developmental sequences; rather, each poem seems a new beginning. Partly, this has to do with the poet's insistent pessimism—the very act of writing poems seems so patently absurd in the face of the world's angry rejection that one must simply begin again and again to write the world. The poems do not attempt to sustain intellectual structures outside themselves; that is not their business. The business of the poems in *At My Ease,* as in much of Ignatow's other work, is to confront situations in which the speaker is at a disadvantage, social or perceptual, and to transform that weakness into a strength through the processes of art. Ignatow's poetics, as described in his journals and in various interviews, typically cast the writing of a poem as an act of perception that might lead to transformation. Or might not.

In a notebook entry from 1959, Ignatow writes, "Those writers to whom words are more important than content earn my contempt. Those writers to whom words are measured by the content at hand earn my respect. Those writers are the only ones that count." This was written about the time that Robert Creeley was creating the dominant aesthetic of the late twentieth century with this credo, derived from Pound and Williams: "Form is never more than an extension of content."

There is an austerity in the poems of *At My Ease,* and in Ignatow's practice, that puts one in mind of Kafka's hunger artist: "No one could watch the hunger artist continuously, day and night, and so no one could produce first-hand evidence that the fast had really been rigorous and continuous; only the artist himself could know that, he was therefore bound to be the sole completely satisfied spectator of his own fast."

JOSEPH DUEMER

■ LITERATURE AND CULTURE

The Confusion Era: Art and Culture of Japan During the Allied Occupation, 1945–1952. Edited by Mark Sandler. Seattle: University of Washington Press; Washington, D.C.: Smithsonian Institution, Arthur M. Sackler Gallery, 1998. 112 pages, paper $19.95.

The seven years immediately following World War II saw rapid, far-reaching change in Japan. In a real sense the country was remade as the Allies imposed a Western-style democracy on what was formerly a feudal state. *The Confusion Era: Art and Culture of Japan During the Allied Occupation, 1945–1952* presents six essays by noted historians and art critics that discuss the broad aims and directives of the Allied Occupation—which the Americans soon came to dominate—and the effects of those directives on Japanese art of the period. The book is a beautifully illustrated, good-quality paperback with images of pre- and postwar life, art, and culture.

The Confusion Era begins with Donald Richie's "The Occupied Arts," an overview of the arts and the Occupation's general policies regarding them. Richie writes that, while visual artists who actively participated in wartime propaganda were rarely "purged" and "benign neglect . . . permeated the Occupation's attitude toward literature and contemporary drama," some censorship was present. The Supreme Commander of the Allied Powers "frowned on paintings of bombers, warships, or imperial archways"; enforced a "wholesale ban on any Japanese translation of Steinbeck's *Grapes of Wrath*"; and "consistently suppressed . . . descriptions of GIs holding hands with Japanese women." The press, ostensibly free, was not allowed to publish criticism of the Allied Occupation forces, and the film industry was censored. According to Richie, all areas of censorship underwent a "similar, problematic transformation: from the search for fascist feudal remains to the great Red hunt. . . . As a result, some of the Occupation's most humane and liberal impulses remained unrealized."

In "Erasing and Refocusing: Two Films of the Occupation," Linda C. Ehrlich compares and contrasts Shinoda Masahiro's 1984 *MacArthur's Children* and Imamura Shohei's 1961 *Pigs and Battleships.* Both are set during the Allied Occupation and concern the "Americanization" of Japan. Shinoda presents a comparatively gentle view of Japan-American relations in a story about the trial of a war criminal, the sometimes bumbling but always powerful American military, and the game of baseball. Imamura introduces a harsher view of those relations in a tale of Japanese thugs who see themselves as American-style gangsters and who "view American culture and 'democracy' as a source of easy money." Produced well after the end of the Occupation, the films, according to Ehrlich, are "acts of remembrance [that] record what was essentially a period of erasing and rewriting."

Changing women's roles in postwar Japanese films is the subject of Keiko I. McDonald's essay "Whatever Happened to Passive Suffering? Women on Screen." American censors helped effect those changes, writes McDonald, by banning "any theme which portrayed favorably the subjugation or degradation of women." McDonald discusses the prewar 1939 film *The Story of the Last Chrysanthemum,* in which a "maidservant lives and dies, entirely devoted to advancing the career of an aspiring Kabuki actor"; she then contrasts it with the relatively recent 1988 *A Taxing Woman,* in which a divorced woman manages to succeed in the world of business. McDonald also examines the work of well-known director Mizoguchi Kenji, whose favorite heroine was "the nobly forgiving, self-sacrificing woman whose destiny is to put men in touch with redemption." While Mizoguchi's ideal woman —such as the female lawyer who defends her doomed, liberal journalist husband in the 1946 *Victory of Women*—appeared more independent than her predecessors, she still practiced "the art of pleasing." It was not until forty years after Mizoguchi that the heroine of *A Taxing Woman* could find corporate success.

In the concluding essay, "My Work in Japan: Arts and Monuments, 1946–1948," Sherman E. Lee offers his recollection of the Allies' well-directed and effective efforts to preserve and protect Japan's national art and monuments. Lee's postwar work in the Arts and Monuments Division was "to inventory and inspect all Japanese art in the country, to determine what works had been destroyed, to assist the Japanese in the protection and preservation of their cultural property, and to encourage the display of Japanese works of art." Clearly evident in the essay is Lee's delight in Japanese art and the Japanese people.

The Confusion Era features excellent visual art: reproductions of paintings and posters, movie stills, and, most notably, beautiful black-and-white silver gelatin prints by Horace Bristol. Among Bristol's subjects are three Shinto priests walking in the rain, a Japanese driver stoking a charcoal-burning automobile, and a road sign bearing directional arrows and the words TOKYO, YOKOHAMA, COCA COLA.

Anyone interested in Japan, the United States, and the relationship that has developed between the two countries will enjoy this book. The essays and the many illustrations broaden our understanding of the new Japan, and the old. American readers will also get a glimpse of how they are seen by the Japanese, and the impact—for good and ill—of American postwar policy.

PHYLLIS YOUNG

About the Contributors

John Balaban is the author of *Locusts at the Edge of Summer,* which was a finalist for the 1997 National Book Award. His translations include *Ca Dao Vietnam: A Bilingual Anthology of Vietnamese Folk Poetry* and *Spring Essence: The Poetry of Hồ Xuân Hương* (forthcoming). His essay in this issue of *Mānoa* is written in memory of his teacher, Nguyen Dang Liem, of the University of Hawai'i. Balaban teaches at the University of Miami.

Tony Barnstone is the editor of *Out of the Howling Storm: The New Chinese Poetry,* coeditor of *Literatures of Asia, Africa, and Latin America* (with Willis Barnstone), and the coeditor and translator of *The Art of Writing: Teachings of the Chinese Masters* (with Chou Ping) and *Laughing Lost in the Mountains: Poems of Wang Wei* (with Willis Barnstone and Xu Haixin). He teaches creative writing, Asian literature, and American literature at Whittier College. His own book of poetry, *Impure,* was recently published by University of Florida Press.

Mario Benedetti was born in Uruguay. A renowned playwright, novelist, essayist, critic, journalist, songwriter, and screenwriter, he has received numerous literary prizes and written more than sixty books.

Kevin Bowen is director of the William Joiner Center for the Study of War and Social Consequences at the University of Massachusetts–Boston. The author of two collections of poetry, *Playing Basketball with the Viet Cong* and *Forms of Prayer at the Hotel Edison,* he guest-edited the winter 1995 *Mānoa* feature on poetry from Viet Nam. He has also coedited two anthologies, *Writing between the Lines: An Anthology on War and Its Social Consequences* and *Mountain River: Vietnamese Poetry from the Wars, 1948–1993.*

Horace Bristol was born in California in 1908. Along with Alfred Eisenstaedt and Margaret Bourke-White, Bristol was one of the first staff photographers hired in the 1930s by the new magazine called *Life.* During the 1930s and 1940s he photographed extensively in Java and then in the American West. When World War II broke out, Bristol enlisted in the U.S. Navy in order to document the war. After the Japanese surrendered in 1945, Bristol made his home in Japan, but continued to travel throughout Asia, creating a distinctive style of photography and an impressive body of work that combined a modernist expression with a journalistic eye sensitive to images of the human condition. He died in 1997.

Sharon May Brown worked for two years on the Thai-Cambodian border as a writer, photographer, and researcher of Khmer Rouge atrocities for the Columbia University Center for the Study of Human Rights. Her photographs have appeared in the books *Seeking Shelter: Cambodians in Thailand* and *The Saving Rain.* Her story "Kwek," about a young boy's rebellion against the Khmer Rouge, appeared in the summer 1999 issue of *Mānoa.*

Choi In Hoon was born in 1936 in North Hamgyŏng Province in what is now North Korea. During the Korean War, he and his family moved to South Korea, where he made his literary debut in 1959. He received the 1966 Tongin Literature Prize for his story "Usŭm sori" (The sound of laughter). He is also a distinguished playwright.

Joseph Duemer has written two books of poetry, *Customs* and *Static.* With Jim Simmerman, he coedited the anthology *Dog Music.*

Gregory Dunne is the author of *Fistful of Lotus,* a handmade book by Canadian printmaker Elizabeth Forrest. His poetry, essays, and interviews have appeared in *Poetry East, Third Coast,* and *Kyoto Journal.* He teaches at Kyoto University of Foreign Studies.

Bruce Fulton is the cotranslator of four anthologies of modern Korean fiction: *Words of Farewell* and *Wayfarer,* with Ju-Chan Fulton; *Land of Exile,* with Ju-Chan Fulton and Marshall R. Pihl; and *A Ready-Made Life,* with Kim Chong-un. The recipient of a 1995 National Endowment for the Arts translation fellowship and the 1993 Korean Literature Translation Prize, he is director of publications for the International Korean Literature Association.

Tom Haar has worked as a documentary photographer in New York, Hawai'i, and Japan, where he was born. He has had solo exhibitions in Budapest, New York, Honolulu, Tokyo, and Seoul. His work in Honolulu, where he has lived with his family for the last twelve years, has concentrated on images relating to the connection between man and his environment.

Sam Hamill is a translator of ancient Chinese, Japanese, Greek, Latin, and Estonian poetry. His recent translations include *The Essential Bashō;* Issa's *The Spring of My Life and Selected Haiku; The Essential Chuang Tzu,* with J. P. Seaton; and *River of Stars: Selected Poems of Yosano Akiko,* with Keiko Matsui Gibson. His forthcoming book of translations is *Three Hundred Poems from the Chinese.* The most recent book of his own poetry is *Gratitude.*

Robin Hemley writes fiction and nonfiction. His works include *All You Can Eat, The Last Studebaker, Turning Life into Fiction,* and *The Big Ear.* Widely published and anthologized, he has won a number of awards, including the 1996 Nelson Algren Award for Short Fiction, a Pushcart Prize, and a *Story* magazine humor award. His most recent book is *Nola.*

Theodore Hughes is a doctoral candidate in the Department of East Asian Languages and Cultures at the University of California–Los Angeles.

Maria M. Hummel has a chapbook, *City of the Moon,* forthcoming from Harperprints. Her poems have recently appeared in *Georgia Review, Meridian,* and the *New Orleans Review.* She lives in Durham, North Carolina.

Im Cheol Woo was born in 1954 in Wando, South Chŏlla Province, where the city of Kwangju is located. He is currently a professor of creative writing at Hansin University. His novel *Pomnal* (Spring day), printed in 1984, was the first fictional work to discuss Korea's Kwangju Uprising. In 1988 he received the Yi Sang Literature Prize for his story "Pulgŭn pang."

George Kalamaras had his work selected for *Best American Poetry 1997.* His new book is *The Theory and Function of Mangoes,* winner of the Four Way Books Intro Series Poetry Award, forthcoming in spring 2000.

Min Soo Kang is a freelance writer who has a master's degree in European history from the University of California–Los Angeles and now resides in Seoul. His work has been published in *American Historical Review,* the *Times Literary Supplement,* and *AZ.* He has contributed essays to two books: *Alter-Histoire,* edited by Daniel Milo and Alain Boureau; and *Revisioning History,* edited by Robert Rosenstone.

Susie Jie Young Kim was born in Seoul in 1971. She is currently a doctoral candidate in the Department of Comparative Literature at the University of California–Los Angeles. Her translations have appeared in *Mānoa* and *Korea Journal.*

Paul Kodama has lived all his life in Honolulu. He began photographing thirty years ago and has taken black-and-white images in many places, including Hawai'i, France, and Italy. He is currently working on images from Rapa Nui and Machu Picchu.

Kong Sŏnok was born in Koksŏng, South Chŏlla Province, in 1963. Her story "Mok marŭn kyejŏl" (Parched season) was first published in the literary journal *Ch'angjak kwa pip'yŏng* (Creation and criticism) in 1993.

Jennifer M. Lee is a doctoral candidate in the Department of East Asian Languages and Cultures at the University of California–Los Angeles.

Robert Hill Long recently received a fellowship from the Oregon Arts Commission. His book *The Effigies* was a finalist for the 1998 Oregon Book Award. A poem he published in *Mānoa* was selected for *Best American Poetry 1995.*

Leza Lowitz is a writer, translator, and editor. She is working with Shogo Oketani to translate the poetry of Ayukawa Nobuo—a project for which they received a 1997 National Endowment for the Arts translation fellowship. Her most recent book is a collection of her poems, *Old Ways to Fold New Paper.* She coauthored the experimental film *Milk,* which was shown at the Berlin International Film Festival.

Ly Lan was born in Binh Nhan Village, Lai Thieu District, Binh Duong Province, Viet Nam. She is the author of eight collections of fiction—including *Singing Grass* (Co hat), *In a Land of Strangers* (Dat khach), *Flying a Kite,* and, most recently, *Le Mai* (Le Mai)—and has won numerous awards for her work.

W. S. Merwin is one of America's preeminent poets and translators. His recent publications include *The Folding Cliffs, Flower & Hand, East Window,* and *The River Sound.*

Mộng-Lan has had work published in such journals as *Quarterly West, Iowa Review,* and *Kenyon Review.*

Harry Morales has translated the work of Ilan Stavans, Eugenio María de Hostos, and Emir Rodríguez Monegal, among other writers. He is a recipient of a Witter Bynner Foundation for Poetry grant for his translations from the Spanish.

Lisa Ottiger was born in the Philippines and grew up in Indonesia and Hong Kong. She has a master's degree in creative writing from the University of Hawai'i and is *Mānoa*'s reviews editor.

Ricardo Pau-Llosa has recently published two books of poetry: *Cuba* and *Vereda Tropical.* His latest book of art criticism is *Rafael Soriano and the Poetics of Light.*

Hiroaki Sato is an essayist, poet, and translator whose recent books of translation are *Breeze Through Bamboo: Kanshi of Ema Saikō, Silk and Insight: A Novel by Mishima Yukio,* and *Rabbit in the Netherworld,* a childhood memoir of the war by Koyanagi Reiko. He is at work on an anthology of Japanese women poets from ancient to modern times. He thanks Kathleen Dooley and Nancy Rossiter for helping him revise the essay that appears in this issue of *Mānoa.*

Andrew Schelling lives in Boulder, Colorado. In 1992, his book *Dropping the Bow: Poems from Ancient India* received the Academy of American Poets prize for translation. Other recent books include *Old Growth: Poems 1986–1994, The Road to Ocosingo,* and a volume of translations, *The Cane Groves of Narmada River: Erotic Poems from Old India.* He teaches at the Naropa Institute.

Arthur Sze has received awards for his writing from the Lila Wallace–Readers' Digest Fund, Lannan Foundation, and the Witter Bynner Foundation for Poetry. His latest book of poetry is *The Redshifting Web: Poems 1970–1998,* from Copper Canyon Press.

Yi Ch'ŏngjun was born in Changhŭng, South Chŏlla Province, in 1939. In 1965 he published his first short story, "T'oewŏn" (Leaving the hospital), which won the Sasanggye (World of thought) Newcomers Literary Award. In 1966, he published the short story "Pyŏngshin kwa mŏjŏri" (The wounded) in *Ch'angjak kwa pip'yŏng* (Creation and criticism), for which he received the 1967 Tongin Literature Prize. In 1978 he won the Yi Sang Literature Prize for "Chaninhan toshi" (The cruel city). He has received numerous other literary awards, most recently the 21st Century Literary Award for his story "Nalgae ŭi chip" (The house of wings).

Phyllis Young lives and works on O'ahu. In 1952 she spent six months in Japan, where her father was stationed in the U.S. Army.

Tsunami Years

Juliet S. Kono

Rich in detail, this collection spans three generations and examines themes of childhood, heartbreaks and affinities, family obligations, love and devotion, death and dying. Cathy Song writes, "Juliet S. Kono's language shimmers with multiple, luminescent layers of meaning, each poem a pearl of truth wrested out of the heart of living."

$10.00 (book) ▪ 173 pages
ISBN 0-910043-35-3

$8.00 (cassette)
ISBN 0-910043-36-1

$16.00 (book and cassette tape set)
ISBN 0-910043-39-6

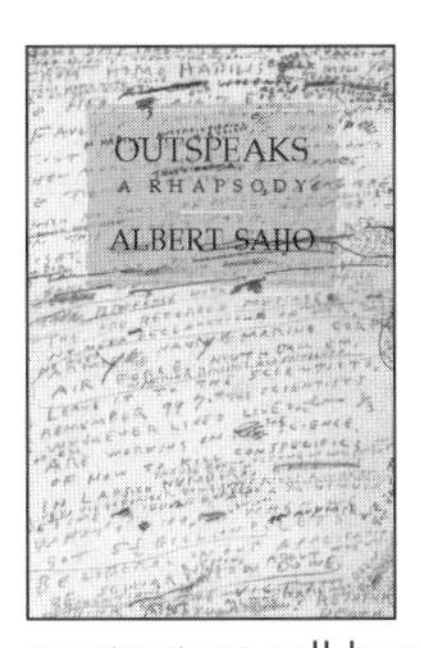

OUTSPEAKS A RHAPSODY

Albert Saijo

A devout poet-philosopher and practitioner, Saijo is committed to illuminating his vision for others through language. Realizing all the while the inherent limitations of this construct we call language, Saijo expounds upon the ineffable as much as is humbly and humanly possible. Lawrence Ferlingetti says, "Albert Saijo has the great vision most poets and painters never had." Saijo is the author of *Trip Trap* with Jack Kerouac and Lew Welch and *The Backpaker*. Of *OUTSPEAKS A RHAPSODY*, Saijo's first collection of poetry, Gary Snyder says: "All CAPS and dashes, Albert Saijo's poem is a great life's strong song."

1998 Small Press Poetry Book of the Year and 1998 Pushcart Prize winner.

$12.00 (book)
ISBN 0-910043-50-7

$8.00 (cassette)
ISBN 0-910043-51-5

$18.00 (book and cassette tape set)
0-910043-52-3

Expounding the Doubtful Points

Wing Tek Lum

This collection of poetry by the 1970 Discovery Award winner speaks of the author's Chinese American heritage: his ancestors in China, his family in Hawai'i, and forging a Chinese American identity. He also speaks of racial discrimination and the obscenity of ethnic stereotypes with astute and unforgiving clarity. "Lum's style is an unembellished line of measured prose, setting out a message in direct declarations...his straight forward descriptions take their impact from that very detachment."—The New Paper

Winner of the 1988 Before Columbus Foundation American Book Award and the 1988 Association for Asian American Studies National Book Award.

$8.00 (book) ▪ 108 pages
ISBN 0-910043-14-0

Subscribe to Bamboo Ridge

All subscriptions are shipped postage paid and are money-back guaranteed.

4-issue (2 year) subscription, $35 (save $15)

2-issue (1 year) subscription, $20 (save $5).

Institutions: $25, 2-issues.

Coming in Spring 2000, Issue #76 *Intersecting Circles: The Voices of Hapa Women in Poetry and Prose,* an anthology of *hapa* women writers edited by Marie Hara and Nora Okja Keller.

Bamboo Ridge Press ▪ P.O. Box 61781 ▪ Honolulu, HI 96839-1781
For more information call (808) 626-1481 ▪ www.bambooridge.com

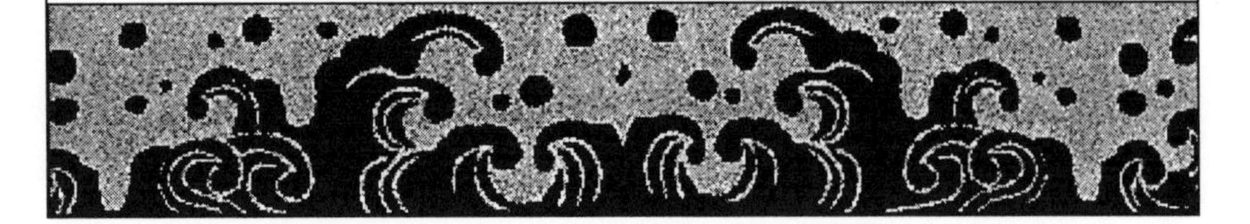